THE
LOST
BLACKBIRD

LIZA PERRAT

Cover design: JD Smith.

Perrat Publishing.
All enquiries to info@lizaperrat.com

First printing, 2020.

ISBN E-book: 979-10-95574-06-4
ISBN Print book: 979-10-95574-05-7

PART 1
1962

1

London East End
January 1962

The girl's father lurches from the flat out onto the landing, where his little girl is playing.

'Bleedin' toys,' he slurs.

At the sound of his voice, she jolts, the breath snaring in her chest. So captivated by her toy blackbird, turning the key on its underside to make it chirp, flap its wings and bob its tail, she'd not even heard him come stumbling onto the landing.

Her father jabs a finger at the wooden toy she now clutches to her chest. He falters, almost topples down the stairs, grabs the railing, steadies himself. She knows it's the drink that makes him wobbly.

'Bloody kid,' he says, 'always leaving yer stuff lyin' around … want me to trip over yer toys and kill meself on them stairs, eh?'

He looms, a monster's shadow, over his daughter hunched on the top step.

'I *didn't* leave my blackbirdie lyin' —' she starts, little fingers clenched around her beloved toy. But the rest of her words snag in her throat as her father bends down, jerks the toy from her grip.

'No!' She stretches up for it but he holds the bird too high.

And the flash from his eyes-on-fire look ripples a fearful quake through her.

The little girl has never owned anything as precious as the blackbird, a present from one of the old people her mother looks after at nights, an ancient man who'd carved it from wood.

It's the only real present she's ever been given, this most beautiful bird in the world.

'Please give back my blackbirdie,' she sobs, but her father ignores the pleas, waves the toy above her head.

'Stop yer grizzlin', girl.'

She cries more.

Lips creasing into a nasty smirk, he flings the bird against the wall.

It clangs like her mother's favourite teacup with the tiny roses all over it.

But Mum's out at the shops. Please come home now.

The shock steals her breath. She struggles to get air in and out of her tight chest. Tears sting her eyes as she gazes at her precious bird lying on the ground, its neck twisted, both feet and one wing broken off.

Her father jerks towards the toy. Lifts a heavy boot, stamps it down. Grinds until the blackbird is squashed. All flat. Dead.

The girl knows she should keep still, quiet, but can't help herself.

'Why you broke my birdie?'

'Teach yer not to leave stuff lyin' around for me to trip over.' His spittle sprays her brow.

'But I *didn't* —'

Her words are drowned again as he lunges at her, palm flat, taut, hair a dark tangle of wires sticking out of his head. Wiggly lines criss-crossing a purple nose. Herring-breath, mixed with what her mum calls the "whisky stink", rushes at her in the sweep of his raised arm.

'Enough of yer lip or you'll get a beltin' you won't forget.'

And when he sways, grabs the rail again, angry face close to hers, the girl knows she has to leap away. Right now!

Younger, steadier, agile, she moves far quicker than he does.

His single shriek springs back from the concrete walls as his head clunks against the stair railing. And down he goes, thudding on each step. Eyes wide, staring. No more scary.

The little girl's heartbeat thrums against her chest as she stands on that top step, panting hard, watching her father bounce and roll. Bounce, roll, bounce, roll, all the way to the bottom, where he has to stop since there are no more stairs, only the doorway to the courtyard that divides the blocks of flats: North, South, East, West.

The stairwell falls silent. The girl looks down at him, his top half sprawled almost across the doorway, legs splayed backwards, upwards. Angles she's never seen before.

And in those seconds, the five-year-old's heart no longer beats at all. The blood inside her turns icier than the January dusk outside. She can't move; can't speak. Can only stare down at her father's unmoving body.

* * *

From inside the flat, the girl's big sister also listens to the silence.

She heard their father staggering about the landing, flinched at his shouts and curses; knew Mum would be counting on her to go out there and defend her little sister. But she couldn't. Just this once she could not face him again.

She cowered behind the closed door, eyes still sore and swollen, cheek still red and stinging from the belting he'd given her before he'd lurched outside and started having a go at her sister.

But silently, she willed her younger sister to shut her trap.

Shush, don't make him angry.

She opens the door now, slowly, glimpses his body lying at the bottom of the steps and stares in horror at the dark halo widening around her father's head.

She grabs her sister's hand and together they sit on the top step and wait for their mother to get back from the shops.

* * *

The girls' mother skitters into view on the ground floor. She almost trips over the twisted body of her husband.

'Albert!' She drops her shopping bag, slaps a palm over her gasp, gaze resting on the ragged circle of blood around his head. She jumps backwards so no blood seeps beneath her shoes.

Annie Rivers doesn't bend down to check whether Albert Rivers is still alive, or dead. She turns her head, looks up at her girls sitting on the top step. 'What the bleedin' hell happened?'

'Dad got too much of the drink in him again,' her older daughter calls down.

'He broked my birdie,' the little one sobs.

Their mother is quiet for a moment, listening to her daughter's small, fragile voice echoing down the stairwell. Shocked, surprised, because Albert's so big compared with her.

How is it even possible?

But yes, she supposes that with the booze already making Albert unsteady, it *is* possible.

She picks up her shopping bag and without another glance at Albert's bloodied head, the awkwardly-angled legs, she steps over him and hurries up to her girls.

She sits on the top step between them, clamps an arm around each girl's shoulder. Tries not to dig her fingernails through the threadbare clothes into their skin. But she presses a little, needs them to listen.

'Right, don't you girls say nothin' to no one, nobody must ever know what really 'appened, alright?'

She takes a breath, gives the younger girl a long stare. 'But if anybody does ask, the pair of you are to say it was an accident.'

2

'I s Mum *ever* comin' to get us?' From Charly's chair beside mine, in the dining room of Easthaven Home for Girls, my little sister looked up at me, wide blue eyes teary.

She sniffed, wiped a snot-crusty sleeve across her runny nose.

Afraid Charly would burst into sobs for the millionth time that day, I gripped her hand, so small I was scared of crushing her bones.

'Mum'll come for us soon,' I whispered, hoping Charly didn't notice the fib in my shaky voice. 'Now be quiet, they're dishin' out our lunch.'

I chewed on a fingernail, my gaze flickering around the gloomy room, terrified Mrs Mersey would catch me and Charly talking.

Because once Mrs Mersey rang the meal bell, you had to stop talking, sniffing and coughing. And there was definitely no crying. You had to go to the toilet and wash your hands. And on the next bell you had to go to the dining room, and if you even sneezed Mrs Mersey would dart you the crow-eye look that knocked your knees together. You were only allowed to speak to say Grace or answer if Mrs Mersey – Mrs Merseyless the Seniors called her, behind her back – spoke to you, which she only ever did to tell you off or punish you.

The Seniors, girls aged eleven to sixteen, moved up and down the trestle table, dishing out some kind of stew with floating blobs of carrot and potato, and greyish-white chunks that might've been pork.

'But Mum only works of a night,' Charly went on, 'and it's daytime so why *don't* she come and get us?'

I silently urged the Seniors to hurry up and finish serving. I wanted to gobble down that stew; to get rid of the gnawing at my stomach, empty since last night because Charly's crying had made us miss yet another breakfast.

Mrs Mersey, who worked at Easthaven on weekends, since there was no school lunch, started saying Grace. 'Bless this food to our bodies, Lord.'

'Look at them birdies, Charly,' Vinnie whispered, from where she sat on my other side. Always helping me get Charly's attention away from the fact that our mother didn't – well, *couldn't* – come for us, my friend waved an arm outside, to the cold February day hanging over the Easthaven grounds like a mouldy blanket.

' … Jesus name we pray.'

This morning's mist had finally pushed off, and Vinnie was pointing out two crows perched on the weathervane.

But that only brought more tears to Charly's eyes. 'My black-birdie's all dead.'

'Oi, don't them trees look funny?' Desperate for my sister to stop crying before Mrs Mersey noticed, I whispered any old thing to Charly, 'cos the trees didn't look funny at all.

The winter drizzle had made them all droopy, branches hanging like thin and naked old-men prisoners looking long-ingly at the high stone walls, wondering if they could climb those creepers and escape over the top.

'We'll get that skipping rope goin' after lunch,' Vinnie said. 'That'll be fun, eh, Charly?'

Vinnie – Lavinia – Anderson had been the one and only good thing about the childcare officer dumping Charly and me at Easthaven Hell for Girls. There was still the ache deep inside me, like one of them wooden trunks plonked on my chest, which had started when that copper took away our mother. But I'd been happy to find my best friend, from our block of flats, sleeping in the same bedroom as me and two other girls. 'Specially since no one had told me where Vinnie had vanished last summer, after her mum and dad's accident.

But that didn't mean I wanted to stay here. No bleedin' way! My mind was the swirly, stormy Thames River, twisting around plots to get away from Easthaven and its hateful care workers, Mrs Mersey and Mrs Benson. War widows, the both of them, and sour and wrinkled as old lemons about that.

'Don't cry, Charly, please,' I whispered as more tears swelled in my sister's eyes. 'Because of yer cryin', we already missed breakfast and I'm that starving I couldn't bear missing lunch too. Please, Charly.'

'Amen,' the girls chanted, as Mrs Mersey finished Grace.

My fingers tingled but before I could snatch a slice of bread and marge from the plate in the middle of the table, Charly's thin shoulders shuddered.

'You keep sayin' Mum's comin' for us,' she wailed, tears leaking down her cheeks. 'But she never does. I want Mum. I wanna go home.'

'Charly, you *have* to stop cryin'.' But after three weeks at Easthaven, I knew the game was up when Mrs Mersey barked at me, 'Lucille Rivers, don't you or that whimpering sister of yours dare touch a single bite.'

Mrs Mersey, sharp and spiky as the shoes she wore, got up, glowering at me and Charly as she walked the length of the trestle table, towards us.

'Better keep yer trap shut this time, Lucy,' Vinnie mumbled.

Mrs Mersey loomed over Charly, waggled a finger at her. 'Charlotte Rivers, you will stop that snivelling at once.'

'My sister don't never answer to Charlotte,' I said. 'We call her Charly, and I'm Lucy.'

'I told you a hundred times, Charlotte Rivers, you ain't got a home no more,' Mrs Mersey went on, ignoring me. 'This is where you live now, and you'll behave properly, like all the other orphans.'

'We *ain't* orphans!' I blurted out.

Charly kept up her stammering. 'I w-want Mu-m.'

Like me, Charly had got the miseries from the first day that childcare officer had brought us here, and things only got worse as one long and awful day stretched into the next, and I couldn't see a way to get away from Easthaven.

Charly's small face was all red-blotched, her eyes blue slits in puffy pastry. Under the table, I kept hold of her hand, squeezing, trying to stop her blubbering.

But she only cried more, which made Mrs Mersey snap harder. 'You ain't got a mother now, no point whining for her like a lost puppy.'

Even though some of the other girls were enjoying the show, glad it wasn't *them* coppin' it, a few looked away, but most kept their heads bent, eating quietly, trying not to be noticed. Jane Baxter, the girl who was always sick, gagged, like she might vomit with the fear.

'Mum, Mum, Mum!' Charly shrieked, kicking her little legs back and forth beneath the table.

The anger spewed out of me and I ignored Vinnie's warning look. 'We have so got a mother,' I shot at Mrs Mersey.

'A common criminal is all that woman is. Not fit to call herself a mother.' Drops of Mrs Mersey's spittle flew from her thin lips.

'My mum done *nothin'* wrong,' I said.

Mrs Mersey grabbed Charly's arm, and one of mine, dragged us away from the table, knocking over our chairs in her roughness.

'How many times have I told you, Lucille Rivers?' Mrs Mersey said. 'You must control your sister's crying. She cannot continue upsetting the other girls. And since you can't stop her blubbering, since you can't control yer own tongue, you'll both miss another meal.'

She shoved me and my poor sister towards a corner of the dining room; corner of which I knew every woody twist and knot. The corner we knew so well our names could've been carved into the wood: "Here standeth Charly and Lucy Rivers for many a Meal".

I wanted to hug Charly tight, to cuddle away all the misery and ache, but I daren't touch my sister. I blinked away my own tears, gulped down my own sobs, tried to ignore the pain in my own chest. I took deep breaths. Vinnie always said deep breaths helped the anger and hurt.

'Now turn yer silly faces to that wall, away from us,' Mrs Mersey said, and stamped back to her place at the head of the table. 'I don't want to have to look at either of you a second longer. Enough to put anyone off their food. And if you don't want to miss tea tonight, you'll keep that trap of yours shut, Lucille Rivers. Nothing but a troublemaker you've been, right from the moment we were unlucky enough to find you two on our doorstep.'

I almost fainted at the thought of missing tea, so I shut my trap, stared at the wall and breathed away the rage churning inside me.

* * *

The smell of stew flared my nostrils, wrenched at my guts, as we stared at the wall. I kept hold of my sister's hand and Charly's sobs calmed to hiccups, then a small whimper, like a little animal trapped in a cage. But she kept up the sniffing, swiping a sleeve across her red, runny nose.

I wanted to shout at her for getting us in trouble, for making us miss all those meals, but Charly was too young to get a grip on her feelings.

Like Charly, I too wanted to cry all the time, but right from our first day at Easthaven, I'd figured out that tears only made Mrs Mersey punish you worse.

Like Charly, I too wanted to go home, even if home was only a "filthy council flat" as that childcare officer had called it.

Like Charly, I too wanted to go back to my old school with my old friends.

But what I really wanted was Mum to put her arms around me, to stroke my hair and whisper, 'Don't worry, only a bad dream, Lucy. You'll wake up soon and it'll all be over, me little love.'

That's what I missed the most, Mum's kisses and cuddles; how she'd tuck Charly and me up in the same bed so we'd keep warm, before she left for her night-job looking after the old people. Oh, it was all *so* unfair.

But – for both our sakes, for our stomachs! – I had to squash my own misery, hate and anger into a tight ball and hurl it over the high wall that surrounded Easthaven. I had to stay strong for my little sister until I could work out a getaway plan.

Ten years old was really too young to be a mother but I had no choice, did I? What with Charly only just turned five, she really needed a mum. And being the mum had been my job since Charly was born: rocking the pram to get her to sleep when Mum was working, our father down the pub. Not that he'd ever looked after baby Charly.

I'd change her nappy, feed her, wash her in the kitchen sink. And when my little sister got old enough to play hopscotch and hide-and-seek outside with me and Vinnie and the rest of the girls from our block, I'd make sure no nasty kids hurt or teased her.

And now that we were on our own, I wouldn't let her down; I'd always take care of Charly.

And of course, I couldn't let on to her that Mum wouldn't be coming to get us at all, if I could believe anything that childcare officer, Mrs Langford, had said.

When she'd ditched us here, she'd said, thankfully out of Charly's hearing, 'Your mother will likely be locked up for quite some years. Manslaughter might not be *murder* but it's still a serious offence.'

'But they'll let Mum out once they realise she *couldn't* have pushed Dad, even by accident,' I'd told her. 'Since she was out at the shops when he fell down them steps.'

Mrs Langford had pushed her lips out and raised her eyebrows, as if I was some idiot who hadn't a clue what she was on about.

But I *did* know what I was on about, though I also knew that by the time Mum could convince them it wasn't even manslaughter, that Dad fell by himself 'cos of the drink, Charly, Vinnie and me would be too old for Easthaven. Because when you turned sixteen, Miss Sutherland, Easthaven house mother who never did an ounce of mothering, kicked you out onto the street to find a job.

We'd be long gone from this place. But gone where? And how could I keep the three of us together?

3

Charly Rivers
London East End
February 1962

'Out you go and play now, get some fresh air,' Mrs Mersey said, shooing the Juniors outside into the freezing playground, after Charly had looked at the wall with Lucy for the whole meal. Mrs Mersey hadn't even let them eat a single bite of bread and butter pudding, which had been the worst thing to miss, since they only got afters on weekends.

Mrs Mersey didn't shove the Senior girls out into the freezing playground of an afternoon on weekends. She made them stay inside washing, scrubbing floors and cooking, which gave them red and sore hands.

The wind's icy fingers cut sharp as a butcher's blade right through Charly's thin coat. She clutched it across her chest, huddling in a tight circle with Lucy and Vinnie, Jane Baxter and the twins, Patty and Suzy Hampton, who had the exact same face and squinty, crossed eyes, and wore the same thick glasses.

Charly's gaze stole up to the high window where Mrs Mersey always spied on them to make sure they weren't making trouble. But for once there was no spiteful face at the window, and Vinnie pulled two slices of bread from her pocket, handing one each to Charly and Lucy.

'Sorry couldn't get you no stew,' Vinnie said. 'Since I ain't got one of them fancy new Tupperware things!'

As Charly swallowed that bread almost whole, Vinnie's big

laugh – a donkey laugh, Lucy called it – made her smile, even though she still felt like bawling.

Suzy and Patty had scrounged bits of potato and carrot, and Charly and her sister crammed the soggy vegetables into their mouths too.

No greedy pig gobbling says Mrs Mersey.

'Anyway you didn't miss much,' Vinnie said, wrinkling her nose, the freckles jumping around her face. 'Stew was same old sludge.' She ruffled Charly's hair. 'But you have to stop yer bawlin', Charly or you 'n Lucy'll starve to death. Promise you'll try?'

'Promise,' Charly said, glancing at her sister, jumping from one foot to the other, gloveless fingers all white knuckles curved around her coat flaps. It *was* Charly's fault they'd missed another meal, she knew that, but hard as she tried, she couldn't stop the tears coming.

'Sorry, Lucy,' she said, with a huge sniff.

Lucy threw Charly one of her pretend smiles. 'I'm betting you'll stop yer crying real soon,' Lucy said. 'We been here three weeks, and I reckon that's about long enough to run out of tears, eh, Charly?'

''Specially if you use up so many every day and every night,' Jane Baxter said, and Charly couldn't work out if Jane was being nice, or having a go at her.

'We know you're tryin', Charly,' Vinnie said. 'You have to try harder, is all.'

They bounced on the spot, trying to keep warm, but the sun had forgotten their playground, and the wind snapped so hard at Charly's toes and fingers that she couldn't feel them.

If only she and Lucy still had their scarves and mittens, but Mrs Langford had been too rushed to think of packing all their things when she'd brought them here from Aunty Edna's flat.

'But I'm s-so c-cold,' Charly stammered, tears stinging her eyes, blurring the playground so everything looked as if it was underwater: trees without their summer leaves, like skeletons with hundreds of little arms sticking out every which way, saggy brown weeds and dead flower heads, thick and high walls. Lucy had told her that even the gardener man's ladder wasn't high enough to get you over them stone walls.

Her sister took her hands, pressed them together, and rubbed. 'Keep wriggling your fingers, Charly.'

'And stamp your feet,' Vinnie said, 'to get the blood to yer fingers and toes so they don't freeze right off.'

Charly stamped her feet harder, terrified her fingers and toes might really drop off. Because, when Lucy escaped them from Easthaven, how could she run away if she had no toes?

Anyway, how could Mrs Mersey and Mrs Benson call a thing a "playground" what had nothing to play with except one almost-broken skipping rope? There wasn't even chalk to draw a hopscotch square. Vinnie and Lucy had drawn one with a stone, but it was so faint you couldn't make out the numbers.

Easthaven didn't have a single ball or cricket bat, or even a dolly, like her Jeannie, who Mrs Langford had also forgotten at Aunty Edna's. And there was no wind-up blackbird, which Charly missed as much as Jeannie, even if the bird was dead.

But she tried not to think about her blackbirdie, because that made her cry more. And Charly never, ever thought about that freezing night just after her fifth birthday; the last time she and Lucy had seen Mum. And the last time she'd seen her father. No, Charly would never think about him again. Ever.

'Who wants to play hide 'n seek?' Patty Hampton said, her and Suzy's snow-coloured braids swinging in the wind. The twins plaited each other's hair every morning, like Lucy used to plait Charly's till Mrs Mersey said it wasn't allowed.

'Not me, I've got a headache,' said Jane Baxter, the girl with a squashed bit of nose and lip. She held her head in her hands like it was as heavy as the ball the boys used to kick around the streets at home.

Charly had never known a girl like Jane who always had an ache somewhere.

'Nah, ain't nowhere to hide,' Vinnie said, waving an arm across the bare playground.

'Anyway, it's our turn for that rope,' Lucy called out to the bunch of girls skipping.

'No it ain't,' said Brenda, a bossy girl who was holding one end of the rope. 'Anyway, yer friend Jane's so ugly I bet she don't even know how to skip.'

'You leave Jane be, it ain't her fault her face is … lopsided.' Charly's sister stomped, the Lucy's-real-angry stomp, over to the skipping girls and snatched the rope from Brenda. 'Our turn!' she called back to Charly, Vinnie, Jane and the twins.

Bossy Brenda tried to yank back the rope, but Lucy – who got real fierce if you mucked her around or gave her lip – shoved Brenda till she tumbled over backwards and everyone could see her white undies.

Charly was glad her sister always stuck up for her and their friends, but she didn't like it when a fight broke out in the playground, which happened most days. It made her want to cry harder, made her hate Easthaven more. Stupid Easthaven and its stupid rules. Like prison, where you weren't even allowed outside the grounds, except to go to school every day.

At home, she and Lucy were never prisoners. Mum always let them run about, not only in the courtyard in the middle of the four blocks, but up and down every street too. Course, she and Lucy never told Mum about playing on the old bomb site, which was forbidden. But that rubbly place really did have the best hide 'n seek spots to crawl into.

But there was no running down streets or swinging around lampposts at Easthaven. If Mrs Mersey even caught you sneaking outside the wire playground fence into the vegetable patch, she'd make you clean the toilets. And one time she'd made Charly do that, the toilet still had a poo in it.

Thinking about home and Mum, and playing with her friends on that old bomb site, a new sob blocked Charly's throat. 'I want Mum, I want my blackbirdie.'

'Your turn to skip, Charly,' Lucy said, wisps of hair slashing her face as she and Vinnie swung the rope in big circles.

'Come on, sing 'London Bridge is Falling Down' with us,' Suzy and Patty said at the same time.

But Charly's sobbing stopped her singing a single word.

'I know you miss your mum and your toys,' Vinnie said. 'But you have to make the best of this place. You got yer sister and me and our friends. That's better than havin' no one, ain't it?'

Charly nodded, made the smallest jump over the rope.

'Besides, I told you,' Lucy said, the wind flapping her coat against her skinny legs as she swung her end of the rope. 'I dunno where we'll go yet, Charly, but we ain't stopping at Easthaven Hell for Girls.'

* * *

Charly trembled, standing before Mrs Mersey in the bedroom they'd made her share with bossy Brenda, Mary Pendleton and another girl she didn't know. She shook not only from the cold, but with fear of the punishment that was coming to a bed-wetter.

'This is the second night in a row,' Mrs Mersey said.

Charly couldn't stop her tears spilling. 'I'm sor-sorry,' she sobbed.

She didn't want to be alone in this cold room with Mrs Mersey. She wanted to be downstairs having breakfast with Lucy and the others, about to go to school.

She wanted to tell mean Mrs Mersey that she'd never wet the bed at home; that it had only started at Easthaven; wanted to say that, since the boiler went on the blink, she froze all night, and that it was too scary dark to get up for the toilet. But Charly's sobs stopped her saying a single word. Besides, if she opened her mouth to talk, or breathe, she might be sick from the smell of Mrs Mersey's pickled herring breath.

'Stop yer blubbering, daft girl,' Mrs Mersey said. 'Strip this bed immediately, and take off that wet nightdress.'

Once Charly had shakily slipped into dry vest and knickers, the damp sheet trailing from her arms, Mrs Mersey grabbed her by the shoulder and shoved her out of the bedroom and down the wide, wooden staircase. She made her go so fast, Charly was afraid she'd trip over the sheet and tumble right down those stairs.

Because if you fell down stairs you died.

They reached the wood-dark entrance hallway. Charly had never seen so much wood inside a house, or one that didn't have a single decoration like Mum's owls or Aunty Edna's teaspoons from all over England. There were just a few photographs on the walls, of people not smiling, like you're supposed to for a photo.

'Charly?' Lucy ran from the dining room towards her. 'Why's my sister standing here shivering in her knickers and vest?' she said to Mrs Mersey. 'Why ain't she dressed for school? Why wasn't she at breakfast?'

'Shut yer trap and mind yer business, Lucille Rivers,' Mrs Mersey said, 'or you'll be standing here in your underwear too. Now off you go to school.' Lucy stood still, breathing hard, staring from Charly to Mrs Mersey. 'Off, off, off, I said!'

Charly caught Lucy's scowl as Vinnie tugged her away, out the front door. Her big sister wanted to stick up for her, but you couldn't disobey Mrs Mersey, or you'd be in for it: no food the whole day, polishing cutlery till you could see yourself in it, and scouring floorboards till your knees were red raw.

'Now, you know what you have to do,' Mrs Mersey said. 'It's not like this is the first time you've wet your bed, is it, you horrible snotty-nosed child?'

Charly sniffed. 'No, please, I'm s-so c-cold,' she stuttered, legs and arms numb, the damp sheet an ice-block in her hands.

'*Tsk, tsk,*' Mrs Mersey said, snatching the sheet, making sure not to touch the damp spot. She threw it over Charly's head. 'Now don't your move a single muscle until I say so. Is that clear?'

Charly nodded through her tears, her words coming out muffled, beneath the sheet. 'What about school? I can't miss lessons.'

17

Charly had loved school at home, even if she'd only been there a few weeks before they'd got sent to Easthaven, but she liked school here even more. Not only was it an escape from Mrs Mersey and Mrs Benson, but Charly loved looking at the picture books. She adored listening to her teacher read stories about those faraway places she visited in her head, a million miles from Easthaven. And every afternoon after school Charly could pretend for the entire walk back that she was going home to their flat, to Mum and Lucy.

'This's the only lesson you'll get today,' Mrs Mersey snarled, and Charly flinched as she heard Mrs Mersey's heavy footsteps on the floorboards. The meanie might be gone, but still Charly couldn't move, couldn't stop trembling in that icy February air.

Perhaps she'd die from the cold. Or the sadness. Could that happen? Charly had heard the expression "freezing to death", but could being really sad kill you too?

I want to go home. I want Jeannie. I want my blackbird. I want Mum.

'Where are you, Mum?' she whispered to herself. 'Please, please, please come and get me and Lucy.'

And, as she shivered and cried and sniffed beneath that wet and smelly sheet, Charly knew she hadn't used up all her tears.

4

'Once you have finished eating, you will all remain seated in the dining room,' said old Miss Sutherland, who Charly and me'd seen only once in our three months at Easthaven Home for Girls.

Right from our first day, when Mrs Langford had "presented" me and my sister, like a plate of stale cakes, to the Easthaven house mother, and she'd sat there in her office, writing on a paper and never looking up, I got it that Miss Sutherland didn't care a bit about us.

'This afternoon, we have a visitor,' Miss Sutherland said, her face wrinkling like an old apple as she smiled. 'Mr Zachary will speak to you about something very important. So you must all behave correctly, as is expected of Easthaven girls. Do you understand?'

'Yes, Miss Sutherland,' the girls chanted.

Snatches of whispers, excitement and questions buzzed around the room; we'd never had visitors.

'What yer reckon this is about?' Vinnie said, nudging me.

'Probably some new rule.' I gnawed at the skin around my thumb, since I'd chewed away the whole nail.

Ten minutes later, all sixteen of us still seated at the table, Mrs Benson, the other care worker who was a smudge less mean than Mrs Mersey, marched into the dining room with a man.

Apart from the gardener, Mr Pottman, we never saw any men, and a wave of giggles rippled across the room.

'Quiet now, girls,' Mrs Benson said, with a stern frown. 'Mr Zachary has come to talk to you about Australia. Who can tell me where Australia is?'

We looked at each other, shrugged. At first no one put up her hand.

'What's Australia?' Charly whispered to me.

'It were an English colony, a long time ago,' I said. 'So me teacher said.'

Suzy Hampton raised a hand. 'It's a faraway country across the sea.'

'With cute furry animals,' said Patty. 'Kangaroos and koalas.'

'Big birds too, emus,' said Vinnie.

'And black people,' Jane Baxter said. 'Aborigines.'

'Yes, that's right,' Mr Zachary said with a wide grin. His teeth were white, not a bit like my father's yellow-brown ones, and he wore a smart suit and a shirt as white as his teeth. Mum would have said Mr Zachary was a dapper dandy.

The dapper dandy opened a small black suitcase, pointed to a Senior girl, Diane, and asked her to come to the front of the room.

'Please hold up each picture in turn,' Mr Zachary said, point-ing to the pile of photographs he'd put on the table. Diane gig-gled, her face going crimson as her hand brushed Mr Zachary's when she took the first picture.

It was of a long sandy beach with clear green water beneath a blue sky. The kind of sky we hardly ever saw in London.

'Australians go to these beaches and swim in this warm sea-water every day,' Mr Zachary said.

'Oi, wouldn't that be smashing, Lucy, splashing about in seawater?' Vinnie whispered.

'There's exotic fruit too, you can simply eat apples and oranges straight from the tree.' Mr Zachary gave us another big smile, and pointed to the next picture. 'Feast your eyes on those sweet and juicy pineapples!'

Diane held up more pictures, of huge parks where children

and dogs played, of farms where men cut wool from fat sheep. "Shearing" Mr Zachary called it. And others of men hacking down tall plants which Mr Zachary said was sugar cane.

There were kangaroos and koalas, and birds, fish and coral of every rainbow colour.

'So, who would like to live in Australia?' Mr Zachary asked.

Every girl in that room shot up a hand but warning bells clanged in my brain.

It all sounds too good to be true. And Australia is a very long way from Mum.

Vinnie frowned. 'I thought you wanted to get away from Easthaven?'

'Course I do,' I whispered. 'But I just don't know … '

Don't know what? Maybe this is *our chance to get away?*

I slowly raised my arm. Charly looked at me, and raised hers too.

'Well, that's wonderful,' Mr Zachary said, with another smirk. 'Because I'm here to find girls who are keen to have this amazing Australian experience.'

'But why do the Australians want us to go and live there?' I asked, finally peeling away that tough thread of thumbnail skin. I pressed my tongue against the stinging spot of blood.

'Because Australia is a new and vast country,' Mr Zachary said, 'and they don't have enough people to fill it up and do all the jobs.'

Suzy Hampton raised her hand, darted a glance at Patty. 'Me sister and I'd like to go but we can't swim.'

'I can't swim neither,' Jane said. 'Swimming gives me tummy ache.'

Several other girls called out that they couldn't swim either.

'Oh don't worry about that,' Mr Zachary said with a flick of his hand. 'The boat journey to Australia takes six weeks, plenty of time to learn to swim in the ship's pool.'

'*Six weeks*?' Jane blurted out. 'I'm sure to get the seasickness.'

'I bet you'll all be having too much fun to get seasick,' Mr Zachary said.

'Where would we live in Australia?' I asked. 'In another orphanage, er home – ' Miss Sutherland forbade us to call Easthaven an orphanage ' – like this one?'

'Certainly not,' Mr Zachary said. 'There'll be no more care homes or orphanages in Australia. You'll live on one of those lovely farms I showed you in the pictures, or with a family who wants to look after you, perhaps one who wants to *adopt* you.'

'Would my sister and me go to the same family?' I asked, squeezing Charly's hand. 'Charly's only five, she needs me.'

'My sister and me ain't never been separated either,' Patty Hampton said.

'We always stay together,' Suzy said.

'Naturally, every effort will be made to keep siblings together,' Mr Zachary said, with another grin.

'That man's a fake,' I murmured to Vinnie. 'Nobody smiles that much.'

Anyway, why would I trust a man? My father could never be trusted – always pissing away the wages, belting Mum or Charly and me. That policeman who'd come the night Dad fell down the stairs couldn't be trusted either. Sure, he'd come across all nice at first, then he'd ignored our screams when he'd taken away our mother. And he'd called Mrs Langford who'd sent us to Aunty Edna's even though I'd known there wouldn't be room for Charly 'n me.

'If there are no more questions,' Mrs Benson said, 'please stay seated, girls, while I see Mr Zachary off the premises.'

Before they'd even left the dining room, excited chatter ticked about me. As I looked around at every glimmering face, listened to their laughter, the hope in their voices, it seemed I was the only girl who had doubts about going to Australia.

* * *

'Can you imagine eating oranges straight off the tree!' Vinnie's donkey-honk echoed off those dining-room walls. 'I've only eaten about five oranges in me whole life.' She leaned across to Charly. 'I bet you love oranges too, eh, Charly?'

My sister glanced at me, nodded. 'I think so.'

'Oranges are me 'n Suzy's favourite food,' Patty said.

'But we ain't never even *seen* a pineapple, let alone taste one,' Suzy said.

'We had tinned pineapple once for special Christmas afters, with evaporated milk,' Jane said. 'When I was still at home wiv me Mum.'

'I bet tinned ain't nothin' like the real thing,' Vinnie said.

Charly tugged at my sleeve. 'Is Mrs Mersey goin' to Australia?'

I patted her hand. 'No, we'll be rid of that old meanie, and good riddance, is what I say.'

'Will Miss Sutherland tell Mum to come for us in Australia?' Charly said.

I took a breath, fought the stone wedged in my chest. If Charly found out our mother was in prison, she'd be even more frightened. She'd cry harder, wet the bed every night. I could never let on to her that Mum wouldn't ever be able to come and get us from Easthaven.

I couldn't tell her that I too was worried once Mum got out of prison, Australia would be too far away for her to find us.

'Well, I still ain't sure we should go, Charly,' I said. 'Nothing good ever happens to us, why should this be any different?'

'But it has to be better than Easthaven,' Suzy said from across the table.

'Nowhere could be worse than here,' Patty said.

'All you been sayin' since you got here,' Vinnie said, 'is that you'll find a way to escape. Isn't Australia our escape?'

'Maybe,' I said, the yeses and the nos colliding in my mind. 'And I s'pose we needn't go to Australia *forever*. We could always get another ship back to England later, to see our mum.' I looked at my sister. 'What do you think of that idea, Charly?'

My little sister gave me a solemn nod.

'I'm so excited we're all going to this paradise together – you, Charly, me, Jane and the twins!' Vinnie said, jiggling about in her chair, grabbing my arm, letting go. Grabbing it again. A right jack-in-the-box.

'I can't wait to get in that warm seawater,' Suzy said. 'To feel the sand … '

' … between me toes,' Patty finished.

Jane's face crumpled. 'I'm *sure* to get burnt and sick in that hot sun.'

'Blimey, can't yer stop thinking about bein' sick for one minute?' Vinnie said.

The hand of the spring breeze pushed a wave of cool air through the cracked-open window, across the dining room, and yeah, I supposed it'd be nice never to feel cold; never to freeze in a bare playground, without a decent coat.

The more I thought about it, the better Australia sounded. I wouldn't be forced to watch Mrs Mersey send Charly and Mary Pendleton – another sickly five-year-old with a runny nose – outside without warm clothes. Poor little Mary coughed all night long too, and Charly and the other two girls in that room were always complaining about the barking dog stopping them sleeping.

And Australia really *was* our only way of escape.

But it's so *far away, six weeks on a ship.*

'That's enough chatter, girls,' Mrs Benson said, sweeping back into the dining room alongside Miss Sutherland.

'Right, before the Juniors return to their gardening tasks,' Miss Sutherland said, 'and the Seniors begin their laundry work, I have something else important to say.'

The chatter ceased, and all heads turned to Miss Sutherland.

'I know all of you would love to go to Australia,' she said, 'but unfortunately not everyone will have that chance.' She held her clasped palms up in front of her, as if praying, and took a breath, splayed her fingers apart. In, out, in out.

'Only a few lucky girls will be chosen, and even those girls must pass a medical test.' Miss Sutherland's eyebrows rose above her glasses. 'And why is that, you might ask? Well, it's because Australia only wants England's healthiest physical specimens.'

Foul-tasting liquid burned my throat, and I was afraid of throwing up the cheese pie I'd just gobbled. Any idiot could see that my sister – a skinny bed-wetter, cry-baby with a constant cold – didn't have a hope of passing any medical test.

And no way could I go to Australia and leave Charly on her own.

5

'**O**i, Lucy, you ain't never told me what yer dad was *really* like,' Vinnie said, a swipe across her forehead leaving a streak of soil. 'Course we all heard rumours, heard he liked the whisky.'

Still clutching the trowel, I sat back on my heels and stared across the garden, pushing away hair strands the spring breeze flicked into my eyes.

April had slid into May, only time of year we were allowed in Easthaven's vegetable patch. But just to work, not to lie in the shade of a tree, smelling a blossom or chatting with a friend.

It was a month since Mr Zachary's visit, and we'd not heard another word about Australia. Nobody was bold enough to ask Miss Sutherland, and no one dared speak to Mrs Mersey or Mrs Benson, and we'd all started to doubt if Australia was ever going to happen. Anyway, there was still the worry of Charly passing the medical test.

'Oi, enough skiving off, you two,' the gardener, Mr Pottman called to us, his face sharpening into a frown.

Vinnie and I lowered our voices, and I took the dibber, began notching out little holes for her to drop the leeks in.

'Everyone in the flats reckoned yer dad was a bit of a misery guts,' Vinnie went on, placing a leek in each of my earthy holes.

A bit of a misery guts!

Our father was a lot worse than a misery guts, though I'd

never told Vinnie or any of my friends. Too embarrassing. Besides, Mum always said, 'don't want everyone knowing our business.'

Her words to me and Charly, after the accident, jangled through my mind.

… you girls say nothin' to no one … nobody must ever know what really 'appened … But if anybody does ask … say it was an accident.

That was right before Iris Palmer, our nosey neighbour who carried around an old potato – "for me *roomatizem*" – had come rushing out of her ground-floor flat and seen my father's body lying in the doorway. She'd looked up to Mum cuddlin' me and Charly on the top step.

'Well, if you ain't fetchin' the rozzers, Annie Rivers, I'll 'ave to do it meself,' she'd called up the stairs. My mother didn't move, didn't answer, so Iris Palmer had sent her spotty-faced son then and there, for the coppers.

But since my father was now "six feet under" as Mrs Langford had put it, who cared if Vinnie knew the truth about him? Besides, I'd been itching to tell her for ages.

'Dad could be nice. Sometimes he'd joke around wiv Charly and me. But the whisky sent him into a right temper. He'd yell at Mum 'n me 'n Charly when he got back from the pub, for *nothin'*. Mum would tell him off for pissin' away all our money … said there wasn't enough to buy food, or for the electricity meter.' I took a breath, twisted that dibber till the hole was deep enough for not one leek, but a dozen. 'That's why she had to work of a night. She hated leaving us alone, or with *him,* after Nan died of the consumption and couldn't mind us no more, but nights was the only work Mum could find.'

Vinnie placed her hand over mine, on the dibber, stopped me digging deeper. I swallowed a sob, shrugged off my friend's hand and flung aside the dibber.

I scooped up a clump of soil, let it slide through my fingers till my hands were empty, and I saw again our lovely Nan, till she got sick and couldn't afford the doctor. I smelt her boiled stew with dumplings that she'd cook for Charly and me, tasted her bread pudding. I saw again that last icy evening with Mum and Dad, on the stairs. And I understood how quickly, how suddenly, a girl could lose everything. The whole bleedin' lot.

'Well now my father definitely ain't comin' home,' I went on, 'and since it don't look like we're going to Australia after all, I'd give anything for Mum and me 'n Charly to go home, all together. And since you ain't got a home no more, Vinnie, you'd come with us too.'

'I wish.' Vinnie dropped in the last leek, gave me a sad little smile. Thinking about her parents, I reckoned.

'Dead and gone in a split second,' Iris Palmer had said.

For as far back as I could remember, Vinnie Anderson had been my best friend. We'd walked to school every day, played together. Until last summer, when we'd been larking about on our favourite bomb site, and Eric – that's Vinnie's oldest brother – rode up on the rusty bicycle her three brothers shared.

Course I knew Vinnie well, her being me best friend 'n all, but I never really knew her brothers. They were always playing cricket with the other boys, no girls allowed! All I knew was they all had the same orange hair and freckled faces as Vinnie.

'You gotta come home, Vinnie,' Eric had said. 'Mum and Dad, they're *gone*.'

'Gone where?' Vinnie had said.

'Gone, you know, *dead*,' Eric sobbed. 'An accident … some car ran 'em down.'

Vinnie frowned, shook her head. 'No, no, that ain't right. You can't just die quick as that.'

But Vinnie's parents *did* die, quick as my father, and that very day my friend and her brothers disappeared from their flat.

'They've taken those kids into care,' Mum had said, when I asked.

Care?

I was confused. Vinnie's mum *and* dad had done all the caring them kids needed, busy as they always were at the fish 'n chip shop.

Nobody could tell me where my friend had gone or if I'd see her again. Without Vinnie's loud laugh, our whole block of flats was suddenly too quiet. And with no freckled face grinning at me of a morning as we walked to school, I'd sunk into the miseries.

'I missed you,' I said, 'when they took you away.'

'Not as much as I missed *you*.' Vinnie gave me a friendly punch on the arm, a heartsick smile. 'We 'ad fun, eh?' she said, 'playin' hopscotch, skippin'.'

'I miss our games so badly,' I said, glancing across to Jane Baxter, crouched over with the Hampton twins, tilling the soil to plant the beans, peas, leeks and cabbages. Even from a distance Jane's moany voice, carrying on about a sore knee or something, annoyed me. 'I miss all of it.'

I even missed our flat, just three cold and cramped rooms, with furniture Mum'd made from boxes and crates and stuff that'd never been furniture in the first place.

I longed for that last freezing winter, when Charly 'n me would cuddle up in bed, my sister clutching her blackbird and both of us hoping Dad would forget we were there, and not bring his temper into our room. I even missed the awful liquorice water Mum made us drink to keep us regular. My legs, always red and chapped from the cold, were even worse at Easthaven without Mum to slather Vaseline on them. And my stomach still screamed with the hunger.

'Well it ain't fair your mum getting locked up when she had nothin' to do with yer dad's accident,' Vinnie said, as Mr Pottman threw us another black look.

I lowered my voice, our heads bent over our bean-planting task. 'No, it ain't fair. Mum told the police Dad fell 'cos he was wobbly with the drink, that she was out at the shops when it happened, but they didn't believe her. Asked her why she didn't try and help him, that's what Iris Palmer had told 'em, that me mum kept sitting there with me and Charly on the step, didn't even check if he was still alive. And then, when Iris Palmer told that rozzer about the fights she heard between Mum and Dad, they reckoned Mum must'a pushed him.'

I took up the dibber again, jabbed away. How easily it slid into that fine, soft soil. Easy as sliding right to the bottom of a staircase.

'I tried to tell the copper he fell on his own,' I said, 'but he said, "how can you be certain, Lucy? You told me you didn't even see it 'appen, that only Charly saw it?"'

'So why don't *she* tell the police he fell?' Vinnie said. 'That's what Charly has to do, sticks out a mile, dunnit?'

I shook my head. 'I tried to get Charly to explain it all to the coppers but she wouldn't say a word about the accident, still won't. She don't never mention our father, like she ain't never had a dad.'

'Remember our teacher told us little kids can block out awful stuff from their mind – like your own dad dying in front of your eyes,' Vinnie said, 'so they don't remember things what could make 'em miserable their whole life.' She sighed, glanced up at Mr Pottman, fumbling in his pocket for pipe and tobacco. 'But I still remember me Mum and Dad clear as day. Eric, Bobby and Danny too.'

'P'rhaps it's only little kids' minds what can block out stuff? Maybe you were already too old when your mum and dad died?'

I stole another glance at Mr Pottman. Instead of giving us mean looks, the gardener was busy lighting his pipe. Puff, puff, frown. Puff, puff, frown, and the breeze snatching away curls of blue smoke. 'So where did them childcare people put your brothers?'

'Some boys' home I s'pose,' she said with a shrug. 'Miss Sutherland won't tell me, won't even let me write to them.' Even as Vinnie turned away, towards Jane Baxter limping from the garden, clutching her knee, I glimpsed my friend's trembling lip.

But like me, Vinnie wouldn't cry. Never would we let a single tear fall on Easthaven grounds. I only wished Charly could hold back her tears too.

'Oi, back to work you two or I'll be having a word with Mrs Mersey,' Mr Pottman shouted. 'It might be Sunday, but this ain't no Blackpool holiday.'

I frowned. 'What's Blackpool?'

Vinnie shrugged again, shook her head. 'When they brung me here, Miss Sutherland said I had to forget about Eric, Bobby and Danny, that Easthaven was me home now.'

'Well let's hope this Australia thing does happen,' I said, gulping down my choking anger. "Cos Easthaven won't *never* be our home.'

* * *

The bell rang for afternoon milk, and Vinnie and I stood, brushing soil from our hands and pinafores.

I didn't tell Vinnie, but I was glad Charly never mentioned our father; never asked where he was, because I had no idea. One thing I was sure though, he wasn't in Heaven, because only good people go to Heaven. God would never open the pearly gates to a husband who punched his wife in the stomach right where a new baby was growing.

Mum had never said so, but I knew those punches – the belly pains and bleeding afterwards that she tried to hide from me – was why there was five years between me and Charly. Unlike most of the mothers from our flats what had a new baby around every two years.

But, unlike all the failed babies, Charly had somehow clung to the insides of Mum's stomach. I'd been afraid she'd be born with a dented face or limb, in the shape of our father's fist, but she wasn't.

'Quite small, but a perfect, healthy little girl,' the midwife had said, and Mum and me smiled at new-born Charly, who'd opened her big blue eyes. I stroked her thicket of almost-black hair, her skin white as last winter's snow before everyone had trampled it to dirty brown sludge.

'She looks just like you, Lucy, me love,' Mum had said, handing Charly to me for my first cuddle. 'And she'll 'ave yer dark curls too.'

As Vinnie and I tramped into the dining room, and Charly scurried towards us from where she'd been cleaning windows with Mary Pendleton and some other five-year-olds, my mother's voice chimed through my mind; chimed in time with those police-car bells, that only got louder. Closer.

I've always tried to protect you both, and I won't stop now. If the police take me away, tell them to take you to Aunty Edna's.

'Why would the police take you away, Mum?' I'd said. 'You ain't done nothing wrong.'

But my mother hadn't said another word, just cried and shook her head, and stayed on that top step cuddling Charly and me. The tightest hug, as if it was the last one she'd ever give us.

And when one of them rozzers *did* take her away, and the other one called in the childcare officer, Mrs Langford, who ordered me to pack some things in a bag for Charly 'n me, the shock and panic gripped my throat so tight I couldn't even ask where they were taking Mum. And I hadn't the slightest clue what to pack.

I flung clothes into a bag, Charly grabbed her Jeannie doll, and her smashed-up wooden blackbird, but my flustering only got worse. This was all way out of my control, and I didn't know what to do, so I just sank deeper into a boggy marsh.

Mud rising up to me knees, waist, neck.

Soon my head'll be under the mud, won't be able to breathe.

I stood in our living room, mind spinning, trying to think, Mrs Langford barking at me to hurry up, that she didn't have all night, so I'd shoved into the bag our only photograph. It was of Mum sitting between Charly and me, smiling, an arm around each of our shoulders.

And once we arrived at Aunty Edna's, that boggy marsh did swallow me right up. 'I can't take 'em, no room here, no food to feed 'em, what wiv me own five,' my aunt kept repeating to Mrs Langford.

Only two days later Mrs Langford had brought us here to Easthaven, and become Liar Langford when every single thing she'd promised – nice and loving care workers, beautiful grounds to play in, a happy place – had turned out to be the most gigantic porky pie lie.

As Vinnie, Charly 'n me hurried down that dim, wooden hallway, I rubbed the numbness from my cold arms. Hard as I rubbed, I couldn't knead away those icy fingers creeping under my skin, clutching at my bones.

Same as that frozen January evening when, straight from the starless square of wintry sky over the courtyard, a soft and ghostly voice had whispered:

You ain't never comin' back home, Lucy Rivers, and you have to take care of Charly now. Forever.

6

'On Monday August 13th of this year, 1962, the following girls will be sailing to Australia on the *Star of New South Wales*,' Miss Sutherland began, standing at the head of the dining-room table.

She cleared her throat, lifting her glasses from the chain onto the bridge of her nose. The bread and marge stuck in my throat. It was over three months since Mr Zachary's visit; three months of fighting off my fear of sailing from England to some unknown place so far away from our mother. But at the same time, Australia was the only way to escape evil Mrs Mersey and Mrs Benson; to stop my little sister crying every day and peeing her bed every night.

'If they don't pick Charly for the test,' I'd said to Vinnie, 'I'm not havin' it either. We have to stay together.'

But – surprise, surprise! – they *had* chosen Charly for the test. Me too, and Vinnie, the Hampton twins, even that moaner, Jane Baxter, deformed face 'n all.

What if Charly failed the test? What if only I passed? Can I refuse to go?

I doubted you'd be allowed to change your mind about such a big decision. So many "what ifs?" One minute I ached so bad to go to Australia, and the next my chest strained with the panic of what we might be going to.

'Hush now, everyone,' Miss Sutherland said. All chatter ceased, and every girl's attention was riveted on the old woman and the paper that quivered between her crooked fingers. I grabbed Charly's hand under the table. My little sister gazed up at me, her blue eyes wide. She had no idea how very important this list was.

'Lavinia Anderson,'

Vinnie's going to Australia!

'Jane Baxter.'

Alphabetical order, so long to wait till the R's!

'Ow,' Charly said, and I loosened my grip on her hand.

'Patricia Hampton, Susan Hampton,'

My heart banged in my chest.

Still nowhere near R.

Miss Sutherland took a breath, pushed her glasses back up her nose again and, in that silent, airless lull, I felt I'd faint right off my chair. In the next second, I'd know if me and Charly were going to this paradise, or staying prisoners at Easthaven Hell for Girls.

Or, God forbid, they'd try and separate us. Mr Zachary said siblings would stay together, but could I believe him?

Miss Sutherland looked back down at her paper. 'Charlotte Rivers, Lucille Rivers.'

Charlotte Rivers. Lucille Rivers.

My mind swirled so fast I couldn't think straight. Then it clicked, Miss Sutherland had read out *both* our names.

'We're going to Australia, *together*, Charly!' I jiggled my sister's hand up and down. 'You, me, Vinnie, Jane and the twins, all of us going to this faraway land where it's sunny all the time.'

But even as I wrapped an arm around my little sister's shoulders, I still wasn't certain this was the right thing to do.

Six weeks on a ship! What if the coppers realise their mistake, and let Mum out today, tomorrow … next week? What if she comes to Easthaven to take us home and we're not here?

But one look at Charly's smile, after months of her teary, red-blotched and puffy face, told me it really was the right thing to do.

'We're going, we're really going!' Vinnie whispered, bouncing in her chair.

The Hampton twins looked excited and even Jane smiled her wonky, squashed-lip grin.

'Hush now,' Miss Sutherland said. 'Now, as chosen girls, I trust you will not let me, or Easthaven Home for Girls, down. You must always be on your best behaviour. Do you understand?'

We all nodded. 'Right then, Mrs Benson will shortly take you to buy some new personal items then, on the thirteenth, a bus will take you to Tilbury Docks, from where your ship will set sail for Australia.'

'Set sail for Australia!' Vinnie breathed out long and hard, her eyes large green saucers. 'Sounds like some romantic picture-house film, don't it, Lucy?'

'You are all dismissed now,' Miss Sutherland said. 'Junior girls out to work in the kitchen garden, Seniors to clear this table.'

Chatter buzzed again as the Juniors filed out of the dining room. Several unchosen girls sobbed with disappointment. Others, who'd passed the medical, frowned in anger, not understanding why they hadn't been chosen to set sail for Australia.

As Vinnie and I attacked a tough patch of weeds, those same thoughts ticked through my mind. It didn't make sense that they'd refused healthy-looking girls, and chosen us, mostly sickly or skinny or with something else wrong.

* * *

'Mr Zachary said Australia's hot like this all year round,' Jane Baxter said, her heat-flushed face crumpling into a frown as she tugged out tomato bed weeds. 'I'll burn right up ... maybe I shouldn't go, after all.'

'Stop yer moanin',' Vinnie said, freckles squishing up in a grin. 'Yeah, it'll be hot in Australia, but we won't care since we'll be swimming in the sea all day, diggin' our toes into the sand, skippin' along the beach and ... and, oh I'm going to do so many things. I wish we was leaving right this minute. I hated Easthaven before, but now I know we're goin', I hate it even worse.'

'What if I get sunburn?' Jane said. 'It could make me really ill.'

'Shut yer gob, Jane,' I said. 'We've had enough of you always pretendin' to be sick.'

'I'm *not* pretending.' Jane's lip trembled as she straightened up from the weeds, stamped away and flopped down in the shade of a big tree.

'Finally my sister and me might get a real family,' Patty said, eyes bigger than ever, behind her thick glasses.

'We ain't never had parents,' Suzy said. 'Well, none we can remember.'

'Well, I'm not as sure as you all, about this,' I said, glancing around for Mr Pottman. No sign of the gardener, so I picked off a tomato. It wasn't ripe, but the hard work had made me so thirsty, I took a bite anyway. 'Miss Sutherland told us Australia only wants healthy physical specimens,' I went on, 'but look at us chosen ones – you twins with yer bad eyes.' I nodded at Jane Baxter lying in the shade, fanning a hand across her face. 'And Jane, born with that gap in 'er lip. Hare lip, they call it, and that hole at the top of 'er mouth. I know she got it fixed, but it were a botch job if you ask me, we all know 'er face still don't look right.'

I pointed across to the playground where my sister sat cross-legged with two other five-year-olds in the shade of a tree, playing with some marbles Mr Pottman had found in the shed. 'And as for Charly who's had a runny nose since the day we got 'ere,' I said, 'you could hardly call her a healthy physical specimen.'

'But remember what Mr Zachary told us,' Suzy said.

'That sisters would be kept together in Australia,' Patty said. 'That'll be why they're sending Charly too, so you two can stay together.'

'All's I know,' I said, 'is that every one of us are either sickly or nuisances. I clear heard Mrs Benson say: "Lavinia Anderson's a right nuisance, talking and laughing so loud and asking about those brothers of hers." And Mrs Mersey's always tellin' me I'm a troublemaker and Charly's a bother what cries too much and still wets the bed at five years old.'

I kept tugging at the stubborn weeds. 'What if them medical tests didn't have a thing to do with finding healthy physical specimens? What if Easthaven only wants to get rid of its nuisances and sickly girls?'

'Well I'm pleased I'm going, I *think*,' Jane said, back with us but not doing any useful weeding. 'But I'm worried my mum won't find me over in Australia.'

'Stop worrying. Miss Sutherland will tell your mother where you went,' Vinnie said, 'and she'll come for you in Australia.'

'I'm wonderin' if our mum even knows Charly and I are going?' I said. 'She surely wouldn't let us go so far away. She'd want us to stay close for when she gets out and we can all go home together.'

'Don't be a silly bugger,' Vinnie said. 'Fer sure they'd 'ave asked yer mum for permission. They can't send kids to the other side of the world without their parents knowing. And you know what? I reckon she'd be really happy you and Charly are goin' to a nicer life.'

'But adults are liars,' I went on. 'Liars and bullies. Apart from me mum, I ain't never met one adult who cared about me, and why would it be any different in Australia?'

'But you heard Mr Zachary … ' Patty said.

' … say that families are ready to take us in,' Suzy finished. 'Even *adopt* —'

'Charly and me can't get adopted,' I cut in. 'We already got a mum!' My insides twisted into a knot of fear; the terror of losing our real mother forever and getting some stranger in her place.

'Mr Zachary seemed a nice man,' Vinnie said, 'telling us Australia needs us to fill it up, and that we'll have a better life than in England.'

'I dunno, that Mr Zachary was too smiley,' I said.

We dumped our pile of weeds into the wheelbarrow, squinting

into the afternoon sun. 'In any case, me and Charly got chosen, and whether me mum's pleased or not, we're goin' to Australia. I gotta get away from Easthaven for Charly's sake, make me little sister into a normal kid again.'

7

'Stay together, girls,' Mrs Benson called, over the noise of Tilbury Docks – men barking orders, horns bellowing, cranes whining as they heaved crates into the air, people panting under the weight of suitcases.

Such a racket compared with Easthaven where it was quiet 'cos nobody had been allowed to talk; so loud that she couldn't hear the thoughts swirling through her mind as fast as the Thames River she'd seen from the bus window on their journey to the docks.

They hadn't been the only ones on the bus. It stopped at Poplar too, where other children had boarded, and another place that Lucy couldn't tell Charly the name of. Every time it stopped, Vinnie's eyes went big and blinky, looking around for her brothers, but Eric, Bobby and Danny never got on the bus.

'Nobody wander off,' Mrs Benson said, frowning at Patty who'd strayed a bit. 'You wouldn't want to miss the boat, would you?'

'You alright, Charly?' Lucy said, taking her hand.

Charly couldn't speak a single word, with the din of the crowd, the ships and their gigantic shadows, the big adventure to Australia.

Vinnie nudged her, threw her a big smile. 'Cat got yer tongue, Charly?'

Charly nodded. Yes, the cat really had stolen her tongue.

'Keep together now,' Mrs Benson said, as she herded their group through the crowd, closer and closer to the *Star of New South Wales*. Charly kept tripping over her feet 'cos she couldn't tear her gaze from the boat, so enormous that, once they got really close, she turned into an ant.

'We're really going on that boat, Lucy?' Charly said, as the cat gave back her tongue. 'It's got *eight* storeys.'

'Decks, they're called,' Lucy said with a smile, and Vinnie, the Hampton twins and Jane giggled.

'And look at those pretty red funnels, Charly,' Vinnie said.

'We ain't never seen a *building* this big, have we, Patty?' Suzy said, bouncing on the spot. 'Let alone a *ship*. It looks so … '

'So safe,' Patty said.

'They said the *Titanic* was safe,' Jane said, 'but it still sank. And I can't swim.'

Vinnie and Lucy rolled their eyes at Jane for the hundredth time that day.

Charly's neck ached from stretching it backwards to look up at the top of the ship, like the other children, all of them knotted together by ladies who looked like Mrs Benson and Mrs Mersey. Charly didn't know any of the children – girls *and* boys – but they were all holding the same shiny new suitcase that she held, in the hand Lucy wasn't clutching so tight it almost hurt.

When their suitcases had arrived at Easthaven, Lucy had helped Charly pack all the lovely new clothes Mrs Benson had taken them to buy: a hat, coat, two pairs of shorts and two blouses. Two dresses, plus a third one, her favourite with the red hearts-pattern, she'd worn today. There was underwear too, a jumper and a cardigan, two nightdresses, shoes, socks and sandals. Even a swimming costume! Charly also had her very own toiletry bag.

She'd never seen so many new clothes, let alone owned them. All her things came from Lucy who'd got them from some bigger girl from their block of flats. By the time Charly wore them they were thin or torn, the jumpers pilly. And she'd never owned a suitcase, new or old.

'These things will be my very own, right from the start, won't they, Lucy?' Charly had said as they'd shut her suitcase, snapped closed the clasps.

'All yours, forever,' Lucy said, and kissed her forehead.

They'd never had anything new in their flat either.

'How I'd love just one new piece of furniture,' Mum would say, gazing around at the upturned wooden boxes that made a bedside table, a coffee table and food shelves. She'd look down at the lino floor cut-offs and shake her head, dark curls trembling on her shoulders.

How pleased Mum would be when she saw all Charly's new clothes. She'd smile and kiss her and say, 'Pretty as a picture, you are.' And Charly would be so happy that she wasn't missing Mum anymore, that she'd let her mother borrow the new suitcase, so she'd have a new thing in the flat. Or, she'd just show Mum everything when she came to Australia to get her and Lucy.

Lucy, too, had kept looking at herself in her new dress, in the bus window, on the ride to the docks. Vinnie couldn't stop laughing at her own reflection, and flying up and down the aisle and twirling on the spot until Mrs Benson had told her to sit down and shut her trap.

Vinnie wasn't looking at herself now though. No, she kept elbowing Lucy, forcing her frowning face into a kind-of-smile face, the one where you want people to think you're happy, but you're really not.

'Stop yer worrying, Lucy,' Vinnie said. 'Can't you wait to explore this amazing ship?'

'S'pose it *does* look amazing,' Charly's sister said.

Now Charly had seen the beautiful boat they'd travel on, and Lucy had promised that Mum would come to Australia to get them, or that they'd come back on another boat to see her, she was as excited as everyone else about leaving.

'Gather close and listen, girls,' Mrs Benson said, raising her voice over the noise again. 'I'm taking the bus back to Easthaven now, so I'll hand you over to your escorts.' She turned towards two smiling ladies.

'Please say good afternoon to the Misses Kirkwood,' Mrs Benson said. 'Australian sisters, a nurse and a teacher, who have kindly agreed to take care of you, along with some other children, on your journey.'

'Good afternoon, Misses Kirkwood,' Charly's group chorused.

'Hi, girls,' the shorter one said, with a white-toothed smile. 'Call me Amelia.'

The sister smiled too, and said, 'Hi, I'm Hazel.'

Charly recognised the sisters' words but the sounds they made were strange and different.

Lucy's sweat-slippery hand still clung to Charly's as they followed the jolly-looking Misses Kirkwood and suddenly they were tramping up the gangway. Almost on the big boat! Charly's heart fluttered as fast as butterfly wings.

Mr Zachary had pointed to Australia on his world map, but Charly really had no idea where it was. All she knew was that this big ship would take them far away, across the ocean, and she couldn't help holding her breath as she stepped onto the *Star of New South Wales*.

Along with her friends and her sister, Charly crowded up on deck, jammed against the rails with so many other children of all ages, even a girl smaller than she was.

The small girl, almost invisible in that tangle of children, was crying her eyes out. Charly wanted to rush to her and hold her hand and tell her it would be alright because mean Mrs Mersey and Mrs Benson weren't coming on the boat, but Lucy kept a grip on her.

'Goodbye,' squawked the gulls, dipping and diving overhead, in the sea breeze.

'Cheerio, you seagulls,' Charly called, waving up at those dark-winged patches on woolly grey clouds. 'Ta ta!'

The ship's siren boomed and Charly snapped her hands over her ears.

A drumming sound from somewhere deep inside the ship started up, so loud that Charly kept her ears covered.

'What's wrong with the boat, Lucy?' Charly said, as the deck trembled beneath her feet.

'Nothing's wrong, silly billy, only the ship sailing away,' her sister said, smiling as the *Star of New South Wales* slipped towards the sea spread out before Charly like a giant, dark green curtain.

* * *

For their first meal on the ship, tea that evening, Lucy read out the menu card: 'Medallions of veal, roasted potatoes, salad-e Po-lo-n-aise.'

'Yum, yum, pig's bum!' Vinnie rubbed together her hands.

'Yum, yum, pig's bum!' Charly said, but an arrow stabbed her heart as she remembered saying that same thing with Lucy and Mum, and laughing, when her mother would get a bit extra in her wages, and got them some nice sausages for tea.

But the stabbing stopped as quickly as it had come when Charly ate the tastiest meat and creamed potatoes ever. The plum tart for afters was sweet and tangy, but best of all was the ice-cream. And you were allowed to eat as much as you wanted.

'Eat slowly or you'll be sick,' Nurse Amelia said, circling their table. Charly tried hard to keep those good tastes on her tongue, but in the end she couldn't help gobbling everything like the others. And she tasted all those ice-cream flavours she'd never even heard of: mango, pineapple, rum, pistachio.

During the feast, the Misses Kirkwood – Amelia and Hazel – went from table to table, telling all the children about themselves. They said they lived in Sydney, a big city in Australia.

'We've been travelling around Europe,' Nurse Amelia said, 'and we get our passage home paid for, in exchange for looking after you all.'

'So if anyone has any problems,' Teacher Hazel said, 'if you feel sick or sad, you must come and see us.'

'Don't be afraid,' Amelia said with a kind smile, 'we don't bite!'

'They speak funny,' Vinnie said, as the sisters moved along to the next table of children.

'They speak Australian,' Jane said. 'Which must be like English, 'cos I understood most of it.'

'It *is* English, silly billy,' Lucy said. 'They just speak with an Australian accent, which I s'pose we'll get used to.'

'I can't believe we can choose who we sit with,' Vinnie said, looking around at all their friends.

'And you're allowed to talk during meals,' Lucy said, throwing Charly a wink. 'Talk, sing, dance, whatever you want.'

Charly was glad about that too, and she hadn't felt like crying once since they'd boarded.

For their whole first afternoon, not a single crew member had frowned or told them off for running along the decks, exploring every nook of the boat, talking and laughing as loudly as they wanted. Billy, one of the stewards, had given her a huge smile and said, 'Hello there, pretty girl, what's your name?'

'Charly Rivers,' she'd said, and her insides had felt warm and sweet as honey.

And she'd caught one of the adult lady passengers staring at her, overheard her saying to a man who was likely her husband: ' … such dark blue eyes and shiny black curls. I bet some family will be so pleased to adopt such a beauty.'

Oh yes, Charly already adored the boat.

She was still licking ice-cream from her lips when a steward started speaking into a black oval-shaped tube, which made his voice louder, so it reached all the children at the tables in their section, and the adults in the bigger part of the dining room.

'The *Star of New South Wales* was once a three-class ship for trade between London and Sydney,' the steward said. 'During World War II it carried Australian and other Allied soldiers, and was then converted to a one-class ship to carry migrants to Australia, to start new lives.'

Lucy patted Charly's hand. 'Our new lives!'

'But you can see how it has been beautifully restored to its original splendour,' the steward went on, pointing to brightly-coloured windows, like in churches, the ceiling which had swirly carvings stuck on it. He waved a hand towards the gloomy paintings hanging on the walls, and to the fancy floor rugs.

Charly was glad when he stopped talking, the orchestra started playing and a lady in a sparkly silver dress sang a song called 'Land of Hope and Glory'.

It was a sad song, but Amelia and Hazel encouraged them all to sing along.

* * *

'Yippee!' Charly cried, clapping her hands when she discovered she'd be sleeping in the same cabin, with three up-and-down beds, as Lucy, Vinnie, Jane and the twins.

'What a big day it's been for our little Charly, eh?' Lucy said. It was true, Charly felt so heavy, she could barely stand up, as her sister helped her change into one of her new nightdresses.

'That's a pretty pattern,' Suzy said, as Charly found a last bit of energy and twirled around the cabin in her nightdress, banging into everyone, and the beds. 'What birds are they?'

'Nightingales, I think,' Patty said.

Another wave of tiredness hit Charly and she sank onto her bed as a picture flashed into her mind of Mum singing her favourite song, about a nightingale.

"Nightingale" was such a nice word that it must belong to a pretty bird – pretty as Mum – though Charly hadn't had a clue what a real nightingale looked like, until she'd worn her new nightie.

Charly saw Mum smiling at her, smoothing the fringe from her brow, kissing it.

'Oi, why the gloom-face, Charly?' Vinnie said, bending down to Charly's bed, tickling her underarms till she giggled and forgot about nightingale songs. And forgot, for a minute, how very tired she was.

'I feel like a princess,' Patty said. 'A right palace, is this ship.'

'I wish we could stay on it forever,' Suzy said in a dreamy voice, as the twins took turns brushing out each other's plaits.

'The sea turns me insides out,' Jane said, pulling a face.

'Nah, you just ate too much, like the rest of us,' Vinnie said, with a hoot.

Nobody flung open the door and ordered them to shut their traps and go to sleep. No nasty Mrs Mersey yelled at Charly that she was a stupid little idiot.

As Lucy took Charly's new hairbrush and brushed out her waves until her hair shone darkly in the little cabin mirror, Charly thought back over her first, wonderful day discovering rooms that were just for playing games, others for watching films, decks to play sport, the library with all those hundreds of books – treasure she wanted to touch, pictures she wanted to look at, words she wanted to learn to read.

Some she recognised from school at home and school at Easthaven, like Dick and Dora, with Nip the dog and Fluff the cat. There was even her favourite Janet and John book, the one with Janet riding a merry-go-round pony. Because Charly's big dream was to one day ride a pony.

'I can't read proper yet,' she'd said to Hazel, who'd been in the library.

'Well, what if I help you learn to read properly?' Hazel said. 'I bet that by the time we reach Australia you'll be reading like a grown up.'

She also told Charly that from tomorrow, she'd be reading a story every afternoon, to anyone who wanted to listen. Charly already loved Hazel, and couldn't wait for story-time to come.

'Into bed you go now,' Lucy said, slotting the hairbrush back into Charly's toiletry bag. Charly might be tired, but she'd never be able to sleep; this was all far too exciting.

Lucy folded back the sheet beneath Charly's chin, and kissed her brow, like Mum used to. The ache in Charly's chest for Mum was still there, but not as bad as at Easthaven.

'They'll send us to the same family in Australia, won't they, Lucy?'

'Course they will,' Lucy said, climbing up to her bed. 'Mr Zachary promised sisters would stay together. And you and me will stay together till you're all grown up. Nighty night now, go to sleep.'

Her stomach full to bursting, the ship rocking as it ploughed through that wide ocean, and cosy in her bed with her sister sleeping right above her, Charly let her heavy eyelids close.

As she drifted into sleep, she was certain she wouldn't wet her bed that night; might never wet her bed ever again.

8

'What would you like to eat, Miss?'

It was our first onboard breakfast, and I twisted around to a smiling, dark-skinned waiter, standing tall and stiff in a uniform as white as his teeth.

He nodded at the table menu card, propped against gleaming silver salt and pepper shakers.

No one had ever given me a choice of what to eat, and my mind went blank, heat rising to my cheeks.

I picked up the menu card, put it back down. 'Can you choose for me, for all of us?'

The waiter smiled again, nodded and spun around on his heels like a dancer.

'Wow, what a feast!' Vinnie cried as he returned with plates piled high with eggs, bacon and sausages. There was toast too, with different-coloured jams, and orange juice and hot cocoa.

'Girls, girls,' Amelia said, hurrying to our table. 'I told you, eat slowly. Many children were sick last night, from over-eating their first meal.'

'Will all the meals be this big?' Suzy asked.

She and Patty were wearing identical apple-patterned dresses, and Nurse Amelia smiled at the twins and said, 'How can *anyone* tell you two apart?'

Suzy pointed to a big freckle beside her right ear. 'That's the only difference.' The twins giggled and pushed their glasses back up into place.

'Yes, every meal will be like this,' Nurse Amelia said, 'so no gobbling, you wouldn't want to make yourself sick and miss a moment of the day, would you?'

We all nodded, since we couldn't speak with our mouths crammed full of that delicious food.

From then onwards, I no longer stuffed myself, and stopped Charly gobbling too, though it was hard to resist tasting all that food we'd never even heard of, and presented so snazzily on white tablecloths with shiny cutlery. At every meal, I'd read out the menu printed on a painted card, like a real painting a rich person would have hanging on their wall.

At home, with our father drinkin' away his wages, Mum tried her best, but could only afford basics like mash, and fatty gristle that passed for minced meat, dripping or sugar sandwiches. I pictured her face – red rings around sad blue eyes, one cheek swollen and shiny with a purple blotch, and a ripple of sadness coiled through me. I put down my fork for a moment, stopped eating the creamy scrambled eggs.

The further away from England we sailed, the more I thought what a shame Mum couldn't be with Charly and me going to a new life in Australia. There were plenty of adults on the ship. Why couldn't she be one of them? My mum deserved better than that awful life with our father. And then to be locked up for an *accident*. It was so unfair.

* * *

One morning, when gales rocked the boat and the decks creaked, Charly scuttled off to the library. Jane and the Hampton twins reckoned the weather was too wild to go out, but Vinnie and I dashed outside.

'Them waves are mountains comin' straight up from the sea!'

Vinnie shouted, as we shrieked and hung onto each other, and gripped the deck rail.

I nodded, breathed deep, in and out, like the ocean's grey-green waves swelling higher than the ship's deck. I licked my lips, tasting the sea-salt tang, let the wind whip my hair across my cheeks.

Amelia and Hazel kept us updated on the ship's route and, after we'd sailed past sunny Spain, told us we were now in the straits of Gibraltar.

'Look, that's the Rock of Gibraltar,' Amelia said, pointing out the famous greyish-white monolith.

'That nice steward, Billy, told me there's monkeys over there,' Suzy said.

'Maybe we'll see one?' Patty said.

'Is the sea like this in Australia?' Vinnie asked Amelia, as we stared down into the Mediterranean Sea. 'I ain't never seen water this blue, this clear.'

'Oh the waves are much bigger in Australia,' Amelia said with a laugh. 'But so much fun to bodysurf.'

I pictured a box of Surf washing powder. 'What's bodysurf?'

'When you catch a wave and ride it all the way into shore,' Amelia said, 'with your body ... no surfboard.'

Vinnie punched me on the arm. 'Did you hear that, Lucy? I can't wait to try this bodysurfin' thing!'

The sea stayed calm and turquoise as we passed through the Suez Canal. Vinnie and I stood at the bows, angling our faces up to the sun bleaching the sky a paler blue.

All along the shore, palm trees swayed and from little boats – like toy ones – sailing alongside our big ship, the locals sold miniature camels, pyramids and brightly-coloured clothes. We didn't have a single penny to buy nothin', but it was fun watching all the haggling over prices.

'I'll never be able to swim like them,' Jane said, as we watched Egyptian boys dive for pennies the adult passengers were throwing overboard. 'Swimmin' hurts me arms, and I can't get the breathing right.'

'You'll all be swimming like Dawn Fraser in no time,' Amelia, our swim teacher, would say at our daily lesson, clapping her hands and praising us with encouraging words.

But it was true that Jane Baxter was the only one of us who still couldn't dog paddle from one end of the pool to the other without a rubber ring. Maybe she couldn't get the breathing right due to the botched nose and lip surgery?

In any case, Jane spent most days curled up on her bed, her face a pale green shade, while Vinnie and I splashed in the pool with the Hampton twins, played quoits and deck tennis, or found a sunny, windless spot under some stairs for a game of Snap.

Every afternoon Charly scuttled off to the library for kids' story-time, and I swear my sister would've spent her whole day in there with Teacher Hazel, if I'd let her.

At the start of our journey Hazel had told us that while play was fun and healthy, we'd have to do some school work so we didn't fall behind the Australian kids.

One sunny morning when Vinnie and me sloped into the library for Hazel's lessons, Charly was already there, sitting on the teacher's knee, a book open on her lap.

'Look at all the books, Lucy!' she cried. 'How will I learn to read 'em all before we get to Australia?' I loved seeing my little sister's wide smile, eyes as blue and sparkly as the sky outside, instead of red, teary and swollen.

It made me think that I *had* done the right thing, getting her away from Easthaven.

'No hurry, Charly,' Hazel said. 'You're already learning your words so fast. Besides, there are plenty of libraries in Australia.'

Hazel went through the usual boring stuff: maths, reading, spelling, geography. To be polite, since Hazel and Amelia were the bee's knees, I sat still, tried not to fidget, or bite my nails which Amelia was always on at me to stop. But I itched to get back outside on a sunny deck, the breeze on my face, salt on my lips.

'"With", not "wiv"', Hazel was saying, determined to rid us of what she called Cockney speak, before we reached Australia. '"Are not" or "am not", instead of "ain't". And stop dropping your "h"s and your "g"s!'

Our onboard lives quickly slipped into the routine of these sort-of-okay lessons, fancy meals, fun, lots of laughter, and peaceful sleep.

The sky stayed bright blue and cloudless, the sun toasted our pale skins. Vinnie and a Yorkshire boy, Tommy Oakley, with the same white skin and orange hair, had burned badly the first week, and Amelia had to slather cream on them. But Tommy and Vinnie's skin was now sun-bronzed, speckled with deep brown freckles.

One evening, as the sun sank over the horizon, striping the pale sky pink and orange, I grabbed Vinnie's arm, and pointed over the railing. 'Look at the dolphins, they're *bodysurfing*.'

The warm breeze tugging our hair, our dresses, we held our breath at the wonder of those smiley dolphins surfing the waves, free in that wide ocean emptiness.

The freedom was what I loved most of all on the boat.

'We were prisoners at Easthaven,' I said, over the noise of seabirds shrieking and dancing on foamy crests of ship wake. 'Even at home, with me dad, it was a kind of prison.' The birds flapped their wings and soared, up and away over the red funnels. 'I don't never want to be a prisoner again.'

'"Don't ever", not "never". Speak proper now, Lucy Rivers,' Vinnie said, with a great belly laugh as a huge albatross glided high above us.

Amelia and Hazel too gave us loads of freedom. They weren't a bit strict, always smiling and joking, but ready with kind words and hugs. All those things we'd never had at Easthaven Home for Girls.

With all the swimming and playing in warm, fresh air, those pasty-faced kids who'd boarded the ship at Tilbury Docks quickly vanished. Eating all that fancy food, every one of us, except seasick Jane, gained weight, and after only a few weeks on the *Star of New South Wales*, our new clothes were already tight.

* * *

Allowed off the boat for once, we were all strolling down the main street of Colombo when Charly clutched at my arm. 'Look, Lucy, big monsters behind us. Oh, oh, they'll squash us!' I swivelled around to see what my sister was carrying on about.

'Oh my God, elephants!' I cried, as Vinnie, Jane and the twins turned too, our mouths gaping in surprise at that herd of huge animals with swaying trunks, lumbering along the main street.

'Elephants, like in Hazel's picture book?' Charly said.

'Yeah, real, *live* elephants,' Vinnie cried.

Jane looked like she might faint with fear. 'We should scoot back to the boat right now, before those beasts trample us.'

But no one moved, our feet magnets to that road, as we stared in wonder at the elephants marching alongside cars, small lorries and people.

'Most smashin' thing I ever seen!' Vinnie said.

'We'll come back and visit all these places properly one day, won't we, Charly?' I said, thinking of all the incredible things we'd seen on our journey – the exciting new places, strange sights, tangy, spiced smells. 'When we come back home to see Mum. You'd like that, wouldn't you?'

Charly nodded, still staring at the elephants.

For the first few days of our journey, I'd missed Mum terribly. But now, even though every night I kissed the photo I'd grabbed from our flat, my mother's face, her dark, wavy hair, her soft and dreamy voice, had faded. Like an old photograph. A shadow just out of my reach, that could never catch up with me.

To my relief, my sister barely mentioned her, and she'd not cried once since we left Easthaven, nor wet the bed. She was happy, settled into our fabulous ship life, learning to read the Janet and John books. Hazel had let her bring one back to the cabin, where she'd slipped it under her pillow, cradling it and smiling to herself as the ship rocked her into deep sleep.

How Mum would love to see us now, like this.

But even as I convinced myself yet again that it had been the right decision, the familiar worry bogged down my mind.

What if she's already out of prison, and searching for us, going crazy with wondering where we've got to?

Back onboard, while we were waiting for ice-cream cones, Vinnie glanced up at the wall clock. 'Look at the time, hurry or we'll miss the start of the film.'

Charly hurried off to the library and Vinnie and I, the twins and Jane dashed down to the picture house. It was the first time we'd ever been inside a picture house and, blinded for a second in the dark, we giggled as we settled, with our ice-creams, into the comfy velvet seats to watch *The Wizard of Oz*.

'The Wicked Witch of the West looked like Mrs Mersey eh, Vinnie?' I said as the film ended, so amazing I could've sat there and watched it all over again.

'Don't you reckon it's like we're on our very own Yellow Brick Road?' Vinnie said, as we emerged into the brilliant sunlight once again. 'On our way to the Emerald City of Australia, eh my friend, Dorothy?'

'I never even knew Yellow Brick Roads *existed*,' I said. Yellow Brick Roads where there were no signs pointing me back to the past – the sadness of losing my home, my mother, the misery of Easthaven – only the way ahead, to the Emerald City.

'What an idiot I was,' I said, as Vinnie and I scrambled upstairs for a round of deck tennis, 'to have got so worried about leaving England.'

9

Lucy Rivers
Sydney
September 1962

'Look, it's the Australian coastline!' Vinnie shouted, pointing into the distance. 'We're here!'

'Are we getting off the nice boat now?' Charly said as the coast loomed closer.

'This is Fremantle, dear,' the friendly lady passenger said, the one who'd called Charly "such a beauty". 'On the west coast. I believe you girls are going to Sydney, on the east coast?'

'Yes, Sydney,' Suzy Hampton said.

'We're all going to live in Sydney together,' Patty said.

'Well the ship will stop in Adelaide then Melbourne before it reaches Sydney,' the lady said with a smile. 'So there's still plenty of time to enjoy yourselves.'

The boat docked, and as a stream of people trooped off down the gangway, I caught the worry on their creased brows; heard the fear in the hushed chatter that had broken out amongst us kids, except for the young ones like Charly.

All we knew about Australia was that it was a place of endless sunshine where you could pick fruit off the trees, where friendly kangaroos hopped about in fresh air, and where people swam all day – bodysurfed even – in warm seawater. A place where farmers and good people were waiting to give us nice homes and families.

But what was *really* waiting for us in Sydney? I had no idea, and no choice but to let the ship sail us to this mysterious place.

At first I didn't realise I was gnawing at the tiny nails I'd managed to grow in the last six weeks. I thought of Amelia's frown each time she caught me biting them, and I slapped my hand away.

It would be sad to say goodbye to her and Hazel, to the stewards and adult passengers we'd become friendly with. I would miss the delicious food, the luxury of the *Star of New South Wales*. The home we'd come to love. Wouldn't it be easier, safer, if we could just stay onboard and keep sailing around the world, around and around it, forever?

'You reckon we'll go to a family?' Vinnie said. 'Or a farm?'

I shrugged. 'I hope we get families who live in the same block of flats, so we can go to the same school ... so we can keep being best friends.'

'We'll always be best friends.' Vinnie squeezed my arm, and I wondered what Mum would think when she found out Charly and me had a new home, a new family. Would she be upset, or happy for us? I flicked those disturbing thoughts from my mind. *In any case, this Australia lark won't be for long, only till they realise she had nothing to do with Dad's accident.*

'I hope the people will be kind to us,' said Jane, 'and take care of me if I get sick.'

Vinnie and I sniggered at each other, rolled our eyes skyward.

* * *

On Saturday, 22 September 1962, through the early lemon-green light, the *Star of New South Wales* sailed under the huge Sydney Harbour Bridge.

'We're here, Charly!' I grabbed her hand, and Vinnie, Jane, the twins, Charly and I jammed up against the ship's rail alongside all the friends we'd made on the journey.

The warm breeze skittering across our faces, we gazed in wonder at the blue harbour water, and the dozens of sailing boats zipping across it.

'We really are sailing into the Emerald City, eh, Dorothy?' Vinnie screeched, over the ship's horn.

'Nothing like grey and foggy England,' Patty said. 'No black, dirty fog where you can't even see your hand right in front of you.'

'I ain't never seen a more beautiful place,' Suzy said. She and Patty were wearing the same dresses, sunny yellow to match sunny Sydney.

'I've never, not "ain't",' Hazel said, with a smile. 'Don't tell me you've already forgotten my lessons?'

Houses with red roofs dotted the hillsides around, between very tall trees whose leaves shimmered silvery-blue in the morning light.

'Eucalyptus trees,' Hazel said.

'But we call them gum trees,' Amelia said.

As the ship slid closer to miles and miles of concrete wharf that Hazel said was called "Pyrmont", people at the dockside started waving and cheering.

I squinted into the crowd, trying to pick out, to imagine, the family taking me and Charly. They'd surely have come to collect us.

Nobody could ever replace Mum but until she could prove she was innocent, Charly and me had no mother. So I supposed a different one was better than none at all. Maybe the father would be nice, and speak softly and play with us, and teach us about all those colourful Australian birds and fish we'd heard of.

We said our goodbyes to Amelia and Hazel, who gave us all big hugs.

'Have fun!' said Billy, our favourite steward, throwing us one of his special smiles.

'Good luck!' the other adult passengers cried, waving and blowing us kisses.

'I wish you all the happiness in your new lives, lovely girls,' the nice lady passenger said. 'And good luck to you, beautiful little one,' she said, planting a kiss on Charly's brow. 'I just know your new family will love you so much!'

I caught the sad look on the lady's face, as if she wanted to pack my sister into her suitcase and take her with her. Wherever she was going. But no way was Charly going anywhere without me. And in that excited tide of people moving towards the gangway, I kept a firm grip on my sister's hand.

My heart lurched with hope, yet my nerves jangled so much, my legs quivering, I could hardly walk down that gangway.

* * *

Men dragged carts loaded with bags across the dockside. Cranes unloaded gigantic wooden boxes onto the wharf. Families stood in clusters amidst their luggage, all looking as worried as I felt, beneath my excitement.

Several stern-looking women holding clipboards were gathering all the kids in front of several large sheds.

'Stay within the designated area and do *not* wander off,' ordered one woman, tall and thin as a long stick.

'Oh no, they look like childcare officers,' I said. 'I thought we'd seen the last of them in England.'

'Are they mean, like Mrs Mersey?' Charly said, as one of the women looked down at her clipboard and began shouting out a roll call, above the dockside bustle and din.

'Don't worry, Australians aren't mean, Charly,' I said, as the woman spoke with that same, strange Australian accent as Amelia and Hazel. She often had to repeat herself as a kid hadn't recognised their own name.

I hoped my sister couldn't sense the tremble in my voice, my rising panic as the women separated boys from girls, and several big men marched some of the boys off in a different direction.

'Didn't Mr Zachary promise they'd keep siblings together?' I mumbled to Vinnie.

'So why're they taking away the brothers?' Vinnie said, and I caught the sadness in her big green eyes for her own brothers.

My heart beat so fast as they tore siblings from one another, nobody explaining why, or saying they'd see each other again.

Some of the girls sobbed, others wailed and one of the women moved amongst us, shaking, slapping the noise-makers. 'Shut up, shut up, shut up,' she snapped.

Thank God Charly and I are sisters, not brother and sister.

Just the thought of being separated from Charly terrified me. But when another woman herded a cluster of girls away from the main group, to another shed, I wrapped my arms around Charly's shoulders, and fought back tears. Vinnie and Jane clung to the back of my coat, Patty and Suzy standing so close to each other they looked like a mirror reflection.

'I'm hot,' Charly bleated, trying to wriggle from my grip.

It really was growing hot, and it struck me then that the peak of the English summer, when we'd left, had been cooler than this Australian spring.

The women separated more girls from the main group, some I knew to be sisters, and my chest tightened as the girls screamed, trying to run back to each other. But those stern women kept them apart.

They won't separate Charly and me, no they won't. Mr Zachary said.

The Hampton twins clung to each other, eyes wide and fearful behind the thick glasses. Jane was sobbing. I could hardly catch my breath, wanted so badly to bite my nails. But I couldn't let go of Charly, even one hand.

Beneath a wave of that hot sun, relief swamped through my sweaty body when one of the women ordered me, Charly, Vinnie, Jane, Suzy and Patty, along with some other girls we didn't know, into one of the sheds.

Once inside, two new women greeted us, one chubby, the other skinny. 'Come in, girls,' they both said. At least they were smiling, and handing out glasses of green drink and square cakes covered in coconut.

'It's a lamington, dear,' Skinny Woman said, at my frown. 'A delicious Australian cake.'

It was spongy, chocolaty, and most certainly delicious and, in that peace and quiet, after the racket outside, I relaxed a little as we drank and ate. Vinnie and I exchanged a small smile. Maybe things were going to turn out alright after all.

'Hush now, children,' Chubby Woman said, as they began splitting us up into smaller groups, 'we've got a lot of you to process this morning.'

I had no idea what "process" meant, but it didn't sound like something you did to people.

Charly started whimpering as Vinnie, Jane, the twins, Charly and I huddled in a hot and airless circle. My breath caught in my throat, as I fought the panic coiling once more from deep inside.

Skinny Woman started reading names from her list. I didn't recognise any of them, except the last one. 'Patricia Hampton,' she said, ticking off Patty's name from her list. 'All of you, go and wait outside, over there.' She pointed to a row of buses that had magically appeared outside the shed.

'But I'm supposed to stay with my sister!' Patty cried, hanging on to Suzy. 'Mr Zachary said siblings would stay together.'

'We're twins,' Suzy said, tears gathering in her eyes, 'we have to stay together to ... to plait each other's hair.'

'I'm sorry, dear, I don't know a Mr Zachary,' Skinny Woman said, giving Patty a nudge. 'Come on now, don't make trouble.'

Skinny Woman tried to unfurl Patty's fingers from Suzy's arm, but she hung on, tears streaming down her face.

'H-he p-promised,' Patty sobbed.

Two big men I hadn't noticed before clamped a hand on each of Patty's shoulders, dragged her outside, and shoved her up the bus steps.

'We th-thought we'd f-finally have a real f-family *together*,' Suzy stammered, her face red patches, glasses all fogged up. 'Where are they taking Patty? Why?'

So dizzy with terror, I couldn't answer her.

'Oh no, poor twins!' Vinnie cried.

Another thing I hadn't noticed were the couples, around ten of them, coming into the shed. All of them looking us up and down as if we were things for sale in a shop and they couldn't decide what to buy.

Whatever are they *doing here?*

The women checked their clipboards and started giving out the youngest children to the couples. One child each.

My mind whirled and buzzed, a runaway spinning top, and I clung more tightly to Charly. Vinnie, Jane and Suzy formed a tight circle around my sister.

Hide Charly, they won't see her. Will forget about her or … or something.

A tall man, with the same dark and wavy hair as mine and Charly's, loped into the shed. Skinny Woman nodded at him and my ears burned to overhear what she was saying to Chubby Woman. 'They must be the last adoption parents, the Wollongong people. But where's the wife? Aren't we supposed to see both parents, before handing over the kids?'

Chubby Woman frowned, checked her clipboard, made a tick and nodded. 'Yes, Mr and Mrs Frank Ashwood,' she said, as the man stepped forward to speak with them.

'My wife's waiting in the car. She's a little overwhelmed by … by all this,' he said, waving an arm at us. I held my breath as he turned back to the women. 'I thought it best she didn't come inside, or she'd want to take ten children!' He gave a short laugh.

'Right oh then, Mr Ashwood,' Skinny Woman said, and nodded at our huddled group. 'Yours is that little dark-haired girl.'

Yours? What do they mean, yours?

My heart stopped, hammered violently. I gagged on the acidy liquid surging into my throat. Swallowed hard.

No, no, don't take Charly, I won't let you take her.

Chubby Woman shoved Suzy, Vinnie and Jane out of the way and tried to pull Charly from my grip. I kept my arms clasped around her. If they wanted to take Charly, they'd have to take me too.

The same burly men who'd torn apart Patty and Suzy stomped over, unclamped my arms from around Charly.

My sister screamed, little hands reaching out, trying to grab at me, but one of the men held her, hurried her towards that Frank Ashwood.

'Please don't take her,' I cried, as the other man seized my arms. 'We're sisters, I have to look after her ... too young to be on her own.'

But none of them listened to my pleas, and as one of the men pushed a struggling Charly into the arms of that tall, dark-haired stranger, my little sister kept twisting around to me, tear-stained blue eyes wider than ever. And I caught the fear in them, a deep terror I hadn't seen before, even on the worst days at Easthaven.

'Take me too!' I shouted at Frank Ashwood, who was struggling to hold the squirming, squealing Charly. 'I'm all she's got, I'm like a mum to her.'

'Don't be silly, Miss,' Skinny Woman said. 'Your sister has a new mum now.'

Frank Ashwood looked straight at me. 'Is the sister being adopted?' he asked Chubby Woman.

She frowned, checked her clipboard. 'No, Lucille Rivers is on the Seabreeze Farm list.'

Frank Ashwood's face crumpled and I thought he was about to take me too, but his gaze flicked away, and he patted Charly's back. 'Shush, little one, it's alright. Shush now.'

Frank Ashwood and Charly had almost reached the doorway when the muscly men had to let me go, to restrain another girl who was also trying to chase after her sister.

I saw my chance, flung open my suitcase, trembly fingers taking the photo of Mum, me and Charly. I folded it, ripped it in half, right down the middle of our mother's face. The part with half of mum and all of Charly, I shoved back into my suitcase. The other part – half of mum and me – I held on to, and sprinted after Charly.

The burly men let go of the girl they were holding, came for me again. I had no clue how I'd get the photo to Charly, but suddenly, that picture of us was the most important thing ever. Not knowing what else to do, I shoved it into Frank Ashwood's hand, just outside the shed door, as the men caught up to me, grabbed me and held me back.

'Please make sure my sister gets this,' I said, fresh tears smarting my eyes.

He didn't nod or say anything, only stared at me, eyes wide, stroking Charly's back and whispering to her as if my sister were some small, fluffy animal.

And, as the men dragged me back inside, the last I saw of Charly was a flying clump of dark hair when her little body curved back to me, arms reaching out, puffy eyes red-rimmed, Frank Ashwood hurrying her away in the opposite direction from the buses.

Everything stopped in that one moment. My world stood still. And there was nothing after that. Nothing at all.

I barely recalled the men bundling me into one of those hot and stuffy buses, along with Vinnie, Jane and Suzy.

And, above the silent screams buckling my mind, Suzy Hampton's cries for her own sister were no louder than whispers.

PART 2
1962 – 1973

10

Lucy Rivers
Southern Highlands, New South Wales
22 September 1962

It was late morning when the bus finally rumbled away from the dockside, out of the city of Sydney, onto a road hedged in by more trees than I'd seen in my whole life.

Suzy hadn't said a word since they'd stolen Patty, just stared, trance-like, out the bus window. She kept her face turned away but her heaving shoulders told me she was still sobbing, silently, for her lost sister.

I wanted to reach across the aisle from my spot beside Vinnie and pat Suzy's arm, tell her everything would be alright. But I couldn't, so paralysed I was with the shock of losing Charly. Besides, after those awful separations on the Pyrmont docks, I figured things might not be one bit alright in Australia.

They'd taken Charly so quickly I hadn't even had time to catch my breath before she'd vanished to some place I could barely pronounce. I wanted to write it down, so I wouldn't forget it, but I had no pencil or paper, so I kept saying the name over and over in my head.

Wollongong. Wollongong. Wollongong.

'So many trees out there,' Jane said. 'Are they poisonous?'

Vinnie raised her eyebrows. 'You ever heard of a poisonous *tree*, Jane?'

'We Aussies call it the bush,' the bus driver said, flinging a meaty arm towards the trees, so thick there was often only an inch of sky between clumps. 'Ya gums, waratahs and wattles. Ya banksias and pines. The good 'ole strine bush.'

'*Strine*?' Tommy Oakley called out. We'd got a bit friendly with Tommy on the boat, and his friend, Nick Hurley, both from a boys' home up Yorkshire way.

'Strine, ya know, Aussie for Os-stry-li-enne.' The driver spelled it out, long and slow, as if we were idiots. And since most of us frowned, shrugged at each other, I wondered if we *were* idiots; goons that got tricked into coming to this hot place with nothing but *strine* bush as far as you could see.

The sun was so bright I had to squint the whole time, and hold up a palm over my eyes.

'If they call this spring,' I said to Vinnie, our shoulders bumping as the bus lurched in and out of cracks and holes, 'how hot will it get in summer?'

'And where's the rain?' Vinnie said. 'This place looks like it ain't never – like it *hasn't ever* – seen a single raindrop.'

'Where are all the people, the Australians?' Vinnie asked, both of us still staring out the window at those trees whose names I'd already forgotten.

'And the buildings, houses, shops and streets?' Jane said. 'And how come there's no fog?'

'It's all so brown and dry,' said Bessy, a Liverpool girl, as the bus rumbled on, outside with the engine noise, inside with our chatter, nervy whispers. A few sobs.

'Not a bit like our green parks back home,' said Helen, Bessy's friend from the same Liverpool girls' home.

'Where are you taking us?' Nick Hurley called out to the driver.

'Place called Seabreeze Farm,' he said. 'Few hours south-west of Sydney, on the Southern Highlands.'

'What's it like, this Seabreeze Farm?' I asked, chewing at a thumbnail.

The driver shrugged. 'Dunno, never been there. But I been told some new owner's setting up his farm there.'

Vinnie nudged me in the ribs. 'Seabreeze, the driver said, must be near the sea eh, Lucy? Might be alright after all.'

'I know you're trying to cheer me up,' I said, 'but don't bother, I'll never be cheery till I find Charly; till I get my sister back.' I took a shaky breath, my chest tight, achy. 'I didn't even get to *see* the wife of that man who took Charly. How will I know her new parents are treating her proper? How can I find her?' I glanced across the aisle again, to the back of Suzy's head. 'Poor Charly, poor Patty, all alone here.'

Apart from losing Charly, it was a terrible worry, not knowing where or what we were going to. The same fear as when Liar Langford took Charly and me to Aunty Edna's, then to Easthaven Home for Girls. But at least we'd been together.

I was glad Vinnie and Suzy were with me now, even that moaner, Jane Baxter, otherwise I might've flung myself under those big dusty bus wheels.

Finally, all of us sweaty, thirsty and tired, the driver turned his bus off the main road at a tin box sitting on a tree stump and a wooden sign that said "Seabreeze Farm". Almost there, kids,' he announced.

At the end of a bumpy track, the bus whined to a stop in front of a large house set on short stilts. Sun glinted off the roof and a wide veranda seemed to run all the way around it.

Two cats prowled across the veranda like stern guards. Another three slept, ears twitching, tails swishing at buzzing flies, in the shade of a big tree with dark, fat leaves.

We clambered down from the bus, hands shading our eyes from the glare as we looked around. 'There isn't *anything* out here,' I said. 'Not a single thing.'

A short, skinny man stood on the veranda, smiling at us. A dog sat at his feet, a chubby woman standing on his other side, whose face we couldn't see because she was staring at the ground. As we shuffled towards them, a flock of huge white birds with yellow head-fans screeched from overhead branches: '*Wark, wark, wark, wark!*'

'Go away, go away!' they seemed to be shrieking.

'Oh, oh! They're going to swoop down and attack us,' Jane said, flinging her arms over her head.

'Go away, go away!' screeched the monster birds.

And I did want to go away – course I did! – but where was there to go? Only dust and purple-brown bush as far as I could see.

* * *

'Welcome, my children, gather round.' The man kept smiling, beckoning us with some kind of stick, towards the farmhouse veranda. As we got closer, I saw it was one of those whips for horses.

'I'm Mr Milton Yates,' he said, all thirty-two of us gathering, hot and straggly, before the veranda – sixteen boys and sixteen girls that Skinny Woman from the docks had counted, when they'd shovelled us onto the bus. 'And this here's Bluey, whose job it is to round up the sheep.' The dog's fur really was a grey-blue shade, and as Mr Yates ruffled its ears, Bluey gazed up at his master, grinned and gave a small bark as if he too was welcoming us into his home.

As Mr Yates spoke, one of his ears waggled. It had a bit missing from the top, like someone had bitten out a chunk. The other, good one, didn't waggle.

One of the sentry cats was playing with a mouse, a paw tapping at the squeaking, little creature as it darted back and forth across the veranda.

Mr Yates spread his sun-brown, skinny arms wide, the veins sticking out like green worms. 'Welcome to Seabreeze Farm.

Our homestead, the paddocks, the billabong, and the bush that stretches right to the horizon. My home that's now *your* home.'

Mr Yates was short, though the big black boots did make him look taller, especially standing on the veranda, above us. He smiled and turned to the woman at his side. 'Isn't that right, Mrs Yates?'

She gave a quick, nervy nod, without lifting her head. I'd never seen a person more tired-looking than Mrs Yates, except Mum when she'd come in from a hard night's work looking after an old person who'd taken ill. The exhaustion didn't show on Mrs Yates' face though, since we still couldn't see it. No, it was in the sag of her shoulders, the hunch of her back, which made her belly bulge. Chubby, limp arms hung by her sides, and she wore a faded, shapeless shift that might once have been navy.

'She looks like Humpty Dumpty,' I hissed to Vinnie, who slapped a hand over her giggle.

Suzy, standing on my other side, let out a hiccupy sob. Her glasses slid down her sweaty nose and she didn't even bother pushing them back up.

'What's wrong, girlie?' Mr Yates said to Suzy, frowning as he flicked the horse whip at a droning fly.

Suzy didn't answer, just pushed back her glasses, squinty eyes crossing. The sentry cat trapped the squeaking mouse, held it between its jaws.

'Suzy's sad 'cos they took her twin sister away from her,' I blurted out, since my poor friend was still too upset to speak. 'Like they took away me own … *my* own sister. Mr Zachary said siblings would stay together in Australia.' I tried to keep the anger, the desperation, from my voice. 'Jim and John Browning got to stay together, Carol and Fiona Mulligan too. Why not Suzy and me? It ain't – isn't – fair, Mr Zachary *promised* —'

'Well, sadly, life wasn't meant to be fair,' Mr Yates cut in, as the squeaking stopped, and the mouse dangled, limp, from the cat's jaws. 'Though life is sometimes *lucky*, and all of you can count yourselves lucky that Mrs Yates and I have taken you in.'

He took a breath, slashed the whip at the same fly. The buzzing stopped, the fly obviously dead, but he kept grinding a boot into that small black body.

'Count yourselves lucky that we saved you from those filthy, overcrowded English orphanages,' he went on, 'offering you a better life here in Australia. Count yourselves lucky that we're being your mum *and* dad. Count yourselves lucky I'm giving you the chance to become a skilled, law-abiding citizen in your adult life.'

I already have a mum! Don't want to be here. Want to be back home with her and Charly. Where is this Wollongong place?

Mr Yates stretched his neck, long and wrinkled as a turtle's, towards us. He stuck his knife-nose into the air and his smile was all crooked, bucky teeth stretched over thin lips. Smiley men weren't honest men and after only ten minutes here I was already wary of Mr Milton Yates.

'*She* might look like Humpty Dumpty but *he's* got a rat face,' I hissed to Vinnie, and Jane let out a gasp, gave me a stare.

'Did you say something, girlie, can we all share the joke?' Mr Yates' small, pink-rimmed eyes stared, unblinking, at me as I fidgeted in the heat, squinted against the sun's glare. 'What's your name anyway?' He grinned. 'I bet I know, it's Miss Gasbag?'

He pointed the horse whip at Jane. 'And I'll wager my money on it, *your* name's Miss Freak-face?' He let out another laugh, sharp gaze roaming across the group, waiting for us to chuckle at his sick and vicious name-joke.

Nobody made a sound. Flies buzzed around the dead mouse, the cat who'd killed it now curled up on one of the veranda arm-chairs. Invisible insects ticked and some other wild bird started up a terrifying laugh.

'*Garooagarooagarooga,*' the bird cackled. '*Garooagarooa-garooga.*'

'I'm Lucy Rivers,' I said, speaking fast so I wouldn't stammer. 'And she's Jane Baxter, and she can't help it if her face —'.

'Well, Miss Gasbag Lucy Rivers, in future, you'll show some

manners and keep quiet while I'm speaking.' I flinched as he kicked the dead mouse off the veranda, onto the dusty earth.

'So, as I was saying,' Mr Yates went on, 'to repay our goodwill and kindness for saving your castaway souls, you will all work hard. I'll be training you boys to be the best farmers on the Southern Highlands and Mrs Yates here will train you girls to become decent farmers' wives.'

He pointed to the two youngest kids, six-year-old Georgie and Sarah. 'And you littlies will have the important task of walking down that track to the letterbox every weekend,' he said, pointing to where the bus had turned off the main road. 'And you'll hand the letters to me – and *only* me. Got it?'

Georgie and Sarah, thumbs stuck in their mouths, nodded solemnly as Mr Yates told them their other important job would be to walk around the farm, filling sacks with sticks for fire kindling.

'Can we write letters home to our mum?' Jim Browning said. 'She'll be worried about me 'n John. We never got the chance to tell her we was, *were*, coming to Australia.'

'Best if you and your brother, the lot of you in fact, forget about England,' Mr Yates said. 'Concentrate on making new lives for yourselves here in Australia.'

'That means we're not allowed to write letters home,' I whispered to Vinnie. Not that I had anyone to write to, besides Mum, and I wasn't even sure whether prisoners were allowed letters.

Mr Yates hurled me a scowl, but kept speaking. 'Every morning you older children will catch the bus to the local high school, while the younger ones walk to the primary school.' He pointed his whip towards four strange-looking rounded huts, past the paddocks of sheep and cows, and a far-off patch of water that shimmered brown in the sun. 'Over behind the billabong there. You'll attend school till you turn fifteen, then you'll work fulltime on the farm as apprentices for two years, training for a proper profession. And when you turn seventeen, I'll guarantee you a good job that'll earn you a decent wage for the rest of your life.' He took a breath, scratched Bluey's head. 'So, how about we all work together to make Seabreeze the most profitable farm on the Southern Highlands of New South Wales? To make of my home – *your* home – an Aussie Shangri-La?'

Several kids shrugged, looked at each other.

'Oh, I almost forgot to mention the best part, didn't I, Mrs Yates?' he said with a silly grin, teeth jutting over the rat muzzle. 'If there's no skiving off, you'll be allowed one hour for play at the end of each day. How good does that sound?'

Nobody said anything. We all shifted in the dust, licked dry lips, batted at flies.

Mr Yates' smile vanished. He cocked his head towards us, cupped a palm around the waggly ear. 'Excuse me, I didn't hear that?'

'Thank you, Mr Yates,' everyone chimed.

'No way are we staying here till we're seventeen!' I hissed at Vinnie, distrusting this man more with every word he spoke.

'And in case anyone gets the idea of running off,' he said, as if he'd heard me, or read the thoughts knotting my mind, 'what do you see out there?' He lashed the whip towards the far-off horizon.

Nobody answered.

'That's right, nothing but bush,' Mr Yates said. 'Bush in which you'd get lost pretty quick, even before you died of thirst or sunburn or snake bite. Do you know Australia is home to a hundred deadly snake species?'

No answer.

'We've got tiger snakes, eastern browns, death adders, red-bellied blacks, all of which kill, *painfully*, in minutes. Not to mention our deadly spiders, the funnel-web, the redback.' He grinned again. 'Ah yes, our friend the redback spider who loves warm, cosy spots. So best be on the lookout in the toilet, alright?'

Mr Yates looked pleased and proud of these deadly things but I shook with the goosebumps that slid down my backbone. Frozen, in this horrible heat.

'Now follow me,' he said brightly, jumping down from the

veranda, boots flicking up swirls of dust, as he beckoned us with the horse whip. 'Mrs Yates and I'll show you around your new home, and your very own bedrooms.'

My stomach hollow, legs trembly, we all skittered after Mr Yates like the sheep scampering about the paddock. Mrs Yates slumped along behind, her gaze still on the ground.

Mr Yates led us past the farmhouse – the "homestead" he'd called it – and down another track, narrower but as dusty as the one the bus had taken. 'That's where you boys will earn your keep,' he said, pointing out tool sheds, the sheep-shearing shed, the dairy, slaughterhouse, and piggery.

Jane stumbled along, whimpering, arms still arced over her head, glancing up at the birds half-hidden amongst the silvery-coloured tree leaves. The noise of the screechy white ones, and others that cackled like mad people, built up and up until it was a roar through my mind.

Mr Yates suddenly stopped, turned around and smiled at Jane. 'Don't be afraid, Freak-face. Australia certainly has many dangerous animals but our cockies and kookas won't hurt you.' He struck up a laugh as crazy as those birds' cackles.

We walked on, Vinnie and I keeping well back in the group, out of Mr Yates' hearing.

'Wish they'd give us a drink,' I said, damp hair sticking to my neck, sweat trickling down my back as we walked on. 'That drink and cake – lamington or whatever they call it – on the dockside seems *days* ago.'

'Mrs Yates will give you all food and drink very soon,' Mr Yates said. Was this man a mind reader, or did he just have sharp hearing? In any case, I'd have to watch every word I spoke.

'Oi, cheer up, you two,' Vinnie said, linking arms with me and Suzy, who was trying to hide a new bout of crying from Mr Yates, though her fogged-up glasses immediately gave her away. 'It might not be too bad here, give it a chance.'

'Yeah sure,' I said. 'Since when have we been able to trust adults, 'specially *men*? And the wife hasn't looked at us once, all she does is stare at the ground. No, soon as I can figure out how to get away from this place without some poisonous snake or spider killing us, and as soon as I can find Charly, and Suzy can find Patty, we're going home to England. *All* of us.'

A little further along the track, we reached the four rounded huts. Up close they were banged up and rusty.

'Your bedrooms,' Mr Yates announced, as if they were posh hotels. 'Come on inside!'

And later, after he'd shown us our sleeping sheds, we gulped down mugfuls of water as the sun slid down that wide, empty sky. The dread crept up on me, slunk beneath my skin and settled there, alongside the sweat, the dirt, the misery.

Deadly snakes and spiders, gigantic screeching birds. Thick and ugly bush that went on forever. I already hated Australia.

'I can tell you right now, Vinnie, this bleedin' place ain't no Emerald City.'

11

'I want to go back to Lucy.' A new sob rose up through Charly's throat as the man carried her further away. He stopped at a big, shiny car and, still holding her, opened the boot, where he stashed Charly's suitcase.

A lady with a puffy hairdo poked her head out of the passenger-side window and cried, 'Oh my God, Frank, it's our little Charlotte!'

Tears wet her eyes, lipsticked mouth all trembly. She kept frowning and smiling at Charly like she'd just found her purse that she'd lost.

From the boot, the man pulled out something wrapped in brightly-coloured paper, tied up with ribbon. 'It's for you, a present,' he said with a smile, as he opened the car door, slid Charly into the back seat and pushed the parcel at her.

Charly folded her arms, shook her head, even though secretly she really wanted to open it. She'd never had a present wrapped up so fancy like this. Even her blackbird hadn't come in paper or ribbon.

'I can't believe it, can't believe … ' the lady went on, reaching around to touch Charly's knees, but snatching back her hand. 'Frank, how did you … ? Oh never mind, she's here now, safe and sound.'

'I want Lucy, I want Mum,' Charly wailed, as the man, Frank, drove away from the docks. Away from Lucy and their friends.

The car was quiet, nothing like the cars Charly would see walking from Easthaven to school, or the ones that rumbled noisily past her and Lucy and Mum's block of flats.

Charly eyed the parcel, reached over, and tore off a corner of bright paper. She peeked inside. A doll.

It's Jeannie, she found me!

She ripped off the rest of the paper.

It wasn't Jeannie, but a horrible dolly with scary, rolling eyes. An ugly dolly that smelled like Aunty Edna's cupboards, which she'd told Charly smelled like that 'cos she was gettin' rid of moffs.

'Oh look, it's Heidi!' the puffy hair-do lady said. 'What a lovely surprise for Charlotte, Frank, wrapping up Heidi for her.'

Charly flung the horrid stinky doll onto the car floor. 'I want my Jeannie.'

'Obviously not such a lovely surprise,' Frank said, eyeing Charly in the little mirror above the steering wheel. 'It's only made her more upset.'

The lady turned back to Charly. 'Heidi's been waiting for you all this time, Charlotte. So I imagine she'll be needing extra cuddles, don't you?'

Charly pushed out her lips into the biggest scowl.

Dolly turned back and they both stared straight ahead at the road as Frank drove past rows of all-the-same skinny houses, like some from back home in England. Squashed-up houses, not big like her block of flats.

Charly hadn't missed Mum too much on the boat, there'd been so many books to read with Hazel, so much tasty food to enjoy, games to play. But now, alone in this fancy, quiet car with the strange Frank and Dolly people, the ache in her chest for Mum and Lucy came back. It knotted her guts, made her feel sick.

'When am I going home? When can I go back to Lucy and Mum?'

Charly couldn't stop her tears flooding out, and Dolly twisted around from the front seat again.

'Look outside at the nice trees, Charlotte,' she said, when there were no more skinny houses.

Charly didn't want to look at the trees, which were not nice, but brown with hardly any green bits like at home, and all droopy, as if they needed a good long drink. And after the trees there were more and more of them, as if those trees went on right to the edge of the earth.

'No trees, I want Lucy.'

Lucy would get her out of this car, away from these people. Lucy had always looked after her when they were playing outside and nasty Iris Palmer would shout at Mum, 'Keep yer filthy urchins indoors, Annie Rivers, drivin' us barmy with their noise.' Lucy had stuck up for her at Easthaven when the girls teased her for being a cry-baby. She'd back-answered Mrs Mersey when she'd punished Charly for wetting the bed, or made both of them stare at the corner of the dining room, instead of eating.

'Whoever is Lucy?' Dolly said. 'Come on, Charlotte, please stop crying.'

'I'm *not* Charlotte, I'm Charly!'

Dolly looked around at Charly again, the brown creamy stuff covering her face crinkling with her smile-frown. 'Your name's Charlotte, how could you forget your own name, sweetie?'

She pointed outside again, at the trees stretching right to a dark blue line that joined the sky. 'Look how lovely the sea is today. I know how much you love the beach, sweetie, splashing about in the shallows, building sandcastles.' She clapped her hands together, which made Charly jump. 'Oh what fun you, me and Daddy will have together, all summer long.'

Charly remembered Mr Zachary's pictures of the seaside. But he'd promised that Lucy would be with her. More big sobs rose in her throat.

Dolly reached over and patted Charly's knee. 'There, there, Charlotte, no need to be upset, everything's alright now.' Charly moved her knee away, slid further across the seat, towards the window, where Dolly couldn't reach her.

The man's head twisted sharply towards Dolly, and Charly caught his frown.

'Eyes on the road, Frank,' Dolly said and Frank looked back at the long road ahead, with not a single building, beneath a sky the brightest blue. The sky had sometimes been that blue on the boat, but never at Easthaven. And never at home with Mum and Lucy.

'Where's Lucy?' Charly sobbed, as they sped past more trees. 'Back home with Mum?'

Dolly stretched back once more, tried to dab Charly's face with a handkerchief. But she couldn't reach her, and dabbed at the air. 'I'm right here, Charlotte, Mummy's right here.'

'I'm *not* Charlotte. You're *not* my mum,' Charly cried, remembering how Mum would dab her knee with her hanky when she'd fall over and graze it.

'Lucy promised we'd go home on another big boat, to see Mum. I want to go back on the nice boat with Lucy.'

'Who is this Lucy she keeps on about, Frank?' Dolly said, puffy hair shaking as she touched her fingertips to Frank's shoulder. 'We don't know anyone by that name, do we?'

'Lucy's my sister. She's ten and I'm five.'

'But you haven't got a sister, sweetie.'

Dolly spoke to Frank again. 'And why is she calling me "Mum" rather than "Mummy"?' She let out a sigh. 'Dear me, well I imagine she's probably just tired after … after everything. And it is quite a long car trip from Sydney.'

'Not to mention the long *boat* trip,' Frank mumbled, but Charly heard, even if he and Dolly did speak funny, like all Australians.

'*Boat* trip?' Dolly's voice cracked. 'Whatever are you talking about, Frank?' She laughed, gave him a friendly slap on the arm. 'Stop saying silly things, you big duffer.'

Frank gave Dolly a Lucy smile; one with only your mouth, not your eyes.

The car hummed along, all three of them silent. Charly

kept sliding her backside off the seat to kick the ugly Heidi doll further away. Almost under the front seat now. Only her legs sticking out.

Frank drove down a steep slope, and soon after, turned the car into a street full of big posh-looking houses made of red, brown, white or yellowy-coloured bricks. Clean and new-looking, nothing like the black-stained, chipped bricks of the houses in England.

'Here we are, Frangipani Drive,' Dolly said. 'Named for those pretty, fragrant flowers we'll be seeing all the way along the street, in a few months. Won't that be marvellous, sweetie?'

Charly had no idea what Dolly was talking about, besides she was too busy worrying about the gigantic birds screeching from the tall trees; birds with scary yellow head-fans and dark Mrs Mersey-eyes.

Charly was glad to be inside the car, away from the terrifying birds. But then Frank parked in the driveway of a red-brick house with a tidy lawn, and Dolly was telling her to get out of the car.

'Come on, Charlotte, let's show you the new house.' She clapped her hands again. 'Isn't it simply wonderful you're finally home?'

Charly shook all over, eyeing the mob of white birds as she stepped out of the car. 'Is Lucy here? Is this Lucy's new house too?'

'This is *our* new house.' Dolly took Charly's hand, held horrible Heidi in the other. Charly had hoped she'd kicked Heidi all the way under the seat, so Dolly wouldn't see her and would forget about the doll. 'Your house, Charlotte, and mine and Daddy's. Remember I told you Mummy and Daddy had moved to a bigger house, with a nicer yard for you to play in?'

Dad's gone, Lucy says. What new house? Why won't Dolly tell me where Lucy is?

Charly couldn't stop her heart thumping, her mind churning with all these thoughts she couldn't understand, as Dolly pulled her across a driveway made of the tiniest stones she'd ever seen.

Frank was unloading Charly's suitcase from the boot. 'My suitcase ... all my lovely new things!' Happy to see it again, Charly went to run after Frank to get her suitcase, but Dolly wouldn't let go of her hand.

'And you can take away that awful thing,' Dolly said to Frank, flapping a hand at Charly's beautiful suitcase. 'I can't imagine where Charlotte picked up something so unsightly.'

'Can't she keep it, surely that can't hurt?' Frank whispered, though Charly caught it. This Frank and Dolly had no idea how to whisper so someone nasty like Mrs Mersey wouldn't hear you.

Dolly let go of Charly's hand and threw her arms in the air. 'Have you gone mad, Frank? We don't even know where she got the suitcase.' She made flicking movements with her hand. 'Now please, take it away.'

'No, no!' Her chest tight, tummy burning with anger, Charly tried again to run to Frank, but Dolly gripped her tight.

'My suitcase ... I want my new clothes!' she wailed, tears blurring crunchy stones, red bricks, the front door Dolly was opening, Frank disappearing somewhere with her suitcase.

'Oh sweetie, why *ever* would you need new clothes?' Dolly said, nudging Charly inside, ahead of her. 'We moved all your beautiful clothes and toys here from the old house. We wouldn't have left your things behind, would we?' She took a quick breath, kept hold of Charly's hand. 'Now let's go upstairs and see your new bedroom.'

Charly stamped a foot. 'But I want my suit —'

'Hush, sweetie, you've never been a whingy child, don't start now.' Dolly tugged her up a staircase. The steps weren't shiny, dark red wood, like on the *Star of New South Wales*, but covered in fluffy brown carpet. Charly so badly wanted to go back to those stairs on the boat. And to Lucy. Vinnie, Jane, Suzy and Patty too.

Where did they go? Will Frank and Dolly take me to see them soon?

12

'There's a spider in this toilet!' Jane cried, that first night in our sleeping shed. 'What if it's one of the poisonous ones Mr Yates told us to watch out for?'

All seven of us scurried into the shower and toilet area, at the far end of the shed. 'Blimey, look at that red stripe, I reckon it's a redback,' Vinnie said, pulling Jane away from the toilet.

'What if it had bit me on the bum and killed me?' Jane wailed, as we tried to get comfy on the hard, metal bunk beds. 'I could've died all this way out in Australia and Mum would never know.'

Vinnie, Jane, Suzy and I had been allocated the same sleeping shed as four girls we'd met on the ship: Bessy and Helen from Liverpool, who were eleven, and sisters, Carol and Fiona Mulligan. Fiona was fifteen and Carol was ten, same as me, Vinnie, Suzy and Jane.

'And now some bug is buzzing in my ear, like it's gone right into my brain,' Jane cried, into the darkness. 'Oh no, it's bitten me. What if it's deadly?'

'Only a mosquito,' said Helen. 'Won't kill you.'

'Unlike the redback spider,' Jane said. 'I'll never use the toilet again … oh, what can I do?'

'Just get used to it,' I said, trying not to sound annoyed. 'Australia sounds like it's *full* of deadly things.'

'I'll go outside and wee in the bushes,' Jane said.

'So a deadly *snake* can bite your bum?' said Bessy.

I let out a short, silly laugh, though I didn't find it a bit funny.

'I don't like it here,' Jane wailed, into the darkness. From her bottom bunk beside mine, I could hear Jane scratching her arms, slapping at mosquitoes. 'And my name's *not* Freak-face. Oh, oh, I want my mother.'

'We all want our mother,' I snapped. Her moaning irritated me more than usual in that hot, airless shed with only two tiny windows, one on either side of the door. Windows which, we quickly figured out when the mosquitos attacked Jane, we had to keep closed. 'And Suzy wants Patty and ... and I want Charly.'

I wanted to yell at Jane to shut her gob, but I bit my tongue. None of this was Jane Baxter's fault.

'You can't always get what you want, Jane,' Vinnie said. 'You ought to know that by now. Anyway, least you still got a mother, not like me.'

'Carol 'n me lost our mother so long ago,' Fiona Mulligan said, 'we don't even remember what she looks like.'

'And we don't remember where we come from, neither,' Carol said.

'Where did my suitcase go?' Jane went on. 'All my lovely clothes from England?'

None of us knew where our things had gone, vanished somewhere between getting on the bus and Mr Yates showing us around Seabreeze Farm.

Suzy had stopped crying, but still not spoken a word since that awful moment they'd ripped Patty from her. The whole afternoon she'd stared at nothing, though her glasses were so dust-caked she couldn't have seen a thing anyway. And she shook her head and pushed me away when I'd offered to brush out her hair before bed, in her sister's place. Though I was half-glad about that, since it made me come over all sad again, and wonder who was brushing out Charly's hair tonight.

Suzy had stayed silent right through tea in the dining shed, same rounded hut thing as the four sleeping sheds, but all thirty-two of us eating together, with Mrs Yates.

Mr Yates hadn't eaten with us, and had only stayed in the dining shed long enough to bark out more Seabreeze rules, along with the daily jobs he expected of us: washing clothes in the laundry, sweeping and scrubbing the sheds and the homestead, tending the vegetable garden, the orchard down near the billabong. We'd collect eggs too, help Mrs Yates cook and bake, and sew our clothes.

'With all those jobs *and* school,' I'd said to Vinnie, 'I can't see when there'll be time for our free hour Mr Yates promised.'

When Mr Yates' black boots had stamped off back towards the homestead, where he'd told us an apprentice girl cooked and served his meals, Mrs Yates spoke her first words to us.

'Call me Bonnie … when Mr Yates isn't around,' she'd said, with a nervy smile as, along with two fifteen-year-old girls, one of them Fiona Mulligan from our sleeping shed, who'd immediately become apprentices, she dished out a mutton, carrot and potato stew into our metal bowls. 'And don't youse go worrying about Mr Yates, bark's worse than his bite. Anyway, enjoy ya dinner,' she said. 'Strewth, the lotta youse must be starving after that long trip.'

'Bonnie seems nice,' Vinnie had whispered, as the apprentices set jugs of water on the tables, along with metal mugs.

'I bet she's only nice when Mr Yates ain't, *isn't*, around,' I'd said, gobbling down the stew, tough and tasteless compared with the delicious ship food. I knew that look on Bonnie's face, when she was around her husband; had seen that fearful, don't-make-him-mad face on my mother. 'She's half-terrified of Mr Yates. Didn't you see the bruises on her arms?'

But friendly Bonnie was gone now, back up to unfriendly Mr Yates in the homestead, and we lay in the hot darkness with the buzzing mosquitoes, the sad-sounding '*wope, wope, wope,*' of some bird, and the send-you-mad whir of those unseen insects Bonnie said were cicadas.

'I've lived in a children's home almost all my life,' said Bessy, from her bunk above Helen's. 'So I don't get why I'm homesick, 'cos I never had a real home.'

'Nobody even asked us if we wanted to come to Australia,' Helen said, 'did they, Bessy? One Sunday they just told us we were going on a picnic.'

'Yeah, some picnic!' Bessy said.

Jane let out another wail. 'My mother will never find me here. Australia's so far away from everything.'

'Your mother never came for you in London,' I said. 'So not much chance she'll come for you in Australia.'

'She *will* come for me … one day,' Jane sobbed. 'She fell on hard times, that's what she said, why she had to put me in the home. But it wasn't forever. Mum promised she'd come for me soon as she gets back on her feet.' She hiccupped. 'My mum *does* love me, even if I wasn't born perfect, that's what she always said. Anyway, didn't Mr Zachary say we'd be going to families in Australia?'

'He said a family or a farm,' Vinnie said. 'But only some of the youngest ones, like Charly, went to families. So he wasn't really telling porky pies, even though I feel like he was.'

'Mr Zachary promised sisters would stay together, and that we wouldn't be going to another home,' I said. 'But with all these rules and jobs, Seabreeze Farm is no different from any other home or orphanage, so that man *was* a filthy liar.'

My chest tightened with rage for Mr Zachary. If I ever got to meet him again I'd punch those white teeth right out of his smiley mouth. I clenched, unclenched my fists.

'Mr Zachary came to our home too,' Helen said. 'Made Australia sound like a beach paradise. But there's no sea here, I feel so tricked.'

'Yeah, so much for the name "Seabreeze",' I said, tossing from side to side, trying to get comfortable on that hard, metal bed with no pillow. But it was impossible, especially since I'd got used to the luxury of the cosy ship bunks. 'There's not a bit of sea in sight, and definitely no breeze!'

'So we travelled all this way, for *six weeks*,' Bessy said, 'only to be put in another home.'

That made Jane's tear-well break open again. As she snivelled into the lonely darkness of that sleeping shed, every ounce of joy I'd known on the *Star of New South Wales* seeped from me. As quick and snappy as a lash of Mr Yates' horse whip.

'What if my little sister suffers, maybe even *dies*, without me to look after her?' I whispered up to Vinnie in her bunk. 'And where did they take Patty?'

But, for once, my friend had no answers; no comforting words that we'd ever see Charly or Patty again.

* * *

We'd been at Seabreeze a few months when, one hot and dry Sunday morning, six-year-old Georgie raced down from the homestead, shouting at the top of his squeaky voice. 'Mr Yates brought us a surprise yesterday, from Wollongong!'

Along with our sleeping-shed friends, Bessy, Helen, and Carol Mulligan, Vinnie, Jane, Suzy and I were rostered on veggie garden and orchard duty, where we grew more kinds of fruit and vegetables that I'd known existed.

'Mr Yates wants us all on the veranda, right now,' little Georgie announced.

'Thank God for that,' Vinnie said, slapping me on the back to dislodge the fly I'd just swallowed. The blazing December sun burning our backs, our shoulders, we'd already been dragging stubborn weeds from the sun-roasted earth for hours, and all of us were relieved to escape the heat, even for a few minutes.

I bent over, finally hacked up the dead fly. We flung down our gardening tools, ran palms across over hot brows and trudged up to the homestead. I was thankful of a break from those flies, as much as from the burning sun. Buzzing in my eyes, up my nose, in my ears, all around me, those Australian flies were nothing like English ones. There was no escaping them, and they drove me bananas.

On our first Saturday at Seabreeze Farm, Bonnie had told us Mr Yates drove down to a place called Wollongong every Saturday to sell our produce and to buy supplies. My ears had burned when she said "Wollongong".

That's where Charly is!

Every Saturday after Mr Yates finished his tasty lunch the apprentices, Fiona Mulligan and another fifteen-year-old, cooked him, he'd strut out onto the veranda, flick a matchstick through his bucky teeth and run his tongue over the rat muzzle. He'd get the boys to load up his open-backed truck thing he called a "ute" with the crates of produce they'd packed, then he'd whistle to Bluey, 'Come on, boy, in you jump.'

As that dog hurdled into the ute's open back I'd say to myself: *if only you weren't here, Bluey, I'd hide under that tarpaulin, and escape to Wollongong to find Charly*. But Mr Yates always took his beloved Bluey with him.

One day though. Just one of these days, Bluey won't go. That'll be my chance.

We never knew what Mr Yates really did, down in Wollongong. But we didn't care, we were just glad to escape the horse whip he lashed around like it was an extension of his arm. Right from the beginning, I vowed that Mr Yates would never see my tears. Like those old bats at Easthaven; brutes like them would never win me over.

Another neat thing about Mr Yates nipping off to Wollongong of a Saturday arvo, was that we got a few hours off the hard work he forced on us before and after school, *and* on weekends.

Not that ploughing, planting, watering, weeding, and harvesting the vegetable garden and orchard was the worst job. No, from Tommy Oakley and Nick Hurley's complaints, the boys worked the hardest: up at four o'clock to milk the cows in the dairy. They'd chop wood for heating, swinging axes, filling wheelbarrows. And all before breakfast. After school Mr Yates made them clean drains, fix fences and sheds, feed cattle and shear sheep. Georgie and the other younger boys would have to pick out the burrs from the shorn fleece and sort it for baling.

'Get a move on, I haven't got all day,' Mr Yates said, as we all flopped down in the shade of the huge fig tree full of shrieking galahs. "A Moreton Bay fig", Bonnie had told us, but we didn't care what type of fig it was, we were just thankful for its shade from the blazing sun when we could sneak away from our jobs for a few moments.

As always, Bluey sat at Mr Yates' feet, but this time the dog wasn't gazing up at his master, he was sniffing at the blanket Mr Yates was holding.

'Whatever's he got?' I said to Vinnie, as Mr Yates slowly unwrapped the blanket to reveal a baby animal, all long bony legs, and big ears. Everyone gasped, a few kids let out *oohs* and *ahhs* and my heart went all melty at the sight of that small and cute animal.

'It's a baby wallaby, a joey,' Mr Yates said. 'Found him in his mum's pouch, after a car ran her down.' He pointed the whip at us. 'So remember, kids, if you come across a dead kangaroo by the roadside, always check the pouch because sometimes the joey's still alive. Like this young fella here.' He stroked between the joey's ears and it closed its eyes. 'So since he's now like all of you – an unwanted orphan – we're going to take good care of him. Same as I take care of all of you.'

'Can we cuddle him?' six-year-old Sarah said, her blue eyes shiny with excitement. This was the first time I'd seen little Sarah and Georgie smile since we'd come to Seabreeze.

'Certainly!' Mr Yates said. 'You'll all get a cuddle when you take turns feeding him. He's so young, we'll need to bottle-feed him with a special extra-long rubber teat to mimic his mum.' He turned to Bonnie, staring at the ground. 'And Mrs Yates will prepare the baby's cot we keep especially for little fellas like him. They get lonely at night, cry out for their mum, so you need to keep them close to you, for night cuddles.' He gave Bonnie a long look. 'Get a move on then, Mrs Yates, stop dilly-dallying.'

'I know how to feed a baby with a bottle,' Sarah said. 'I always gave me baby bruvva his bottle.'

'Can I go first?' Georgie shot his hand up into the air. 'Can I feed the baby wallaby right now?'

Images of Charly flashed through my mind. How I'd give my baby sister her bottle at night when Mum had to look after the old people. My chest tightened, and I fought to breathe, as always when I thought about Charly, and Mum, locked up when she'd done nothing wrong.

'How about we give this fella a name first?' Mr Yates said. 'Let's vote on it: Jim, Joe, John, James … what'll it be?'

'Joe!' Tommy cried. 'Joey Joe!'

Mr Yates grinned. 'Sounds good to me, Joey Joe it is then. Right, follow me, those of you who want to learn how to make up Joey Joe's bottle. Then you'll all get straight back to work, no excuse for skiving off.'

We all trooped into the homestead, where usually only girls aged ten and over were allowed, for cooking and sewing lessons, to scrub and polish windows and floors, and the job I hated most – cleaning Mr Yates' room and changing his bedlinen.

13

'Don't like herrings.' Charly scowled, pushed away the plate Dolly had put in front of her at tea time.

It was right after she'd shown Charly a pink room upstairs, which she'd told her was her bedroom, and which, to Charly's horror, she wouldn't be sharing with a single other girl. Night-time was far too scary to sleep on your own.

Charly had hated all the clothes in the wardrobe. 'Not mine!' she'd said, but Dolly kept insisting they were, even though Charly had never seen these dresses and blouses and shorts that stank like Aunty Edna's moffs cupboards. Same stink as horrid Heidi, who Dolly had put on the bed Charly would sleep in on her own.

'I want to go back to the boat,' Charly had kept saying. 'Want to sleep in the cabin with Lucy and Vinnie.'

But Dolly pretended she couldn't hear a word, even though Charly spoke loudly. Even yelled, once.

She'd also kept asking for her suitcase, but Dolly made out she couldn't hear that either.

Dolly slid the plate back towards Charly. 'But you *adore* pickled herrings, Charlotte, one of your favourite foods.'

Charly shook her head, clamped her arms across her chest. Fresh tears burned her eyes.

Dolly took away the herrings and placed some carrot sticks,

in the shape of a smiley face, onto Charly's plate. 'Now I *know* you love raw carrots,' she said with a grin.

Charly's tears pushed against her eyes, made them go bulgy, like they'd pop right out of her aching head. 'Only like *cooked* carrot.'

'Really, Charlotte.' Dolly flung her arms into the air again. 'I don't understand why you are so grumpy and hostile.'

'I'm Charly, not Charlotte!'

Frank shook his head, which he did a lot. 'Can't you just ask her what she wants to eat? Don't you think we've had enough tears for one day, Dolly?'

Dolly flung her arms in the air, which she did a lot too, stamped across the green floor and stared into the kitchen sink. Her fingers gripped the edge, as if she couldn't stand on her own, shoulders and puffy hair quivering like the wings and tail of Charly's blackbird. Before it had got killed.

If only she had her beautiful blackbirdie, even all smashed up, she didn't care. And Jeannie and Lucy and Mum, Charly could stop her blabbering.

Dolly spun back around to face Frank. 'I simply don't understand what's got into her. First she doesn't even want to look at any of her toys or clothes. Second, she refuses *all* her favourite food. And third,' arms flying again, 'I have no idea where she got this silly idea of calling herself "Charly"?'

''Cos that's my name!' Charly wished Dolly would stop talking about her as if she wasn't sitting at the table right there with her in this kitchen with a strange green floor and yellow cupboards.

Frank patted Charly's arm, winked at her. 'I fry up a mean melty cheese and bacon sandwich,' he said. 'Want to try one?'

Charly didn't want any of Frank and Dolly's food, or their clothes or toys, but it was ages since that drink and cake on the docks when they'd taken her away from Lucy, and she was starving.

She nodded, and Frank's sandwich, which he toasted for her in a big frypan, was definitely melty and tasty.

* * *

'Beddy-byes now,' Dolly said, after she'd put Charly in a bath full of bubbles and washed her, as if she was still a baby, then made her put on a pink nightdress that also smelled like Aunty Edna's moffs cupboards.

'Such a big day it's been for our little Charlotte, a big day for *all* of us, you must be exhausted,' Dolly said with a smile, folding back the pink puffy bedspread, patting the pink sheet.

'Can I read a book?' Charly pointed to the shelf full of them, the only good thing in the pink room. She couldn't wait to look at every single Janet and John book.

'*Read*?' Dolly said. 'You can't read yet, sweetie, but you'll learn soon, when you start school, just the day after tomorrow.'

'I can *so* read ... a bit,' Charly said, pulling out her favourite – the one with Janet riding a pony. There hadn't been any ponies on the boat but maybe there would be some in Australia.

'Teacher Hazel was teaching me to read,' Charly said, 'on the boat.'

'Well, let me read it to you,' Dolly said, tucking Charly into bed.

Charly could have read a lot of the Janet and John words, but she was too tired to argue with Dolly, so she let the nice words flow over her, soothe her aching head. Her raw eyes. Her throbbing heart.

Frank loped into the bedroom, kissed Charly's brow, and smoothed back her hair that had fallen across her eyes. 'Goodnight, Charlotte. Tomorrow, after a big sleep, I'll show you all your toys in the backyard, I bet you'll love playing with them!'

Charly was too tired to shout at Frank that she wasn't Charlotte.

Dolly kissed her too, stroked her arms, and patted her on the leg, like Hazel did on the boat. But not like Miss Sutherland, Mrs Mersey and Mrs Benson from Easthaven who'd never patted any girl's leg. Not once.

Dolly snuggled Heidi into Charly's curled arms and switched on a lamb statue on her bedside table. 'All cosy with your little friend, Lambie night-light, sweetie,' Dolly said, and blew her another kiss from the doorway.

As soon as Dolly disappeared, Charly flung moff-smelly Heidi onto the floor. She didn't want to sleep in this big pink room on her own. It might be nicer than the bedroom she'd shared at Easthaven, but there were no friends in it. And no Lucy.

Where did they all go?

The bed was soft and comfy though, and Charly was so tired from wondering when they'd be going home on another boat to see Mum, and from asking, 'Where's my suitcase? Where's Mum? Where's Lucy?' that her whole body ached. Invisible fingers pressed on her eyelids.

As her eyes closed, she caught Dolly's whisper, outside the door.

'She's made some imaginary friends, Frank ... Teacher Hazel and a sister, Lucy. But I've heard that's normal for an only child.'

14

A girl's freckly face popped up over the fence. 'Hello, what's your name?' she said to Charly.

It was the morning after Charly's first night without Lucy, and Frank was pushing her on a swing on the square of grass he called a "backyard".

'Higher, higher!' Charly cried, her heart going boom, boom as Frank pushed her so high she could see into the backyards of the houses on each side. Those backyards were big too, but Frank's had more toys in it.

'My name's Simone Maree Jardine,' the freckly girl said. 'I'm turning six next birthday and I live at 9 Frangipani Drive and you live at 11 Frangipani Drive so we're next-door neighbours.'

Simone Maree Jardine spoke like everyone in Australia, except that her words tumbled out all at once, with no commas or full stops as in the proper sentences Hazel had taught Charly. But her voice wasn't like Frank's sad one, or Dolly's that jumped up, down and sideways like the jack-in-the-box in the toy room on the *Star of New South Wales*.

Charly might come to like Frank, and his kind words. His nice, soft voice, how he held her hand gently, not like Dolly, who squeezed far too tight, same as Lucy.

Yesterday morning on the dockside, Charly'd tried so hard not to let go of Lucy's hand but they'd been too strong for her. A sob rose in her throat, but that thrilling up-and-down swinging swallowed the sob, and no tears burst from her eyes.

'So are you ever going to tell me your name?' Simone Maree Jardine said.

'It's Charly.' Frank didn't correct her, and Dolly was too far away, right up the top of the backyard, to say, 'No, sweetie, your name's Charlotte'.

After breakfast, when Dolly had tried to force Charly to eat some awful black stuff she called Vegemite, insisting Charly loved it, Frank had given her a bowl of yummy Rice Bubbles cereal, then he'd taken her outside to show her the backyard.

He'd smiled at Charly, pointing out the swing, the see-saw, the sand pit, the big slide. 'It's all yours, to play as much as you want.'

'Higher, higher!' Charly called again.

Frank pushed the swing harder, Simone Maree Jardine's head bobbing with the up-down movement. The warm morning sunshine tickled Charly's face and some bright red, blue and green-coloured birds dangled from tree branches and twittered loudly.

Mid-swing, from her great height, Charly was a queen, ruling the world she gazed down on: her shiny playground. Nothing like the cold and bare Easthaven playground. But at least Lucy had been there. And the other girls.

Where are *they?*

Maybe Frank would tell Charly where Lucy was, if she could get Dolly to go away. But in the one afternoon and night she'd spent at the red-brick house, Dolly had barely left Charly alone for a second.

Charly glanced up the backyard at Dolly, smiling and waving to her and Frank, in between hanging out washing on a line she called her "Hills Hoist", which was in the shape of an Indian tepee Charly had seen in a storybook. Nothing like the washing lines the mothers back home would stretch across the buildings.

Charly smiled to herself as she remembered running with

Lucy and Vinnie under all those washing lines, laughing as they slapped at the clothes, sheets and nappies. *Slap, slap, slap.* She remembered how they'd scoot past babies in their prams getting the sun, and tickling those little kicking feet till the baby shrieked. She giggled, thinking how they'd pinch a few peas from a mother sitting out in the sun shelling them.

And in winter, when it was too cold to play outside, she remembered how she'd loved sitting with Lucy and Vinnie on the landing, their coats warming their legs, sharing a bag of chips and crackling slathered in salt and vinegar, that Vinnie'd got from her mum and dad's fish 'n chip shop.

'Are you *ever* getting off that swing to talk to me?' Simone Maree Jardine leaned her arms along the top of the fence and frowned, her freckles squashing into brown patches.

'Beaut idea,' Frank said, slowing down the swing. 'Why don't you get to know Simone while I finish working on your doll's house?'

Charly nodded and leapt from the swing, mid-air, flying free as a bird until her feet hit the soft grass. Frank disappeared into the garage and Charly, still wobbly from flying, staggered towards the fence.

'Charly's a boy's name,' Simone Maree Jardine said.

'No it's not, I'm a girl.' Charly glanced up at Dolly again. Still hanging out her washing. Still too far away to hear her.

Up close, she could see that Simone had more freckles than Vinnie, but not the same hair the colour of carrots. Simone's was darker, same red as the sand in Egypt.

Is Vinnie with Lucy? Where are *they?*

'I know you're a girl,' Simone said. ''Cos your mummy told mine she had only the one daughter. And you can be my best friend because Mummy said you must need a best friend 'cos you're new.'

'I'm not new,' Charly said. 'I'm five, six next birthday. And Lucy is ten, eleven next birthday.'

'But you're new *here*, in Frangipani Drive.' Simone pointed up the backyard, all the way past the play things and the Hills Hoist to the big red-brick house. 'Some other people lived here before you. And Mummy and Daddy were glad they left because they were New Australians who had a barking dog, and who laughed and sang late at night, and played dreadful loud music.' Simone took a quick breath. 'I saw your mummy and daddy when the big truck brought your furniture from your old house. But how come I never saw you before? Don't you go to school? Have you been hiding?'

'I *do* go to school,' Charly said. 'But I didn't go to school on the boat 'cos Hazel gave us our lessons, and I wasn't hiding. I was at Easthaven, then Mr Zachary showed us pictures of beaches and Lucy and me went on a big boat with Vinnie and Jane and the twins. Do you know where Lucy's gone?'

'Who's Lucy?' Simone said, 'and why do you speak funny?'

'I don't speak funny, *you* speak funny. Lucy's my sister and I have to find her because we're going home on another boat to see Mum. Lucy promised.'

'But your mummy's up there.' Simone pointed to Dolly, still snapping pegs onto wet clothes. Dolly wasn't watching her that second, but Charly still felt her gaze. She'd felt it every second since that terrible moment when Lucy had to stay on the dockside and Frank had bundled her into his quiet car.

'She's *not* my mum.'

'Course she is, you duffer,' Simone said. 'Can I come over to your backyard and do the see-saw with you? Mummy says your yard is fitted out like a verytable playground. That you have everything a child could want, and more.' Simone frowned and waggled her longest finger at Charly. 'But you can't buy a child's love, you know.'

The see-saw was shiny red, nothing like the see-saws Vinnie's brothers would make from a plank of wood and an upside-down dustbin. They'd fit three kids on each end, as well as one brother walking up and down the plank, showing off how he could keep his balance.

'*Garooagarooagarooga, Garooagarooagarooga.*' Charly jumped, looked up to the tree Frank had told her was a gum tree.

Simone laughed. 'Don't be a scaredy-cat, it's only Mr Kookaburra, look there he is.'

Charly followed Simone's finger, pointing up to a brown bird with a patch of blue on its wings. From the high branch, it stared right down at Charly, laughing at her. It *was* scary, but less scary than the big white birds from yesterday.

'How come you've never heard a kookaburra laugh?' Simone said.

Charly shrugged as Dolly left her empty washing basket on the grass and strolled down to her and Simone.

'Hello, Simone dear,' she said, one hand on Charly's shoulder, the fingers of her other hand running through Charly's hair, as if untangling it. But there wasn't a single knot, since Dolly had brushed her hair almost right out of her head that very morning. 'Why don't you come over and play, Simone? It will be lovely for Charlotte to have a friend before she starts school tomorrow.'

'Charlotte?' Simone said, the freckles bumping into each other as she struggled to climb over the fence. 'She said her name's Charly.'

15

Lucy Rivers
Southern Highlands, New South Wales
February 1963

'Coast's clear. Quick, go now!' Vinnie hissed from our hiding spot behind the bougainvillea that climbed up a veranda post and tumbled down a side wall of the homestead.

I gave my friend's hand a last squeeze and, heart thwacking against my chest, sprinted across to Mr Yates' utility van, parked in front of the veranda. The back of the car was already packed with crates of fruit and vegetables, eggs and other stuff he'd sell down in Wollongong.

Today I was escaping Seabreeze, going to Wollongong to find Charly. And to find a post office to send Mum a letter. Last night, when Bluey looked poorly and was off his food, I'd hoped he mightn't go with Mr Yates today. So I'd torn out a page from a school notebook, and written a letter to my mother at our old address.

Mum mightn't be living there now, I knew that, but maybe, *somehow*, my letter would find her. There was also the hope the rozzers had figured out their mistake and let her out of prison. Then she *would* get my letter, and take the first boat to Australia.

I had no stamps or envelope but I'd tell the post office people I'd forgotten my purse, promise to pay next time I was at the shops, like Mum used to do at the butcher's, and hope they took pity on me.

My head moving left and right like a hunted animal, I scrambled up the side of the ute, and slithered beneath the tarpaulin that covered the back, where Bluey usually sat with the goods.

'*Still* not hungry, what's up, old boy?' Mr Yates had said yesterday afternoon, stroking and kissing that mutt, all sleepy in the shade of the fig tree. 'Eh, Bluey, tell Daddy what's up.'

Bluey had bleated a small whine, laid his head back on his paws and gone to sleep.

'If he's not right by Monday, I'll have to take him to the vet,' Mr Yates said to Bonnie, who'd scuttled onto the veranda with a bowl of something. She nodded, knelt beside the dog, and tried to get him to take some of whatever was in the bowl.

I'd known it then. This could be my big chance.

Crouched beneath the hot, airless tarp, Mum's letter stowed in my pinafore pocket, creeks of sweat trickled down my back, my brow, my armpits.

Mouth dry, tongue furry, I heard Mr Yates' boots stomping on the dirt, louder the closer he got to the ute. 'Now you take good care of that dog, Bonnie,' he said. 'If anything's happened to him when I get home tonight, you know what'll happen, don't you?'

I didn't hear Bonnie's answer, none probably, but pictured her standing on the veranda, feet turned inwards, wringing chubby hands through the faded pinafore, and staring at the ground.

Don't look him straight in the face. No, Mum never did either. Don't want him to think you're giving cheek.

The blood beat hard in my temple, the breath snagging in my throat as Mr Yates fired up the ute. He crunched it into gear, started a U-turn.

I had no idea how I'd find Charly but I'd work that out once I got to Wollongong. All I could think about now was making the most of this lucky break. And not getting caught.

'*Woof, woof,*' Bluey barked. '*Woof, woof.*'

Oh no, damn dog, you're supposed to be sick and sleeping!

But Bluey must've made a sudden recovery as his barks grew louder, more urgent. So loud he must be right behind the ute by now, chasing it down the drive.

Mr Yates slammed on the brakes, lurching me forwards, and backwards as the ute came to a stop. Dust seeped beneath the tarpaulin, tickled my parched throat. I wanted to cough so badly I was gagging.

Mr Yates' boot-steps scuffed through the dirt, circling the ute. I held my breath, muffled a small cough.

The dog barked louder. The tarp flew off and I stared into Mr Yates' pink-rimmed eyes.

He grinned like he was pleased to see me. 'Well look who we have here, it's Gasbag.' His spittle sprayed my cheeks with each short, fast breath. 'I don't remember inviting you to Wollongong?' His eyebrows shot up. 'Oh but maybe I did, and silly me forgot. Do you think I forgot?'

My heart too swollen, too fearful to answer, I shook my head, scrambled out of the ute and stood there in the dust, waiting for his whip to slash the back of my knees.

Mr Yates clicked his fingers at Bluey, who jumped into the ute. No whip. No punishment threat. Nothing.

Without a backward glance, Mr Yates drove off down the driveway, Bluey's head poking out from a corner of the tarp. Ears stretched back in the rush of air, that mutt smiled his doggy grin at me.

* * *

Worrying why Mr Yates hadn't whipped me, I almost didn't enjoy our Saturday afternoon of freedom. That man "executed discipline" for far lesser offences than trying to escape. So why not me?

Knackered from our morning duties – cleaning the chook pen, lugging laundry baskets outside – in a savage heat that made my vision blurry, my head thump hard, we spent most of the afternoon lounging in the veranda shade.

'Here youse go,' Bonnie said, pouring us all glasses of her

tangy homemade lemonade. She then cut slices of the jam sponge cake she'd baked as soon as Mr Yates had taken off for Wollongong.

'Surely it can't get any hotter?' I said, cramming a fistful of cake into my mouth. I stroked my favourite cat, an extra fluffy one with eyes the yellow of dandelion flowers.

'It was bad enough in November and December,' Vinnie said, gobbling down her cake.

'And January,' Tommy said. In Bluey's absence, he threw the mutt's ball to Joey Joe, who bounced after it, a paw tapping it along the veranda.

Nick gave the wallaby's ears a friendly tweak, and my heart swelled with pride that we'd saved that little creature from certain death, six months ago. Just the other day Mr Yates was telling us that only now, at around eight months old, would Joey Joe've been able to survive outside his mum's pouch.

'Oh God, January,' I said, remembering my scorching birthday a month ago when Jane, Suzy and Vinnie had covered my bunk with sweet-smelling, creamy yellow honeysuckle flowers. 'But February's even hotter!'

I knew my friends had simply plucked the flowers from the honeysuckle vine that climbed across our redback spider-infested toilet – the "dunny" Bonnie called it – masking the stink a bit on the hottest days. But they'd thought of my special day, and that's what counted.

And, like she would do on the closest Saturday to everyone's birthday, Bonnie had whipped up a chocolate cake and magically found some candles. Blowing out those eleven candles reminded me of Charly's birthday, within a few days of mine. I thought of my little sister every single one of those blazing, unbearable days, but missing her sixth birthday made her absence seem like the searing pain of a sliced-off foot or hand.

How is she? Where *is she?*

Thinking of Charly made me think of Mum.

Does she know we're in Australia, that I'm a prisoner, a slave?

Does she know they lied and separated us; that Charly has a new mother?

Mum would not be happy about any of that; she'd always counted on me to look after Charly. And as the burning summer months slid by, it became more and more likely that I'd lost Charly and Mum forever. Sometimes I wished I could crush my love for both of them from my heart, it would be easier then, to be stuck here without them.

Like every Saturday, our smashing time with Bonnie was over too quickly and, in the dying heat of the violet dusk, we chased about finishing jobs, making sure everything was neat and tidy for Mr Yates' return.

Fretting over my punishment that was surely coming, I took deep breaths, tried to calm the pulse that thudded in my temple.

But when he got back that night, Mr Yates still didn't whip me. No surprise though, the way he tumbled out of the ute, lurched up the veranda steps and slurred at the screen door, 'Where the hell are you, Bonnie?'

'How can anyone be that drunk and drive a car?' I hissed to Vinnie from our spying spot behind the fig tree. 'Come on, let's get closer, I need to know what he's planning for me.' We crept across to the veranda, peered through the cracked-open kitchen window.

Bonnie was cowering in a corner, behind a chair – a useless shield, since Mr Yates flung it aside and loomed over his wife.

'No dinner for me, you fat cow? After slogging away all afternoon, chasing around Wollongong selling our produce, buying supplies for you and that ungrateful bunch of kids?'

He bent down, slapped Bonnie's cheek. I clapped a palm over mine, feeling the same sting as when my father had slapped Mum.

'S-sorry, M-Milton,' she stammered, as his fist crunched into her face. 'Y-your t-tea's … plate … Aga.'

'How can she let him hit her like that?' Vinnie whispered, though there was no chance he'd hear us above the racket he was making. 'Why doesn't she leave him?'

I shrugged. 'Mum never left Dad even if he knocked her, and us, around. Once I asked her why, but she just mumbled something about "nowhere else to go".'

'Get out of my way,' Mr Yates snarled, lurching back towards the screen door.

My guts churned with hatred for that brute, kicking Bonnie as she lay in a crumpled heap on the floor. She was so nice to us and I felt guilty too, that I'd called her Humpty Dumpty that first day.

Vinnie and I scuttled behind the bougainvillea clump as Mr Yates came staggering out onto the veranda, glass of whisky in one hand, battered wireless in the other.

He often sat out on the veranda drinking whisky on these summer evenings when the worst of the day's heat was over. As usual, he fiddled with the little dial till the radio voice came clear.

'Bloody communists!' he barked, a hand cupped around the torn, waggly ear. The announcer was speaking about the Cold War, the White Australia policy, but we really had no clue what any of that was.

' … loyal to Britain … mother country.'

Mr Yates shook a fist, and Vinnie's clammy hand gripped mine. 'When're we going back to *our* mother country?'

'One day,' I said, with a sigh. 'But for now, there's nothing we can do to get back there, *or* to help Bonnie. And that monster hasn't mentioned any punishment for me, so we might as well get to bed, it'll be six o'clock in the morning before we know it.'

Vinnie kept hold of my hand as we slunk through the darkness to the sleeping shed.

I sank onto my bunk beneath Vinnie's, dead beat from worrying about a flogging that never came. Against the drone of mosquitoes, the whir of cicadas, the scratch and rumble of possums across the roof, it was like trying to doze off inside a hot and noisy stove.

But I ended up sleeping heavily, convinced Mr Yates had forgotten all about my failed runaway.

* * *

The next morning at breakfast Mr Yates still didn't punish me. He didn't even come to the dining shed, like most meals, to lecture us on something or other.

'The drink made him forget,' I said to Vinnie. 'Like my father would forget stuff after a whisky binge.'

'Fingers crossed,' Vinnie said, as we gobbled down our porridge.

But as we left the dining shed, setting off to our different chores – because Mr Yates made us work even on Sundays – his skinny figure blocked my path. 'You're on homestead duty today, Gasbag. You'll clean my bedroom.'

He crossed his arms over his chest, the riding crop dangling down his front. 'Only this morning when I got out of my bed,' he said, 'I thought to myself, poor girl's looking a bit peaky, she could do with an easy job.' The buck teeth juddered between his lips as he smiled at me. 'Off you go then, and you might want to thank me for almost giving you a day off.'

'Yes, Mr Yates,' I said, trying to ignore the strange gleam in his pinky eyes, legs quivering as I skedaddled up to the homestead, not even daring to glance back at Vinnie.

And once I reached his bedroom, my gaze settling across the giant mess, I knew he'd tricked me.

Every last thing, from drawers, dresser and cupboard, was scattered across the floor, the bed upended. Dirty crockery, clothes, shoes, pages and pages of newspapers, were strewn about. It would take me hours to tidy up and scrub everything clean. Mr Yates must be laughing right down to his black boots.

I hate you!

I sighed, looked around at the shambles; had no idea where to start. My gaze came to rest on the locked cupboard where Mr Yates kept the telephone that only he was allowed to use. Bonnie had told us he wouldn't even let her use it, and that he kept the key in his pocket, on the ring with all the other farm keys.

I tiptoed over and around the clutter to the phone cupboard, trying not to break anything, or cut my bare feet. My ears burned, my mind alert for any noise. But the homestead stayed silent. Mr Yates would be out in the paddocks, or around the dairy or piggery, at this time of day, checking on the boys' work. And I'd seen Bonnie hanging out sheets, with an apprentice girl.

I tried the cupboard handle which, of course, didn't budge. Riffling through the dressing table mess, I found a tie pin, tried to slot it into the lock. In it slid, easily. Heart pummelling against my chest, I fiddled about, trying to get the lock to open. It held fast.

I soon realised there was no point, and slumped to the floor amidst the jumble. Tears stung my eyes, sobs clogged my throat.

You don't even know the Ashwoods' address, or phone number, you daft idiot.

And, in that instant, I understood Mr Yates' second cruel trick of the day.

16

Lucy Rivers
Southern Highlands, New South Wales
February 1963

❮ … and don't any of you *ever* forget that England did not want you.' Mr Yates' boots thud-thudded on the dining shed floor as he strolled up and down before us, seated along the hard benches.

I'd spent all morning clearing up his bedroom, the whole time stopping myself from taking a hammer to the telephone cupboard; frustrated I couldn't phone those people who'd taken Charly. I'd opened another cupboard, surprised it wasn't locked when I saw that's where he kept his hunting rifle.

I'd stared, long and hard at that rifle, murderous thoughts ticking through my brain. Then, with a sigh, I'd closed the cupboard.

We all sat, still and silent, listening to Mr Yates rant on, our Sunday lunch – the usual tough mutton with potatoes – growing colder on our metal plates. But no one complained since lunch was always better than the breakfast porridge sludge.

'England threw you from the nest like baby birds who cannot yet even fly!' Mr Yates cried.

Bluey sat on one side of Mr Yates, staring up at his master. Bonnie stood on his other side, stumpy hands clasped across the washed-out blue shift. She kept her head bowed, tried to hide the puffy, purple eye his fist had made last night.

Loyal as Bluey, Bonnie was, though Mr Yates never laid a hand, fist or a boot into his dog.

'England rejected you!' Mr Yates' voice rose as he repeated the same thing, only slightly differently, as every one of his Sunday lectures. 'You would've been homeless, with no one to look after you, to feed or clothe you, if Mrs Yates and I hadn't taken you in. And at our own expense.'

Mr Yates stabbed the horse whip into the stuffy air; the whip I'd never seen him without in the five months we'd been at Seabreeze Farm. His ratty stare settled on each child in turn, for Mr Yates was searching out the bored, the sleepy, the smirkers, who – without the slightest warning – he'd slash across the shoulders.

That was the thing we'd learned about Mr Yates: one minute he'd be showing you how to bottle-feed Joey Joe, the next he'd whip you for being lazy or cheeky. Two different people sewn into one, and it was terrible living with the fear of never knowing which one you were facing.

'What more could a child want besides a mother and father, a roof over its head, food and a bed?' Mr Yates' lips stretched behind the bucky teeth into that wide grin that was no smile at all. 'So, my children, before you enjoy my good farm nourishment let me hear your thanks. Thank you, Australia!'

'Thank you, Australia!' everyone cried. Except me, and Suzy Hampton.

Mr Yates strode over to Suzy, glowered down at her. 'Didn't hear you, girlie, say it again.'

Shoulders trembling, poor Suzy stared, in silence, down at her lunch plate. She hadn't spoken a single word through those whole five months, except the occasional sobbing fit that sent her all shaky. Suzy's body might still be with us, but her mind had vanished to some place so far away not even Vinnie's donkey laugh could reach.

'You'll speak to me if it's the last thing you do on this earth,' Mr Yates said, and slashed a single, cutting stroke across Suzy's arm. She flinched, didn't say a word.

Mr Yates turned his gaze back to me. 'And you, Gasbag, I didn't hear you thank Australia either?'

In the silence that followed, before I could stop myself, I blurted out, 'No thanks, Australia!'

'Oh, oh!' Jane gasped, threw me a fearful look.

'What's your problem, Freak-face?' Mr Yates barked at Jane, who went so pale I thought she might faint.

During our early Seabreeze days, Jane had complained about every ache and pain, and moaned for her mum.

'No use bellyaching about your mother, Freak-face, here's something to really whine about,' Mr Yates said, whipping the back of Jane's knees. She'd cried the whole day but since then she only complained when Mr Yates wasn't around.

'Shut yer gob, Lucy,' Vinnie hissed, elbowing me in the ribs, her eyes big green saucers in a freckly maze.

Too late, Mr Yates' gaze had already shot to me. Two poison arrows. But I didn't care anymore. After five hot and weary months of work drudgery, I'd had enough of Mr Milton bloody Yates. And Seabreeze bloody Farm.

A deadly hush fell over the dining shed. I gnawed on a nail.

'*What* did you say, Gasbag?' Mr Yates' voice was a husky whisper. His face darkened to a thundercloud, like the ones that would gather over the horizon, clump together, and slide towards Seabreeze. Slowly, but coming all the same. There was no escaping the storm.

'I said, "No thanks, Australia".' I tried to keep the quiver from my voice; to sound bold, as if I wasn't afraid of shitting myself. Because if Mr Yates thought you feared him, he only whacked you harder, longer. I resisted wiping clammy hands down my pinafore.

Everyone held their breath. The shed grew hotter by the second, the asbestos roofing trapping the day's heat, tighter, closer, adding to the heat of yesterday. To the heat of all those scorching yesterdays. And outside, in that still air with not a shred of breeze, flies buzzed, cicadas trilled from the eucalyptus gums, and a bird let out a single, sad chirp.

Same as every other day in this bush place, lost and forgotten if not for a wooden sign and a tree-stump letterbox at the end of a dusty track.

'You said, "No thanks, Australia"?'

I gave him a firm, defiant nod.

He tapped the crop on the floor, grabbed a rickety chair from a corner, and beckoned me towards him. 'Right, come here, and don't complain I haven't warned you, over and over, about your cheek. After all I've given you – a home, food, clothes – a man can only take so much disrespect. I just do *not* understand your thanklessness, Gasbag.'

Everyone lifted their bum and I slid back the bench seat, the screech loud in that silence. Head held high, hands clenched to stop me biting my nails, I walked towards Mr Yates.

'Bend over the chair,' he said, foul breath hot on my cheek, small pinky eyes stabbing holes through mine. Rat whiskers twitching. 'Lift up your dress, and pull down your undies.'

Pull down my undies?

I thought I'd heard him wrong. Mr Yates only ever whacked knees, arms and shoulders. Never bare bums.

I frowned. 'What here, in front of *everyone*?'

The dining shed remained silent though fear bounced off every wall. Along with mine, I smelled their terror, tasted it like the maggot-ridden mutton Mr Yates often forced us to eat. Bonnie glanced up at me, tears springing to her eyes. She looked back down at the floor.

Mr Yates smiled. 'Your crime – attempting to run off like some common criminal from Seabreeze, from the roof I so *kindly*, so *selflessly*, put over your head – surely merits extra punishment, don't you think?'

He swivelled back to all those bowed heads, gazes fixed on lunches from which the steam had fizzled out. 'You all agree with that, don't you?'

No answer.

'You didn't think,' he said, returning his gaze to me, torn ear waggling, 'that I'd forgotten your silly escape attempt, did you?'

My blood settled, so cold I couldn't speak, or move; couldn't believe he wanted me to show off my bare bum to every Seabreeze boy.

The heavy silence hung over us like that baggy spider's belly in our sleeping shed, right before it had burst open and a flurry of baby spiders scampered out. I shivered with the gooseflesh.

Mr Yates sighed, annoyed at my silence. 'So don't try my patience any more than you already have. Now, dress up, undies down, bend over the chair.' The riding crop hung loose, by his side, but I caught the quiver in it, the tremor of the white-knuckled hand that gripped it.

Bonnie glanced up at me again. Even as I knew it was useless, I threw her a silent plea.

Help, Bonnie, only you can help me!

Bonnie did shuffle forward, stood between me and her husband. 'Punish me instead, Mr Yates ... I should've stopped Lucy from trying to run off ... all my fault.'

Without a word or even a glance, Mr Yates placed a palm on Bonnie's arm and shoved her aside. 'Bend over *now*,' he said to me in a quiet snarl.

Bonnie looked so sad for me, so hurt, I might've felt bad for her, if I hadn't been shrinking with shame as I bunched my pinafore around my waist, bent over the chair and slipped down my undies.

Undies dangling around my ankles, I clutched the chair legs, and as I stared at the floorboards, inches from my face, I understood Mr Yates' special pleasure was not only to punish you, but to shame you in front of everyone.

I realised too, that Mr Yates never punished you straightaway; never flogged you on the spot. No, he'd make you sweat on it for hours, sometime a whole day or night. Then he'd whip you at a meal, in the dining shed. That waiting was often worse than the punishment.

My breast nubs hurt, pressing against the hard chair and I pictured my burning cheeks flushing to the colour of the canned beetroot Bonnie sometimes put on our school sandwiches.

Only last week, Bonnie had told me, Vinnie and the other girls eleven or older, that she wished she could get us a camisole. 'A thing you wear before ya first bra,' she'd said with a motherly smile. 'I'd get youse all one if only Mr Yates'd take me shopping with him of a Saturday.' But Mr Yates had never taken Bonnie to Wollongong. He'd never once let her leave Seabreeze Farm.

True, there wasn't an inch of privacy in our sleeping shed, but at least we were all girls. There were sixteen boys at Seabreeze, and, as I glanced sideways, I caught a few leery gazes, whistles from Jim and John Browning.

Mr Yates spun around, pointed the riding crop at the Browning brothers, but didn't say a word. His terrifying look buttoned the boys' lips. Just one brief glance was often enough to make most of us quake or cry or wet our pants.

But not me.

No, Lucy Rivers had grown up with a bullying father. *She* wasn't about to bow down to this one even if, deep inside, he terrified her.

I'd stood up to Mr Yates every time he'd flogged me around the knees. I'd never cried, had held my promise that bully would never see my tears. Now was no different. A few more swats? I could take it, no worries, as Bonnie always said.

Bonnie made another move toward us. Mr Yates flicked the crop at her as if his wife were some annoying blowfly. 'Best get out of the way, Mrs. Yates, or you'll end up with a hiding too.'

Bonnie lurched backwards and the first thrash of the whip shot a red-hot, jagged pain from my bum right through my backbone, up to my shoulders, my neck, the top of my head.

Knee lashings were caresses, compared with this.

I gripped the chair legs tighter as the second lash shuddered inside my skull, sending me dizzy, and bolted back down to the soles of my feet.

It was not only the pain of horse whip on skinny flesh, almost bare bones. No, it was the agony too, of my shame; my black rage against Mr Yates. Pain I knew, in that instant, I'd never recover from.

But pain that still wouldn't make me scream in front of my torturer.

The third blow split my skin, spots of blood dripping onto the floor beside me. Yet still I willed myself not to cry out, though inside, I was screaming, dying.

The whipping stopped.

Mr Yates bent down, grabbed my hair, spoke softly close to my ringing ear. 'Maybe you'll think twice now, Gasbag, about making smart-arse remarks *and* about running off.'

A droplet of spittle escaped the muzzle, a blob settling on my cheek. 'And from now on, I'll be watching you like a hawk till the day you leave Seabreeze Farm, your home for which I get not an ounce of thanks.' He took a breath. 'Do you understand, you ungrateful, selfish bitch, one more cheeky remark, one more runaway attempt, and this beating will feel like feather strokes?'

I couldn't move; couldn't speak. Just hung over that chair, my backside on fire.

Until those flames fizzled out and I saw nothing. Heard nothing. And there was only darkness.

Is this what it's like to die?

17

Charly Rivers
Wollongong, New South Wales
February 1963

'Isn't he smashing?' Charly cried, showing her father the little red pony she'd just won in the lucky dip at the fair.

'Wow, he really *is* something,' Daddy said, with a grin.

Charly had been at the red-brick house for one whole summer. An entire hot summer of Daddy and Mummy Dolly calling her "Charlotte". In the end she'd got tired of telling them she was "Charly", and now just went along with everyone thinking her name was "Charlotte".

'Look, Simone, isn't my pony lovely?'

Simone crossed her arms and put on her pouty mouth. 'I want to win a red pony too.'

'Come on, girls, let's get out of this heat,' Daddy said. 'Who's on for an ice-cream and a drink?'

He held one each of Simone and Charly's hands as they struggled through the crowd of people at the showground. The sun burned her face and she was glad when they finally sat in the shade of a tree, with drinks and ice-creams, on grass that the sun had turned dry, brown and rough.

The ice-cream dribbled down Charly's chin, her neck, her arms, and she and Simone had to lick the cones really fast. They had a race to see who could finish first. Simone won, and forgot about wanting a red pony.

Charly dragged her sticky ice-cream fingers across the grass, slurped the last of her iced green drink and stroked the pony's mane. He wasn't anywhere near as lovely as her wind-up black-birdie she'd left in England, but still, she loved the pony. Even if it was only a toy – course she knew he wasn't real! – but she pretended he *was* an alive pony that she'd ride one day when it grew into an adult pony.

'When can I ride a *real* pony?' she asked Daddy.

'Yeah, why *won't* you let us ride the ponies over there, Mr Ashwood?' Simone said, pointing across to the dusty ring where a line of kids was waiting for pony rides. 'Charlotte 'n me are six now, that's way old enough to ride a pony.'

'Yes look, Daddy, some of those children waiting are younger than us,' Charly said, slurping the last of her iced drink. 'It's not fair.'

'You'll ride a real pony when you're older, girls.'

'When we're in First Class, Daddy?'

'Yippee, that's next week!' Simone said.

Daddy laughed. 'Well maybe not *that* soon.'

* * *

When the fair was over, Daddy drove them home and parked his car in the driveway. Charly got out with Simone, breathing in the lovely scent of the creamy-yellow frangipani flowers. Simone had to go back to number 11 to tell her mum she was home safe and sound, and Charly dashed inside to show Mummy Dolly the red pony.

Charly's new mother had insisted on being called "Mummy". But Charly already had a mother – the one Lucy was taking her back to England to see, on another boat – so she'd decided to call this one "Mummy Dolly". But only inside her head, since the new mother hated being called "Mummy Dolly".

Charly only had one father though, so he was "Daddy", not "Dad" or "Daddy Frank".

Mummy Dolly hadn't wanted to come to the fair with them.

'I've got far too much housework, and would you look at this *mountain* of ironing!' she'd cried, flinging an arm at the clean washing basket, which you were never allowed to mix up with the dirty washing basket, that stayed in the laundry.

'Do you really need to iron socks and undies, Dolly?' Daddy said, as he came in from the garage.

Charly waved the little red pony at Mummy Dolly, who slammed the iron down onto her ironing board. She gasped and snatched the pony from her.

'Get rid of it, Frank, burn it.' She held Charly's pony upside down between thumb and forefinger, by one hoof, her other fingers spread wide as if the toy was dirty and ugly. 'Take it down to your incinerator right this minute.'

Charly could tell Daddy didn't want to burn her pony in his incinerator at the bottom of the backyard, but he always did everything Mummy Dolly wanted, especially if she cried.

So he did burn the little red pony, but that very evening, Daddy started building Charly a life-sized rocking horse-pony which he promised to paint red when it was all carved out. Far more beautiful than the little toy pony.

'And don't think, for a minute, you're bringing that rocking-horse into the house either, Frank,' Mummy Dolly said, hands on her hips as she watched him from the garage doorway, since she never went inside.

And when Mummy Dolly stamped back up to her kitchen, Daddy smiled at Charly and said, 'I think we should stable your rocking-pony right here in the garage. What do you say?'

18

'Where am I?' I opened my eyes, went to sit up. The fierce pain in my backside immediately brought back the agony of Mr Yates' thrashing and I slumped down again.

'You fainted in the dining shed.' Vinnie's voice. 'We carried you to your bunk.'

'You were a bit heavy but we managed.' Jane's whiny voice.

'Poor Lucy, what an evil brute.' Vinnie again.

And Suzy staring down at me, brow puckered, silent. Carol, Fiona, Helen and Bessy all hovering too, worried looks twisting their faces.

Suzy's shaky hand took mine, gave it a gentle, silent squeeze. Tears filled her eyes and Bonnie circled her chunky arms around Suzy, patted her back.

'Downright passed out with the pain, you did. Here, take this, one of Mr Yates' pain pills I sneaked ya,' Bonnie said.

I fought the red-hot agony as my friends helped me sip lukewarm water to swallow the pill. 'Thanks, Bonnie, hope it works fast.'

'And them cuts'll need disinfecting,' Bonnie said, as gentle hands eased me onto my side.

I winced beneath Bonnie's tender dabs at my bum. 'I know it stings like billy-o, but I need to hurry a bit ... Mr Yates don't know, I'm not supposed ... '

116

Liza Perrat

'Don't want to get you in trouble, Bonnie,' I said.

'You rest up, and don't be worrying yourself about me, sweet chook.' Bonnie called all us kids "chook" which was Australian for "chicken". 'I can take care of meself.'

'No you can't, Bonnie,' Fiona Mulligan said. 'We're not stupid, we know Mr Yates beats you too.'

'How can you stand being married to such a brute?' Bessy said.

'And why do you call him "Mr Yates" and not his first name?' Vinnie said.

'Aw strewth, Mr Yates, Milton, can be a good bloke,' Bonnie said, 'when he's not wearing the wobbly boot. Means well, reckons he's giving youse kids a better life than those orphanages back in Pommie land.'

'Well it's *not* a better life,' Helen said. 'He works us like dogs. We're that wrecked we can hardly stay awake at school.'

'I didn't even get to *go* to school,' Fiona said. 'Straight into apprenticeship which is just slave labour but for longer hours.'

'And the food's even worse than back at Easthaven in England,' Jane said. 'My stomach's always aching from the bad food.'

'Yeah, why won't Mr Yates let us, and *you*, eat all that good farm food, like he does?' Carol said.

'I told you why,' said Fiona, who'd told us about Mr Yates' meals made with real butter, fresh eggs and veggies, and tender meat cuts, ''cos he sells the best produce and leaves the grungy leftovers for us.'

'So all our hard work does is line his pockets,' Carol said.

'And I'm so much further away from my mother in Australia,' Jane moaned. 'She'll *never* find me here. I bet she's searching for me right now.' She touched a fingertip to the squashy spot between her nose and lip. 'Even if I wasn't born perfect.'

'Don't be a silly bugger, Jane, fer sure ya mum wants ya. 'Course she'll find ya one day.' Bonnie patted Jane's back. 'Now let me get this mercurochrome onto Lucy's cuts,' she said, 'and best stay on ya side till it dries.'

I nodded. 'Hurts too much to move anyway.'

117

'I know Mr Yates is a bit strict sometimes, bit harsh,' Bonnie said, dabbing on the soothing red liquid, 'but he tries his best. Suffered himself, ya know, in that Korea War, ended up a prisoner, which was no Sunday picnic. Anyway, I'm sorry for youse all, sorry on his behalf.'

'But why don't you leave, Bonnie?' Vinnie said. 'You're not a prisoner here, like us.'

'And go where?' Bonnie said. 'Seabreeze Farm's home. When me own mum and dad chucked me out at sixteen – 'cos they reckoned I was dumb and no use to them on our property out Dubbo way – Mr Yates was right kind to take me in, as his wife.'

Vinnie rolled her eyes. 'Yeah, like he was kind to take us in.'

'Sure, it got a bit lonely out here beyond the black stump, got me down a bit, till youse kids came along,' Bonnie went on. 'But I always had me cats for company.'

As I lifted my gaze to the open doorway, to that wide, empty farmland, the endless miles of scrubland beyond; to the yellows, browns and blue-greys stretching away to meet a blue sky, more and more bleached out as the day went on, I realised that Bonnie was as much a prisoner of Mr Yates, and Seabreeze Farm, as us.

'Anyway, best you rest on ya bunk a few days, sweet chook,' Bonnie said, groaning as she heaved herself up from the floor. 'I'll try and get back to see ya later ... I'll pop one of me sleeping pills into Mr Yates' whisky,' she said with a giggle.

She pulled two tablets from the pocket of the faded shift, pushed them into my hand. 'Here's a sleeping pill, and an extra pain pill for later.'

'Thanks, Bonnie,' I said, as she shuffled off. She stopped in the doorway, turned back to me, pointed up, outside.

'*Wiohwi, wiohwi, wiohwi ... trrrrrr, arrrr.*'

'Listen, prettiest song you ever heard – a blackbird. I bet he's singing just for you, Lucy.' She smiled and lumbered back outside into that fierce sun.

From my first day at Seabreeze, I'd hated Mr Yates as much as I'd felt sad for his wife. Just as I'd sensed my mother's fear of our father, I figured out Bonnie's dread of Mr Yates. Sometimes though, I wished she'd stand up to him, stop being such easy prey. If she fought back, he might bully her less.

'We'd better get back to work too,' Carol said. 'Mr Yates wants us to shovel all that chook-pen manure into the wheelbarrow, and dump it in the veggie garden.'

Carol shuffled off with Fiona, Bessy and Helen, and Jane and Suzy went back to their task of scrubbing down the homestead kitchen.

'The girls are covering for me in the laundry, so I can stay a bit longer,' Vinnie said, sitting cross-legged on the floor, stroking damp hair from my sweaty forehead. My special friend, Vinnie, the only person in the whole world who truly cared about me.

'I get that you hate Mr Yates for whacking you so hard, *and* baring your bum to the whole world,' Vinnie said. 'I'd have died on the spot, but you'll really have to shut your mouth, Lucy … next time he might kill you.'

'I'll kill that bloody monster first,' I said, my body so hot with pain I worried I might die from it. 'Anyway, I'm not even embarrassed anymore, only angry. Mad that we travelled right to the other side of the earth to live in another place like Easthaven. Angry when I think how free we were on the *Star of New South Wales,* so free I never wanted to be a prisoner again. But here we are, caged up like zoo animals.' A sob rose in my throat. Out of Mr Yates' sight, I let it escape.

'Aw don't you cry, Lucy Rivers,' Vinnie said, stroking my arm. 'Or you'll make me cry too. And remember we promised, no crying?'

'I've lost *everything,*' I sobbed. 'My home, my mother, my sister, my *country.*' I beat my fist against my chest, trying to shift the stone wedged there that made it hard to breathe. 'Now there's nothing left in here … only an empty space.'

'I got nobody either,' Vinnie said, with a sad smile as she stood up, smoothed down her grey pinafore. 'But we still got each other, eh? Anyway, I better get back to that laundry, but you stay here, the laundry apprentice girl said to tell you you're excused from duty this afternoon.'

Just the afternoon? Won't it take weeks – months! – to recover from this?

* * *

I must've slept a few hours, thanks to Bonnie's sleeping pill, but a full bladder woke me. The pain splintering me, I heaved myself up to go to the dunny.

It was all I could do not to collapse back onto the bunk and scream out, yet somehow, gripping the ends of the beds as I stumbled, bent over, tears stinging my eyes, I fumbled out to the Belongings section of the shed.

Besides four bunks, each sleeping shed had one of these sections where every child had two shelves on which to store our stuff. After this Belongings section was a roofless bathroom containing one dunny, a sink and a shower.

There was no comfy settee, no floor rugs, or pictures on the walls. Not a bit of cosiness. My mother could never afford fancy furniture or decorations though she'd still managed to make our flat cosy. But here at Seabreeze, the sleeping and dining sheds were hot, bare and ugly. We lived like Mr Yates' farm animals, the only difference was that he never beat them.

I ducked around a cobweb, stepped over the scatter of dried-up insects and, like always, kept a watch on Raymond Redback spider as I eased my throbbing bum onto the seat.

It was Vinnie who'd named our resident spider who lived in a corner, trying to make us laugh instead of shake with fear every time we used the dunny. No one was game to stomp on the spider, or to ask Mr Yates to get rid of it, so we just took extra care not to annoy or disturb Raymond Redback. And we got the hell out of that dunny as quick as we could.

In that heavy air, the silvery gum-tree leaves drooping

through the open roof, I kept an eye out for stray snakes that would slide through the gap beneath the door to coil up in a sheltered spot.

I rinsed my hands, flung water onto my hot face, and breathed in the honeysuckle scent as I lurched back to my bunk.

I gently lowered myself back onto my side. Outside, a kookaburra laughed into the hot stillness, a cockatoo shrieked. Bluey barked, and was silent.

From the eucalyptus gum overhanging our shed, I couldn't see him, but the blackbird struck up his mellow song. '*Wiohwi, wiohwi, wiohwi, trrrrrr, arrrr.*'

I thought of Charly and her beloved wind-up blackbird that our father had so cruelly smashed.

As the blackbird sang, my heart softened, dampening the fury inside, making way for the tears. And there I lay all afternoon, in that sweltering shed, crying till my eyes were swollen and sore, and my chest ached.

But the blackbird's chirp must have lulled me to sleep again, as the next thing I knew, I opened my eyes to the yellow-mauve twilight.

Beyond the shed door, I caught the bright needle of the first twinkling star and our night friends, the possums – who we'd once feared to be burglars! – thundered across the roof.

Mozzies buzzed. I eased myself to a sitting position, braced myself to get up and close the door or we'd all be covered in swollen, red bumps by morning. Especially Jane.

Once my eyes focused, I smiled at Joey Joe standing in the shed doorway, rubbing his front paws together. But our wallaby friend wasn't alone, and my heart juddered in my chest as I realised Mr Yates was standing beside Joey Joe.

'Thought a visit from Joey Joe might cheer you up,' he said, with a bucky grin as he stroked the wallaby's soft head. The blood thudded in my temples and my breaths came short and fast. Terrified of saying the wrong thing, stunned by Mr Yates' friendliness just a few hours after such viciousness, I kept my gob shut. But the words screamed through my mind.

Mr Hates, you'll be now, since hate's your air, your food. Your everything.

'Go on, in you go and see Lucy,' Mr Hates said softly, giving the wallaby a little push towards me. Joey Joe hopped into the shed, sat beside my bunk like a real, comforting friend.

'And you might want to check out the Southern Cross, so bright tonight.' Mr Hates waved a hand at the darkening sky. 'See that cross-shaped constellation up there? Part of the Milky Way … best-known star pattern in our Southern Hemisphere.'

I nodded, imagining lines drawn between those five winking stars. They really would make the shape of a cross.

Without another word, Mr Hates stamped off along the dirt path.

I clicked my fingers at Joey Joe. 'Hello there, my favourite wallaby, you really do cheer me up.'

And as I stroked his furry head, I hung on to all the precious things in my sad life – Joey Joe, my friends, Bonnie, the invisible blackbird, the amazing Southern Cross constellation – and that's what got me through that afternoon after the beating.

Later that night, after I'd taken another pain pill, and my sleeping-shed mates had fallen, exhausted, into their bunks, I groped beneath my mattress, trying not to wince with the pain, till my fingers curled around the torn photo. As every night, I kissed Mum's half-mouth, stroked half of her: some hair, an eye, half a nose and mouth, half her body, the arm she'd tucked around Charly's shoulder. That way I might dream about her, and about my sister.

Had that man, Frank Ashwood, given the torn photo to Charly? Would he and his wife tell her she had a sister, and, since I couldn't get away to find Charly, might they come and find me at Seabreeze one day? Did they even know I was here?

I almost wished I'd die from my wounds during the night. Because if I didn't, there was no way I could survive living at Seabreeze Farm for six more years.

19

From the school gates, Mummy Dolly sniffed away her tears as she waved and blew Charlotte a kiss. 'Have a lovely day, sweetie.'

'Bye, Mummy.' Charlotte waved back and she and Simone skipped off across the playground. She hugged her coat around her, warm enough to keep out the cold wind that had whistled right through July and into August, and had even blown down a gum tree in Frangipani Drive.

'Why does your mum *always* cry when she says bye-bye?' Simone said.

Charlotte shrugged. She didn't understand either, why Mummy Dolly cried almost every morning, especially when Charlotte kept telling her how much she loved school, which wasn't a fib. *And* since she was seven years and seven months old, not a baby.

She'd adored school right from her first day, in kindergarten. She'd loved listening to her teacher reading from the Ladybird books, the Dick and Dora Happy Venture ones, and the little Golden Books whose spines gleamed in the sunshine. The same books that Hazel had taught Charlotte to read from, in the ship's library.

The kindergarten teacher had let them paint pictures with their fingers! They'd been allowed to dress up as Disney characters, too. Charlotte was always Snow White, because her teacher said her hair was dark and shiny as Snow White's, her skin as milky, her lips the same crimson. That had made Charlotte's insides feathery warm.

Charlotte had loved First Class even more, when her teacher had written on her report card:

Charlotte is the best reader in the class and already shows much literary talent.

Mummy Dolly hadn't cried at that. No, she'd smiled and said to Daddy, 'Our clever little Charlotte.'

'Hurry up,' Simone said, 'or we'll miss play time.' She grabbed Charlotte's hand and they raced across the playground to their friends, who were jumping over an elastic held tight by one girl at each end.

It was true, Mummy Dolly did cry a lot, but she also laughed and smiled. And sometimes all three at once. She never shouted at Charlotte, like Mrs Mersey and Mrs Benson from Easthaven. Mrs Jardine next door shouted at Simone sometimes, for leaving her toys lying around.

That's not to say Charlotte's mother wasn't firm. Every time Daddy took her and Simone to North Beach, Mummy Dolly would waggle her pointer finger at Charlotte and say, 'Only swim between the red and yellow flags. And no gobbling rubbish from that kiosk.'

Her mother was firm about food too and only allowed her to eat certain things, even though Charlotte thought that seven-soon-to-be-eight was old enough to decide what you wanted to eat. But if she asked for something different, like something she'd tasted on the *Star of New South Wales*, her mother would get upset and refuse.

'Stop whining,' Mummy Dolly would say. 'You were never a whingey child, don't start now.'

Thankfully Charlotte had grown out of those clothes Mummy Dolly had made her wear at first; clothes that smelt like Aunty Edna's moffs cupboards. She was happy to have new ones; new as the lovely clothes in her vanished Easthaven suitcase. In the beginning she'd kept asking for it but her mother would frown and say, "what suitcase?" Daddy kept shaking his head, so Charlotte had given up asking.

Charlotte and Simone joined the girls playing elastics and singing about London Bridge falling down. But Charlotte's chest closed up tight as she remembered singing the London Bridge song with Lucy and Vinnie.

When she'd first arrived at the red-brick house, Charlotte had kept her sister's face sharp in her mind. That hadn't been hard, as people always told them they looked alike – same dark blue eyes and wavy black hair, but now Lucy's face, and those of her Easthaven friends, had gone hazy. She was squinting at them through the fog that clung all winter to Mount Kembla, Mount Keira, Mount Nebo and Mount Ousley, towering over the city of Wollongong. No matter how hard she tried to hang on to them, their faces were sliding from her mind like the *Star of New South Wales* sailing further and further out to sea.

Not that Charlotte had forgotten Lucy – *never* would she forget her big sister or her real mum – but since Mummy Dolly and Daddy had never answered her when she asked about them, she'd got tired of asking.

Charlotte had stopped speaking about her life in England and on the boat as that had upset Mummy Dolly, who'd kissed and cuddled her even more. So tight that she squashed Charlotte's breath from her, though it was kind of nice, at the same time.

As much as Mummy Dolly and Daddy loved Charlotte, they made her feel bad for thinking about her other life; never wanted her to talk about it, so she kept it quiet. Locked it away in her mind during the day when she was at school or playing on her backyard slide with Simone.

But at night, when Mummy Dolly made her put away whatever book she was reading, Charlotte would let the memories spill through her mind: her real mum, Lucy and Vinnie, the bomb sites where they'd played hide 'n seek and built towers from rubbly bricks, leap-frogging across the courtyard, swinging around a lamppost till she was dizzy. She thought too, about all those amazing places they'd seen on the *Star of New South Wales*.

Her memories were so bright at night, Charlotte sometimes couldn't get to sleep. She'd cuddle up to Heidi, whose eyes weren't a bit scary anymore but who would never be as nice as Jeannie, and she'd tell Heidi stories about them all, then make up extra ones, which would make Charlotte fall asleep.

Tears gathered behind Charlotte's eyes. But she was no crybaby, like at Easthaven; like Simone's little brother, Edward, so she blinked them away and sang the London Bridge song loudly, to hide the tremble in her voice.

'Are you one of those ten-pound Poms, Charlotte?' said Sally, a new girl at school who was eight, a year older than Charlotte and Simone. 'You've got a Pommie accent, same as Debbie and Sharon Buckland.'

'What's a ten-pound Pom?' Charlotte asked.

'My father said they're people who came on boats to Australia from England,' Sally said, 'almost for free, *and* they stole all the Australian people's jobs.'

'Is that the boat you went on?' Simone said. 'The boat your mummy told mine they took you on a cruise over-the-seas, last summer holidays?'

'No that was a *different* boat from the one I went on with Lucy.'

'Lucy's not real,' Simone said, as she jumped over the elastic Charlotte held tight around her ankles.

'Is so! Lucy's my *sister*, I keep telling you.'

The bell rang. Sally shoved the elastic into her school case and Simone and Charlotte hurried into class since their Second Class teacher, Miss Tindale, did not tolerate latecomers.

Charlotte breathed in that lovely blackboard-chalk smell as she sat at the desk she and Simone shared.

'So where *is* this Lucy-sister?' Simone said. 'We never see Lucy 'cos she's *nowhere*. Your mummy told mine that Lucy's an imaginary sister you invented because you haven't got brothers or sisters.' Simone crinkled her nose, freckles squishing together.

'But you wouldn't want a brother like Edward, who cries and dribbles. And Mummy says five is far too old to wet yourself so she'll have to take Edward to the doctor.'

'Oh yes *far* too old,' Charlotte said. She might have told Simone about Lucy but she'd never tell her best friend, or *anyone*, how Mrs Mersey had made her stand the whole morning with her wet sheet over her head.

At lunchtime, they ate their sandwiches beneath the jacaranda tree, which Charlotte had loved sitting under since she'd first seen its pretty mauve blossom carpet last November.

Charlotte loved the yummy sandwich Mummy Dolly packed into her lunchbox every day, of crusty bread slathered with cheese and Vegemite. She could hardly believe it when Daddy told her how she'd hated Vegemite when she was a little girl. There was also a crispy red apple, and two of her favourite nutty, chewy Anzac biscuits that Mummy Dolly baked once a week, and which Daddy told her the brave Australian soldiers had eaten in the war.

Charlotte got to thinking again, about Mrs Mersey calling her a bed-wetting cry-baby, and she wanted to shout at Mrs Mersey that she hadn't wet the bed a single time since Lucy had escaped them to Australia. But most of all, she never wanted to go back to Easthaven.

If Easthaven was even real, that is, since whenever Charlotte said the word "Easthaven", Mummy Dolly would let out a shrieky laugh.

'None of that is real, sweetie,' she'd say. 'It's all simply in your dreams.'

20

'Hey, Vinnie, Jim and John Browning didn't get on the bus.' I twisted around in my seat, pointing at the brothers sprinting off in the opposite direction from the school bus, and disappearing into a roadside tangle of wattle trees. 'You reckon they're running away, or what?'

It was a warm September morning, the sky a deep blue, the air shifting as winter turned to spring. The driver didn't stop his bus rumbling down the main road towards school, past the wattles pouring out yellow blooms, honeyeaters crazily sucking up the pollen. And the pink and white jasmine, and the bottlebrushes, where rainbow lorikeets feasted on the red flowers.

'Run away?' Tommy Oakley said, from the seat behind me and Vinnie, where he sat beside his mate, Nick Hurley.

'Where would they go?' Nick said.

'That's if they really *have* run away,' Vinnie said, blinking and fluttering her eyelashes at Tommy. She'd started making those silly eyes at Tommy ten times a day, which annoyed me, though I had no idea why.

'Yeah, like the rest of us, they don't know anyone in Australia … no family, no friends,' I said. 'Why do you reckon *I* don't try and escape again? Because there's nowhere to run to, that's why, and not even considering the deadly snakes and spiders that'd prob'ly kill me first!'

Mr Hates' bare-bum beating might have happened a whole

128

year and seven months ago, but still I dreamed of getting away from Seabreeze. Never would I forget, or forgive, that monster for whipping me so hard I'd had to hobble about for ages like an old person, barely able to sit.

Bonnie had smoothed ointment on the cuts every night, and sneaked me a homestead cushion for the hard dining-shed bench. My friends helped me with my farm jobs, carried my school case, told me everything would be okay soon.

I was grateful but I was so wounded inside that their pity made me want to bawl.

My welts finally healed to shiny red stripes hidden beneath my undies. The deeper scars, the ones inside my head, I kept hidden too. But those wounds never healed, only gaped, raw and festering. And thirsty for revenge.

My shoulder bumping against Vinnie's as the bus bounced along the pot-holed road, I sniggered to myself, remembering my little Mr Hates-revenges. How I'd spat in his eggs and bacon when I'd helped the apprentice girl make his breakfast. How, when Vinnie and I were on homestead duty, I'd polished his boots with my own pee, and smeared a whisker of Bluey's shit under his pillow.

Vinnie was horrified, but couldn't help giggling at those small triumphs that helped me get through each miserable day.

The brakes whined as the bus came to a stop outside the school, and the kids poured off. There was no sign of Jim and John Browning at school, so it was pretty obvious they *had* scarpered.

'They won't get far,' said a fat bully boy who called us Seabreeze kids "orphans the cat dragged in". 'You skinny orphans stick out a mile with them bowl haircuts, scraggly uniforms and holey shoes. And anyone can pick the Pommie accent a mile off.' He laughed at the crowd of town kids hanging off his taunting words as we, the sorry-looking Seabreeze mob, veered off to our classroom, in our second-hand uniforms, carrying our battered cardboard school cases, all donated by the townspeople.

Right back to the day we'd started high school, and the headmaster had thrown us Seabreeze kids together in the one cramped and hot classroom – whatever class we were supposed to be in – the town kids had teased us about the "dumb orphan kids' class".

At swimming lessons at the local pool, they needled us about our uncool, baggy swimsuits. 'Cossies we call them in Australia,' they sneered. 'Not swimming costumes.'

* * *

'I'm sorry to say that only *one* student, out of the lot of you, passed yesterday's spelling test,' Mr Harding said. From the pile of test papers on his desk, the teacher held up two.

'Tommy Oakley and Nick Hurley, with nine out of twenty, *almost* passed,' he said. 'But the rest of you – Vinnie Armstrong, Lucy Rivers, Jane Baxter, etcetera, etcetera, didn't even come close. And don't go blaming your Pommie accents on bad spelling, again,' he said, waggling a finger.

Like every teacher, Mr Harding believed we'd all been turfed from our homes in England, or came from broken families, or really were orphans. They didn't bother teaching us anything besides basic reading, writing and arithmetic, so we had no clue about the world beyond Seabreeze Farm. They never expected us to pass any exams, and mostly we didn't.

He shook his head, held up each paper in turn, all covered in red-pen scrawls. 'All of you, nothing but a discredit, besides Suzy Hampton, who – God only knows how, with her muteness – passed with flying colours … nineteen out of twenty. Well done, dux of the class as usual, Suzy!'

Mr Harding no longer expected an answer from Suzy, or a smile for his praise. As always, she kept her nose in her books, worked hard, got the best marks. In the beginning, the teachers had tried to force her to speak but soon realised there was nothing left of our friend – on the inside or the outside – and gave up.

And as for the boys, who'd already been awake for five hours by the time they got to school – to milk cows and chop wood – the teachers just left them snoozing on their open textbooks all afternoon.

* * *

Just when I couldn't bear another minute of boredom, the lunch bell rang. There was still no sign of the Browning brothers.

'Looks like they really have escaped,' I said to Vinnie, as we scurried up to the girls' change rooms, where the town kids left their school cases if they did lunchtime sport. 'I so wish it was us gone from here.'

'You forgotten how Mr Yates punished you last time?' Vinnie said, taking up her lookout post outside the door.

'I know,' I said, rummaging through case after case, on the prowl for a tasty lunch. I really wanted to try and escape again, but even a year and a half after my failed attempt, I still didn't have the guts.

'Score!' I cried, holding up a fresh-smelling tomato, cheese and ham sandwich, and a crisp-looking red apple. I shoved the bounty into my own school case, and replaced it with my sad Seabreeze sandwich of stale bread and a thin slice of dried-out Spam.

'It *does* look yummy, but you really shouldn't steal,' Vinnie said, for the millionth time.

'I'm not, it's a swap … our sarnies for theirs. Anyway, why should those town kids get tasty sandwiches and not us? What's fair about that?'

Sometimes – not often, since Vinnie was a smart lookout – a girl would catch me going through her case. But after the first one, who I'd punched and made her nose bleed, they all pretended not to notice and let me get on with it.

While Vinnie's head was turned, I pinched a few pennies from a purse, quickly closed the case and moved on to the next one. Vinnie's favourite sandwich was Vegemite and cream cheese, and a green apple, so I figured I'd have to search a bit longer before I found my friend's lunch.

Vinnie might know about the sandwiches, but I never let on to her about the pennies I pilfered and stashed in a rag at the back of my Belongings shelf. I was saving them for "a rainy day" as Bonnie would say. And why not? It wasn't right, those mean town kids having the lot – fancy school lunch, new uniform and shiny shoes every year –- while we had nothing. That we were cold the whole winter, and hungry, except on Saturday after-noons when Bonnie brought out her hidden stock of goodies.

* * *

That bully was right, and the police did pick up John and Jim Browning only a few days later. They didn't catch the brothers because of their second-hand clothes or their bowl haircuts, but because a Bowral shopkeeper caught them nicking a bar of chocolate.

When the police brought them back to Seabreeze, Mr Hates was in the middle of cursing Vinnie and me for doing a bad job of scrubbing the homestead windows.

'You call that *clean*, Armstrong and Gasbag?' He swiped a hand down a window, leaving a brown streak on the spot I'd been scrubbing. 'Do it properly, or you'll be eating broth for a week, you pair of dirt clods.'

We only had to clean the insides of the windows, since wire mesh covered the outside, to keep out insects. At the start, I'd thought of that mesh as prison bars, but now I knew those flyscreens were a luxury. The hot, fly- and mozzie-infested summers would be more bearable if our sleeping-shed door and windows had screens.

It was a hot spring Sunday, the midday sun reflecting off the windows, into the homestead. Vinnie and I dabbed at our sweaty faces, but still beads of it trickled down my face, my back. Still my pinafore stuck to my clammy body. Still we worked hard, ever fearful of his whip, even as our minds and bodies screamed with exhaustion.

'Well look who we have here,' Mr Hates said with a smile, gaze turning to the police car pulling up in front of the veranda. He opened the screen door, strode towards them.

'Officers, so kind of you to bring back my boys.' A grin stretched his lips over the rat muzzle as the Browning brothers, heads bent, got out of the car. 'I've missed my boys, been so worried about them.' He circled an arm around a shoulder of each boy, gave them friendly pats. 'Come on inside, officers, my wife'll get you a beer, and these boys look like they could do with a nice cold drink ... Bonnie, where are you, my dear, we have guests?'

'Liar. Fake. Monster!' I flung aside the scrubbing brush as they all filed into the homestead.

Vinnie touched her fingertips to my arm. 'Shut yer trap, Lucy.'

Mr Hates didn't flog the boys immediately, and certainly not while the police were there. No, he let them sweat it out. And, that afternoon, he took Jim and John Browning rabbit shooting.

'He's not supposed to carry the rifle like that ... always warning us it's dangerous,' said Nick Hurley, as Mr Hates trooped off across the paddock, the Browning brothers skittering along in front of him, flicking fearful gazes over their shoulders.

It was true, Mr Hates wasn't carrying the rifle as he usually did, the "broken" part resting in his elbow crook, barrel pointed at the ground. He held it straight up, with both hands, like it was aimed at the back of the boys' heads.

And, at the end of the afternoon, when the three hunters returned with limp rabbits and the smell of fresh blood dangling over their shoulders, both brothers had pissed their shorts.

'Crazy, isn't it?' I whispered to Vinnie, as we sat on those dining shed benches, our evening soup going cold, while Mr Hates whipped the brothers, still wearing their peed-on shorts. 'Them getting punished for doing exactly what Mr Zachary told us we could do in Australia – eat fruit straight from the tree?'

21

Lucy Rivers
Southern Highlands, New South Wales
August 1965

'This could be it, our chance of rescue, Vinnie,' I muttered, as the visitors arrived, the only people who'd come to Seabreeze in three whole years.

It was almost a year after the Browning brothers' failed runaway and we all stood there, that icy Friday afternoon after school, trembling with the cold.

'We gotta tell those people what it's really like here,' I said, the tyres on their shiny black car kicking up dust, which made us cough and splutter into that chill August air. 'Surely they'll rescue us if they know we're slaves?'

Overnight, the mist had rolled in from the western plains, hanging about the Southern Highlands long into the morning, until the cutting fingers of the wind pushed it away, over the sea. Now, a sickly yellow light had wrapped itself around the homestead and farmland, those tin sheds trapping the cold as tight as the summer heat.

'You be careful,' Vinnie said, 'Mr Yates'll be watching us, especially *you*. He'll never give you the chance to talk to them on your own.'

I gnawed on a thumbnail. 'Well I'll give it a damn good try.'

Same as our first day at Seabreeze, Mr Hates had lined us up in front of the veranda with Bonnie. Now only three rows, since eight kids, including Fiona Mulligan, had turned seventeen in the last two years, their apprenticeship over, and Mr Hates had sent them away to jobs on large properties somewhere in New South Wales. We hadn't heard a word from them, which made Carol Mulligan slump about the place, miserable for her sister.

We had no idea who these visitors were or where they'd come from. All Mr Hates had told us, five days ago at breakfast, was that some people would be coming to visit.

'To see the wonderful life Mrs Yates and I have given you all, out of the goodness of our hearts,' he'd said, with a flick of the horse whip. 'Which you'll not forget, especially in the presence of our guests.' As always, we watched our porridge grow colder, soggier, harder to swallow.

'We'll all be excited to show our guests around Seabreeze, won't we?' he went on. 'And we'll all be polite and friendly when those guests eat dinner with us, won't we?'

Since the beginning of the week, Mr Hates had put us all on extra slave duties, before and after school. We scrubbed the homestead, polished every floor and doorknob. Nick and Tommy repainted the peeling weatherboard. We cleaned the sleeping sheds, dining shed, the bathrooms. There'd been no hour off at the end of any day.

'You'll remain in your uniforms ... and your shoes, after school on Friday,' Mr Hates had said.

'So the visitors won't know he only lets us wear shoes to school,' I'd whispered to Vinnie. 'Even in winter!'

'And so they don't see our daggy pinafores,' Vinnie muttered back.

The two grey pinafores, which Bonnie and us girls sewed, were the only clothes we owned besides second-hand school uniforms. The boys had one pair of shorts, one pair of trousers and two shirts, all in the same dull grey as our pinafores. Bonnie and some apprentice girls had also knitted each of us a grey jumper, baggy enough to fit for several winters.

'I know I can count on *all* of you to be on your best behaviour for our guests,' Mr Hates had said, flicking his pink-eyed gaze to me, 'because if any one of you makes the slightest remark out of line, the lot of you'll come a cropper. And who would be selfish enough to punish her mates?'

He knew I wasn't dumb enough to make any smart-arse remarks. Out loud that is. Mr Hates would've flogged me to death if he knew how much hatred for him was locked away in my mind.

All bucky-toothed smile, Mr Hates strode towards the visitors, a hand stretched out to greet them. It was the first time I'd ever seen him without the horse whip that still sent ice blocks sliding down my backbone.

Bonnie, wearing a red-rose patterned dress I'd never seen, stood awkwardly behind her husband as he smiled and shook hands with the man and woman, who kept darting glances at us. The man patted Bluey, ruffled his ears. Bluey licked his hand.

'Anyway, where did all this stuff come from?' Vinnie whispered, nodding at the teddy bears the youngest children held, the ribbons in the little girls' hair.

I shrugged, kept my eye on those visitors – both the same age, around forty I guessed – as Mr and Mrs Yates. I couldn't miss the slightest chance to speak out.

Beneath that wild yellowy sky, the steely wind ripped through the dry air, circled the trunk of the Moreton Bay fig tree as if it was chasing something. Shivering in our thin uniforms, we stared in envy at the man and woman, snug in warm coats, gloves and hats.

In the beginning, we couldn't wait for that first scalding Seabreeze summer to be over, but quickly understood that winters were no better. We were shocked to find it colder than England, icy frost sparkling on the ground. Bonnie dabbed vinegar onto our chilblains, shaking her head and stumbling over her sorry excuses when I pleaded with her to beg her husband to let us keep on our school shoes.

But Bonnie was as helpless as us when it came to Mr Milton Hates, which made me frustrated. I knew she loved us, so why couldn't she try harder, be stronger? She might be dead scared of her husband, but I was starting to think that was no excuse, she should still try and stick up for us.

No way would I end up like Bonnie; no way would I let a man knock me around or tell me what to do.

' … and each child has an assigned task to train and prepare them for the working world once they leave the comforts of Seabreeze,' Mr Hates was saying, as we followed him and Bonnie, and the guests – Mrs Sampson and Mr Rogers – around the farm. Mrs Sampson kept turning around and smiling at Joey Joe, hopping along beside us.

'And this here's Joey Joe, our resident wallaby I saved from certain death as a little orphan,' Mr Hates said, as Georgie and Sarah, skinny eight-year-olds now, skipped along beside our beloved wallaby, patting him. 'I like my children to have their own pets … teaches them to treat animals with respect.'

Vinnie and I rolled our eyes at each other as Mr Hates looked away. 'I've explained to them that it's a harsh world out there if you can't find work,' he went on. 'I wouldn't want that for my children, so I guarantee them all employment at age seventeen, once they've finished their two-year apprenticeship here at Seabreeze.'

He waved his arms in the air, spicy with the smell of the wood the boys had cut that morning, pointing out the chook pen, the piggery and dairy, the veggie garden and orchard, the cows and sheep in the paddock. 'Seabreeze generates a wide range of produce, some of which we consume here, the sale of the rest of which is a vital source of Seabreeze's revenue.'

'Liar,' I hissed, Vinnie and I keeping to the back of the group, out of Mr Hates' earshot. We barely saw any cream, since he sold gallons of it to private families and, despite the many orchard trees, we hardly ever got to eat fresh fruit. He sold most of the chooks' eggs too.

'And I'm proud to report,' Mr Hates went on, spinning around and smiling at us, 'that all my children are doing well at school.'

I almost snorted out loud.

It was torture, walking around freezing, forced to listen to Mr Hates' lies, but I kept reminding myself that these visitors might be our only chance of rescue. After three long years of anger and frustration at Mr Zachary's rotten trick, we'd had to accept Seabreeze Farm as our home. Our pitiful home where bells rang to mark every moment of our wretched lives: get up, get dressed, do your jobs, go to breakfast. Go to school, with *more* bells. Evening bell. Bedtime bell.

Is this my chance to never hear another bell? But how? Vinnie's right, Mr Hates will never leave me alone with the visitors.

But then he did.

* * *

The grand tour was over. Mr Hates had made Seabreeze Farm look like the paradise Mr Zachary had lied about, giving the guests only glimpses of our cold and uncomfortable sleeping and dining shed.

Since the five cats were curled up on every armchair, we stood on the veranda with Mrs Sampson and Mr Rogers, sipping cups of Bonnie's freshly-brewed tea and munching on delicious lamingtons. As if that's what we did every day after school.

Like the bold magpies strutting about pecking cake crumbs, Mr Hates was crowing to Mr Rogers about how terrific the boys were at school cricket and rugby – another huge porky since they were always too tired for any kind of sport. The woman, Mrs Sampson, moved amongst us, speaking to us in turn.

'What's your name, dear?' she said to Jane, as I pushed my way towards her. 'Are you alright?'

'It's Jane Baxter, Miss, and I'm not alright, I've got bad stomach ache.' Jane had been complaining of belly ache all day but it was probably only her rags, since that girl complained every single month since she'd got the curse.

'Aw, I'll make ya up a comfy hot water bottle tonight,' Bonnie said to Jane.

'But it really hurts,' Jane went on.

I wished Jane would shut up and let me speak. We all had our sicknesses, on the outside and the inside. We were all ill with grief, overwork, not enough food or sleep. And sick from no love. Bonnie tried her best but Mr Hates always stopped her giving us any special attention.

'And what's *your* name, dear?' Mrs Sampson asked, turning to Suzy. 'How old are you?'

'Her name's Suzy – Susan – Hampton,' I said, circling an arm around my friend's shoulder. 'I'm Lucy Rivers, and Suzy's the same age as me, thirteen. But Suzy doesn't speak ... hasn't said a single word for three years, since they took away her twin sister, Patty, on the docks in Sydney. We haven't heard a thing about Patty ... or about my sister, Charly.' A quick breath and my words tumbled out in a panicked jumble. 'We miss them so much ... real worried ... could you find —?'

'Susan Hampton's sister, and yours, have gone to good homes,' Mr Hates cut in, cunning as a dunny rat. I hadn't been aware of that sly snake slithering up behind me. 'We tried to keep siblings together, like the Mulligan girls – until the older one left to go to a rewarding job – and the Browning brothers,' he nodded at Jim and John, 'but sadly that wasn't always possible.'

Wasn't possible. I'll bet nobody even tried!

It had simply been good luck if you ended up with your sibling and bad luck if you didn't.

Mrs Sampson patted Suzy's arm, gave her a sympathetic frown. But I had no idea if she'd try to track down Patty and Charly.

'And how do *you* like living at Seabreeze Farm, dear?' Mrs Sampson asked me.

My lips quivered. I itched to spill the whole awful truth, almost yanked up my school dress, ripped down my undies and showed her those angry welts, scars that would never disappear. But Mr Hates' words rang, loud as the farm bells, in my mind.

If any one of you makes the slightest remark out of line, the lot of you'll come a cropper.

Everyone's gaze fell on me, all of them hoping my big mouth wouldn't get them punished. The veranda was silent, except for the chill wind surging through the treetops, slashing hair wisps across my face, scudding swabs of shorn-fleece clouds across the sky.

I'll never get another chance.

I inhaled sharply, gaze flickering to Mr Hates. His look froze my blood. I cleared my throat and said, 'I love all the pretty-coloured birds, trees and flowers, and our wallaby, Joey Joe, is a beaut friend. And Bonnie – Mrs Yates – is a real mother to all of us. We love her very much.'

I sent a silent "sorry" to my real mum, Annie Rivers locked in some cold, dark cell somewhere, or out of prison and searching wildly for Charly and me, and not finding us.

Bonnie blushed, threw me a small smile. Mr Hates scowled. It was an awkward moment.

* * *

'Come along, everyone, Mrs Yates has our dinner ready,' Mr Hates said with a smile, beckoning us all inside. He patted each cat in turn and we all crowded into the homestead dining room. Joey Joe hopped inside too, taking up his usual spot in the kitchen on a rug in front of the Aga cooker.

'We only use the dining shed for breakfast, and lunch on weekends,' Mr Hates lied, as he put some jolly music on the gramophone player.

The apprentice girls, wearing white aprons, served us from the huge platters of roast lamb with heavenly-smelling mint sauce, mixed vegetables lathered in butter, and crunchy potatoes.

The table was set with posh white cloths and we got to eat with shiny knives and forks, on china plates, and to drink from real glasses.

'What a treat!' Vinnie said.

'It's like being on the ship again,' Bessy said.

My mind flitted back to that blissful voyage, Charly and me still together.

Two of my lost little sister's birthdays I've missed. She'll be eight and a half years old. Does she look the same? Is her life better than mine at Seabreeze? Maybe Charly's life is so smashing that she's forgotten all about me, and our mother back home?

Several times I'd thought of asking one of the school kids to post a letter to Charly, or Mum, but I'd never had a single school friend, only enemies from nicking their sarnies and pennies. Besides, I had no idea of Charly's – the Ashwoods' – address. A tight fist clutched at my heart and my teeth ripped off a sliver of thumbnail skin.

Ouch! I winced, sucked on the spot of blood.

'Leave room for my wife's delicious pavlova,' Mr Hates said, from the head of the table. 'Bonnie makes the best dessert from here to Alice Springs.'

He patted Bonnie's hand, kissed her cheek. Startled at this show of tenderness, I stopped mid-chew, and Bonnie blushed, stared down at her plate.

We'd tasted pavlova on the *Star of New South Wales*, but we never had desserts like this at Seabreeze, except occasionally on a Saturday afternoon.

The soft, crunchy meringue, juicy passionfruit and strawberries, and freshly-whipped cream was as delicious as I remembered. And I savoured every mouthful.

After dinner, Mrs Sampson and Mr Rogers shook hands with Mr Hates and Bonnie, waved goodbye to us, and the black shiny car sped off into the night.

The visitors hadn't even reached the end of the dirt track, when Mr Hates went around yanking the ribbons out of the little girls' hair. 'Gather up all those teddy bears, Bonnie,' he barked. 'And take off that dress, best keep it in case we get more visitors.'

The white tablecloths and crockery vanished, the gleaming cutlery, the fancy food, and the next morning we were left with our usual metal bowls and mugs, and sludgy porridge. And the flimsy hope that those visitors might rescue us.

22

That burning February morning, Charlotte plonked beside her father at the kitchen table. 'It's Simone's birthday soon, what's a good present I can get her?'

It was almost the end of the summer holidays, Charlotte and Simone about to start their last year of primary school.

Through the kitchen flyscreen, frangipani scent heavy on the breeze slipping sparks of sun through the eucalyptus leaves, a magpie swooped low, clacking her bill. And, despite the strips of fly paper Dad had hung from the ceiling, thick with dark, winged bodies, flies ticked and hovered around the fruit Mum was slicing for her pavlova.

'We're going horse-riding for Simone's party,' Charlotte said. Thirsty after another hot night, she gulped down the orange juice Mum had squeezed for her, and munched on the melty-butter and Vegemite toast Mum had set out on a plate. 'So, any ideas of a present I can get for Simo —?'

'*Horse-riding*?' Mum shrieked, like the sulphur-crested cockatoos circling the gum tree as if, like every person, bird and animal, desperate to escape the sweltering heat. 'Oh, Charlotte, I doubt you'd enjoy *horse-riding*.'

'What? I'd love it, Mum! I'm always asking to go horse-riding with Simone, and I don't get why you never let me?'

Face white, Mum glared at her, fruit knife quivering in her hand. The passionfruit she held in her other hand shook too.

144

She waved the knife at Dad. 'Don't simply sit there, Frank, say something.' But her dad's gaze remained fixed on the newspaper, face deepening to crimson behind the pages of the *Illawarra Mercury*.

Charlotte caught the bold, black newspaper headline:

John Gorton sworn in as Prime Minister of Australia after disappearance of Harold Holt.

Harold Holt had made national headlines last December. Not for being Prime Minister, but because he'd disappeared while swimming in Victoria. They said that even though the Prime Minister was a strong swimmer, a rip probably swept him away. They'd called off the search for his body just after New Year 1968.

Charlotte found it very scary that a person could vanish like that. Here one minute, gone the next. How many people were there in the world who simply disappeared, their families never knowing what happened to them?

'Come on, Frank,' Mum cried. 'Back me up!'

The newspaper crinkled in Dad's hand. 'It's Simone's birthday, Dolly, I'm sure it'll be safe. What are the chances —?'

'*Safe*? Since when has horse-riding been *safe*?' Knuckles white gripping the knife, she shook it at him. 'I'm sorry, Charlotte, I forbid it.' She turned back to the bench, stabbed the knife into the strawberries. *Chack, chack, chack*, on her chopping board.

'But why not, Mum? I'm *eleven*, not a little kid.'

No answer. *Chack, chack, chack.*

Charlotte stamped her foot, tears stinging her eyes. 'That's so unfair, you're so mean! Simone came to my party but I can't go to hers ... all my other friends are going.' She breathed deep, tried to swallow her anger. 'You're always saying to get my head out of books and play outside, that it's not healthy to stay in reading all day. And now, when I want to go out horse-riding, you won't let me, I don't get it?'

Amongst all the books in her bookcase, including all twelve of Arthur Ransome's *Swallows and Amazons*, the Rosemary

Sutcliff and Cynthia Harnett books, she pictured her favourites, the whole row of Enid Blyton's *Famous Five*.

'If you don't let me go to Simone's horse-riding party,' she said, 'I'll never go outside again. I'll read in my bedroom my whole life, and it'll be your fault if I get sick.'

Mum's lips pursed, shoulders hunched, knife still chacking on the board.

Charlotte turned to her father, put on her most pleady voice. 'Dad, please, you *have* to let me go.'

Dad cleared his throat, still wouldn't look up from the newspaper. 'You'd best do what your mother says, Charlotte.'

'Best do what your mother says,' Charlotte said, pulling a face, mocking his voice. 'It's always the same, do what she says, do what she wants, don't make Mum cry or scream or get sad.'

Mum's fruit knife clattered onto the kitchen floor. 'Oh Frank, I simply can't bear this,' she wailed, catching hold of the benchtop. 'I think I'm going to faint.' Her legs buckled. Dad bolted from his chair, caught her before she hit the green lino.

'You just rest,' he said, carrying her into the living room and laying her on the couch. 'I'll make you a strong cuppa.'

From the kitchen-living room doorway, Charlotte scowled, angry, upset. But most of all, confused.

'*Why*, Dad? Why won't you let me go? What's wrong? Something is wrong, I know it is. Why won't you tell me?'

'Alright, Charlotte,' he said, ignoring Dolly's warning glance, 'you deserve to know the truth.'

23

'Come on, Jane, fun's starting, Mr Hates just drove off to Wollongong.' I shook her arm, tried to get her off her bunk but, her face puckered in pain, Jane wouldn't budge.

'My stomach hurts,' Jane moaned, hunched on her side, clutching her stomach.

'Aw come on, it's only the rags,' I said, sick of Jane moaning about her belly ache all week. 'You know all of us have to put up with that, you heard Bonnie say the curse goes on *every* month for years and years.'

'It's not the curse,' Jane said. 'The pain's more kind of, on the side.'

'We'll save you something nice to eat then,' Vinnie said, as we hurried from the sleeping shed with Suzy and Carol, a skip in our step because it was Saturday afternoon.

When Mr Hates' ute, with Bluey in the back, had chugged off, excited chatter broke out and everyone dropped whatever job they were doing, and scurried up to the homestead.

Bonnie had said Wollongong was about one and a half hours' away, which amounted to three hours of driving, plus a bit longer to sell produce and buy supplies. But Mr Hates was always gone much longer.

'Bet he goes drinking in a pub,' I'd told Vinnie. 'Like my father did. It's obvious from the state of him when he gets back.'

But we really had no idea, nor the slightest care, what Mr Hates did the rest of the time.

Nothing ever came of those visitors, Mrs Sampson and Mr Rogers. We never heard another thing about them and no more people came to Seabreeze. The months went by, then two and a half more years, and no other chance of rescue or escape, or of trying to find Charly and Mum. No one in the whole word cared about us, except Bonnie, a prisoner like us.

I still kissed that torn photo of Mum and Charly every night, and stroked their faces, but it was becoming harder to remember them. As if my family, my other life, had never happened, and my real life had started that terrible day we arrived at Seabreeze Farm.

As we went into our sixth year at Seabreeze, I no longer believed anything good could happen to us. I'd lost all hope; all belief in people. Dreams of escape still tormented me, though, but the same hurdles jolted me to my senses.

No money. Where would I go?

I didn't know a single person in Australia, besides Charly. But more than anything, I was terrified that even if I managed to get away from Seabreeze, the fangs of a deadly snake or spider would kill me within minutes.

It was another blistering afternoon, almost the end of the school holidays for most kids, but not for the Seabreeze slaves. Not that we went to school any longer, since last year when Vinnie and I, Jane, Suzy, Carol Mulligan, Tommy Oakley and Nick Hurley, had turned fifteen, and become apprentices. But I remembered those schoolkids boasting to each other about camping trips, splashing in the sea, eating ice-creams. Having fun.

School had been torture, what with teasing kids and snarky teachers, but at least it had got us out of slavery for a good part of the day; out of the sun that crushed the zing from me.

A year ago, Mr Hates had sent the Liverpool girls, Bessy and Helen, away to some property no one knew where. Nobody arrived to take their place, or Fiona Mulligan's, and our sleeping shed was emptier, sadder, without them. A few more seventeen-year-old boys had left too, with no others coming to fill their bunks. We were down to sixteen kids, with the same amount of work as for thirty-two. But nobody dared point that out to Mr Hates.

'Letter for you, Carol!' Bonnie cried, scurrying out onto the veranda as we sank down in its welcome shade. Since Georgie and Sarah were twelve now, Bonnie had told them to show her the mail they collected from the box before they gave it to Mr Hates. She'd nick any rare letters addressed to a kid, sneaking them to us on Saturday afternoons.

Nobody had ever written to me though, and I thought back to my one, useless attempt to write to my mother. There'd never been another chance; even Bonnie wasn't allowed to write letters.

Carol tore open her letter, Joey Joe stretched out on the veranda beside her, Tommy and Nick stroking our wallaby mate, Georgie and Sarah throwing Bluey's ball to him.

'Oh yippee, it's from Fiona!' Carol's face glowed like the blaze of pink bougainvillea draping the homestead walls right through spring, summer and autumn. Bonnie had told us that bougainvillea was one of Australia's most sturdy plants, flourishing even in the face of drought and neglect.

Carol took a breath, read her letter aloud.

Dear Carol,

Sorry I've taken so long to write, four years! They wouldn't let us write letters on the cattle station where, thank God, I no longer am. So this's the first chance I've had, and I hope Bonnie manages to get it to you.

I was living on this huge property near Broken Hill, which I suppose you never heard of. Well, neither had I, but you never want to go there, it's a pig's bum hot and ugly place right near the South Australian border, so hot that Seabreeze was almost cold, in comparison. So hot that I'd sometimes pass out with the heat. The other girls said I'd get used to the weather and the hard work, much the same as Seabreeze: sewing, cooking and serving food, cleaning, washing, ironing clothes. Same drudgery, same slavery. At least the owners didn't beat us, like Mr Yates, but they weren't nice either. And I never got used to it, hated it the whole time, especially since I was so far away from you. Anyway, I was so glad when my four years' service were up, and I could get away from that hell-hole.

Like everyone who leaves here, I hitched a ride seven hundred miles (!!) with a truckie and ended up in Sydney – address on the back of the envelope.

Thankfully I found work as a nanny to three sweet kids, with this lovely family. They live in the best house you've ever seen, with a view right across Sydney Harbour. Oh, Carol, it's magnificent!

Anyway, I've spoken to the wife, Mrs Castlemaine, about you and guess what? She said she could give you a job too. Only housework and laundry mind, but we'd be together again. And you wouldn't have to go to some terrible cattle station.

I know you're only sixteen, still a whole year until Mr Yates lets you go, but just think of it, in only a year we could be together again. We'll swim in the rock pools, jump over beach waves, walk in the parks, eat ice-creams strolling around Sydney Harbour. It'll be so much fun, please say you'll come?

I hope you and the girls are okay? I suppose Bessy and Helen are gone too, by now? I miss them, like I miss Vinnie, Lucy, Jane and sweet, silent Suzy. Please say hi to them from me.

Anyway, now you have my address, write soon, Carol, please. I haven't had a single letter in four years. Miss you so much!

Love forever,

your sister, Fiona.'

'And she's put ten kisses,' Carol said, pressing the letter against her heart.

Goosebumps flared on my arms, and tears glimmered in Carol's eyes as she folded the letter and slipped it into her pinafore pocket.

'So that's the kind of cattle station Mr Hates will send us to when we turn seventeen next year,' I said, stroking my favourite cat, the fluffy grey one with sharp yellow eyes.

'Another hot and ugly prison,' said Nick, 'in the middle of woop-woop.'

'The *third* prison of our life,' Vinnie said, as something bigger than a lizard, a snake no doubt, rustled in the bushes beside the veranda.

None of us wanted to stay here but the few letters we got from the kids who'd left were filled with this kind of news, so we were afraid too, of leaving.

'Well I hope Mr Yates sends me to Sydney, to Fiona,' Carol said, taking one of the black cats onto her lap.

'Not a bloody chance,' Tommy said, the boy who had the same orange hair as Vinnie, same green eyes so large he always looked surprised, and who, it was obvious from their sly grins, was as keen on my friend as she was on him.

'Why would he send you where you want to go, Carol?' Nick said. 'When has that brute done anyone a favour?'

'You'll have to run away,' I said, 'if you want to get to your sister in Sydney.'

'Run away?' Carol tickled the black cat under its chin. 'I couldn't do that ... wouldn't know how.'

'Yeah, not everyone's as brave as you, Lucy,' Nick said, giving me a strange smile. I couldn't tell if he was having a go, or praising me.

'I hate being apart from Fiona,' Carol went on. 'She's the only family ... '

Carol's voice dwindled away as she caught Suzy's silent, grief-filled stare.

Charly's face rushed into my mind and, once again, I asked myself if her new father, Frank Ashwood – I'd never forgotten his name – had given her the other half of my photo.

Eleven years old, she'd be now. A year older than me when we boarded the *Star of New South Wales*. No longer a little girl.

Would I even recognise her?

And Mum, surely she's proved her innocence by now, and they've let her out of prison?

But if Mum *was* free, she mustn't know we were in Australia, or she'd have come over by now. 'I love you girls to the end of the earth,' she always said. Well, Australia really *was* the end of the earth, so she'd have come to Seabreeze for me; she'd have got Charly back.

Mum's sister, Aunty Edna, would've told her that the child-care officer, Liar Langford, had taken us to Easthaven, so my guess was that Miss Sutherland had *not* told Mum they'd shipped Charly and me to Australia.

It was torture, the wondering, the not knowing if Mum was worrying about us. Living with the doubt every day. Making nightmares of every sleep.

Every time I had to clean Mr Hates' bedroom, I thought about breaking into that phone cupboard, but still I hadn't the foggiest how.

'What's with the misery-guts faces?' Bonnie said, plodding out onto the veranda with two apprentice girls, carrying trays loaded with the goodies Bonnie stashed away all week, a little after each of her husband's meals.

Once she and the girls set down the trays brimming with juicy watermelon, plums, grapes and pineapple, jam sponge cake, cheese, chewy Anzac biscuits and sweet dark chocolate, Bonnie fetched Mr Hates' radio.

Since we had no television, and now no school, that battered little wireless was our only contact with the faraway, outside world. Cockatoos screeched, dived and wheeled through the hot air, kookaburras cackled like mad things and rainbow lorikeets squealed so loudly that Bonnie had to turn up the radio to full volume.

I smiled to myself, remembering how terrified we'd all been of the sulphur-crested cockatoos, the blue-tipped kookaburras, the ground-hugging pink and grey galahs. All those brightly-coloured birds I'd come to love, along with my blackbird who sang me his song. I'd still never seen him but I pictured him sitting on a branch of our sleeping-shed gumtree, dark and proud, and his sparkly chirp lifted my spirits on the really low days.

'… *Viet Cong and North Vietnamese People's Army of Vietnam launched one of the biggest military campaigns of the Vietnam War*,' the radio-announcer said, '*against the forces of the South Vietnamese Army of the Republic of Vietnam, the United States Armed Forces, and their allies.*'

Sure, we'd heard about this war in Vietnam, wherever that was, but didn't get what the hullabaloo was about, or why Australians were fighting there. All we'd gathered from the radio was that the Aussie soldiers were right pissed off about it.

Bonnie sat cross-legged with us on the veranda, no simple feat with her thick legs, feeding cheese bits to Joey Joe and the cats, as we gobbled down the bounty we waited all week for.

Bonnie threw off her apron, showing off the red rose-patterned dress we saw only on Saturdays, and put her favourite song on the gramophone, 'Itsy Bitsy Teenie Weenie Yellow Polka Dot Bikini'. We all laughed at the silly lyrics, but joined in as she sang.

Bonnie's lovely voice had surprised me. Always low and nervy around Mr Hates, her singing voice was loud, clear and sure.

Tommy put on 'The Twist' and grabbed Vinnie. Grinning like goons, the pair twisted about and, in one black and white swarm, the magpies lifted off from the veranda.

Nick Hurley went to take my arm to dance but I pulled away, escaped to an armchair with the fluffy cat. Nick's eyes, same amber colour as the cat's, looked sad, beaten down.

This wasn't the first time I'd seen Tommy and Vinnie holding hands, laughing together, staring into each other's big green eyes. I was happy for Vinnie that she had a cool, friendly boyfriend like Tommy but I had no itch for Nick Hurley to be *my* boyfriend.

How could I be sure he wouldn't turn into a man who'd drink away his wages and slap my face? A husband who'd die falling down stairs, for which I'd get blamed – imprisoned!– and make orphans of my kids? A man who'd bullshit me about some far-off paradise. Or the worst kind of man who'd beat me senseless with a riding crop?

No thanks, I'll stick to Lucy Rivers. At least she won't let me down.

I stayed on the chair with the cat, watching everyone giggle, stomp and twist across those wooden boards, Vinnie's chortles ringing over the farmland, the thick scrubland beyond.

Music jingling on that hot air, the perfumes of the honeysuckle and orange jasmine flaring our nostrils, Joey Joe bounded amongst us, that wallaby enjoying himself as much as the humans.

The only time in the week when Bonnie sang, smiled and laughed, she danced like a young girl, not a bit like Humpty Dumpty.

It could always be like this, Bonnie, if only you had the guts to get away from him.

But I'd got weary of telling her that.

***

'Who's up for a dip in the billabong?' Tommy cried, as everyone fell down in a sweaty, exhausted heap once the music finished.

To shrieks of 'Yes!' we all hurried down to the sheds to change into our cossies.

Bonnie came to our shed with me, Vinnie and Carol, to check on Jane, who was still lying on her bunk. She pressed a palm against Jane's cheek. 'Crikey, she ain't got half a fever.'

'Stomach still hurts,' Jane moaned.

Bonnie wiped a cool cloth over Jane's brow, gave her more castor oil. Jane managed to swallow the thick foul-tasting liquid then slumped back down.

'You rest, sweet chook,' Bonnie said. 'I'll get me chores done real quick and be back in two shakes of a lamb's tail.'

'I'm sure you'll be better soon, Jane,' I said.

'Then you can swim in the billabong with us, before Mr Yates gets back,' Vinnie said. 'Shame to waste a Saturday afternoon being sick.'

'I'm *not* pretending,' Jane said in her small, bruised voice. 'I really *do* feel awful.'

'I know,' Vinnie said.

But we weren't sure, really. Jane Baxter had been sick with something or other as far back as our Easthaven days. But was she just sick in her mind; sick and sad at being locked up here at Seabreeze Farm?

Down at the billabong, Tommy and Nick had slung a rope over a tree and attached an old tyre to it.

'Come on, Vinnie!' Tommy grabbed her around the waist with one hand, the other clutching the rope. My friend let out a bellow as Tommy sailed them both, on the tyre, way out over the billabong. She shrieked again as he let go and they dropped into that mud-brown, cool water.

'Your turn, Lucy,' Nick said, and went to hang on to me like Tommy had held Vinnie.

'No!' I cried, quickly grabbing the rope. But as I swung out on the tyre on my own, I thought it might've been more fun holding on to Nick Hurley.

Joey Joe, who followed us everywhere like a dog, stood at the water's edge, rubbing together his front paws as if clapping at our antics. And, as he twitched his ears, I could've sworn he was grinning at us having such a gas time with an old tyre and a bit of rope.

Even Suzy threw us a half-smile, as if it had escaped her lips before she could catch it. She might never speak, but Suzy always joined in our Saturday games, mucking about down at the billabong, kicking a football around the paddock, hitting a cricket ball with a makeshift bat, planting branches for wickets.

There was no sign of the kangaroos yet, who gathered to drink at dusk, like a group of people in an English pub. Maybe in Australian pubs too, if they existed.

The roos always hung around the billabong, hardly ever venturing over the orchard fence.

'Scared of Mr Yates' rifle,' Tommy had said, which might've

been true, since when one of those kangaroos had bounded over the fence, he'd ended up in Bluey's food bowl.

Vinnie gazed at Tommy's sun-bronzed, muscled body, and nudged me in the ribs. 'What a hunk, eh?'

'Whatever you reckon,' I said with a sly grin.

The yellow sun soon became a bright orange ball, sinking over the far western horizon. Our signal to head back to the homestead.

We stopped off at the orchard on the way back. Tommy and Nick climbed a tree, picking off apricots, throwing handfuls down to us. We sat on the ground, showing Georgie and Sarah how to use a rock to crack open the stones to prise out the kernels which we gave to Bonnie to season her stews.

When we reached the shed to change out of our wet cossies, Bonnie was bent down beside Jane's bunk again, trying to force a spoonful of chicken broth between her lips.

'I gave her another pain pill,' Bonnie said, as Jane managed a few mouthfuls, whimpered and slumped down in a crunched-up ball. I laid a hand on her arm, flinched at her burning hot skin.

'I want my mum,' Jane wailed, eyes shiny with fever. 'Please, somebody find her.'

'Don't know about her mum,' Bonnie said, 'but we should call the doc. She's been sick the best part of a week.'

'Didn't your husband take the phone cupboard key?' I said.

'Yeah, sure he did,' Bonnie said. 'But as soon as he comes home I'll give him a gobful, *make* him call the doc.'

* * *

As always, our fun ended too soon. Mr Hates' ute rumbled down that dusty track and, once more, a quiet unease seeped across Seabreeze Farm.

But, worse for the drink yet again, Mr Hates took no notice of us as he stumbled from his ute, Bluey on his heels, and lurched up the veranda steps, and through the screen door.

Vinnie and I listened from our usual hiding spot, behind the jungle of bougainvillea.

'Strewth, Milton, Jane's got the fever, white as a ghost, cryin' out with the pain,' Bonnie was saying. 'She's real crook, needs the doc.'

'Always on my back, woman,' Mr Hates slurred, as we crept across the veranda, peered in the kitchen window. 'You think I enjoy coming home to you whining about those bloody kids? After everything I do for them, what I sacrifice to give them a good life?'

'Sacrifice? You're shitting me!' I hissed.

'Deep down, them kids *are* grateful to you,' Bonnie said, 'but Jane keeps wailing for her mum.'

'Freak-face is *always* wailing for her mother, always whinge-ing about something. You should know that by now, you dumb cow.' He took a quick breath. 'Anyway, why did those Poms send me such a sickly, deformed kid? "Only the healthiest physical specimens", they promised.' He waved the riding crop at Bonnie, who stumbled backwards, almost tumbling over the Aga. 'And look what we ended up with along with Freak-face – Lavinia Anderson who cackles like a banshee, Susan Hampton, a mute who can't see past her own hand and Gasbag Rivers who does nothing but scowl and back-answer me. Those Poms cheated me, Bonnie. Yes, cheated me out of my money and useful work-ing hands.'

Mr Hates patted Bluey, tickled between his ears. 'There's nothing wrong with Jane Baxter, just a waste of the doctor's time and my money to get him all the way out here. Now where's my dinner, it's been a long and tiring day.'

'You *gotta* get the doc out for Jane,' Bonnie said, in her most pleady voice. 'Poor chook can't help it if she don't look the full picnic.'

'Who are you to tell me what I should and shouldn't do for

those ungrateful little blighters?' he said. 'I'll do what I want and *how* I want.'

The crack of his whip filled the kitchen as he brought it down on Bonnie's arm. She cried out, and Vinnie and I leapt back a step.

'He's not going to get the doctor,' Vinnie said.

'He is if I can help it,' I said. Without another thought, I hurried across the veranda. 'Bonnie's right,' I called, through the screen door. 'Jane really needs the doctor, so you'd better call him now!'

My breaths came fast, staggered. They caught in my throat, chest tightening as, in the silence that followed, I realised I'd shouted an order at the evil monster. I had no clue what made me do it; what made me risk the worst punishment.

Mr Hates stamped towards the door. The blood stopped flowing through my body. But when that ratty face glared at me through the flyscreen, his look blacker than the night sky, I stood firm. Not a single tremble.

'What the hell are you doing here, Gasbag?' he said. His voice had lost most of the slur. 'When you're supposed to be asleep in your bunk? And what *business* is this of yours, anyway?' Thick eyebrows rose above the pinky eyes. 'Besides, I never thought you were that keen on Jane Baxter? You and the Anderson girl, always rolling your eyes at her.'

Voice low, steady, he said, 'Now get back to your shed and mind your own business.' He waved me off with a lash of the riding crop, and Vinnie and I scurried back to the sleeping shed, to the sound of crockery smashing, more shouting, Bonnie's cries.

'Bastard,' I muttered. 'We'll just have to take care of Jane ourselves, and hope she gets better.'

Back at the sleeping shed, Jane was still sweating and shivery. Not one bit better.

Through the night, Vinnie, Suzy, Carol and I took turns sitting beside her bunk, dabbing a cool cloth to her face, trying to get her to drink the chicken broth Bonnie had left. Coaxing her to swallow another pain pill.

When it was my turn, I sat there watching Jane, listening to the possums scratching at the roof, the cicadas, sugar-gliders, bandicoots and rats all scurrying about their night lives.

'The pain pill must've worked,' I whispered to Vinnie as finally, in the yellow glow of that bright full moon, Jane dozed off.

'She'll be better in the morning,' Vinnie said as I dropped, exhausted, onto my bunk beneath hers. 'You'll see.'

But at dawn, as the fingernail moon faded in the pearly sky, the rooster crowed, and the birds struck up their daybreak cackle, Jane Baxter lay, ice-cold, in her bed.

24

'Try to understand, Charlotte,' Dad began. 'After what happened to you —'

'Oh dear, Frank, must we really talk about that terrible time?' Revived after two Anzac biscuits dipped into her cup of tea, Mum's face back to its normal pink shade, she sat up on the couch and pursed her lips at Dad.

Charlotte sat in an armchair facing her parents, sitting side by side on the couch. 'What happened? *What* terrible time?' She glared at her mother, then her father, who looked down at the shag-pile carpet.

'Seven years ago – you were only four years old – we took you for a pony ride,' Dad said. 'Something scared the pony and it bolted. You fell, hit your head on the ground.'

Mum's lips quivered. Dad kept patting her arm, like stroking a kitten.

'The bump on your head was so severe, you were ill for a long time,' Mum said, a tear rolling down her cheek. Her voice dropped to a husky whisper, as if it was almost impossible for her to speak. 'We were terrified we'd lose you.'

'Is that why I was in hospital for a long time?' Charlotte said. 'You never said why, only that I was really ill.'

'That's right,' Mum said. 'We'd even moved house by the time you recovered. You came straight here to Frangipani Drive from the hospital.'

'How come I don't remember this pony accident?' Charlotte patted her head, felt all over, but there was no bump. No lumpy scar. Nothing. 'I have memories of some things from when I was a kid … strange things that don't make any sense, but nothing about falling off a pony.' She frowned, trying to concentrate. 'I don't get it, why can't I remember a thing like that?'

'Because you hit your head so hard,' Mum said, 'the doctors said you may not recall the accident, or anything before that time. That it was nature's healing way. A miracle it was, a true miracle.'

Charlotte squeezed shut her eyes, tried to force her mind back to when she was four years old, before she'd even started school. How frustrating not to have a single memory of an accident that had almost killed her.

'All I remember from around that age is this giant, luxurious ocean liner,' Charlotte said, snapping open her eyes, fixing her gaze on her mother. 'How much fun it was.'

'Oh that would be the cruise Dad and I took you on to Noumea,' Mum said, 'wasn't it, Frank?' She threw Dad a sharp glance, but he was still staring at the carpet.

'There was a friendly lady in the ship's library,' Charlotte said. 'I'd sit on her lap in the library, while she read to me. What was her name, again? It started with an "H" I think.'

'Oh, I can never remember people's names,' Mum said, with a wave of her hand. 'But you certainly loved reading, even as a very young child.'

Until this moment, Charlotte had forgotten so much about that ship, things that came back now: hurtling around the decks, splashing in the pool, feasting on tasty food. She'd always sat at a table with other children, rather than her parents.

Where had her parents eaten then? In a separate, adults dining room, maybe?

She might have forgotten a lot about the cruise, but Charlotte had never forgotten the girl on the ship – older than she was, but with the same black wavy hair and dark blue eyes. Like the fat blue-tongued lizard in their yard disappearing from the sun to the depths of the hydrangea bush, a picture of this girl would slither into her mind, then, before she could focus properly, it would slide away.

The memory came as a flash exploding in her mind – a picture of this girl gripping Charlotte's hand so tightly that even now she felt the pain of squashed fingers.

There was a lady too, in some of the flashes, with the same dark hair and blue eyes. She cuddled her, spoke in a soft voice, but Charlotte could never make out a single word or see her face properly. Like the lady was wearing a bride's veil.

Another girl was sometimes with them, with carrot-coloured hair, a freckly face and a loud laugh.

These images followed Charlotte like a long, afternoon shadow. But when she spun around to face them, to touch them, they'd shrink away, out of her reach. Until they were gone. And there was nothing left, only an empty spot, heavy with the space where they'd been.

'Is that what ghosts are?' she'd once asked Mum. 'And who are these ghosts?'

'No such thing as ghosts, sweetie,' Mum had said, 'they're simply something you've read in a book, or a dream. Don't fret now, those kinds of dreams are quite normal for an only child.'

Charlotte tore her mind away from those strange, watery dreams, back to the living room, and her parents staring at her from the couch.

Charlotte thought of the beautiful rocking horse Dad had carved for her, that Mum had made her keep in the garage. But Charlotte hadn't cared where it was kept, she'd just loved rocking, chattering away with her father as he hammered, chiselled or repaired something at his work bench.

'Is that why you built me the rocking horse, Dad?' Charlotte said, 'not only to make up for incinerating that plastic pony I won at the fair, but because I'd never be allowed to ride a real one?'

Her father gave a small nod, but still wouldn't look at her.

Why can't you look at me, Dad? What's wrong? Something *isn't right. Something else.*

'I simply couldn't bear having anything in the house,' Mum said, 'to remind me of that ghastly accident.'

'I get that,' Charlotte said, 'but I was only four then, a little kid. You *do* realise that I'll be starting high school in just one year?'

Mum shook her head. 'I'm sorry, I cannot take the risk of another accident.'

The scarlet rage rose in Charlotte, made her breathe fast. She glared at her mother, bolted from the armchair, stomped out and slammed the living-room door behind her. She thumped upstairs, into her bedroom, flopped down on her bed and snatched up the *Famous Five* book from her bedside table.

* * *

Charlotte turned each page of the story, tramping through English countryside so green and damp and lush compared with the burnt brown land of Australia.

She chattered with Julian, Dick, Jane and George, and patted Timmy the dog. She cycled and swam with them, drank refreshing ginger beer at the picnic and, that night, camped in a cottage that was far older than the whole country of Australia.

That faraway place, England, felt so close it could be at the end of Frangipani Drive.

Charlotte's parents might have taken her on a cruise to Noumea, but they refused to take her all the way to England.

'Oh no, England's *much* too far away, and *so* rainy and cold!' Mum always said, when Charlotte asked.

If her mother wouldn't always rant on about getting her head out of her books and going outside with Simone, for the sake of her health, Charlotte would have happily spent every day of those blistering summer holidays lost in a new *Famous Five* adventure.

Charlotte didn't know why she longed to be in England – for real, not only in stories when she *imagined* she was there, sharing the *Famous Five's* exciting adventures, the fog shrouding her, the rain wetting her skin, seeping through to her bones. Why did that invisible magnet tug at her, turn her stomach into a jumble of butterflies?

Why, when she thought of those places, did she shiver with goosebumps? Not the usual chilling bumps, but gooseflesh that made Charlotte's insides both cold and warm at the same time.

25

'Jane can't *truly* be dead?' Carol sobbed. 'Why … please someone tell me why?'

But none of us spoke. We all just stood, in horrified silence, around Jane's bunk, staring down at her waxy, blue-lipped face, not knowing what to do.

Carol's sobs rose to screams, the noise ringing in my ears, clanging about my brain so that I feared it might explode.

'Shut the fuck up, Carol!' I snapped, still too angry to be sad; so furious at Mr Hates for refusing to call the doctor last night. I bit my nails harder, teeth tearing at the skin around my thumbnail.

But Carol didn't shut up and her din brought every other kid running to our shed. Bonnie waddled in, hair on end, faded blue dress inside out. 'Strewth, what's all this racket about?'

'It's Jane, we think she's … we're *sure* she's dead!' Carol cried.

'No, no, no!' Bonnie shuffled to Jane's bunk, knelt down, took Jane's wrist. All of us crammed into that tiny shed, we fell quiet, even Carol. Bonnie held one palm over Jane's lips, placed the other on her chest.

Maybe we'd been wrong. Jane was simply in a deep sleep. But I'd felt her icy hand, knew there was no mistake.

Bonnie shook her head, touched her palm to Jane's brow. 'Gawd, right sorry I am … sorry I couldn't save you, poor sweet chook.'

'She might still be alive if you'd had the guts to stand up to your bully husband.' The spiteful, accusing words blasted from me before I could stop them. 'I tried, but we all knew *that* was useless,' I said, 'but you could've done something, Bonnie. I dunno, got his rifle, or stolen the phone key, called the doctor while he was asleep, or *something*!'

Bonnie stared at me, too stunned to speak.

'Shut yer trap, Lucy,' Vinnie said. 'We all know Mr Yates beats her black and blue if she stands up to him.'

I stared back at Bonnie's pudgy, tear-streaked face, and, riding on my anger, a wave of pity and frustration hurtled through me. 'I'm sorry, Bonnie I shouldn't have said that, it wasn't fair.'

'It's al-alright,' Bonnie stammered, wide bosom heaving. 'Youse are all upset … and it *is* my fault. You're right, Lucy, if only I'd had the guts to stand up to him, like you did.' Bonnie's voice rose to a wail, sobbing for Jane, for herself. I felt like a right bitch.

'You tried,' Vinnie said, circling an arm around Bonnie's shuddering shoulders, as Mr Hates stomped into the doorway.

Hair sticking out like a bird's nest crushed in a storm, he wore only shorts, a white singlet and the boots. No socks. But he held the riding crop. Probably slept with it.

'What the hell's —?' he started, gaze coming to rest on Jane.

I threw him my darkest scowl. 'Our friend is dead. But if you'd called the doctor, Jane might still be alive.'

Speechless for once, Mr Hates breathed hard, looking from Jane's body, to me, to Bonnie.

'Well, I'm calling the doc *now*,' Bonnie said. She stood up, padded towards her husband. 'Even if it *is* too late. So you'll give me that phone key, Milton.' She held out a chubby hand, her voice calm, defiant.

Surprisingly, Mr Hates took the heavy ring of keys from his pocket, removed a small one and placed it in Bonnie's hand.

Half an hour later, the doctor arrived.

'That looks like a magician's bag,' Carol whispered, as the doctor pulled a stethoscope from his black bag. 'Maybe he could do a trick and bring Jane back to life?'

That's a stupid thing to say, I almost snapped at Carol. But I just shook my head as the doctor listened to Jane's chest, pressed his fingers to the side of her neck, then fired questions at us.

"How long had Jane been ill? What were her symptoms? Where had it hurt? Did she have a temperature? What had she been given for the pain?"

Once we'd answered him as best we could, he straightened up, brow crumpling into a frown.

'My guess would be complications of appendicitis,' he murmured. 'Ruptured appendix, and peritonitis. Which is known to be dangerous, and can be deadly ... I'm very sorry about your friend.'

'*Appendicitis?*' I cried. 'Plenty of schoolkids got that but they didn't die. No, they had an operation – that's what they said – then they came back to school, alive and well.'

My hatred for Mr Hates burned, hot and acidy, in my heart. I smelled it, tasted it, coiling from me, thick and deadly as a bushfire. He'd killed Jane as surely as if he'd beaten her to death with his horse whip.

'This is all *your* fault,' I hissed at Mr Hates. I ignored Vinnie's wide-eyed look, willing me to shut up.

The doctor shot me a look.

Mr Hates' rat muzzle dropped open in shock, face flushing red as a rooster's comb. But, in that instant, I wasn't scared of him; knew he wouldn't whip me in front of the doctor. Oh no, appearances meant everything to Mr Hates. Besides, I was beyond fear, beyond caring about his punishments, the shame he'd drown me in, later.

'Jane is dead for nothing!' My rage boiled over into a black fury. Anger that Jane would never get the chance to grow up with the rest of us, as sorry as that growing up was.

'No, it's m-my f-fault, doctor,' Bonnie stammered, right back under the spell of her husband's evil gaze. 'I knew Jane was v-very ill ... should've insisted we call you sooner.'

'But you *did* try to get him to call the doctor,' I said, anxious to make up for hurting Bonnie's feelings. I turned to the doctor. 'But her husband beat her, like he always beats her if she stands up to his bullying.' I pointed to the angry red marks across Bonnie's arm. 'Look, that's a whip mark from last night. He hits her all the time, gives her cut lips, black eyes.'

The sleeping shed fell silent. Nobody, including the doctor, knew what to say.

'I'll need to make some calls,' he finally said, frowning at Mr Hates as he shoved his stethoscope back into the black bag.

'I'll take you to the phone,' Mr Hates said. And, as he led the doctor up the dirt pathway to the homestead, without a backward glance at any of us, I began to tremble. And then I cried. Sobbed for Jane. Sobbed for myself. Sobbed for all of us.

* * *

A police car hurtled down the driveway, and an ambulance. They sprayed up more dust along that rutted track than in our whole five and a half years at Seabreeze.

I'd only ever seen one dead person, my father. I thought I wouldn't be able to look at Jane, but I couldn't stop staring at her. She did look like she was asleep, as I've heard people say of the dead. And peaceful. Poor tortured Jane, always sick, forever waiting for her mother, was finally at peace.

The ambulance men covered Jane with a blanket, and as they slid the stretcher into the ambulance, my invisible blackbird friend struck up his song. Not his usual mellow chirp, his '*tchink, tchink*' alarm bell or the anxious '*tsooi, tsooi*', but a deep and sad warble.

Jane's special send-off song.

'Will there be a funeral?' Carol asked Bonnie, when Jane was gone, as quickly and suddenly as the dust puffs the ambulance tyres flicked up as it rolled away.

'Where will it be?' Vinnie said.

'Will we be allowed to go?' I said.

We kept firing questions at Bonnie, but she just looked tearfully at us, sighed and shrugged.

I knew it was wrong, but still I couldn't help my annoyance, my frustration. How could Bonnie stand by, day after day, letting her husband crush her to snivelling, shrugging pieces? No way would I ever put up with that.

And later, as we shuffled towards the dining shed for Sunday lunch for which nobody was hungry, even though we'd missed breakfast, Jane was still so heavy on my mind that I didn't notice Mr Hates creep up behind me.

That was his thing, appearing out of nowhere to punish you for something. But I was in no doubt I was about to cop it for opening my big mouth, both last night *and* this morning.

'How can you even think to speak to me like that?' he said, breath warm and sour on my cheek. He sounded more frustrated than angry, as if I truly did confuse him. 'And in front of the doctor? Me, who's been your father, your saviour, for five and a half years? I will never understand your hostility, Gasbag.'

And, in that moment, I understood Mr Hates truly believed he *was* doing us a favour, offering us a better life at Seabreeze. Hard work was what we owed him for his roof over our head. The family he'd given us. Obviously he didn't think small and tasteless food portions, uncomfortable metal mattresses, cold showers, or exhaustion, mattered.

I looked Mr Hates straight in the eye, kept my voice calm. 'You're no father to me, to any of us. You're an evil fucken brute.'

The whip came down fast and hard on my shoulder, before I could even finish the word "brute". It knocked me flat, and while I was down, he kicked me in the ribs. 'Ungrateful bitch, after all I've given you, selfish little *cunt.*'

'Stop, Milton!' Bonnie shrieked, hurrying over to us. 'Or you'll kill her too.'

'Leave Lucy alone!' Nick cried, and I think Mr Hates *would* have killed me, if he and Tommy hadn't dragged him off me. The boys each holding one of his arms, Mr Hates stood there panting, rat muzzle drizzling saliva, sweat beading the scarlet face.

Tommy and Nick had got so tall this past year, muscles thick and rounded, that short and skinny Mr Hates was no longer a threat to them. And Mr Hates knew it, sensed the danger if he crossed the boys. So he trod carefully around them, no longer raised his whip to them.

Eyes rolling, pink and frantic like the crazy eye of that kangaroo he'd caught in his orchard, Mr Hates pushed away Tommy and Nick; shoved Bonnie aside so roughly that she tumbled onto the dirt.

'You, Gasbag, you and Lavinia Anderson, and the mute one, Hampton,' he snarled, 'you can forget lunch. Get back to your sleeping shed and strip Jane Baxter's bunk this minute.'

He stamped away, calling over his shoulder, 'And burn her sheets, burn everything. You never know what vermin that girl was harbouring.'

I wanted to scream at him that I was pretty sure vermin didn't cause appendicitis, but I couldn't get the words out. Jane's death, and this latest beating, had sucked the fight out of me. For now.

'You gotta get away from that monster, Bonnie,' I said, as Vinnie and Suzy helped me up from the ground, and I pushed a clump of sweaty, dark hair from my face. 'Or he'll kill you one day.'

'Told ya, I got nowhere to go ... no one'd give this dumb cow a job or a roof over her head.'

'You're a bonzer cook, and you sew and do lots of things, sure you could get a job,' Vinnie said, helping me brush the dirt and dust off my pinafore.

'I ain't never been on me own,' Bonnie said. 'Always been with me family in Dubbo, all of us helpin' out on the property. I wouldn't know what to do on me lonesome.'

'Didn't I give you girls a job?' Mr Hates called, from the veranda. He lashed the horsewhip, and I cradled my painful ribs as we scurried back to our sleeping shed.

The only mirror Mr Hates allowed at Seabreeze was the one in the homestead bathroom, which we only ever saw when we had to clean the place. But as I dabbed water onto the whip marks grazing my shoulder while Vinnie, Suzy and Carol stripped Jane's bed, and took her belongings outside, I caught a glimpse of myself in the reflection of one of the small shed windows.

My face was dust-caked, streaked with sweat, bowl-cut hair hanging in a filthy, limp tangle. Bruises were already blooming on my shoulder, my ribs.

An image of rosy-cheeked, plump-faced Lucy who'd got off the *Star of New South Wales* five and a half years ago flashed into that window. I looked at her standing beside this hollow-cheeked girl with the sun-roughened skin. The blistered bare feet, the bowl haircut, the stained grey pinafore that hung from her skinny body like a sack.

But it was the eyes that showed how Lucy Rivers felt, deep inside. The misery, the hopelessness, the exhaustion, reflected in them.

* * *

That night, as we dropped onto our bunks, thunder murmured from far across the scrubland. The warm evening breeze rose to a hot wind, rattling the window frames, the door, sending our possum mates scuttling from the roof.

Jane's death had left me so stunned, I couldn't bear to be on my own. My ribs were too sore to climb up to Vinnie's bunk so she'd slid into my lower bunk, beside me.

In the sliver of moonlight cutting through the window, Jane's bunk looked sad and empty. Mr Hates had even made us burn her school shoes, so that, in such a short time, there wasn't a single thing left of Jane Baxter. Like she'd never existed.

'Even back at Easthaven we never believed Jane when she complained about this pain or that ache, did we?' I said, a gale whistling through the treetops. 'We ignored her, thought she only wanted attention because of her … her wonky face. I feel so guilty, what terrible friends we were.'

'No friends at all,' Vinnie said, and I caught the sob in her voice. 'From now on, I'll never ignore anyone who complains of being sick.'

'Poor Jane,' Carol said, from her bunk. 'She just wanted to be loved, like the rest of us.'

As the thunder grumbled louder, closer, I remembered only the good things about Jane: how she always smelled nice, her pretty pale blue eyes and long dark lashes. I pushed from my mind the annoying moaning, how her stream of sicknesses – and never knowing if they were real – had frustrated me.

'I hope that brute feels guilty for not calling the doctor,' Carol said.

'He won't,' I said. 'Jane dying has only proved, even *more*, the bastard doesn't give a shit about us.'

I gritted my teeth, tried to swallow my hatred for him, to ignore the pain in my ribs. The murder in my heart.

In our early Seabreeze days, when I'd first seen Bonnie's bruises, the red welts on her neck, the blood blisters on her lip, images of Mum after my father's drunken beating would flood my mind. And I'd hated Mr Hates. Then, after that terrible bare-bum whipping, I'd wanted him dead. But now that he'd murdered Jane, I wanted his death to be horrible, agonising.

'I want to kill Mr Hates,' I said, 'to split open his skull with the wood-chopping axe and watch his brains and blood and innards spill out. I want to see him suffer.'

'Don't be daft, Lucy Rivers,' Vinnie said. 'They'd lock you up for murder.'

'What's the difference, we're already in prison? And it'd be easy, he doesn't even keep his rifle locked up, unlike his *telephone*.'

'But you still can't, you're not a murderer,' Carol said.

'Put that stupid idea out of your head right now,' Vinnie said.

'Well the only way you can stop me from shooting him – or I can stop myself – is to get away from Seabreeze,' I said. 'If I stay, I'll kill him. I know I will. So, too bad for the deadly snakes and spiders, we're getting away from here.'

'Have you forgotten you already tried escaping?' Vinnie said.

'That Jim and John Browning failed too? Have you forgotten those school bullies telling us we stick out like sore thumbs, that everyone recognises us in a flash from how skinny we are, our daggy clothes, our shitty haircuts?' Vinnie sighed, rolled over, away from me. 'You *really* want to get us killed with your crazy ideas, Lucy?'

'You *really* want us to be Mr Hates' slaves for another whole year?' I snapped. 'Only for him to send us to some awful cattle station, like Fiona, and probably Helen and Bessy and the others too? And remember when Carol was reading her sister's letter, you said, "the *third* prison of our life".'

I grabbed Vinnie's hand, squeezed it, trying to make her look at me, to understand we had to try again to get away. 'We're smarter than those Browning brothers, smarter than I was before. We won't get sprung.' I glanced across at Carol. 'And if you want half a chance of getting to Fiona in Sydney, you'd better come with us. Suzy, you're coming too, five and a half years is long enough not to speak a single word.'

I tugged on Vinnie's shoulder, till she rolled back over to face me. 'And what about splashing around in that warm seawater Mr Zachary promised us? Isn't it time we *finally* got to an Aussie beach?'

A crack of thunder right above our shed made me jump. The first raindrops clacked onto the roof. Those storm clouds wiped out that fingernail of moonlight and, like a magic spell, Jane's bunk vanished in the sleeping-shed darkness.

26

Lucy Rivers
Southern Highlands, New South Wales
February 1968

Our chance of escape from Seabreeze came on a hot, still morning, the following Sunday. Mr Hates would be busy for hours with the older boys, finally rebuilding the dairy shed which had blown down in the storm the night Jane died. A storm that had lasted all of ten minutes before the wind pushed it out over the ocean, the scatter of raindrops teasing the sun-baked earth, the wilting plants and flowers.

'We gotta go *now*,' I said to Vinnie, Suzy and Carol, after breakfast. 'Mr Hates won't miss us till lunchtime.' For sure, he'd come after us as soon as he saw we weren't in the dining shed for lunch, but for a few hours we'd be free as the cockatoos wheeling through the sky.

'Give me your cossies,' I mumbled to the girls, through a mouthful of toothbrush and paste. My heart walloping against my chest, I shoved our threadbare cossies into the small cloth bag I'd snaffled from the laundry, along with the rag in which I'd tied those pennies stolen from our school days. Anxious to get away, there was no time to think what else we might need.

'I'm still not sure this is a good idea,' Vinnie said as, the blood pulsing through me, we slipped away down that tree-lined, rutted dirt track.

'Look, Vinnie, I know we don't have anywhere to go, that there isn't a single person in this whole country who might help us escape, but, like I already said, we'll work it out once we get far enough away from Seabreeze, from *him*.'

Once the homestead was out of sight, we relaxed a little, grabbed each other's hands, whooping and sprinting towards the main road. Suzy wasn't laughing, but in her silent way, she was as pleased as us to be getting away from our miserable lives.

But our joyful shouts weren't only happy ones. They also masked the worry of what we'd do, where we'd go. And they hid our deep fear of being caught, and taken back to Seabreeze.

I kept glancing over my shoulder, expecting to see Mr Hates' ute screeching down the track. But no one came after us, and my heartbeat slowed a little as we reached the wooden "Seabreeze Farm" sign at end of the dusty track.

'So, left or right?' Vinnie said, as we stood in the measly shade of a willow tree.

'Which beach are we going to, anyway?' Carol asked.

'We go right,' I said. 'Same as when we caught the bus to school, but then we keep going, and hitchhike to a beach in Wollongong. I know there's nice beaches there, those town kids always raved about their holidays at Wollongong beaches, remember?'

Vinnie stared at me. '*Wollongong*? You still think you can find Charly after five and a half years? And even if, by some miracle, you did find her, she won't look the same you know. You mightn't even recognise her.'

'What other choice've we got?' I said. 'Where else do you know of, that we should go?'

Vinnie shrugged, squinted into that sun, rising quickly in the morning sky. Soon it would be blazing, making us tired and thirsty.

'Anyway, how do you hitchhike?' Carol asked, as we hurried along the roadside.

'When we were still at school, some girls were boasting about how they'd hitchhiked to Sydney for some music festival,' I said. 'It's easy, just stick your thumb up, like this, and when a car drives past, if they've got room, they pull over and give you a free ride to wherever you want to go.'

Vinnie, Carol and Suzy stuck out their thumbs too, as we kept walking, staring down that long, empty road, tar shimmering in the morning sun.

'Shit, it's Mr Yates!' Carol cried, as a utility van exactly like Mr Hates' sped towards us. My heart thundered in my chest, and I shook with fear and panic, as we scurried from the roadside, behind a dense clot of stringy-barked eucalypts.

And there we crouched in the lantana, bee flies buzzing about our heads, grasshoppers tickling our ankles. He'd surely have seen us, the only people for miles on that lonely road.

The cicadas beat a rhythm to match my heart fluttering in my chest. I could hardly believe our escape was over before it had even begun.

I fretted too about snakes slithering through the lantana, fangs drooling deadly venom sinking into our flesh.

But that ute careered right past us. It wasn't Mr Hates, but a younger, fat bloke and, only a few minutes later, I yelled, 'Quick, thumbs out!' as a lorry came barrelling towards us, its front gleaming silver in the sunlight.

The lorry pulled over and the driver wound down his window. His grin showed off yellowy-brown teeth, a front one missing. His gaze travelled across our identical pinafores, our bare feet. 'Where youse girls off to?'

'Wollongong,' I said. 'Can you take us all?'

'Bit of a squeeze but I reckon there's room. Yeah, jump in, all of youse,' he said. 'Don't mind Woofy here. Woofy by name, woofy by nature, but he won't bite ya bum.'

As we piled into the lorry, Vinnie and I wedged in the front beside Woofy – who really did stink – Suzy and Carol in the back, I was so excited, and fearful, at the same time, I almost peed my pants.

This is it, we're going, really leaving Seabreeze!

The driver wore dusty boots, a navy singlet and washed-out

grey shorts, paunchy belly sagging over the top. A tattooed hand reached over Woofy, gave my thigh a friendly slap. 'Comfy there?' he said.

Goosebumps slithered down the leg he'd touched and I tried not to shiver, even as it got hotter by the minute. More and more stifling in that cramped and airless lorry.

'Where youse live then?' the driver asked. 'Bowral? Mittagong?'

'Yep, around here,' I said.

'So whereabouts in Wollongong should I drop youse?'

'At the beach please,' I said.

'Which beach would that be?' he said with a gappy grin. 'There's miles and miles of beaches along the Aussie coast, unlike Pommie land.'

'How did you know we —?' I started, till Vinnie poked me in the ribs.

'A girl don't lose her accent *that* easy,' the driver said with a wink, another slap on my thigh.

'The best beach then,' I said, my leg jerking beneath his touch, glad we'd soon be away from this man and his thigh-slaps and his smelly dog. Though I *was* thankful for the lift.

'We're going to swim in warm, clear seawater,' Carol said.

We travelled along in silence for ages. The driver whistled some tunes I'd never heard, slapping my thigh from time to time. Woofy breathed his stink right into my face, his fur rough on my skin, slippery with sweat.

'Here youse go, young sheilas,' the driver said, finally, pulling up at the end of a street full of cars whizzing by, and van-type vehicles with surfboards strapped to the top of them.

'Walk to the end of this street and youse'll reach North Beach,' he said. 'But watch out for them waves. Stay between the red and yellow flags, or a rip could pull youse out to sea.'

'What flags?' Vinnie said, and it was my turn to poke her.

'Yeah, sure,' I said, as we climbed down from the lorry. 'And thanks for the lift.'

'Youse better take these sarnies,' he said, handing me down a pack of sandwiches. 'The wife made 'em up, fresh this morning. A swim in the surf gives a girl one hell of an appetite.'

He grinned again and Woofy gave a short bark. 'Enjoy ya swim,' he called with a wave as the lorry pulled back out into the traffic. And he was gone.

* * *

Not since we'd sailed into Sydney Harbour back in 1962 could I remember being so amazed at the Pacific Ocean. My lips stretched so wide in a grin, I thought they'd crack.

'Oh wow!' Vinnie said, as we stood with Suzy and Carol on a grassy spot above the sand crowded with people and beach umbrellas, the sea spread out like a massive turquoise cloth edged in white lace.

'We made it!' I cried, breathing in that warm, salty air. I grabbed Vinnie's arm, jumped up and down. 'And no deadly snake or spider killed us on the way.'

'How inviting the sea looks!' Carol said.

Even Suzy smiled at the curling waves, the smooth yellow sand, the shrieking children and smiling mums and dads.

From the pine trees, a magpie sang its deep '*iaouw, iaouw*,' kookaburras and honeyeaters laughed and chirped.

'Reckon we've found our Emerald City eh, Vinnie?'

'Well that sea *is* the colour and sparkle of emeralds,' Vinnie said, and let out one of her donkey laughs from long ago, before Easthaven. 'So you must be right, Dorothy.'

I nodded, felt so giddy in that air seething with salt, the pulse of people having fun, the swell and dip of crashing waves, the '*hark, hark*' of gulls overhead, boasting snow-white underbellies.

'Wish we had groovy tie-dyed tops and Jesus sandals like them,' I said, scowling at a group of girls who were staring at us, giggling at our faded, and very un-groovy, grey pinafores.

'I don't care,' Vinnie said. 'It's just really far out that we got here. Come on, let's try that bodysurfing thing Nurse Amelia was going on about, on the boat.'

'Not yet,' I said, pointing at the red telephone booth. 'I want to phone the Ashwoods, those people who stole Charly.'

Vinnie stared at me. 'Can't you phone them later? Aren't we in a hurry to splash in that warm seawater? We've only waited five and a half years for this, Lucy.'

'This is my first chance,' I said. 'And nobody's going to stop me trying to find Charly, right now.'

Of course we'd seen phone booths before, had overheard school kids talking about those directories inside where you looked up numbers, but none of us had ever been inside one.

Suzy, Carol and Vinnie stood outside as I flipped the directory pages until I spotted the name Ashwood. There were two "Ashwood, F." listings. From my pocket, I plucked the rag of stolen pennies.

'Oi, where'd you get that money?' Vinnie said.

'Never you mind, just be thankful I saved up for our rainy day.' I winked at my friend, then frowned in concentration, trying to work out how to use the phone. But it was hopeless, I had no idea, and neither did Vinnie, Carol or Suzy.

I slipped back outside and stopped a friendly-looking couple strolling towards us.

'Excuse me, can you tell me how to use this phone?'

The man and woman didn't say anything at first, gazes roaming over our grey pinafores. The man frowned, as if unsure he'd heard me right. 'How to use this phone?'

I cleared my throat. 'Yes, we're visiting for the day, and the phone booths where we live – far away – are different.'

The couple frowned at each other, but the woman ended up showing me how to use it.

For the first "Ashwood, F." number, it rang ten times. I sighed, pressed the silver B button and when my coin fell into the chute, I dialled the second number. Someone answered after the first ring. My heart skipped as I pressed the A button.

'G'day?' A woman's voice.

'Hello, is this the house where Frank Ashwood lives?'

'I'm sorry, dear, my hubby's Fred. Bye-bye now.'

My shoulders drooped as I hung up, shook my head at the girls waiting outside.

'That first number was probably the right one,' Vinnie said. 'Come on, we'll try again after our swim.' She pointed to a pale-brick dome-shaped building. 'Look, there's a toilet and change room.'

'*... dong, the wicked Mr Hates is dead,*' we sang, to the tune of 'Ding Dong The Witch is Dead'.

Our laughter tinkling on the warm, blue air, we almost fell over each other as we changed into our cossies and sang, Suzy mouthing the words.

'Oh shit, we forgot to bring a towel,' I said.

'Who cares?' Vinnie said, as we hurried down the steps onto the sand. 'This sun will dry us off in seconds!'

'*Ouch, ouch, ouch,*' we all squealed as our feet hit that burning sand, scalding even our soles, tough from years of going bare-foot, except to school.

27

Charlotte Dolores Ashwood
Wollongong, New South Wales,
February 1968

'Mum won't allow me go to your horse-riding party,' Charlotte told Simone that afternoon, as she spread out her favourite beach towel, the dolphin-pattern one, on the burning North Beach sand.

'But why not?' Simone said, flicking her towel down beside Charlotte's. 'Your mum and dad let you do everything you want, like they *give* you everything you want.'

'Because I fell off a pony when I was four, and almost died.'

Beyond the sand crowded with noisy families, brightly-coloured towels and striped umbrellas, Charlotte glimpsed her father already pounding through the surf, diving under waves, swimming out to the rolling, foamy breakers.

'So now I know why I was in hospital for so long before we moved next door to you,' Charlotte said, as two kids raced by, kicking up sand onto their towels. '*And* why I can't remember this pony accident, or the house we lived in before Frangipani Drive.'

'Why's that?' Simone frowned at the kids, brushed the sand from her towel.

'Because I hit my head so hard it wiped out my memories of the accident, and before it too,' Charlotte said. 'Mum told me that's what the doctors said.'

'So maybe your brain went weird from the accident?' Simone

said. 'That's why you keep remembering, or dreaming or – like your mum reckons – *making up* that sister, and other stuff?'

'Mum reckons I dream a lot, about ships and people and other things because I read too many books. She says my stories come alive in my dreams.' Charlotte shooed away a fly, her mind stuck on that imaginary sister Mum said she'd made up because she was an only child.

Why then, if she's imaginary, does that sister seem so real?

'Anyway, it's so unfair your parents won't let you come to my party,' Simone said, as they sprinted across the scalding sand, down to the shoreline. 'You were only a kid, as if you'd ever fall off a horse now.'

'That's what I told them,' Charlotte said. 'Pfft, as if ... '

After the horse-riding party blow-up that morning, the day had only got hotter, without the slightest whiff of sea breeze. They all drooped. Mum with her saggy shoulders, Dad with his sad eyes. Charlotte with frustration and anger over Simone's party.

The backyard gum, wattle and jacaranda trees drooped too, in search of the tiniest drop of water.

The red bottlebrush flowers were long gone, the rainbow lorikeets, pink and grey galahs and sulphur-crested cockatoos had fallen silent. Even those noisy kookaburras didn't let out a single laugh. Like the heat had stolen every last petal and bird call.

The hot tension – no one speaking to each other – stretched right through the house like chewed gum, until Dad had finally coaxed Charlotte away from her *Famous Five* adventure. 'Go and get Simone, let's go to the beach for a swim.'

Charlotte was still angry, and even though North Beach would be packed with annoying little kids, she couldn't pass up the chance of cooling off in the billowy waves.

'We'd best let Mum rest,' Dad had said, leaving Mum with another cuppa – "lots of milk and sugar please, Frank" – and her box of Vincent's Powders. He always said Mum needed a rest after any kind of upheaval.

* * *

'Well I can't change the plans now, the horse-riding's all organised,' Simone said, as she and Charlotte stood on the shoreline, eddies of seawater cooling their hot feet and ankles. 'You'll just have to talk them into letting you come, tell them no way can you miss your best friend's birthday.'

'I'll try and talk them into it,' Charlotte said, as they waded out through the shallows. 'Well, Dad at least. He's easier than Mum.'

The sun burning the part in her hair, Charlotte watched four thin and gawky girls run into the surf, holding hands as they jumped over the tiniest waves.

One had bright orange hair. The second one had the same dark, wavy hair as Charlotte's, the third one's was plain brown. The fourth girl's hair was very white, and she squinted behind the thick glasses she'd forgotten to take off before swimming.

A set of different-coloured-hair Barbie dolls, except those girls weren't one bit glamorous like Barbie.

Even though they looked older than Charlotte and Simone, they shrieked and giggled like little kids. A spark shot through Charlotte; there was something familiar about them. Not their daggy cossies and even daggier haircuts, something else, but she didn't know what.

'Look how skinny they are, like they don't get enough to eat,' Simone said, nudging Charlotte, 'and their hair's like someone plonked a bowl on their heads and cut around it. Those cossies look second-hand too, as if they come from the olden days.'

Charlotte looked away, didn't want the girls to catch her staring, which Mum said was the height of rudeness. But an invisible thread tugged her gaze back, and she couldn't stop herself watching the girls wade out into knee-deep water, squealing every time a small wave knocked them over.

They shrieked and laughed and held on to each other as if they were scared but, at the same time, having the best fun. That exciting, but terrifying, rollercoaster sensation. Maybe they'd never been in the surf before? Charlotte couldn't imagine that, a life without the beach.

'They probably live inland or somewhere,' she said to Simone, 'and just came to the beach for the day.'

'Yeah, well come on.' Simone grabbed Charlotte's arm, dragging her gaze from the straggly girls larking about in the shallows. 'There's a break in the swell, let's swim out.'

'Last one out's a rotten egg,' Charlotte shouted as they swam out towards the crashing breakers.

Simone and Charlotte had learnt to swim at five years old and, since then, had swum almost every day of their lives, except through cool and windy July and August. They pounded through the surf, and Charlotte forgot all about the odd-looking girls.

She and Simone trod water, waiting for the sets of waves, oil tankers hugging the horizon sailing to and from the Port Kembla Steelworks, where Dad worked. They dived beneath waves that were about to break and leapt over the swollen ones coiling above them – invisible wave hands lifting Charlotte up to their dizzy peaks, she felt like a queen, gazing down over the whole beach.

An image burst into her mind – imagining herself a queen, ruling the world. Where was that, and when? Oh yes, Dad pushing her on the swing when she was little, looking down across the backyard, her playground with dozens of toys. Much nicer than that other cold, ugly and bare playground.

What other cold, ugly and bare playground?

28

"Stay between the red and yellow flags, or a rip could pull you out to sea", that's what the lorry driver told us,' I said, as we stood knee-deep, seawater cooling our legs and hands.

I sensed the others, like me, itched to rush right out to those crashing breakers, but even after school lessons, none of us were confident swimmers, and those rough waves looked scarier, bigger the closer we got. So we stayed in the shallows, ducking down, cooling our bodies.

'I wish Fiona could be with us,' Carol said.

'Don't worry, from her letter it sounds like she's going to some nice beaches in Sydney,' I said. 'And you'll be there with her real soon.' Though I had no idea how Carol would get from Wollongong to Sydney. Like everything, we'd work it out later.

'Well I wish Tommy could've come with us. He'd *love* this beach,' Vinnie said.

'I told you,' I said, 'if Tommy came, Nick and some of the others would've wanted to come too. And if that many knew about our escape plan, it'd surely have got back to Mr Hates. I couldn't risk that.' I ducked down again, the salty water cooling my hot body.

'Anyway, I said you can write to Tommy as soon as we find a job, and a place to live. Bonnie'll give him the letter the first

Saturday. Then he, and Nick and anyone else, can hitchhike here from Seabreeze like we did.'

'I know, and I *will* write to him,' Vinnie said. 'But I'm really going to miss our nights sneaking out to the orchard.'

'Yeah, what *do* you two get up to out there in the middle of the night?' Carol said, as we took more cautious steps towards those huge curling waves, heaving themselves up to breaking point. 'Pashing off and stuff?'

Vinnie's freckled face turned a deep crimson. 'That's how we started but then we … well, we went the whole way.'

'What, like real screwing … *sex*?' I said. 'Why didn't you tell me? I thought we had no secrets?'

'I was going to,' Vinnie said with a giggle. 'Give a girl half a chance.'

'So what was it like?' Carol said.

Vinnie looked out to the horizon where blue sky met dark green sea. 'When Tommy and me do it, it's like … like only me 'n him in the whole world,' she said with a sigh. 'So cool, like no other feeling.'

Vinnie sat down on the soft seabed, only her shoulders out of the water. She leaned backwards, let that salty water rush across her body, her face. She lifted her head, swept back an arc of orange hair.

'You should try it with Nick,' she said. 'Tommy told me Nick reckons you're a choice chick, and he's not just on the make.'

'That's not half obvious,' Carol said, splashing her hands through the water. 'The way Nick Hurley stares at you the whole time.'

'Nick Hurley? You're mad,' I said. 'Why would I want *him* for my boyfriend?'

'"Cos a boyfriend might make you … I dunno, less angry at the world,' Vinnie said.

I gritted my teeth. 'I'm *not* angry at the worl —'

'You so are!' Vinnie laughed, splashed water in my face.

'Anyway, I haven't met a single bloke I could trust, and I'll *never* have a boyfriend,' I said. 'So you shut up about Nick Hurley and let's try this bodysurfing thing.'

Amelia's words rushed into my mind like that water over our legs – soft, gentle, cooling, with a rush of memories of me and Vinnie standing on the deck of the *Star of New South Wales*. And of Charly.

Sorrow squeezed my heart; made me more determined to find my sister.

Might I really see Charly again, this very day?

We tried to copy the other people riding waves into shore. But that swirling seawater chucked us about like rag dolls, dumped us down to the sand-rippled bottom, choking our lungs, filling our hair and cossies with clumps of sand.

But still we shrieked and giggled like those kids building sandcastles on the shore, hitching up our cossies after each wave, which the worn elastic dragged down to our knees.

Now that I was away from Seabreeze, gazing out over the shimmering sea at that far-off horizon, I didn't want to be Lucy Rivers anymore, but a new girl. With a new life, far away from the one I'd been frozen in, too afraid to escape from.

For sure, I'd tried to tune out the fear and excuses that scratched at my mind and stopped me trying again to escape. But my rage over Jane Baxter's death had given me a shitload of courage.

I was sad I hadn't been able to say bye-bye to Bonnie. Sweet, sad, silly Bonnie, who'd made living at Seabreeze bearable.

I'd write a nice long letter to her once we got settled in Wollongong. And who knows, maybe our bravery escaping Seabreeze and Mr Hates would rub off onto Bonnie?

* * *

'I'm starved,' Vinnie said, tugging me towards the shore.

The surf had made me hungry too, not to mention thirsty

from all that salt water I'd gulped trying to bodysurf, and as we lurched and stumbled from the water, Bonnie Yates flitted from my mind.

From the wet shoreline, Suzy picked up a pretty white and brown shell, held it to her ear. A smile spread across her face and she pushed it towards me. I too held it to my ear.

'Wow, you really *can* hear the whooshing ocean,' I said. 'Like Hazel told us, remember?'

Vinnie and Carol took turns listening to the shell as we walked back up the beach towards our pile of grey pinafores, and the stolen pennies tied in the cloth, that I'd buried beneath the clothes.

'Back in a sec,' I said, veering off to the change rooms. 'I need a drink.'

'Better hurry,' Vinnie said with a grin, 'or we'll gobble all the lorry driver's sarnies.'

I hurried over to the change rooms, where I'd spotted a bubbler earlier, and drank thirstily from the fountain. I still hadn't thought about what we'd do after the beach, had no clue how we'd cope. We knew nothing about this outside world, not even about phone booths. But I wasn't too worried, as a thought kept niggling my brain; the feeling that I'd find Charly today. That, somehow, her new family would rescue us.

Surely if we found that man, Frank Ashwood, and told him about our Seabreeze prison, he wouldn't make us go back there. He'd have an idea about jobs for us, a place to live in Wollongong.

I couldn't wait to get back to the phone booth and call the number again. Because today really was a day of miracles.

29

In a few quick strokes, Charlotte's father was beside them, grinning, splashing water into their faces. She pushed the unsettling flashes of those four girls – unknown but so familiar – from her mind as she and Simone shrieked, splashed him back. Charlotte pushed his head under, let him come up for air. Dunked him again.

'Hey if you drown me,' he said, when he surfaced, 'who'll buy you a sausage roll at the kiosk? Come on, let's get hot chips too.'

They bodysurfed into shore, squealing as they flew free on the crest of the wave that bounced them up and down. A free ride, all the way into shore.

'I was thinking about your pony accident,' Simone said, when Charlotte's dad strode off, up to the kiosk. 'You know, you hitting your head and forgetting everything.'

'And?' Charlotte said, streaking a fresh layer of zinc cream across her nose.

'It made me remember something I overhead Mum telling my dad, but it was ages ago. I didn't take much notice at the time, thought maybe I'd heard wrong. But now it's come back and it's weird.'

'What's weird?' She threw the zinc cream tube to Simone.

'I'm pretty sure Mum was telling Dad that the pony accident, and that hospital thing, is all a lie. It never happened, and is just some story your parents made up for adopting you. She

189

reckoned that's why they always spoiled you, to make up for you being adopted.'

'What do you mean, *adopted*?' Charlotte frowned at her friend, pushed stray hair strands from her face. Charlotte knew what "adopted" meant. Heaps of kids at school were adopted. One family – the Radstones – had *five* adopted kids. 'Why would your mum tell your dad such lies?' Charlotte's chest was tight, her breath catching in her throat.

'Cos you weren't there when your parents moved into the Frangipani Drive house —'

'That's because I was sick in hospital!' Charlotte snapped. 'Then I got better, and came straight home to the new house. I never went back to the old one. No way am I adopted, I can't be!'

Simone truly could say the stupidest things. 'And anyway, why would Mum and Dad make up a story about me falling off a pony, and being in hospital for ages? They'd have just told me, and everyone, I was adopted, like all those kids at school.' She took a breath. 'No way am I adopted, Dad would've told me, he doesn't keep secrets from me.'

'I remember Mum saying she thought you were adopted because you spoke funny when we first met you,' Simone said. 'You know, with a Pommie accent … not like an Aussie. Course, I was too young to remember *that*, but my mother isn't a liar. And I'm pretty sure that's what she said to Dad.'

'Don't be an idiot, I've always spoken like this, same as you and all Aussies.' Charlotte took a deep breath and gathered up a clump of sand, itching to throw it in Simone's silly face.

'Well you should ask your mother to see your baby photo albums,' Simone said, 'then you'll know the truth.'

Against the '*hark, hark*' of gulls overhead, something from long ago – she must've been about six or seven – clanged into Charlotte's mind.

Are you one of those ten-pound Poms, Charlotte … you've got a Pommie accent?

She couldn't remember who'd said those words, but now they

swirled through her head as clear as the sun-streaked sea before them.

Everyone had heard about ten-pound Poms but Charlotte hadn't remembered, until now, that someone had actually called her one.

Why ever would they have said that? Was Simone right, did she have a Pommie accent? How could that be?

Dad came back from the kiosk and as they sat on their towels, savouring the tomato sauce-soaked sausage rolls, the hot, salty chips splashed with vinegar, Charlotte's mind churned again with those doubts. Those unanswered questions.

Why would someone lie about me having a Pommie accent? And why don't I speak like a Pommie now? Can you lose an accent?

And why, when Charlotte was lost in her *Famous Five* adventures, did she feel that magnetic tug towards England? How come she felt she really *was* there?

She looked across at Dad, licking the salt and grease from his fingers. She could hardly make a scene here, on the beach. But the worm wriggling through Charlotte's mind made her wonder if she wasn't challenging her father right now because she so badly didn't want it to be true. No, she definitely did not want to be adopted; did not want to be a ten-pound Pom. Because whichever way Charlotte twisted it about in her mind, it wouldn't make any sense.

Besides, she hated the idea that Simone, who could be bossy, even for a best friend, might be right. But Charlotte was hanging out to get home and ask her mother about baby photo albums.

* * *

'There's those girls again,' Simone said, nodding at the skinny girls, crouched on their haunches on the sand, not far from them.

'Only three now,' Charlotte said, as they started to pack up their beach things, families gathering buckets and spades, shell collections, and complaining kids. 'Where did the fourth one go?'

'Dunno, but it looks like they don't even own a towel,' Simone said as she and Charlotte shook the sand from theirs, folded and slipped them into their denim beach bags. 'They're just crouched there, all dripping wet, and breaking up a sandwich, or something.'

'Maybe they're too poor to have a sandwich each?' Charlotte said, slipping into the groovy lime green Sportscraft dress Mum had bought her last week.

'And did you see, they don't even know how to *bodysurf*?' Simone said. 'They didn't go out past the shallows.'

'I feel sorry for them,' Charlotte said. 'Who doesn't know how to bodysurf? Who doesn't even own a towel?'

'*Or* funky cossies,' Simone said.

'Let's get a move on, girls,' Dad said, pulling shorts and T-shirt over his wet cossies. 'And stop staring, Charlotte.'

But Charlotte couldn't stop staring. Her feet were stuck to the sand, like it was quicksand, sucking her to the spot.

It was as if she knew those three girls, and the dark-haired one who still hadn't come back from the surf club or wherever she went. But how could she? Nobody from their neighbourhood, and definitely not from Frangipani Drive, dressed like that, or had such awful haircuts. And she didn't know a single person who couldn't afford to buy a beach towel or decent cossies.

As if Charlotte's mind and body had separated, she took her beach towel from her bag. The palm of an invisible hand pressed against her spine, nudged her towards the girls. She couldn't have turned back even if she'd wanted to.

'Here, have my towel.' Charlotte held it out to the three girls. 'I've got another one' – she stopped herself saying "plenty more" – 'at home.'

'You're *giving* us your towel?' the carrot-haired girl said, green eyes wide in surprise, as if nobody had ever given her anything. The white-haired girl said nothing, stared at her feet.

'Wow, that's kind of you,' the brown-haired girl said.

'Come on, Charlotte,' Dad called, already halfway up the beach.

'Yeah, thanks, that's real cool of you,' the carrot-haired girl said, with a big smile, and a wave as Charlotte plodded across the sand, away from them.

She glanced back over her shoulder, but Simone tugged at her arm. 'Come *on*, Charlotte, what are you staring at? Why ever did you give them your towel – that dolphin one was your favourite – and you don't even *know* those girls?'

But Charlotte couldn't stop looking at the girls, and rubbing her goose-fleshed arms, as the hot sun began its westward arc over Mount Kembla.

The dark-haired girl was back with the other three, and they were taking turns drying themselves with her towel. Their towel now. Charlotte was glad she'd given it to them; it made her feel good inside.

She and Simone were quite a way off now, but Charlotte caught the dark-haired girl's stare, so long and hard that icicles slid down her back.

She turned away, kept walking beside Simone, but the sand was blurred, hazy, like looking at the rippled seabed. Up ahead, her father had already disappeared along the path behind the kiosk.

'Come *on*, slow coach,' Simone said. 'Or I'll chow down the whole lot of that chocolate ice-cream at home.'

But Simone's voice was small, quiet, behind the voices and pictures blazing through Charlotte's mind.

A woman is shoving Charlotte down a steep staircase.

Don't make me go fast, I'll trip over the sheet. Don't want to fall down the stairs. You die if you fall down stairs.

You'll stand there with that wet sheet over your head until I say so … don't take it off.

Can't see anything, only the stink of stale pee, clinging to me.

Can't stop shivering, so cold. So very cold and sad.

Charlotte held her breath, trembled in that dying heat. Tried to focus on those images, vanishing as quickly as they'd come.

She and Simone reached the grassy spot beside the kiosk. Breathless, a weird kind of ache pressing on Charlotte's chest, she turned back, glanced one last time at those four strange girls.

And, as she and Simone skittered off to catch up to Dad, two sparrows danced on the grass – to and fro, to and fro. Skipping towards each other, then away. Back together, then away again.

30

'Where'd you nick that towel from?' I grabbed it from Vinnie, rubbed it through my wet hair. In the time I'd been to the bubbler, and back to the sand, the fiery sun had already dried the water in a salty crust onto my body. 'Nice one too ... pretty dolphin pattern.'

'I'm no thief, like *some* of us,' Vinnie said with a grin, as we slipped on the grey pinafores over our cossies. 'A girl gave it to us.'

'That's her,' Carol said, pointing way up the beach, as two girls stepped from the sand onto the grass beside the kiosk.

I squinted through the crowds leaving the beach. The girl was a fair way off but I could see she had the same black, wavy hair as me, and looked about eleven years old. The age Charly would be now. She even walked like Charly. I shuddered, my pulse quickening.

Does she really *walk like Charly, or do I so badly want it to be my sister, I'm only imagining it? There must be hundreds – maybe thousands! – of curly-haired eleven-year-olds in Wollongong. What are the chances? And who's to say she's still here ... the family could have moved away by now?*

I could run after the girl; could catch her if I sprinted. No. Yes. No.

Yes!

I inhaled sharply, about to dart off, but a hand grabbed my arm. A larger, much stronger hand than Vinnie's.

I swivelled around to two serious-faced men wearing the same blue uniform as those policemen who'd come to Seabreeze when Jane died. I hadn't even noticed them approaching us across the sand, and a tangle of fear knotted my stomach.

'Let me go,' I said. 'Why are you holding my arm? I need to catch up with someone.' I waved my other arm towards the girl, now out of sight behind the kiosk. 'I think I know her … think she's my sister. Please … have to catch her … lost her before.'

From the way the policemen, and Vinnie, Carol and even Suzy, frowned at me, my words must be spilling out in a jumble of nonsense.

I tried to pull away again, but his grip held firm. 'You're not going anywhere just yet, Miss,' he said.

'But I have to! She might be my sister. Please, let me go!' I shouted, still trying to pull away from him.

'Quieten down now, Miss, you're making a scene,' the cop said. 'People are staring.'

Mind swirling like a wild, raging river, my gaze wheeled about the beach to see if I could glimpse the girl again. But she was gone, and people *were* ogling us, and talking amongst themselves. I wanted to scream, to sob my heart out. To yell at them that it was *so* unfair.

'Please, why are you stopping me?' I said, trying to dampen my anger; to keep my voice even, calm. 'What do you want with us?' But even as the words tumbled from me, a tight fist closed around my heart and I suspected our game was up.

But who'd told the cops about us? How did they know we'd run away from Seabreeze? Then, one glance beyond the cops told me who the filthy snitches were.

The couple who'd showed me how to use the phone, only a few hours ago, stared at us, the man frowning, the woman gnawing at her top lip.

'Those people called us, they were concerned about you girls,' the second policeman said, his gaze roaming across our identical, grey pinafores. 'Wondered if you were lost or something.'

'You're shitting me,' I said to the man and woman. 'Why would *you* be worried about us? *Nobody* cares about us.'

Nobody besides Bonnie, but Bonnie should worry about herself, not anyone else.

'Where do you girls live?' one of the policemen asked. 'Do your parents know you're at the beach?'

'We live here, in Wollongong,' I said. 'And for sure our parents know we're at the beach. Anyway, we're all sixteen, way old enough to go places on our own.'

'The thing is,' the other policeman said. 'We had a phone call a few hours ago, from a Mr Yates, reporting that four of his girls had gone missing from their home, Seabreeze Farm. He's very worried, has rung many police stations in the area. And his description sounded a lot like you four … same dresses, same accents.'

'We're not *his* girls,' I snapped, even as I knew it was over; that those prison gates were slowly but surely, closing on us again.

'No *not* his girls,' Vinnie said, 'all we are is slaves on his farm … works us like dogs.'

'Doesn't give us enough to eat,' I said, jabbing a finger at our bare feet. 'Only lets us wear shoes to school, even in winter.'

'He flogs us with a horse whip,' Vinnie said, looking at me. 'My friend here's got the scars to show for it.'

Suzy remained silent but nodded at the garble of our words.

'Well, what say you girls come with us,' the first policeman said, 'and we'll figure out what's the best thing for you?'

Right, as if we had a choice? And, as they led us away from the beach, past the man and woman, I scowled, spat at their feet. 'Bloody dobbers.'

A little further along, still glaring at the couple over my shoulder, blood still simmering, I realised that Carol was no longer with us.

We all looked around, the policemen too, but Carol Mulligan had vanished.

* * *

At the police station, just around the corner from the beach, the cops plonked me, Vinnie and Suzy in an office with only a desk and four chairs. A policewoman, who actually smiled and was friendly, brought us orange fizzy drinks and a plate of biscuits, plain and tasteless and nothing like Bonnie's yummy Saturday biscuits.

'Where the hell did Carol run off to, and *why*?' I said, as we munched biscuits, drank, and waited.

'S'pose she twigged the game was up,' Vinnie said with a shrug, as a fly smashed itself against the window, trying to get in. 'But good for her, I only hope she makes it to Sydney and to Fiona.'

Suzy stared at her feet, the toes of one foot brushing the sand from her other foot. Slowly, gently, silently, she shook her head, shrugged. She looked even more miserable than usual.

'I'm so bloody stupid!' I said, snaffling the last biscuit. 'We look *exactly* like runaways in these identical pinafores. I should've got different clothes for us ... didn't plan our getaway properly.'

'Don't blame yourself,' Vinnie said. 'Anyway, where would you've got other clothes?'

I shrugged. And we waited. And waited. Outside the window, a butcherbird impaled some insect on a branch of the jasmine, using it like a fork to hold his prey while he devoured it.

I stood up, paced about. 'What's taking those cops *so* long?'

'Maybe they're finding a better place for us to live,' Vinnie said, 'since we told them the truth about Seabreeze.'

I let out a snort. 'Yeah, *sure*. Right this minute, they're finding us a palace with slaves of our own.' Annoyed at her denseness; frustrated I'd bungled our escape, terrified about what would happen to us now, I couldn't help snapping at my friend. 'And since when do we trust adults, especially *men*? They've duped us from the beginning, right from those cops who took Mum away, and Liar Langford promising us Easthaven would be a *nice* place. Then those cold and mean Easthaven bitches, and Mr Zachary. And the worst of them all, Mr Monster Hates. And now, today, that bloody couple who dobbed us in.' My hands bunched into fists and I wanted to punch something, someone. 'All of them, liars.'

Another half hour ticked by. I jumped up again, called out into the corridor. 'Oi, what's going on? What are you going to do with us? Where —?'

A figure filled the open doorway, snapping off my words. My blood turned to ice as I stared into the grinning rat-face of Mr Hates.

31

Charlotte Dolores Ashwood
Wollongong, New South Wales,
February 1968

Home from the beach, Charlotte left her dad parking the car in the garage out of the heat, and darted straight to the kitchen, where her mum was kneading pastry.

The little radio that sat on top of the fridge was blaring out one of those old love songs Mum loved listening to while she baked, ironed or cleaned. Charlotte snapped off the radio, folded her arms across her chest. 'Simone's mum reckons I'm adopted, and that I never fell off a pony, *or* went to hospital.' Her breaths came short, quick. 'That it was all a cover-up for adopting me when I was five years old.'

'*Adopted*? Don't be ridiculous.' Mum smiled but Charlotte caught the quiver of her top lip. 'Everyone says you're the spitting image – a mixture – of your father and me.' Pearls of sweat dotted her brow, eyebrows puckering into a frown as she concentrated on that pastry.

Flour, knead, roll. Flour, knead, roll.

The kitchen, hot with the day's trapped heat, fell silent, but Charlotte had to admit she did have her parents' dark blue eyes and almost-black, wavy hair. She had her mother's build, one size smaller than most of the girls in her class. And Mum was always saying she had Dad's feet and hands.

'How can you not be our own flesh and blood, sweetie?' Mum pointed a floury finger at the table. 'Why don't you sit down and taste one of those delicious chocolate crackles we made yesterday, I hope you didn't fill up on rubbish from that dreadful beach kiosk?'

Was Mum trying to change the subject, going on about the Rice Bubbles crackles she knew Charlotte loved? She didn't sit down.

'Why would Simone lie to me? Why would Mrs Jardine say something like that?'

'Well, Simone may be your best friend,' Mum said, fanning the rolling pin at a buzzing fly, 'but she's always been a teensy bit jealous, right from when we moved here. You're smarter, prettier, than Simone. Also, she'll be hurt you're not going to her party and probably just made up something like that to hurt you back. Her mother can't truly believe such rubbish. Anyway, I told Irma Jardine, right back when we moved into Frangipani Drive, that our little girl was recovering in hospital and would soon be coming home.' She shook her head, went back to rolling the pasty. 'I simply can't imagine why Simone, or her mother, would say you were adopted.'

Dad strode into the kitchen. '*Adopted*?' He snagged a beer from the fridge, pinged it open, took a long swill.

'Why's your face all red, Dad?'

'Nothing, it's just this heat.' He looked from Mum to her, rubbed a hand through his sweat-slick hair and took another gulp, frowning as if he truly had to concentrate on something as simple as drinking beer.

'Simone also told me Mrs Jardine said I spoke with a Pommie accent when I was little,' Charlotte went on. She plonked down at the table, pushed away the plate of chocolate crackles. 'And she wasn't the only one, this girl at school said it too, ages ago.'

'Don't be so ridiculous.' Mum shook her head, spoke like she thought Charlotte had gone completely bonkers. 'You haven't got an accent, you speak exactly like any other Australian girl. Can't you see that for yourself?'

That was true, she did sound like everyone else. But still, something wasn't right. She could tell by the twitch of her mother's lip, and how Dad refused to meet her gaze; the way he edged towards the door, hoping Mum wouldn't notice he wanted to disappear down to his garage.

'Prove it, prove I'm not adopted,' Charlotte said as, outside, the first gust of a southerly buster hurled pockets of dust and dead leaves across the backyard. 'Where are my baby photos? Why haven't I ever seen them?'

'Well, because you never asked, I suppose,' Mum said, washing her hands, soaping them up to a lather. 'Right, come back here, Frank, don't you run off to that garage, I need you to fetch those photo albums from the box in the wardrobe, so we can put these silly ideas out of Charlotte's head right now.' She took a quick breath. 'And I've got a good mind to go next door and have a stern word with Irma Jardine. Fancy her spreading such a rumour.' She dried her hands, snapped the towel at another fly. 'And here's me, imagining the Jardines were our friends.'

'Calm down, Dolly,' Dad said, and swallowed the last of his beer. 'I'll get the albums.'

* * *

'See, there you are as a newborn,' Mum said, as she opened the first page of the album she'd taken from the stack Dad had piled on the living-room coffee table. This one was marked "1957" in Mum's neat handwriting. 'There's me pregnant with you ... oh look at my enormous tummy!' She giggled. 'Dad's taking the picture, obviously.'

In that muggy, evening heat, Charlotte sat beside her mother on the couch, just the two of them since Dad had succeeded in escaping to his garage. Outside, the southerly had blown up to a gale that whistled through the gum and jacaranda trees, slunk beneath the roof eaves and rattled the whole house.

She squinted at the next photo Mum pointed to. 'And there's me holding my new, precious daughter.' She smiled, went to pat

Charlotte's knee but, as if she were afraid she might push her away, her hand hovered.

The black and white photo did show a baby with a mop of dark hair, but it could have been any baby.

How can I be sure it's me? But who else could it be?

Charlotte turned each page with her mother, saw that baby grow into a toddler, sitting on her father's shoulders, laughing, pulling at his hair. Dad twirling a little dark-haired girl around in what looked like a yard. But it wasn't the Frangipani Drive backyard.

'They were taken at our old house,' Mum said, as if she could read Charlotte's thoughts.

'Where was the old house?' Charlotte asked, 'in Wollongong?'

'Yes, in a different suburb though. We wanted a nicer, bigger place, and found it here, in Frangipani Drive. And it was closer to your father's job.'

Like almost everyone's father at Charlotte's school, her dad worked at the Port Kembla Steelworks – beating heart of the city of Wollongong, a school teacher had said. She wasn't exactly sure what he did in Port Kembla, which was full of chimney stacks and smelly brown smoke. She only knew that he had an important job, walking around in big boots and a hard hat checking that furnaces and other things were working properly.

Charlotte peeled back the plastic on one of the album pages, took a photo out, stared at it more closely: her and Dad on the sand at North Beach, beside a huge sandcastle with a deep moat. 'Look at you two, thick as thieves,' Mum said with another giggle. 'I often thought Dad had more fun than you, building those sandcastles.'

Charlotte smiled too, remembering building those elaborate castles with her father. She turned over the photo, read her mother's neat cursive writing:

Charlotte & Frank, North Beach, Jan. '61

'You'd just turned four that very week,' Mum said.

'It's so weird I don't remember any of this, or the pony fall and the hospital.'

'I told you that's quite normal,' Mum said. 'Remember the doctor said the head bump could make you forget the accident completely, and everything before it. Besides none of us recalls anything much from before the age of five, apparently.'

So Simone was lying. I'm not adopted. So much for being my best friend. I'll never speak to you again.

* * *

A few weeks later, the day of Simone's party, Charlotte was glad when she woke to rain pelting her bedroom window.

'Ha! So much for horse-riding, that'll teach you to be jealous and tell spiteful lies, Simone Maree Jardine,' she said to herself, with a smirk. From her bedside table, she plucked *The Jungle Book* and opened it to the book-marked page.

She hadn't even wanted to go to Simone's stupid party in the end; hadn't spoken to her since she'd lied about the adoption and the Pommie accent thing.

And she'd told Simone she could find a new best friend.

She was still miffed at her parents though, for refusing to let her go to the party for what she believed was a silly reason. So Charlotte had decided she'd become a jockey when she left school, to annoy them. She dreamed about winning Australia's greatest horse race, the Melbourne Cup, and becoming famous. That would teach her parents to tell her what she could and couldn't do.

Besides her beloved *Famous Five* collection, *The Jungle Book* was one of Charlotte's old favourites. She loved reading about the adventures of the little orphaned baby, Mowgli, left in the deep jungle of India. And how the jungle animals brought him up to be one of them, and were then afraid he might never want to return to his own people, in the Man-village.

But the elephants were Charlotte's favourite characters, Hathi most of all. As always when she looked at pictures of those great beasts, without knowing why, she felt sad, lonely and faraway.

Another picture flashed into her mind – elephants plodding along a road. Not through Rudyard Kipling's jungle but down a real city street alongside cars and people. However could elephants be in a street? But Charlotte saw the big lumbering animals as clearly as if she was holding the mind-picture in her hand.

A hand grips mine. Mum's?

But it's not Mum's voice whispering in my ear: We'll come back … visit all these places properly, won't we, Charly? Charly … Charly … Charly.

Was that from some other story? Or was she thinking about that Noumea cruise?

Who is Charly?

Mum poked her head around the bedroom door, startling Charlotte. 'Time for brekky, can't stay up here all day, reading, even if it is raining.'

'Did we see elephants on the cruise, Mum?' she asked.

Her mother frowned. '*Elephants*? I don't think so, why do you ask that?'

'Because I had this picture in my head of walking alongside elephants on a road with cars and trucks and people.'

Mum laughed, flicked a wrist. 'Simply another of your vivid dreams I suspect, sweetie. Now come downstairs and see how the rain's revived the frangipanis. They smell quite delicious.'

Another dream, that's what you always say.

'Be down in a minute,' Charlotte said, flicking through a few more pages of *The Jungle Book*.

But she couldn't concentrate on the story. She was thinking about those photo albums Mum had shown her. Every year of her life in order. Each birthday and Christmas. Outings to the beach, picnics, holding glowing school reports.

But not a single photo of the Noumea cruise.

32

Lucy Rivers
Southern Highlands, New South Wales
February 1968

Suzy, Vinnie and I squashed into the front seat of the ute beside Mr Hates, the silence on the way back to Seabreeze sitting heavy, grim. Mr Hates didn't speak, knuckles taut on the steering wheel, staring at the road ahead through the gigantic umbrella of gum trees.

I didn't dare speak either, not to Mr Hates, nor to Vinnie and Suzy. I nibbled at my nails, trying not to dwell on the whipping we were in for, surely as bad as when he'd given me the bum scars. The shiny red bumps that ached all winter.

I hadn't been surprised when those dickhead cops had ignored our complaints about Seabreeze Farm. Why would they believe us "vagrants" as I'd heard them call us, over the polite and smiley Mr Hates?

'So sorry for the bother with my girls, officers,' he'd said. 'Please forgive me.'

One of the cops had smiled and said, 'No bother, sir. We'd hate to think of your girls roaming around Wollongong, lost and homeless.'

'Especially when they have the most privileged home with me, at Seabreeze Farm,' Mr Hates had said.

Despite Vinnie's warning look, I couldn't help blurting out, 'Privileged home? We're nothing but slaves, I told you, he beats us with a horse whip! Wanna see my scars?' I went to hitch up my pinafore, but Vinnie frowned, tugged down my dress.

Mr Hates' face had taken on the saddest, most disappointed expression. 'I have tried to do my best for Miss Rivers, officers. Sadly though, the poor girl has a disturbed mind and is prone to violent tempers, not to mention removing her clothes in front of total strangers. Once again, please excuse her bad behaviour.'

I breathed fast, boiling with my poisonous hate for that man, but there was no point arguing. And, in that moment, the helplessness of it all swamped me like one of those whopping beach waves.

A wave broken on the shore, spent of its water, its strength, the energy seeped from me. The long, hard days of physical labour, the crap food, the lack of sleep. The heat. The cold. The weariness wrapped itself around my skinny body and squeezed me until I had to struggle to hold myself upright.

And, as the police had walked us out to Mr Hates' ute, I'd thought the very worst bummer of this whole day, even worse than the failed runaway, was that I might have missed out on finding Charly by a minute.

* * *

The ute groaned its way up the steep and windy road to the Southern Highlands.

The sun had almost sunk behind the western bushland as we passed through the town of Mittagong and I knew, from when we'd caught the school bus, that Mr Hates would soon turn off onto the dirt track that led to Seabreeze Farm. Almost home.

I'd long ago accepted that Seabreeze was my home, though still, after five and a half years, I wanted to go home to England. But then it struck me again, how bloody unlikely I'd ever get home, back to my mother.

I've let them down. Mum, for not looking after my little sister, and Charly for not keeping her with me. Bad daughter. Terrible sister.

I kept thinking that since Mum hadn't come to Australia and found us, she must still be in prison. Or she *was* out and, as I dreaded, that old Easthaven bat, Miss Sutherland, hadn't told her we'd been shipped out here.

Or maybe she did come, and she's searching for me and Charly this very minute? Will she ever find us?

Still nobody spoke. I sneaked a glance at Vinnie sitting beside me, and Suzy, next to the passenger door. I caught Mr Hates' cold stare, and my sweat turned to ice, spiders scurrying down my arms. His look alone could still do that, which both annoyed and terrified me.

I shifted my gaze to the windscreen again, to the people striding along the footpath, crossing at traffic lights, hurrying to buy last-minute things as the shops closed. All of them chatting, munching snacks, returning to their homes, their families. Free people. My insides frothed with jealousy.

The traffic light ahead turned orange and Mr Hates slowed down, brakes whining as we stopped. He flicked his gaze the other way, to the shops, and I dared another glance at Vinnie and Suzy.

Are they as bone-weary, as desperate and helpless, as me?

A strange look crossed Suzy's face. A shadow? A light? No, something dark. Behind the thick, dusty glasses, her eyes were blank. Dead-fish eyes, like I was staring down a hollow corridor, right into her brain. Suzy was that beach shell she'd picked off the sand, earlier. But there were no whooshing waves when I held it to my ear. Only silence.

Before I could say anything, or reach over to pat her leg and reassure her, Suzy flung open the door. She tumbled out onto the road, scrambled upright and started running. Not looking back, just sprinting along that footpath.

'Suzy!' I shouted, but still she didn't look back. She kept running, faster than I'd ever seen her move.

'What the *fuck*?' Mr Hates bolted from the driver's side, chased after Suzy, left the ute at that red light, humming away, blocking traffic that had pulled up behind. People beeped horns. Someone called out, 'Oi, shift ya ute, mate.' But Mr Hates ignored it, sprinting after Suzy.

Vinnie and I jumped from the ute too. I grabbed my friend's arm. 'Come on, let's run too!'

'Run to where?' Vinnie resisted my tugs.

'Dunno, don't care, let's just *go*, Vinnie!'

'Those cops'll only pick us up again,' she said, 'and then we'll be in for even worse punishment. Anyway, we need to stay here, for Suzy, when he catches – and *punishes* – her.' Vinnie pointed up ahead. 'Look, he's almost caught her.'

I didn't know what to do, so I stood with Vinnie on that footpath, squinting into the fading light, watching Mr Hates gain on Suzy.

'Can you believe she actually did that?' I said. 'Suzy, of all people?'

'You think you know a person,' Vinnie said, 'but sometimes you really don't.'

Mr Hates was only a yard from Suzy when she stopped, pivoted about to face him.

In the streetlight that had flickered on, her face was flushed pink, damp blonde hair strands streaking her cheeks. Mr Hates reached out to grab her.

And, in that last second – for the first time in five and a half years – Suzy Hampton spoke. 'No!' A single, strangled word, but it came out strong, the meaning clear, as our friend jumped off the kerb, right in front of a passing car.

In the seconds that followed, as Vinnie and I ran towards that scene, I didn't know if it was the sickening screech of tyres, my screams, Vinnie's, or Mr Hates' cursing, that shrieked through my brain. Or all of them, mingled in that most grim and shocking sound I'd ever heard.

'Don't look, Vinnie. Don't look at her.' Breathless, we panted hard, faces buried in each other's shoulder.

I can't look. Won't look.

But I did.

33

A few nights after Suzy's grisly death, I tossed about on my metal bed in that hot and airless sleeping shed. Like every night since Suzy died, Vinnie had sneaked out to the orchard.

'Being with Tommy helps me forget about her,' she said. And, my other shed-mates either gone from Seabreeze, or dead, I ached with the sadness, the loneliness.

Still no punishment from Mr Hates for my second failed runaway, but I could hardly worry about that, so deep in shock I could barely speak, walk or eat, after the horror of seeing Suzy's crumpled body on the road.

A light tap on the cracked-open window made me jump. 'Hey, Lucy, it's Nick, open the door.'

'What for? Go away.'

'I thought ... thought you might wanna come to the orchard?' Just above a whisper, his voice was soft, gentle, pleading. 'We could, you know, be there together ... same as Tommy and Vinnie?'

I got up, flung open the door. 'Are you crazy, Nick Hurley?' Why would I want to do *that* with you?'

He shrugged, creamy skin and dark hair shiny in the streak of moonlight, raspberry-red lips stretched in a nervy smile. 'We wouldn't have to do anything ... only, you know, talk, hold hands or something?'

Nick looked as miserable as me and, as he stretched out a hand, I couldn't stop myself taking it, following him down the dirt track to the orchard.

Vinnie and Tommy's whispered giggles pealed though the fruit trees. We couldn't see them, but I was dead curious to know exactly what they were doing. What this screwing thing with a boy really was. Nick smiled, sat down and patted a spot beside him. I sat, not too close to him.

I breathed in those mixed smells of fruit, damp grass and animal manure as Nick circled an arm across my shoulder, patted my arm. I wanted to pull away, but couldn't. 'I'm sorry about Suzy … I know she was a good friend.' I let him pull me closer in a cuddle. His touch, the heat of his body, split apart my heart like Bonnie's Saturday marshmallows over the fire.

'I'm sorry too,' I said, as he lifted my chin, and his soft lips clamped onto mine. I went to pull away, but pashed him back, let the warmth flush from my lips, right down through my body, to the top of my thighs. I let him run shaky hands all over me, to kindle a fire deep inside me.

Night creatures ticking and rustling all around us, we threw off our pyjamas. Nick pulled me down next to him, kissing, stroking me all over. He lay on top of me, our hot, naked skin touching.

I gasped, knew what Vinnie meant now – just me 'n him in the whole world – and I wanted more. I wanted it all. I wrapped my legs around his back, held on tight as he pushed against me.

And then, suddenly, all I felt was a warm, sticky wetness between my thighs. Nick rolled off me, lay on his back panting, staring up at the sliver of moon.

'Oh shit,' he said. 'Sorry, couldn't stop … '

Confused, I frowned at him. There must be more to this sex thing? Surely it wasn't supposed to end like that?

I shoved him away, jumped up, struggled back into my nightie. 'Well that was a whole lot of *nothing*,' I said, so mad, so frustrated, so *embarrassed* how he'd fired me up, only to blow out the match a few seconds later. 'I don't know what the hell Vinnie is raving about, but I won't be doing that again, fucken waste of time!'

I ran back to the sleeping shed, ignoring Nick's pleading voice. 'Lucy, I'm sorry. It's not supposed to be like that. Come back, please!'

But I didn't, and I didn't understand what had happened in the orchard, but I'd never speak to that drongo Nick Hurley again.

* * *

The six o'clock morning bell woke me with a jolt.

I reached up to the top bunk, shook Vinnie's arm. 'Time to get up, sleepy head.'

'Leave me alone,' Vinnie mumbled. She'd stayed out way longer than me last night, so must be even more flagged out. Vinnie didn't know I'd snuck out with Nick and I wasn't about to tell her. No point, since I wasn't ever going to bother with sex again. If that's what it *had* been.

But no way could Vinnie sleep in, since Mr Hates didn't make exceptions for grief. For us, the deaths of Jane and Suzy changed nothing of our Seabreeze life. We'd lost them, we missed them terribly, we felt more alone than ever, but we weren't allowed to mourn them.

No, Mr Hates barked out the same orders, wielded the same riding crop, forced us to work in that same hot and dusty bleakness. And today Vinnie and I had the worst job – scrubbing the entire homestead, including Mr Hates' bedroom.

I rubbed my sleepy eyes and as we trudged out to the bathroom, Vinnie and I wrenched our gazes from those vacant beds.

'How will we tell Patty her twin killed herself?' Vinnie said, splashing cold water on her face.

'We won't.' I ran a comb through my hair, a sob catching in my throat at the sight of those empty towel hooks and Belongings' shelves. 'Because I bet we'll never see Patty again.'

Our feet dragging up the pathway to the homestead, Mr Hates, on his way down to the paddock, threw us a smile and a wave as if we were his mates. And the weight of all my losses – Charly, Mum, Patty and Suzy, Jane, Carol even – a stone pressing down on my shoulders, hunched me over like a sad, old person.

'I still can't believe he hasn't whipped us for trying to escape,' Vinnie said, as Mr Hates stalked away, riding crop thrashing about like a conductor's baton.

'Bastard enjoys torturing us with the wait, remember?' I said, patting Joey Joe, bounding along beside us. 'As much as he enjoys the actual punishing. You don't really think his pride would let us – *me*, because he'll know it was my idea – get away with it? Not a chance! You bet that devil is saving up something really evil just for me.'

* * *

'Maybe Mr Hates hasn't punished us because, deep down, he feels guilty about Suzy killing herself?' Vinnie said, both of us down on all fours, scrubbing Mr Hates' floorboards. It was late afternoon and we'd left his hated bedroom till last.

'*Humpf*, not a chance,' I said. 'Remember how he told those cops who came to the accident that Suzy was odd, miserable? That he was saddened, but not surprised, she'd taken her own life?' I sat back on my heels, swiped damp hair strands from my face. 'I wish they'd asked *us*. We'd have told them why Suzy killed herself.'

'But those cops didn't want to talk to us,' Vinnie said. 'And Mr Hates didn't want them to either, and we were too shocked to think of saying a single thing.'

'For sure he didn't want us to talk to them,' I said, flinging aside the scrubbing brush. 'More chance the truth about Seabreeze might get out. God, this job's a drag, I can *smell* that monster in here. Gives me the shivers.'

'Let's hurry and finish then,' Vinnie said, fetching clean bed-linen from the hallway cupboard. 'Sooner we're out of here, the sooner I can see my Tommy again.' From the window, Vinnie threw a smile and a wave to Tommy, who was repairing the front fence with Nick.

'Ooh, *my* Tommy,' I said, scowling at Nick as he waved at me, and ripping off Mr Hates' stale bedlinen.

'Isn't Tommy the grooviest guy ever?' Vinnie said, her freck-led face turning scarlet.

'S'pose so.' I shrugged, fanning out the bottom sheet over the mattress. With Suzy, Jane and Carol gone, it was hard to feel an ounce of happiness for anyone, even my best friend. And after the shame of last night, I kept pushing Nick's face from my mind; ignored his sweet smile and soft voice.

'I wish I could tell Jane and Suzy I miss them,' I said, as we tucked in the top sheet. 'Put some sweet-smelling orange jas-mine on their graves and tell them how sorry I am they're gone.'

'Did you ask Bonnie about a funeral?' Vinnie said, 'or where Suzy'll be buried?'

'Yeah, but Bonnie was too chicken to ask Mr Hates.' I breathed hard, tried to squash my frustration over Bonnie's simple mind; not to hold it against her. 'Like she never asked about Jane's funeral or burial place.'

'But without a grave to visit, it's like Jane and Suzy never existed,' Vinnie said, flinging on the bedspread. 'What if we make our own graves for them, not real ones of course, but a nice spot to remember them?'

I rolled my eyes, chucked the dirty bedlinen into the wicker basket. 'Yeah, Mr Hates'll be hunky dory with that. Anyway, right now I just want to wipe from my mind the horrible picture of Suzy's body.'

'Come on, we should finish up here,' Vinnie said, 'and head to the dining shed. Bonnie and the apprentices'll have dinner ready.'

As we packed up the cleaning gear, throwing dirty cloths

and brushes into the mop bucket, I tried to focus on something else – the shrill click of cicadas beyond the flyscreen, the gentle breeze through the fig and gum trees – but still I couldn't stop thinking of Suzy's legs bent out at that strange, awkward angle, her arms not where they should be. Her glasses smashed into a million shards.

Acidy liquid burned up my throat, a droplet of sweat burned the corner of my eye and, from nowhere, an image of my father lying at the bottom of those stairs burst into my mind. His bent legs, the grim halo of blood around his head.

'Thinking of Suzy makes me remember my father's accident.' I had no idea why my voice had dropped to a whisper, there was no one else in the homestead, though Mr Hates would be back any minute to chow down his dinner.

'Remember I told you, Mum couldn't have pushed him, even *accidentally*, because I clearly remember she was out at the shops?'

'Only about ten times,' Vinnie said.

'Well, I've been wondering, *again*, why those cops reckoned Mum accidentally pushed him, and, thinking back, I reckon it was our bitch of a neighbour, Iris Palmer, who put that idea into their heads.'

Vinnie nodded. 'Old bat always hated us kids for making too much noise.'

'Since it was Iris Palmer who fetched the rozzers in the first place … well, her son did.' I shook my head, still bitter at the unfairness of it all. 'But Mum would *never've* killed my father, even if he was a shitty husband. She was like Bonnie, putting up with the crap 'cos she reckoned she had no choice. Like Bonnie'd never hurt Mr Hates, when he's the shittiest husband ever.'

Thinking about my father's accident brought Charly's smashed up blackbird flickering into my mind.

And, back over the years, across the oceans, I snatched a glimpse of my mother's face, the buzz in my ears of her hurried, hushed words. And everything became as clear as that North Beach seawater.

Neither of you are ever to speak of this ... nobody must know what happened ... but if anybody does ask, it was an accident.

I grabbed Vinnie's arm. 'Bloody hell, I get it now.'

'Get *what*?'

'It was *Charly* who pushed him down the stairs, because he smashed her toy bird. And when Mum came home, she guessed straightaway what my sister had done, and took the blame ... went to prison to protect her daughter.'

As Vinnie and I shuffled towards the doorway, carrying the basket and mop bucket, my head thumped like someone had whacked me with a hammer.

'And Mum taking the blame for Charly, leaving us with no parents, is what got us sent to bloody Easthaven, then me to Seabreeze. So, you know what, all of this – my shitty life – is my sister's fault.'

'Don't you reckon it's a bit late to think about all that now?' Vinnie said. 'Anyway, Charly was only five, too young to blame for anything.'

'Not too young to kill someone,' I said, the love for my sister suddenly poisoned with splodges of doubt about her. 'And if Charly could do something like that at only five, what the hell's she growing up into?'

My mind reeled and spun with confusion. For sure, I still loved my sister but thinking how she'd got adopted rather than sent into slavery, I couldn't dampen the burning anger.

'Charly's probably having a bonzer life with her adopted parents in Wollongong and I bet she's completely forgotten she ever had a sister.' The bitter words spewed from me like a gobful of lemon juice.

But I didn't have a second longer to stew about Charly, as heavy boots clomped along the hallway, stopped at the doorway.

'Ah, thought I might find you both here.' Mr Hates strolled into his bedroom, creepy smile not reaching his eyes. 'You really thought you'd get off scot free with yet *another* runaway attempt, Gasbag? Such an ungrateful bitch you are.'

Gripping the riding crop, he folded his arms across his chest, leaned back against the door, ankles casually crossed. 'And look what came of your silly escapade, you as good as killed your friend. Susan Hampton would never have leapt in front of that car if she hadn't left Seabreeze, which I'm guessing was not her idea.'

Mr Hates' hushed voice terrified me more than his shouting.

'Get down to that dining shed, Anderson.' He flicked the whip at Vinnie. 'Your escape artist friend will join you shortly, once I'm finished with her.'

He shoved Vinnie out into the corridor, threw the bucket, mop and washing basket after her. 'And best you keep your mouth shut in that dining shed,' he said, 'or you'll be back here with your fiery little friend.'

He locked the door behind Vinnie, pocketed the key, turned back to me.

'And don't *you* think about shouting either,' he said, still smiling, saliva oozing from a corner of the rat muzzle as he raised the whip. 'One lash in the right place could kill a girl, you know.' He lowered the whip and softly, gently, stroked it across my brow, down my nose, over my cheek, around my lips. The touch of a feather. I shuddered.

I daren't make the slightest noise, or breathe, and forced myself to meet his evil, pink-eyed stare. No way would he make me buckle, on the outside. But inside I quaked, my guts loose as jelly, for I knew Mr Hates really *might* kill me this time. So best to shut my cake 'ole, get the punishment over with, and just get on with my miserable life.

'Kneel down over there,' he said, pointing the crop to a spot beside his freshly-made bed. 'Facing me.'

Still holding his stare, I back-pedalled, knelt beside the bed, braced myself for the whip lashes to come.

From a pocket, Mr Hates pulled lengths of twine, the rope Tommy and Nick had been using to fix the fence only an hour ago.

I so wish the boys were still out there, they'd help me, stand up for me, like when Mr Hates knocked me to the ground after Jane died.

But the boys had gone to the dining shed, along with Vinnie and Bonnie and everyone else.

His breaths coming hard and fast, sweat flecking his brow, Mr Hates bound my wrists, my ankles. Lips curving into another mean smile, he laid the riding crop on the bed. Then, with quivery fingers, he unbuckled his belt.

So he's going to flog me with his belt this time.

I almost shit my undies, imagining the pain, the damage, that buckle could do.

From another pocket, he pulled a handkerchief, which he placed across my eyes, bound tightly at the back of my head. I smelled and felt his snot on it, gagged. Forced myself to swallow my puke. I tried to shout for Bonnie – for anyone – but he jammed a hand across my mouth.

'No point calling for help,' he said, 'they can't hear you.'

My limbs ached with the lack of blood. I tried to struggle but it was pointless. I was his prisoner. My body tightened into spasms, as his breath came hotter, faster, staler and I knelt there and waited for the whip to lash down onto my bare flesh.

34

Charlotte Dolores Ashwood
Wollongong, New South Wales
February 1968

'Why are there no photos of the Noumea cruise?' Charlotte said to her mother.

Busy scrambling eggs for breakfast, one hand on the frypan handle, the other swatting her wooden spoon at a fly, Mum spun around to face her. 'No photos, what do you mean, sweetie?'

Dad sat at the kitchen table, drinking his cup of tea, the *Illawarra Mercury* newspaper rattling in his hand.

'There are photos of every minute of my life in those albums,' Charlotte said. She gulped down Mum's freshly-squeezed pineapple juice. 'But not a single one of that cruise … that's strange?'

Dad cleared his throat. 'Because silly me dropped the camera into the sea, while we were walking up the gangway.'

Mum dished out scrambled eggs onto the plates, slices of toast already on the side. 'Oh yes, I remember now. I was hopping mad at you, wasn't I, Frank?'

'You certainly were,' Dad said with a smile, chomping down his eggs.

'Well, like I said at the time, I think it's a shame we have no photos of that holiday,' Mum said, sitting at the table, sipping her tea. 'Without photos, memories simply fade away. We need pictures to keep past times in our mind.'

'I still remember lots of things about the cruise,' Charlotte said. 'Running up and down all those decks, splashing about in the pool, Dad haggling with the locals to buy me that shell necklace I so badly wanted.'

Mum smiled, waggled a finger at her. 'And eating ice-cream and pizza till you were sick, even though I warned you.'

'I was so amazed at all those books in the library. I think I learned to read on that boat.'

Mum frowned, shook her head. 'That cruise was Christmas of '63, you'd already been reading for over a year by then, Charlotte.'

Charlotte scraped the last forkful of creamy egg, piled it onto toast. 'That's weird, I clearly remember learning to read on that trip.'

'Don't be a duffer,' Mum said, and looked at Dad. 'Charlotte was a very early reader, wasn't she, Frank?'

'Sure was,' Dad said, wiping his mouth. 'Right, I'm off to work.' He grabbed his work briefcase, kissed Mum and her, and headed down to the garage.

'I remember the ship's bright red funnels too,' Charlotte said, helping Mum clear away the breakfast things.

'Red?' Mum frowned. 'No, the funnels were black, sweetie.'

'No, Mum, they were red.' Charlotte dumped the plates into the sink. 'And I remember the name of the ship too. I can still see it printed on the side: *Star of New South Wales*.'

'No, no, no, it was *nothing* like that,' Mum said, rinsing the plates. 'It was Fair-something, or some Italian-sounding thing. Oh I don't remember exactly, but the name definitely didn't have "New South Wales" in it.'

'It definitely *was* called the *Star of New South Wales*,' Charlotte said, stashing HP Sauce and Vegemite in the pantry.

'Maybe that was another boat, in a book or a dream?' Mum said. 'As I told you, without photos to back up your memories, they fade away until one day they've completely disappeared.' She handed Charlotte her sandwich and apple lunch and kissed her cheek. 'Now hurry, sweetie, don't be late for school.'

Charlotte stuffed the book she was reading – *The Weirdstone of Brisingamen* – into her school case and headed off down Frangipani Drive. It was only a fifteen-minute walk but she'd be glad when this year, and boring primary school, was over, and she'd get to catch a bus to Wollongong High School.

She spied Simone up ahead, halfway down the hill, but didn't call out to her, or hurry to catch up. It was almost a month since that day at North Beach, but Charlotte would never forgive Simone for spouting such mean lies.

Trudging down the hill, the growing heat already bubbling the tar on the road, instead of being sad about losing her best friend, Charlotte thought about the amazing story she couldn't wait to get back to. Colin and Susan, *The Weirdstone of Brisingamen* characters, had become her friends. She sensed those eerie creatures chasing her too, across Alderley Edge. She was right there with them, in England. Same as in her *Famous Five* adventures.

Susan. Susan. Susan.

The name thumped in Charlotte's mind in time with her school shoes on the footpath. She knew someone called Susan. Nobody at school, or Frangipani Drive, so where? She frowned, trying to think of a Susan she knew.

Yes, that was it! Susan from the Noumea cruise. But they'd called her "Suzy" and her twin sister, Patricia, was "Patty".

A picture of the twins flashed into her mind: snow-white braids, eyes squinty and crossed behind thick glasses. And, as she reached the school gate, ignoring Simone's dark stare, Charlotte knew Mum was wrong.

Clear as the sea on a sunny day, Charlotte saw those bright red ship funnels, and the name – *Star of New South Wales* – printed on the side.

It wasn't from a story she'd read, not from a dream she'd had. The *Star of New South Wales* was real, and Charlotte had been on that ship with twins called Suzy and Patty.

Was Charlotte's mother losing her mind, her memory? Or was she lying? But why ever would Mum lie about silly things like that?

35

Lucy Rivers
Southern Highlands, New South Wales,
February 1968

Mr Hates had bound my eyes with his snotty hanky, but still I squeezed them shut, held my breath for the blows to fall; for that belt buckle to tear gashes through my skin. Instead of blows, I felt his hot, stale breath on my face as he grabbed my hair, wrenched my head backwards.

Dribbles of his sweat splatted onto my cheek. I went to shake my head, to move the sweat bead, but he clutched my hair and the beads itched my cheek.

He let go of my hair for a second, and I heard shuffling, fiddling around. Then, before I could take another breath, he jerked my face up towards him. Then I felt it, smelt it. A thick stream of piss, directed straight into my face.

My heart stopped beating for a second. Then my blood beat so fast, so hot with shame and anger, I feared my veins, my head, my whole body, would explode.

I tried again to shift my face from the arc of piss, but he gripped my hair, almost yanking it from my skull. I kept my eyes shut, the hanky already sodden. I opened my mouth to scream. His piss filled it up. Stomach heaving, I gagged, spat. But still I couldn't move my face. I wriggled my wrists and ankles so hard, I thought my bones would snap, but the rope bindings held firm. I was as helpless as a rabbit in Mr Hates' rifle sight.

'Ah,' he sighed, as his stream dwindled off to droplets, which he shook over my face. 'That felt good.'

I heard the bedroom door fly open, Bonnie's voice: 'What the fucken hell are you doing to her, you monster?'

Vinnie's cries. And my friend ripping off the piss-soaked handkerchief. Fumbling with the twine to untie my wrists and ankles, rubbing the blood back into my limbs. Her soothing words. 'It's alright, Lucy, we're here now. You'll be okay.'

Despite the deep pit of humiliation gaping my insides, leaving me speechless, I glanced beyond my friend, to Bonnie, who was aiming Mr Hates' hunting rifle at his face.

'How could ya do such an evil thing? You wouldn't even piss on an *animal*,' she said. 'Now mop up ya mess all over this floor or I'll blow ya evil brains out.' I'd never heard Bonnie speak like this, voice oozing hatred, scorn, disgust.

As if Bonnie hadn't spoken, or wasn't aiming a rifle at him, Mr Hates took no notice of his wife. His gaze stayed on me, ratty face glowering with a sickening, triumphant smile.

'And you, Anderson, didn't I tell you to keep your mouth shut?' he said, shifting his gaze to Vinnie, who'd backed away, towards the door. 'But you couldn't help yourself, could you? Had to bring stupid mama bear, Bonnie running up here.'

Vinnie said nothing, just stared at him, wide-eyed, from the doorway. I wanted to spit on him – no, *shit* on him. I scrambled to my feet, rushed to the hallway, past Mr Hates, Bonnie and the rifle, and Vinnie. Tears blurring my vision, I stumbled into the bathroom.

I puked into the toilet, threw up until my emptied-out guts ached.

I didn't glance at myself in the mirror above the sink, couldn't bear to look at that girl shamed in the worst way ever. Between gulping sobs, I held my face under the hot water tap. I soaped it up, rubbed and scrubbed, until my cheeks were raw and red.

'You okay, Lucy?' Vinnie's soft voice, her hand patting my back as I hunched over the sink.

I nodded 'But I'm not going back to his bedroom … can't bear to see that monster's victory smile for another second.'

'Things sound a bit freaky in the bedroom,' Vinnie said, taking my hand, leading me back down the hallway. 'Come on, we'll just listen outside the door.'

'Blow my brains out?' Mr Hates was saying. 'You wouldn't dare.'

'Oh wouldn't I?' Bonnie's voice.

I couldn't resist, peeked around the doorframe.

Mr Hates held up a hand. 'Don't be a dumb cow, Bonnie. You'd be nothing without me. All of you, you'd wither and die.'

Bonnie took a step towards him.

'You know you're never going to use that thing ... since when have you ever fired a rifle?' I caught the tremble in his voice. A stain of fear?

'Never,' Bonnie said. 'Tonight will be me first go.'

'Sure it will, you stupid, fat cow.' Mr Hates let out a hollow bellow, lurched at Bonnie, tried to snatch the rifle.

At first I didn't understand what had happened, why my heart pounded, my ears buzzed, echoing with a deafening noise. Until I saw Mr Hates' knees buckle, and he crumpled to the floor, staring wide-eyed at Bonnie as if in surprise.

So stunned that Bonnie had actually got the guts to shoot him, I couldn't utter a single word. All I could do was gape, along with Vinnie and Bonnie, down at Mr Hates, and the flower of blood blossoming beneath his shirt.

* * *

'Oh, Bonnie!' Vinnie cried, her eyes wide green saucers. 'You shot him!'

Still aiming the rifle at Mr Hates' chest, as if she feared he might still be alive, Bonnie took slow steps towards her husband. Avoiding the blood, spreading in a dark halo around his body, Bonnie stepped over him, placed the rifle on Mr Hates' pillow. She bent down, pressed fingertips to the side of his neck.

'Is h-e ... d-ead?' Vinnie stammered.

'Yep, he's gone. Gone straight to Hell,' Bonnie said, her voice flat, calm.

Still wearing my piss-stained pinafore, I walked over and spat on him. I ripped the stinky dress over my head, threw it onto Mr Hates' – no, Mr Yates' – dead face.

'Did you see that, Lucy?' Bonnie said. 'I stood up to him … like I should'a done before, when Jane got sick. She might've lived – Jane *and* Suzy – if I was brave, like you.'

I stared at Bonnie, still too shocked from Mr Yates' humiliation, the shooting, to speak.

'Well you were *very* brave tonight, Bonnie,' Vinnie said.

'I killed him to stop you doing it, Lucy,' Bonnie said, pulling two clean sheets from the hallway cupboard, as if she was simply about to change a bed, and hadn't just shot a man. 'Vinnie kept telling me you'd kill him one day,' she said, wrapping one of the sheets around me. 'So now ya don't have to. I should'a done it years ago. For all of youse, and for meself. I'm only right sorry this had to happen to you, I only wish Vinnie and me had got back here quicker.'

She took a towel from the hall cupboard, held it out to me. 'Go get yaself a shower, sweet chook.'

I didn't know what to say to Bonnie. "Thank you" was weird, though I truly was thankful, felt not an ounce of sadness or grief. But I still couldn't think straight, could only stand there, speechless, gripping the sheet around my underwear, and holding the towel in the other hand.

Tommy and Nick loped into the bedroom, stared down at the bloodied corpse.

'Jesus Christ, was that a gun shot? What the hell happened?' Tommy said.

'Is he *dead*?' Nick said.

'Yep, dead. I shot him,' Bonnie said, as casually as she might say "it's a nice cool day out there".

Nick looked at me, wrapped in the sheet. 'Did he hurt you, Lucy? What did that bastard do?'

'Nothing,' I said. 'Don't worry … I'm fine.'

'Why are you wrapped in a sheet —?'

'I'm *fine*,' I snapped, hurrying back to the bathroom.

'I'll fetch your other pinafore,' Vinnie said.

As I stood under that hot, cleansing water, scrubbing my whole body, my face again, I regretting snapping at Nick. He was only trying to be nice, caring.

I slipped into my other pinafore Vinnie had fetched, and we went back to the bedroom.

'None of the others should know about this,' Bonnie said, and I sensed, as she covered Mr Yates' body with the other sheet, that his murder would be our secret.

'What'll we do with him?' Vinnie said.

'You boys dig a hole and bury him,' Bonnie said. 'I'll send the others off to bed with a hot choccy and a story about Mr Yates havin' to shoot a deadly snake ... hissing and set to attack youse. Had no choice but to kill it. Then I'll get me Ajax onto those stains in the bedroom, and make us some pancakes. Reckon we deserve a treat after this, don't youse?'

So that's what we did. While Bonnie lumbered down to the dining shed, Vinnie and I stood with Tommy and Nick beside the fig tree, choosing the best spot for a grave.

'Here?' Tommy jabbed the spade at the earth. 'Soil's a bit less bone-dry near the trunk, than out in full sun.'

Nick shook his head, stabbing another spade at the hard earth. 'Nah, too near the tree roots ... fig trees spread wide, underground.'

'Anyway, not *beneath* the tree,' Vinnie said, as Bonnie came puffing up the path from the sleeping sheds. 'That's where we sit, to get out of the sun.'

'Make sure youse dig deep,' Bonnie said, 'don't want Bluey here sniffin' him out.' She patted the dog, who'd followed her down to the dining and sleeping sheds.

'Here then?' Tommy said, a little further away. We nodded and he and Nick began digging. It was a hot night, that solid, sun-roasted earth like splitting rock, and the boys were soon sweating and panting.

Vinnie and I sat down, Bluey parked between us. I patted him, felt sorry for that mutt, but not sorry enough to want his master back.

After an hour, the hole barely deep enough for a rat let alone a man's body, Vinnie and I went into the kitchen and made icy drinks for the boys, where Bonnie was turning out pancakes.

'How can Bonnie act so normal, so cool, right after shooting her husband?' I said as we went back outside. 'She's not the least bit shaky.'

'Maybe the shakes'll come later,' Vinnie said, as we set down the tray of drinks. 'It hasn't sunk in yet.'

Faces sweat-shiny in the moonlight, Tommy and Nick guzzled their drinks. Bonnie came out with plate of steaming pancakes smothered with honey and fresh strawberries. 'There youse go, bog in.'

I'd missed dinner. Vinnie and I had barely eaten since Suzy's death, but now we gobbled down those soft and light pancakes like the half-starved animals we were. Bluey didn't get the slightest morsel, nor any of the five cats, hanging around us.

Finally, the sheet-wrapped body lugged straight from bedroom to grave, was covered with soil. There was no cross, or anything else to mark Mr Yates' resting place. Just Bluey sitting beside it, moonlight shimmering his fur a shiny grey-blue.

Nobody but us knew about the murder, and since we all knew how to keep our mouths shut, we were sure we'd got away with it.

36

Lucy Rivers
Southern Highlands, New South Wales
February 1968

The following morning Bonnie made a breakfast announcement. 'Mr Yates left Seabreeze, took off early this morning, he did.' A nervy smile, hand-wringing, licking her lips. 'He's gone to live with … with a new wife down Wollongong way so we'll have to fumble along on our own.' She flung an arm towards the fig tree, where Bluey was still sitting from last night, letting out the occasional howl. 'And youse'll have to take extra care of Bluey-boy, who's really gonna miss his master.'

Excited chatter struck up along the trestle tables. No more Mr Yates! They couldn't believe their luck.

Vinnie smiled at Tommy, who threw her a wink. But I couldn't smile or really feel happy. Don't get me wrong, I was thrilled the monster was dead but Mr Yates' filthy deed still had me upset, angry, and paralysed with shame.

After our breakfast of fresh bread, honey and jam, first break-fast ever of no porridge, when the schoolkids left and the others started their jobs, Tommy and Nick coaxed Bluey away from the grave with a bone. They took him down to the paddock, where they were fixing fences.

Bonnie wanted Vinnie and me to help her turn Mr Yates' bedroom upside down. 'Long as you reckon you can cope with going back in there, Lucy?'

'Yep, sure I can cope,' I said, shrugging off the army of spiders scurrying down my back.

'Reckon he stashed away heaps of stuff over the years,' Bonnie said, unlocking the wardrobe, the desk, the set of drawers, and the phone cupboard. I squinted at the floorboards beside the bed, but the only sign of last night's shooting was the faded Ajax circles from Bonnie's scrubbing brush.

'Ah ha! Just as I thought, look at this bounty,' she squealed, a smile lighting her face as we pored over boxes of ribbons, teddy bears, white tablecloths and crockery, sparkly cutlery and glassware. All that fancy stuff Mr Yates had brought out years ago, for those visitors.

'Check out this!' I said, pulling wads of cash from another box.

'Wow, where'd he get all that dosh?' Vinnie said.

'Squirrelled away from produce sales, over the years,' Bonnie said. 'Saving it for his rainy day … now *our* rainy day.' She clapped her pudgy hands together. 'This'll keep us going till I can think of another way to get us money.'

* * *

It quickly became obvious, from our fun-filled, shambly days, that Bonnie hadn't the foggiest idea how to run a farm. He'd controlled everything – finances, animals, jobs, us. So even with Mr Yates gone we still had to work hard; still baked our bread, kept chooks for eggs and meat, grew our fruit and veggies, a lot of which Bonnie managed to sell to shops around the place, along with the cows' milk.

'Me hubby's loot ain't gonna last forever,' Bonnie said, 'we'll sell off the sheep and the pigs.'

All that meant fewer outdoors jobs for the boys. But they were still busy, though now they tackled their work willingly, whistling and chattering, with no fear of a beating if they took a drink break in the shade, or a cool-off swim in the billabong.

And since Tommy and Nick had taught themselves to drive

Mr Yates' ute, Bonnie would give them cash to drive into town for extras. Sometimes Vinnie and I went with them to get stuff like undies, bras and Modess sanitary pads. The material shop was one of our favourites, and we'd choose groovy patterns and brightly-coloured fabric, then spend hours sewing fancy new clothes for everyone.

Instead of trying to escape after these outings, we were happy to return because Seabreeze had become our real home. Bonnie was free to be a mum, to kiss and cuddle, joke and laugh with all her sixteen kids.

But the worry still smudged our jokes, our laughter; the fear still simmered beneath our skin like Bonnie's slow-cooking stew. Dread that the cops would somehow discover Bonnie's crime lurked like a heavy storm cloud, especially in *my* mind, when I thought of my mother.

'Mr Yates and meself couldn't have kids,' Bonnie told us one evening as we cooled off on the veranda in a rare breeze. Mr Yates' battered wireless played tinny music and fruit bats squealed and zoomed through the fig leaves, mini-aeroplanes dive-bombing the purple twilight sky.

Bonnie shrugged. 'Dunno why, but kids never came to us.' She slapped a palm against her thick thigh. 'Probably me own fault … this fat, useless body. And I know Mr Yates' ways weren't the best, but he only knew how to take the tough stand.' She took a breath. 'As I told youse before, he was only a kid when they took him prisoner in Korea, and that … that bullet took off a bit of his ear.'

She sighed into the balmy night air, heavy with the scents of orange jasmine and honeysuckle, and fell silent, maybe thinking her husband hadn't been so lucky with that other bullet.

Bonnie might have suffered rare twinges of guilt for shooting her husband, but the rest of us – me especially – didn't feel a thread of remorse. That didn't mean I'd stopped thinking about him though. Mr Yates couldn't hurt me anymore, but still I felt the shame, the disgust. He'd stolen my childhood, my freedom, two of my friends, but the night he pissed on my face, he stole the worst thing from me. My pride. And, even as I couldn't explain to myself why, my pride seemed the most terrible thing to lose.

Yes, that evil man might be gone but his shadow still crawled after me. His ghost still wielded the whip, stomped about the homestead, up and down the dining shed, so clearly that, for no reason, my heart would jerk in my chest.

Bluey too, couldn't forget his master, lying graveside for hours on end, chin resting on his paws.

37

Lucy Rivers
Southern Highlands, New South Wales
May 1968

'Whoopee!' Tommy yelled, him and Vinnie clutching the tyre, sailing out over the billabong. Vinnie's bellow slid across the brown water like a skimming stone, bounced into the thick folds of green, violet and ochre-coloured scrubland beyond. Still clinging to each other, they shrieked again as they dropped into the water.

I stood on the bank, ready to take the tyre rope before Nick tried to convince me, yet again, to swing out with him.

This was the first time Vinnie and I'd worn the snazzy bikinis Bonnie had crocheted for us, and I felt pretty groovy, but there was still no way I'd let Nick Hurley near me.

'Come on, Lucy, one little swing together,' he said. 'I won't try and kiss you.' He grinned, face gleaming in the afternoon rays, honey-coloured eyes shining. 'Even though I really, really want to kiss you again. I promise it won't be like that night in the orchard.'

The tyre sailed back to the bank, and I grabbed the rope, swung out wide over the water. 'In your dreams, Nick!' I shouted, hiding my secret smile, the warm glow that someone actually wanted to kiss Lucy Rivers.

But that smile slipped from my lips quick enough. It couldn't be real, Gasbag Lucy Rivers didn't deserve anyone kissing her.

It was the end of a warm May afternoon, three months after Mr Yates' death. Vinnie and I'd peeled off our sweaty work clothes, slipped into the new cossies and raced down to the billabong. We picked a few plums and nectarines as we passed through the orchard, letting the juice dribble down our chins as we ate that delicious fruit.

Once everyone'd had a few swings on the tyre, we dried off and changed into our new trendy, checked shifts. Tommy and Nick loped off to feed the animals, and Vinnie and I tramped up to the homestead kitchen. Bonnie was frowning, sitting in her chair in front of the Aga, and stroking one of the cats curled up on her lap.

'What's wrong?' I asked, pouring out three cups of tea from the pot brewing on the table. Bonnie rarely frowned these days.

'Norman's just phoned me,' she said. 'He's phoned a few times in the last three months since Milton … '

'Who's Norman?' I said, placing the teapot back on the table.

'Norman Yates, Milton's brother,' Bonnie said. 'Youse chooks don't know him 'cos he's been away from Australia about ten years, working in some Asian country.' She stroked the cat harder. 'Milton and Norman spoke on the phone every month, and now he keeps asking me why he hasn't heard from his brother … why Milton's never here when he calls.'

'What did you tell him?' Vinnie said, splashing a cloud of milk into each cup.

'Same story I made up for the rest of the kids,' Bonnie said, sipping her tea, a hand resting on the cat's head. 'That Milton pissed off to Wollongong with some floozy.' The cat swiped a paw at her, leapt off her lap. 'But I don't reckon Norman believed me.'

'Why wouldn't he believe you?' Vinnie said, filling a huge saucepan with water, to cook spaghetti for our dinner, and clanking it onto the Aga.

''Cos he kept on at me,' Bonnie said, 'asking the same questions over and over.'

* * *

233

All of us ate together in the homestead these days, no more hot and airless dining shed and hard bench seats, but sixteen was still too many to sleep inside. So Bonnie had bought us proper mattresses and a pillow, and a warm cover for winter. She'd got hot water installed in the bathrooms, what luxury! And Nick and Tommy had put flyscreens on the windows, so we could keep them open on hot nights.

'Bonnie talking about this Norman brother phoning her,' Vinnie said, as we lay on our comfy mattresses that night, after a tasty meal of spaghetti with bacon and tomato sauce, 'makes me wonder why you don't try and phone Charly, since we can use the phone now? For years, you wanted to find your sister and now, suddenly, you don't want to even *try*,' Vinnie went on. 'She was only five years old and maybe – like you reckoned for so long – your dad's death really *was* an accident? You can't know for sure that Charly pushed him.'

I stayed silent for a moment, listening to the possums scratching on the roof. We'd been over this many times since we'd got phone access, but still Vinnie couldn't change my mind.

'So why didn't my sister ever say to the police that he fell on his own?' I said. 'My life could've been so different. No Easthaven, no Australia and no Mr Milton Fucken Yates.'

'Maybe Charly really did block it out of her mind,' Vinnie said, "cos it was too awful.' She took a breath, our bunk rattling as she turned over, bent her head over the side, and said, 'Anyway, even if Charly *did* push him, you *have* to forgive her. It wasn't her fault your mum took the blame. Don't you reckon it's kind of the same thing, Bonnie killing Mr Yates, and risk getting caught, so you wouldn't have to?'

'*I* didn't kill him.'

'But you wanted to, you *would've*, if Bonnie hadn't done it for you. Admit it, Lucy, you would have.'

'Okay, maybe I would've.'

'And don't tell me you don't still love Charly,' Vinnie said. 'You can't turn off love for a sister like a leaking tap.'

'Course I still love her, but after she wrecked me and Mum's life I just can't bring myself to phone her. What would I say?' I took a breath, pressed a palm against that aching spot deep in my chest. 'Anyway, Charly's another girl now ... a girl who no longer has a sister called Lucy.' I took a breath. 'Maybe I *will* call her one day, just not yet.'

* * *

A few days later – another May day as rainy as I remembered England in spring – we'd forgotten all about Mr Norman Yates' phone calls, and a letter arrived from Carol Mulligan. She said she'd hitchhiked to Sydney, found her sister, Fiona, and was working for the same family. She sounded happy as Larry, and we were all so pleased for her.

The drought had broken, the blistering summer finally slipped away, cooling breezes fanning scrubland and treetops, and we were sitting on the veranda listening to the rain pounding the tin roof like horses' hooves. It was amazing to watch those muddy rivulets stream tracks across the dried up, dusty ground, to see grass and plants shoot up overnight. It was a relief to sleep without that shed heat, to feel cool rain on my skin after months of unbearable heat.

The shower stopped and Vinnie ducked back out to keep digging the holes to plant the orange jasmine Tommy and Nick had brought back for us yesterday. The bushes that would grow into special, fragrant shrubs for Jane and Suzy. We'd never found out about a funeral or burial site for either of them so, the soil now rain-softened, we'd decided to plant a memorial for our lost friends.

The rain had brought more and more brightly-coloured birds that now fluttered about, chirping so loudly that Seabreeze Farm had its own, continuous orchestra.

'Remember how scared we were of them,' I said as a kookaburra laughed from his gum-tree branch, and a sulphur-crested cockatoo screeched back. I smiled, thinking how much I'd come to love them all.

''Specially poor Jane,' Vinnie said, as we tamped down the soil around the orange jasmine bushes.

'Hey, you'll never guess what we got!' Tommy shouted, as he and Nick pulled up at the homestead in the ute.

Vinnie straightened up, swiped a frizzle of orange hair from her brow. 'What *is* it?' she called out, as Tommy and Nick lugged a box from the back of the ute.

'A television set!' Nick said.

'A *television*?' Vinnie and I cried at the same time. None of us, not even Bonnie, had ever watched a television show, and we hurried over to the veranda.

'Careful, don't drop it,' Vinnie said, as he and Nick carried the box containing the precious object onto the veranda.

'What do you think we are, drongos?' Tommy said with a laugh.

Bonnie hurried from the kitchen, wiping her hands on the apron she wore over one of the bright, swirly-patterned dresses she'd sewed herself. Gone was the faded navy shift; never seen again since the night we'd buried Mr Yates.

'Get that television wired up quickly, boys,' she said. 'I baked us a fruit pie to celebrate our first television show.'

'You knew about this, Bonnie?' I said.

'Who do you reckon paid for it?' Nick threw me a wink, the cutest smile. I shivered with goosebumps, looked away.

'Wouldn't Jane and Suzy've loved this?' I said as we all crowded into the living room, chattering as Tommy fiddled with the dials.

'Poor Jane ... poor Suzy,' Vinnie said.

'I'll never forget them,' I said, the sadness surging inside me. A towering beach wave dumping me onto the seabed, stealing my breath. 'Wherever I end up.'

Wherever I end up, and where will that be?

We couldn't stay at Seabreeze Farm forever, I knew that, but none of us had made any plans for the future. We knew nothing about the world and I reckoned we'd all be lost out there, like that day at North Beach when we couldn't even use a phone! So here we stayed, safe, enjoying each day, never giving a thought to the next one.

But I couldn't damp out the fear smouldering inside me, the worry that our nice Seabreeze Farm life might end as suddenly as our nice life on the *Star of New South Wales*. Because how did someone like me deserve to be happy?

Everyone clapped as the television picture came clear and, munching slices of Bonnie's fruit pie, we watched an outta sight show called *Skippy the Bush Kangaroo*.

Joey Joe heard Skippy's clicking *tcha, tcha, tcha* sounds and bounded inside, head cocked, rubbing together his front paws.

'Joey Joe's so brainy, he could be the *Skippy* kangaroo,' Georgie said, stroking him.

'*Skippy the Bush Kangaroo* will be his favourite television show,' Sarah said, clapping the wallaby's paws together, which Joey Joe never seemed to mind.

'Hey, Joe, move it, boy,' Tommy said, but Joey Joe, parked right up close to the set, refused to budge and we spent the whole episode peering around, and over, that wallaby.

After the show, Georgie and Sarah raced outside, tore off gum leaves, held them to their lips and tried to whistle like Sonny from the show. Everyone laughed at them hopping around with Joey Joe, trying, and failing, to leaf-whistle, then belting out the *Skippy the Bush Kangaroo* song.

Vinnie and I set the homestead table for dinner with the nice white tablecloth, proper plates and glasses we now used. Our metal bowls and mugs, that had looked like animal-food containers, we'd chucked out along with our daggy grey pinafores. And, as Vinnie called everyone in to eat, that was another thing I was glad of – no more bells clanging all day long.

We gobbled down the tasty shepherd's pie, keen to go back to the television set. But we never did get to watch more television that night, because after dinner, a white car pulled up outside the homestead.

* * *

'Who the hell is *that*?' I squinted into the veranda light as a short, thin man wearing a fancy suit and hat got out of the car.

I didn't recognise the man but there was something creepily familiar about the way he stalked across the driveway. A flurry of insects scrambled down my arms.

'That's weird,' Vinnie said, as she kneaded the dough for tomorrow's bread. 'We never get visitors.'

Bluey bounded over to the man, wagged his tail, which he never did for strangers.

'Well g'day, Bluey,' the man said, patting the dog. 'Haven't seen you in over ten years. Look at you, an old boy now.'

'Bonnie?' I called, fingers kneading the dough faster, harder, 'there's a man outside … someone Bluey knows.'

Bonnie hurried into the kitchen, peered through the window. 'Aw strewth, it's *Norman*.'

'Shit,' I mumbled, seeing that Norman Yates did resemble his brother, only in city-type clothes. And no horse whip.

Bonnie scurried outside. 'G'day, Norman.' She smiled, opened wide her chubby arms as he reached the veranda steps. She didn't kiss or hug him, didn't invite him inside. 'What can I do for ya? As I said, all them times you phoned, Milton's not here … gone off to live in Wollongong with some floozy.'

'And you know what, Bonnie,' Norman said, 'I thought to myself, how odd that story sounds, given Milton's attachment to Seabreeze. His lifelong dream, wasn't it, to own his own farm? So I got to thinking the police might be able to help me find my brother, since you were unable to give me an address.'

Bonnie breathed harder, kept a straight face. Stayed silent.

'And incredibly,' Norman went on, 'they haven't been able to locate Milton anywhere in Wollongong.' The same bucky teeth as his brother jutted over his top lip. 'Doesn't that strike you as odd, Bonnie?'

He ruffled Bluey's ears. 'And even odder that Milton wouldn't take Bluey with him. I was under the impression that man and dog were inseparable.'

'How should I know why he didn't take Bluey?' Bonnie said with a shrug. 'Maybe his new woman's allergic to mutts?'

Bluey, hearing his name, sloped off and, to my horror, plonked himself down beneath the fig tree.

Norman folded his arms, kept his gaze on Bonnie. Nick and Tommy, who'd been fixing the leaking homestead dunny, loped out onto the veranda and stood, one on either side of Bonnie.

Gradually the rest of us joined them, all of us staring at Norman Yates. Nobody spoke. A flying fox streaked overhead, fruit bats swooped through the Moreton Bay fig. The silence stretched, settled into that woodsy, furry-animal night smell.

'Anyway, who are all these children?' Norman Yates said, gazing around at our silent circle, as if he'd only just noticed us.

'They're my sweet chooks,' Bonnie said, with a short, high-pitched laugh, gaze flickering to Bluey, still beside the grave. 'Well, not really mine. Mr Yat – Milton and I took them in, orphans from England.'

The brother's eyes widened. 'All the way from *England*? Milton did mention getting young workers for his new farm project, but I never imagined … '

'Milton got to hear of some scheme where England was sending orphans to better lives in Australia,' Bonnie said. '"To turn poor and unlucky children into upright and productive citizens of the Empire", were his words.' She smiled at her circle of supporters, flinging a meaty arm around Sarah's shoulders. 'I'm dead against the idea of me kids working, but you know Milton, bit of a stubborn old mule when he got – gets – an idea into his head.' Bonnie flicked a wrist as if Mr Yates' tempers were nothing more than a kid's tantrums.

'Bonnie's told you everything she knows,' Tommy said.

'Yeah,' Nick said, 'sorry we can't help you.

We all nodded and, in that instant, I was thankful we'd kept the shooting a secret. Norman Yates was so unnerving that the younger ones could easily have given away the game.

Norman shook his head. 'I must say all this sounds most strange. Why would my brother not contact me?'

'And I'm right sorry we can't help ya with that, Norman,' Bonnie said.

He stared at Bonnie for a long moment, gave a deep sigh and turned around to leave. Vinnie and I exchanged a relieved glance.

But he didn't leave. He strode over to Bluey, still sitting beneath the fig tree. He patted the dog again, scratched his head.

'Surely the grass has grown back?' Vinnie whispered. 'All this rain … '

'Shut up, he'll hear us.'

The blood thundering in my ears, legs trembling, I gnawed at my nails, gaze fixed on man and dog.

Bluey looked up at Norman, sniffed his master's brother, let out a small whine.

Bonnie's shoulders bent over in the slightest hunch, but she held her head high, her gaze steady, firm.

The dog fell quiet.

And only when Norman Yates strode back to his white car and drove off without a word, or a backward glance, did we breathe again.

Bonnie grinned. 'Right, who's on for a hot choccy before bed?'

38

Annie Rivers
London East End
May 1968

Through the mist, the splintery spring rain needles jabbing her arms, Annie Rivers reads the sign on the fancy-looking mansion. 'Easthaven Home for Girls.' She peers through the gate set into the stone wall, to a driveway lined with neat shrubs and flowers.

Yes, this must be it, the place her sister, Edna said the child-care officer took Charly and Lucy. Over six years ago now but to Annie it's a lifetime ago.

Looks like a decent sort of place, Annie thinks, even if them high stone walls do make it look like the prison they'd let her out of, only yesterday. Finally, after six long years of trying to tell them she was innocent of manslaughter, they'd believed her.

A blade slices into her heart as she thinks about the years she's missed out on and she hopes the Easthaven people have been taking good care of her girls.

But I'm here now, and can't wait to see them, can't wait another second!

Yesterday, the moment they'd set her free, Annie went straight to Edna's, hoping to find her girls there. But when they weren't, she wasn't too surprised, what with her sister and those kids all cramped in that tiny flat. And a husband who'd up and left with some young slip of a thing, leaving poor Edna with nothing to live on.

Annie tries to push open the gate. Locked. Her fingers hover over a button. She presses it.

No answer, but a woman appears, holding an umbrella, and walks down the driveway towards Annie. The rain comes down heavier, stabbing at Annie's face, her neck.

'Can I help you?' the woman asks. She doesn't unlock the gate, doesn't invite Annie in out of the rain.

'I hope so, I'm Annie Rivers, and I've come for me girls, Lucy and Charly Rivers … I was told you had 'em here?'

The woman frowns. 'I'm Mrs Mersey, resident house mother here at Easthaven. Who did you say you're looking for?'

'Lucy, she'd be sixteen this past January, and me little one, Charly, eleven. Sadly their father died and I … I couldn't look after 'em at the time. But I'm here now and I'd like me girls back please.' Annie wipes a sleeve across her face but the rain wets it again, as quickly.

Mrs Mersey frowns. 'Oh yes I remember now, back when Miss Sutherland – rest her old soul – was house mother. Annie Rivers, locked up for the manslaughter of her own husband, *tut, tut* dreadful thing. Poor Charlotte and Lucille Rivers, losing both their dad and mum all in the one day.'

'I'll have you know that was one big misunderstandin',' Annie says, her face burning with that familiar shame. 'I never killed me own husband, not even by accident. And they acquitted me, so if you'll be kind enough to get me girls, I'd like to take them with me.'

'They're not here,' Mrs Mersey says, holding the umbrella lower, gripping the handle tighter.

Tyres hiss as a car passes on the wet road. A thread of panic coils from deep inside Annie. 'Where are they then?

'For a start, once an Easthaven girl turns sixteen, she's out on her own, so your Lucille wouldn't be here anyway, even if she hadn't, very sadly, passed away.'

In that second, as the woman pronounces those words – the terrible thing you can never change – Annie's heart stops beating. 'Passed away, like you mean … no, surely not … *dead*?'

A wave of ice freezes her body, sends it numb so that, at the same time, she can't feel a thing but every part of her aches. She clutches the gate to stop herself collapsing onto the ground. 'B-but h-how … what happened? She was j-just a y-young girl, healthy! Where'd they bury her, my Lucy?'

'If I recall, it was a nasty bout of 'flu what took her,' Mrs Mersey says, 'very sad, as I said, but I'm afraid I have no idea where she's buried.'

'No idea? But it must be written down somewhere? I gotta know where my girl is laid to rest!'

Mrs Mersey shakes her head. 'I'm sorry, I don't have any information.'

'And what about Charly, she must still be here?' Annie takes a deep breath. 'Oh God, don't tell me she's dead too?'

'To my knowledge, your youngest daughter is still alive,' Mrs Mersey says. 'But with so many poor and orphaned girls out there, needing homes, new families, you can't expect her to still be here after *six* years? No, she was adopted by a family, up north somewhere.'

Annie's hand keeps slipping off the gate. '*Adopted*? *Where* up north?' She runs her tongue over her lips, glad of the cool moistening rain.

'Once again, I'm proper sorry, Mrs Rivers, but it's against the rules to give out adoption information.'

Annie swallows hard, afraid she might throw up through the gate, all over Mrs Mersey's shiny shoes, which is really what she wants to do.

'But there's gotta be a record of where Charly went … what family adopted her?'

Mrs Mersey shakes her head again, looks away, down the rain-slick street, clearly anxious to be rid of Annie. 'That information is confidential. Now, Mrs Rivers, while I'm very sorry for your loss … losses, I'm a busy woman with sixteen girls to take care of.'

'You can't send me off like that,' Annie says. 'I got rights, I never gave up my Charly for adoption, and I want her back!'

'I really must get back to the house, the girls need me,' Mrs Mersey says. 'Sorry I can't help you but my advice is go home, out of this rain, make yerself a strong cup of tea and forget about your youngest. She's gone to a good family, is having a better life.' She turns, hurries back along that perfect driveway.

'Come back!' Annie shouts, against the noise of the rain. 'How dare you …?'

But Mrs Mersey has disappeared into the posh mansion and now Annie does let go of the gate. She crumples to the wet pavement. She doesn't feel the rain pelting her curled up body, doesn't feel wet, sad, or angry.

She feels nothing.

39

Lucy Rivers
Southern Highlands, New South Wales
May 1968

The morning after Norman Yates' visit, a car sped down the track kicking up so much dust we could barely see it was a cop car.

Vinnie and I were collecting eggs in the chook-house. Surrounded by soft clucks and the grunts of the only pig left at Seabreeze, we'd been chatting easily, convinced we were safe when Mr Yates' brother had driven off last night. But now the fear and worry swallowed us again as two cops – one tall and rakey, the other short – got out of their car and stalked towards the veranda.

'Better go and see whatever *they* want,' I said, as Vinnie and I hurried up to the homestead, carrying our baskets of eggs.

I tried to ignore the pit in my gut; tried not to think our luck might be blowing away like dandelion seeds on a breeze. That our cool Seabreeze life with Bonnie might be ending.

'Mrs Yates … Mrs Milton Yates?' Rakey Cop asked as Bonnie, who'd been cooking a rabbit stew, came out onto the veranda, wiping her hands on her apron.

'That's me, officers, can I help you with something?' Bonnie patted Joey Joe, sitting on his haunches beside her like a furry sentry.

'A short time ago we had a phone call from a Mr Norman Yates,' Short Cop said. 'Who's worried about his brother, told us he's had no news from him in over three months.'

'That's correct, officer,' Bonnie said. 'I was only sorry I couldn't help Norman with any information about Milton. As I told him when he turned up here last night, me husband up and left me for some floozy down Wollongong way.' Bonnie spoke as if her husband had truly offended her. 'And I'm betting that floozy's a lot younger, thinner and prettier than yours truly,' she said, jabbing a finger at her chest.

My fear deepened as the cops' gazes roamed across all of us clustered on the veranda. Eyeing us as if we were guilty of something, their stares trying to prise from us what that might be.

'Mr Norman Yates holds down a responsible job,' Short Cop said. 'Not a man to worry over nothing.'

'And it *is* strange that we haven't been able to locate your husband in Wollongong,' Rakey Copper said, 'don't you think, Mrs Yates?'

Bonnie gave him a firm nod. 'Yep, real strange.'

Rakey Cop pointed to Mr Yates' ute. 'Your husband didn't take his vehicle when he left?'

Bonnie's face flushed pink for a second, before she recovered from the one question for which she'd not prepared an answer. 'Oh that old thing.' She flicked a wrist as if the ute wasn't worth mentioning. 'I think it's kaput. Anyway the floozy came and got him in her own car … saw her with me very own eyes.'

'What kind of car was that, Mrs Yates? What did the woman look like? Did you know her?'

'It was a blue car. And I told youse, she looked like a floozy,' Bonnie said. 'And nope, never laid eyes on her in me life. Prob'ly some woman he met of a Saturday, when he went down Wollongong way to sell produce, get supplies.' She took a breath. 'And now I know that *supplies* wasn't the only thing he was getting down there.' She shook her head, put on her most miffed face.

I quashed a smile, proud of Bonnie's quick thinking, her steady voice. Maybe she wasn't so dim, perhaps it had been *him* making her act like a kangaroo short of a paddock?

'And you're certain you saw him leave Seabreeze Farm with this … this woman?' Short Cop said.

'I'm not blind or stupid, officer,' Bonnie said. 'I know what I saw.'

'Did he take anything with him? Belongings, a suitcase?'

Bonnie nodded. 'Yeah, took a bunch of his clothes, in a suitcase. That's how I knew he was up and leaving me. But he never said a word, just left, like that.'

'Right, well then, it seems Mr Yates has vanished into thin air,' Rakey Cop said as they strutted, in true cop style, back to their car. 'But if we hear anything, we'll let you know.'

'And vice versa, officers,' Bonnie said, with a solemn nod.

We let out sighs of relief but, as the rakey one opened the driver's door, he turned back to Bonnie, squinted into the sun's glare. He frowned, as if concentrating on the farm noises – the cluck of chooks, the clank of a milk pail in the dairy, a lizard scuttling through dead leaves, out of sight of a currawong.

'Oh, just one last thing, Mrs Yates. Norman also found it odd that his brother left without his beloved dog … told us they were never separated?'

As if he'd known they were talking about him, Bluey stalked out of the homestead, let out a low growl.

'It's alright, boy,' Tommy said, he and Nick stroking the dog.

My legs quivered. I silently prayed Bluey wouldn't go near that grave, and howl or whine, but Tommy and Nick held him close, patted his flank, whispered reassuring words into his ear.

'Well, as I told Norman,' Bonnie said, 'his new woman's prob'ly allergic to dogs.'

We all held our breath, hoping those cops would get back in their car, piss off and leave us alone.

But they didn't.

* * *

'Well, since you have no idea of your husband's whereabouts, Mrs Yates,' Rakey Cop said, as they strode back to the veranda, 'you won't mind if we have a poke around the place, will you?'

I shot a terrified glance at Vinnie as Bluey escaped the boys' grip.

'Come here, Bluey-boy,' Tommy said, clicking his fingers, but Bluey trotted over to the Moreton Bay fig tree, lay down beside Mr Yates' grave, and rested his head on his outstretched paws.

'That's what Norman Yates said, didn't he?' Rakey Copper said to his mate. 'That the dog was acting weird, whining in a spot beneath a fig tree?'

As if Bluey had heard him, he let out another whine. Then, to our horror, that mutt lowered his head and started digging. I clutched Vinnie, afraid I'd faint on the spot. Bonnie sank into an armchair, shaking all over. Tommy and Nick tried to pull the dog away, to stop him digging, but there was no way.

Hands on hips, the cops stared and frowned at the earth where Bluey was digging. Overhead, a crow cawed its ugly, '*Ah-ah-ah,*' as they bent down, felt the soil, parted the newly-grown grass. They mumbled to each other. Looked back at Bonnie; at all of us.

'Well, since your husband left with another woman,' Rakey Cop said, 'you won't mind getting me a shovel, Mrs Yates? Won't mind if we have a dig around with your husband's dog?'

Bonnie remained silent.

'Something wrong, Mrs Yates?' Rakey Cop called out to her. 'Don't tell me this farm doesn't have a shovel?'

'I got no idea where me husband kept his tools,' Bonnie said, voice trembly.

'Should we look around these sheds, find a shovel ourselves?' Short Cop said.

Like us, Bonnie must've seen that everything was quickly sliding out of control. She nodded at Tommy. 'Get them a shovel, Tommy.'

And after that it took those cops less than half an hour to dig up Mr Yates' remains. And his horse whip.

'It was m-my … all my f-fault,' Bonnie stammered, before the cops said a word; when they just stood, staring down at the sheet-wrapped body. 'My kids had nothing to do with it.'

'Mr Yates was a monster,' I said. 'He beat Bonnie, beat us all, for nothing! He blindfolded me and … '

My voice trailed off, humiliated and embarrassed, like it had been my fault. I couldn't tell them about him pissing in my face.

'It was self-defence,' Nick said. 'After he hurt Lucy real bad.'

'Nothing but an evil brute,' Vinnie said.

'Yeah, he would've killed us, killed Bonnie, if … ' Oh what was the point? It was obvious the cops were ignoring us.

'None of you make the slightest move,' Rakey Cop warned, the short one staying beside the body, as if we might try to hide it, while he hurried to the car and spoke into the radio.

Within fifteen minutes, Seabreeze Farm was swarming with cops and cars.

'What'll happen to me sweet chooks?' Bonnie said, voice heavy, shaky, as they handcuffed her. 'They need me, their mum … can't stay here on their lonesome.'

'Don't you worry, Mrs Yates,' Rakey Cop said, looking me, Vinnie, Tommy and Nick up and down with a smirk. 'Several of them look quite old enough to be on their own. Besides, someone from Child Welfare will be out as soon as possible, and they'll find another home for them.'

And before we had a chance to say goodbye to our beloved Bonnie, to give her a good-luck hug and kiss, they stuffed her into the police car and sped away from Seabreeze.

40

Lucy Rivers
Southern Highlands, New South Wales
May 1968

Two days after the police took Bonnie away, a Child Welfare woman arrived and gathered us all on the veranda. She told us Seabreeze Farm would be sold.

'A buyer has already expressed interest,' she said. 'He's coming for a look around this afternoon. So within the week, those of you aged sixteen and over will be placed in employment on properties around New South Wales.'

The following day, the younger ones, including Georgie and Sarah who'd become brother and sister to us, were shipped off, we had no idea where. The rest of us awaited our fate like sheep lined up outside the slaughterhouse.

'I can't sit here and wait for them to send me to some awful cattle station, like where Fiona Mulligan went,' I said to Vinnie the next morning. 'I reckon we split from Seabreeze right now, unless we want to end up slaves again. We'll hitch-hike down to Wollongong, we've done it before. Bonnie's taught us stuff so we'll get a job – cooking, cleaning, or sewing in a factory or something. And we'll find a place to live.'

'Wollongong?' Vinnie said. 'I thought you didn't want to find Charly?'

'I *don't*.' I tried to keep the bite from my voice. But, as always when Vinnie mentioned Charly, she grated at a raw nerve.

How can you forgive someone for wrecking your life, even if she is your sister? Even if, deep inside, you do still love her?

It was hard to cast out my thoughts of Charly, and maybe I would try to find her once I got set up in Wollongong, but right now I had other problems.

'We should go to Wollongong because it's the only place we know, sort of,' I said, 'and it's a big enough town to find a job.' I grabbed my friend's arm. 'Come *on*, Vinnie, let's go now, this afternoon? You heard that woman say they'll send us away *within the week*, so let's bug out before they get the chance?'

Vinnie's green eyes glimmered with tears, and she shook her head. 'There's been some news since the new owner came yesterday. Tommy and I, and Nick, are staying here, at Seabreeze, and so can you, if you want.'

I frowned. 'Staying *here*? But why, *how*?'

'Well, and this is the good news … part of the good news.' Despite her tears, Vinnie's face lit up, like I hadn't seen since we were ten years old, mucking about in the flats' courtyard. 'I'm pretty sure Tommy and me are having a baby,' she said, patting her belly.

'A *baby*, shit, no!'

'Tommy's over the moon, me too. Oh Lucy, we're going to have a real family of our own.'

I scowled. 'You're too young to have a kid.'

'I'm sixteen, Tommy too. And his mum had him at seventeen and my mum was eighteen when she had my oldest brother.'

I glared at her. 'So, what's having a baby got to do with staying at Seabreeze?'

'Tommy and Nick spoke to the new owner yesterday, told him how they do all the farm jobs, repairs and everything … and how you and me know all about chooks and veggie gardens, cooking, sewing and stuff. So the bloke, real friendly he was, agreed to keep the boys on as caretakers.' She clapped her hands together. 'And he'll give us jobs too, we'd get paid a real wage. Think of that, a proper job!' She pressed her hands into prayer position. 'Please say you'll stay with us, Lucy?'

I glanced away, across the farm, and the dense scrubland

stretching right to the horizon. 'I can't stay … too many fucked-up memories. And what if everything that new owner promised is a lie? Have you forgotten that adults are liars, especially men? What if the Welfare *do* send you away, separate you and Tommy? You can't take that risk. I'm telling you, we gotta piss off right now.'

Vinnie clamped her hands on her hips. 'Well Tommy and me and Nick are taking that risk, and you should start trusting people. You can't go around angry and bitter your whole life.'

'When people show me I can trust them, then maybe I will,' I snapped, blinking back tears.

'Aw, that's a pity, 'cos Nick really digs you, Lucy. He'll be cut up you're leaving. I told him I was sure you'd agree to stay, in the end.'

'Why would I stay here for Nick Hurley? I don't dig him, and anyway, boys only want girls for one thing … that stupid thing they call shagging. No way, there's not a single reason I should stay at Seabreeze.'

'Not even *me*?' Vinnie said, touching her fingertips to my arm. 'We've always done everything together, since we were five years old, haven't we? You can't split on me now, Lucy Rivers.' She took a quick breath, pressed her fingernails against my skin. 'What if you don't find a job or somewhere to live? Please stay with us … I'm sure it'll work out.'

I shook my head. 'It's too risky, and if you've got any sense, you – and Tommy, Nick even! – will get the hell out of here too.'

Vinnie threw her arms in the air. 'Oh God, do what you want, you always do anyway, you … you stupid, angry idiot!'

'*You're* the idiot.'

Pulse thudding, sadness, anger and frustration heaving my heart in my chest, I stomped off to the sleeping shed, shoved my few possessions into the rainbow-coloured bag Bonnie had crocheted for me.

Vinnie stood in the shed doorway, tears streaming down her cheeks as I brushed my hair, fast growing out from the bowl-cut

Mr Yates had forced on us. I gathered the dark curls up in a ponytail, slipped the left-over money Bonnie had given me for our last shopping trip into the pocket of my funky red and white checked dress. No way was I going out into the real world looking like some poor, orphan dag.

'So you reckon that *is* Charly's towel … that it *was* her at North Beach that day?' Vinnie said, as I shoved the dolphin-pattern beach towel into my bag.

I shrugged. 'Might be, might not be. But I need a towel, and this one will do fine.'

'You'll at least phone me, when you find a place to live?' Vinnie said.

'Why, Vinnie? I'm only a stupid, angry idiot.'

I pushed past her, hurried up the pathway.

'Well I hope that Yellow Brick Road takes you to your Emerald City, *Dorothy*,' Vinnie shouted after me as I set off down that dirt track without a backward glance at my friend or Seabreeze Farm.

* * *

My heart heavy after my argument with my best friend, but light with the thought of, finally, leaving Seabreeze, I trudged down that pot-holed track towards the main road.

Vinnie Armstrong had been by my side forever. And now she wasn't. For the first time in my life I was on my own. A thought that, now I'd left Seabreeze, terrified me.

Was Vinnie's plan to stay really too risky? Might they get shipped off to some awful cattle station, slaves once again? Or did I only want her to come with me because I'd be so lonely without her, in that strange, outside world?

For all Seabreeze Farm's misery, apart from our last few months alone with Bonnie, there were some things I would miss: those tall gum trees with their weirdly-shaped trunks and strong-smelling leaves. And how, in a fluttering breeze, the leaves looked silver, grey and green all at the same time.

I would miss hanging out with my friends in the fig-tree shade, drinking Bonnie's lemonade, munching her Anzac biscuits and lamingtons. I would miss the songs of the kookaburras, galahs and cockatoos, the willie wagtails and honeyeaters. The beautiful song of my blackbird, who I never did get to see.

I would miss watching the kangaroos drinking at the billabong at dusk, and our – bad! – singing, and dancing on the veranda. I'd even miss Raymond Redback spider, who never ended up biting a soul.

And, if I was honest, I would miss Nick Hurley; the cosiness of someone caring about you, wanting you. Even if you weren't convinced it was real.

As I reached the "Seabreeze Farm" sign at the end of the track, I patted the tree-stump letterbox. My world was turning upside down yet again. Though if I thought about it, my world had been fudged my entire life.

With my normal clothes and the weight I'd gained since we'd started eating properly, I looked almost like any other sixteen-year-old. And that made me feel normal, and walk with my head held high instead of staring down at my bulging kneecaps and the grimy, curdled skin of my bare feet.

I took a deep breath, shredded the old Mr Yates-skin. And Dorothy strode out onto the Yellow Brick Road and stuck out her thumb for a lift.

* * *

I only had to wait ten minutes before a car pulled over. A fancy black one. The driver wound down the window. He looked about twenty-something, dark hair slicked back from his forehead, a large cross dangling from a gold chain about his neck.

'Where to, pretty girl?' His smile showed off white, straight teeth.

'Wollongong?' Wary that I was, I couldn't help the glow that spread through me. Only Nick Hurley had ever called me "pretty girl".

'Cool, that's where I'm headed, jump in.' As he leaned across, opened the passenger door, I caught a glimpse of a sparkly gold watch. In those crease-ironed black trousers and very white shirt Mum would've said he was a dapper dandy.

The car was spotless, with the faint smell of that eucalyptus cleaning stuff. Nothing like Mr Yates' battered ute. I'd never been in such a posh car and I wanted to lean back, relax in the comfy seat. But, unsure about this man, I perched on the edge of it.

'What's your name?' he said, flashing me another smile. He took one hand from the steering wheel and held it out for a handshake. 'I'm Benito, but you can call me Ben.' I shook the soft, smooth skin of that hand. Nothing like my sun-bleached, rough, working hands.

'I'm Lucy.'

'Pretty name for a pretty girl.'

This Benito might be friendly, but who could tell what men were really like, behind their flashy smiles?

But no worries, if things turned bad, I'd jump out at a red traffic light. Easy. I was sure I could outrun this Benito – Ben – faster than poor Suzy Hampton had tried to outrun Mr Hates.

He pointed to the cooler of drinks on the floor beside me. 'How about you open me a Coke, Lucy? And help yourself to one.'

'Okay.' It was a mild May day, but the argument with Vinnie had left my throat dry as the bottom of cocky's cage. I opened Benito's can, passed it to him, opened another for myself, and for a few moments we drank in silence as the car purred its way down the Macquarie Pass bends.

Ben lit a cigarette, took a few puffs and passed it to me. I didn't smoke much, we'd never got the chance on the farm and I'd only smoked a few cigarettes at school, to look cool in front of those orphan-teasing town bitches. But this one smelled and tasted different from those school fags.

'So, Lucy, off to see your boyfriend in Wollongong?'

I shrugged, puffed on the cigarette, tried not to cough up my guts. 'Maybe.' Why should I tell this stranger my life story?

The scrubland whizzed by. I smoked some more, mellow, relaxed, and when Ben turned up the volume of the car radio, I sank back into that comfy seat, and we sang along together to the lyrics of 'Pretty Woman'.

I'd vowed not to say a word to anyone about my past, but I felt miserable about the fight with Vinnie, and Ben was so friendly, so easy-going that I ended up blurting out my whole sorry story.

I told him about Easthaven Home for Girls, being shipped to Australia, the slavery of Seabreeze Farm. I didn't mention the part about Mr Yates pissing on my face. Never would I tell a single soul what that barbarian had done to me. Because I kept trying to tell myself it never happened. That Mr Milton Yates had never existed.

The super-strong fag left my mouth and throat dry, and I swallowed the last of my drink. 'There's no boyfriend, I'm going to live in Wollongong,' I said. 'Get myself a job, place to live.'

'Really? Well I might be able to help you with that,' Ben said. 'I know a woman who has a free room in her pad. Nothing fancy but it'd be a good start for a girl on her own.'

'I don't have a lot of money but I'm no sponger, I'll find a job. I've got skills, training.'

'No need to worry about money,' Ben said, a thick gold bracelet flashing as he gave my thigh a friendly tap. 'My friend, Eileen – that's her name – doesn't ask much for rent money. Only that you're nice to her guests. That you give them some extra attention when they visit.'

'What guests?' I grinned, had a flash of Lucy Rivers dressed up in some black and white maid's uniform, serving tea and fluffy cakes to important people in a parlour, or wherever posh people took afternoon tea.

'Special guests,' Ben said, stubbing out the fag in the ashtray. 'Don't worry, Lucy, Eileen's a beaut bird who treats her girls well … good food, fancy clothes too, if you want.'

Wow, a place to live, food – clothes even – it all seemed too far out. Maybe it *was* too good to be true? Another trap like Mr Zachary's paradise?

'No thanks, Ben, it's cool, I'll find my own place to live.'

'I'm sure you will but it's not that easy to find lodgings,' Ben said. 'You could always stay at Eileen's for your first few nights till you find a pad? You know, take the pressure off arriving on your own, in a new place?'

My heart fluttered in my chest – the wings of a bird stuck in a hot, airless cage. In my panic, not to get sent to yet another place of slavery, I'd convinced myself I'd find a job, a place to live. But maybe Ben was right, and it wasn't that easy. Now that I was away from the safety of Seabreeze, and Vinnie, I wasn't so confident. Besides, it's not like I had a lot of choices.

Should I jump at this offer ... or take my chances on my own?

'Okay thanks, Ben ... just for a few nights till I get myself sorted.'

He flashed me another toothy smile, and that warm rush, like when Nick Hurley stared at me when he thought I wasn't watching, whizzed through my body again.

41

Charlotte Dolores Ashwood
Wollongong, New South Wales,
February 1972

'This album's *sooo* funky,' Simone said, as she put on Elton John's *Madman Across the Water*, released a year ago, in 1971. 'Thanks for the cool birthday pressie, Charlotte.'

Charlotte smirked, remembering Simone's fifteenth birthday party last Saturday, and how her stuck-up cousin, Kirsty – who Charlotte knew pretty well as she'd often come to Frangipani Drive over the years – had sneaked in a bottle of vodka.

They'd all got blitzed, thought they'd got away with it, until Kirsty had vomited pizza all over Simone's bed, and Mr and Mrs Jardine had put an end to the party.

That brought to Charlotte's mind her friend's eleventh birthday, four years ago now, and how pleased she'd been when rain had spoiled the horse-riding outing. What a bitch, but Simone's lie about the adoption, Pommie thing, had been bitchier.

They'd stayed enemies for a whole year, but in the end it had been too boring trying to find new best friends, too hard to stay mad at each other. Besides, they were only eleven back then. Just kids.

Dad had kept saying that everyone has their faults, and that she shouldn't be too harsh on Simone.

Singing along with Elton John, Simone grooved around her bedroom and Charlotte plonked their tray of afternoon snacks on her desk.

Simone and Charlotte had just started Fourth Form at school, after the hot summer holidays tanning their bodies, spying on muscly, sun-bronzed boys, and bodysurfing at North Beach. But that late February afternoon was as blistering as the past few months, and they kicked off their sweaty school shoes and socks and flopped across Simone's bed.

'Any idea what we could write for this kooky English class project?' Simone said, sticking back a corner of her *The Seekers* poster, of the band posing on some bridge in London, that had come unstuck from the wall.

'We?' Charlotte said as they listened to the 'Madman' song, sipped cordial and munched Sao biscuits slathered with butter and Vegemite. 'You want me to write *your* story as well as mine?'

'Yep, you're the brainy one.' Simone laughed, and dug her elbow into Charlotte's ribs. 'The one who's got more books in her bedroom than the entire Wollongong Library. I bet you'll be a famous author one day.'

'Who knows?' Charlotte said. 'Anyway, I've given up the idea of becoming a jockey to annoy Mum and Dad. I figured you need to start riding really young to be good enough. And since horse-riding's always been out of the question … '

Her voice straggled off as Charlotte thought about what their English class teacher, Mr Safari, had said in class that morning.

'Find an old object at home, from your parents, an older relative or friend, even at the rubbish tip. Study this object, imagine where it might have come from, then invent a story around it.'

Most of the class had groaned. But not Charlotte, who loved inventing stories, and couldn't wait to find the coolest object ever.

'I can't even think what object to use for *my* story, let alone yours,' Charlotte said, swallowing the last gulp of cordial. 'We don't have old things, you know my mother throws out all the junk. No useless, tatty things cluttering up her clean and tidy house.'

'What about under your house, behind the garage?' Simone

said, biting into another Sao. 'That part where your dad stores all those old boxes and stuff?'

'I've only been in there once in my whole life,' Charlotte said. 'Since Mum freaked out. "A red-back spider'll bite you, a funnel-web spider'll kill you".'

Staring out of Simone's bedroom window, at the mushrooms of brown smoke swelling from the Port Kembla Steelworks into that bleached-out afternoon sky, the wilting gum-tree leaves, the heat shimmering the dead grass, the frangipani flowers sagging with thirst, Charlotte thought about old objects, like the Egyptian pyramids the History class teacher had told them about. However could something be four thousand years old and still standing? Nothing in Australia was anywhere near that old.

When the teacher had showed them slides of the pyramids, a cool feather had flickered across the nape of Charlotte's neck. And a picture of Egypt bloomed in her mind – palm trees along a shoreline waving in a hot, soft breeze. Dark-skinned boys diving for coins, through turquoise-coloured water.

Such good swimmers, they are!

The boys diving for pennies, the small boats selling miniature camels. It was all so familiar, as if Charlotte really had been to Egypt. But that was impossible. The only time she'd been overseas was on the Noumea cruise with Mum and Dad.

She saw the funnels – fiery red funnels her mother had insisted were black – as the ship slipped away from those palm trees on the Egyptian shoreline. She shook her head, it was all so confusing.

'Australia's such a young country,' the teacher had said, 'so our history is modern.' He'd told them about white men massacring the poor Aborigines, then European migrants coming to jobs in Australia after World War II destroyed their own countries.

Included in these migrants were the ten-pound Poms, which they all knew about. The parents of at least five kids at school had paid only ten pounds to come to Australia, the government paying the rest.

As a cockatoo screeched outside the window, Simone's lies that had caused their huge argument, slipped into Charlotte's mind again.

I remember Mum saying she thought you were adopted because you spoke funny when we first met you ... with a Pommie accent.

And more of the same words at school, ages ago.

Are you one of those ten-pound Poms, Charlotte ... you've got a Pommie accent?

She shook her head. That girl, whoever it was, must've been talking about someone else, since Charlotte had already asked Mrs Jardine about it. And Simone's mum had said, 'Oh I don't recall saying anything like that, Charlotte.'

She glanced at the gold-plated Seiko watch Mum and Dad had got her for her birthday last month. 'I'd better get home soon or Mum'll have a fit worrying where I am.'

She dragged herself off Simone's bed, stuffed the white bubble socks into her school shoes. 'Spiders or not, I might check out that place under the house, see if I can find something old.'

Shading her eyes against the last of the sun's glare as it sank over Mount Kembla, Charlotte hurried next door to number 11, where Dad was running the mower across the front lawn, all pale and brown and screaming for water. He smiled, held up a hand.

She waved back, and as her footsteps crunched along the gravel driveway, the sound of other footsteps grinding along that same driveway chimed in her ears. Those steps didn't march in time with hers though, but were longer, slower. Then she saw the person – a man carrying a brown suitcase. She couldn't see the face, but was it Dad?

She frowned, trying to focus, to trap that image in her mind, but it slipped away as quickly as the last burst of sunlight behind the mountain.

* * *

Sweat plastering her school uniform to her back, Charlotte swiped at a cobweb, wiped a palm across her damp brow as she stepped from the small doorway at the back of Dad's garage into that cemented space under the house.

The only light came from a tiny, grime-stained window on one side, which gave onto a frangipani bush in the yard. She smiled to herself. She might've only been in here once, but the thick dust told her that Mum and her can of Mr Sheen had never set foot here in the ten years they'd lived in Frangipani Drive.

She shuffled between saggy cardboard boxes, trunks, tatty bags, her breaths shallow so as not to choke on the stifling air swarming with dust motes. It stank of mothballs too, the same ones her mother hung in the wardrobes.

… get rid of moffs … moffs … moffs …

Someone had said that, though Charlotte couldn't think of anyone who said "moff" instead of "moth".

She had no idea what object she was looking for. So far, there was nothing she wanted to touch, let alone write about, for the English class story. But she figured she'd know the right thing when she saw it.

She stumbled towards the back section, lined with shelves bowing under the weight of cardboard boxes.

On the top shelf, a box marked in Mum's neat lettering: FRANK CHILDHOOD MEMENTOS, caught her eye. She reached up to it; there *had* to be an interesting object in there.

As she lugged the box down from the shelf, onto the floor, something that had been wedged behind it shifted, tumbled into the space the box had left. Charlotte leapt out of the way as an old suitcase crashed down onto the FRANK CHILDHOOD MEMENTOS box.

She knelt down, coughing and sneezing, and blew off a thick smudge of dust.

A scrap of the name tag remained on the handle. Charlotte held it up to the square of light, squinting to read the writing. The first name had been worn – or eaten! – away but the surname clearly said "Rivers".

A person called "Rivers" had owned this suitcase. Charlotte frowned, didn't know anyone by that name; had never heard her parents talk about anyone named "Rivers".

She forced the rusted clasps, the suitcase opened. It was full of a little girl's clothes, moth-eaten, musty-smelling and a bit old-fashioned, like the brown cardboard-type case itself.

She couldn't understand why, but Charlotte's hands shook, heartbeat thumping against her chest as she picked up each item of clothing: shorts, blouses, dresses, shoes.

How small everything is. How old was the little girl who owned these things? Who was she?

There were nighties too, underwear. Charlotte's trembling fingers opened a dusty toiletries bag containing a flannel, hairbrush, toothbrush and a tube of dried-out paste.

Her mind ticked and whirred as she touched dark strands of hair snagged in the hairbrush. She pulled at threads, that tangled between her fingers.

A girl is helping her pack the lovely new clothes into her brand new suitcase.

The girl grips her hand, won't let go. Squeezing, hurting.

Stay close, Charly.

A shudder beneath her feet, engines throbbing. What's happening?

Someone whispering into her ear, lips almost touching the lobe. A voice? The wind rocking the big boat? A seabird soaring overhead?

Don't worry, Charly, only the ship sailing away.

Charly, Charly, Charly.

Who is Charly? Charly's a boy's name.

Someone tugging the girl's hand from hers.

Please don't take her … we're sisters … I have to look after her … too young to be on her own.

A chunk of hair covers her face as twists around to the girl, screams exploding her eardrums.

Gusts of wind back-pedalled Charlotte down a long, white

corridor, bare except for the closed doors along either side, and darkness at the end, filled with the girl's shrieks. She tried to stay still; to keep in the light, white part of the corridor but the wind tunnelled her backwards, into the darkness.

Charlotte breathed slowly, in and out, eyes squeezed shut, hands pressed over her ears. But the girl's screams chimed on. One continuous, clanging bell. Until the bell fell silent and she was struggling to hold on to those quietening voices, those fading images, sliding from her focus. A desert mirage, the closer she got, the further it slipped back. And then, was gone.

She waited till the dizziness passed, then continued riffling through the suitcase. She spied the corner of a scrap of paper that had slipped down one side, pulled it out. Charlotte stared at the shadowy black and white image of a photo torn in half right down the middle of a woman's face.

Despite the heavy, airless heat, she shivered as she stared at half of the woman's smiling face, her arm draped across the shoulder of a girl with dark wavy hair, same as the woman's.

What was on the torn-off part? The rest of the woman and someone else? Charlotte searched the suitcase but there was no missing half.

She flipped it over, read the writing: *Lucy 9, Annie, Char* —. And below that, *August 19* —.

The heat burned through Charlotte as if someone had flung her into a hot oven, throat so tight she had to grapple for breath. She pressed a palm against her heart; against the hole that gaped inside.

She felt sick, actually ill. And terrified. She licked her dry lips, swallowed hard. And she knew. As quick and agonising as a hammer-blow to her head, Charlotte knew these clothes, the suitcase, were hers. And the people in the photo were her mother and sister.

She knew that she, Charlotte Dolores Ashwood, was Charly.

42

Charlotte Dolores Ashwood
Wollongong, New South Wales,
February 1972

Charlotte's legs shook so violently as she lugged that brown suitcase through the garage, up the steps and into the house. Afraid she'd lose her footing and tumble headfirst back down the stairs, she gripped the rail. Why was she so terrified? It wasn't as if she'd ever fallen down stairs.

But someone had. She remembered now. Someone *had* fallen down some stairs. Right to the bottom. And died. Who *was* that? Someone from one of her books, or yet another foggy dream?

But she couldn't think about dreams right now, Charlotte needed to know if her suspicions about the brown suitcase, about everything, were true.

Pulse pumping, she dragged the case into the living room, where Mum was sitting at her Singer machine, set up on the dining-room table. She was sewing Charlotte a pair of denim shorts from the groovy fabric they'd got at the material shop. 'Is this my suitcase? I found it in that storage area behind the garage.'

Mum glanced up at Charlotte over her glasses. 'Don't be silly, obviously it's not yours, sweetie, though I haven't the slightest idea who that dreadful old thing could belong to. Besides, whatever were you doing under the house? I told you, there could be poisonous spiders in there.'

With a shaky finger, Charlotte pointed to the worn name tag. 'So you don't know anyone by the name of "Rivers"?'

'Absolutely not.' Mum's gaze snapped back to her sewing. 'And please take that grimy thing outside, Charlotte, it'll dirty the carpet.'

'And you definitely don't know anyone called "Lucy" or "Annie" or a name starting with "Char"?' Charlotte pushed the half-photo close to her mother's face. 'Look, it's written on the back. *Lucy 9, Annie, Char – August 19 —.*' She took a shaky breath. 'That's my real mother, my sister and *me*, isn't it?'

Mum shook her head, didn't look up, pressed the sewing machine pedal harder.

Zzzz, zzzzzzzzz, zzzzzzz.

Frowning in concentration, she guided the fabric beneath the needle.

Jab, jab, jab, jab.

'The suitcase *must* belong to us, if it's in our house?' Charlotte insisted. 'And since it's full of a little girl's clothes, I think it belongs to *me*.' She willed Mum to look up, to tell her the truth, but she kept her head bowed.

'Well, maybe Dad knows?' Charlotte said, as Dad came loping in, can of beer in one hand, blades of lawnmower-flicked grass stuck to his sweaty cheeks.

'What does Dad maybe know?' Her father sank into the armchair her mother kept covered with an old towel, especially for these after-yardwork rests.

'Who the people are in this photo, and whose suitcase this is?' Charlotte said. 'It belonged to someone called "Rivers". How come it's under our house? Is it mine? Am I Charly?' She inhaled sharply. 'Was Simone *really* lying, when she told me her mum thought I was adopted?'

'Oh dear, Charlotte, haven't we already been through this adoption business?' Mum said, head still bent over her sewing. 'I thought you'd forgotten about that ridiculous notion years ago?'

Zzzz, zzzzzzzzz, zzzzzzz.

Dad frowned, shook his head, didn't know what to say, but Charlotte caught the shifty, fleeting look he flicked at her mother. 'Dolly?' Dad said, dark eyebrows shooting up.

The sewing machine noise stopped. Mum snipped off the thread and the quiet that fell between them was especially silent, and still, in that west-facing living room that trapped the day's heat. Held it there all day, till it almost suffocated you, until the evening sea breeze stirred away the burning rays.

'Oh, I know!' Mum blurted out, face breaking into a smile. 'The suitcase surely belonged to the people we bought the house from. I do recall now, they left quite a bit of junk under the house.' She looked at Dad. 'The laziness of some people, you simply wouldn't credit it, would you, Frank?'

Dad said nothing. Drank his beer, face flushed a darker pink.

'So you're *sure* the suitcase isn't mine?' Charlotte said. 'That these people have nothing to do with me?'

'Oh sweetie, how could it be yours?' Mum said. 'I'd *never* have bought you such an awful thing. And why ever would I leave your clothes under the house? You know I get rid of everything once it's no longer useful.' She got up, grabbed Charlotte's hand. 'Now you really should forget this silly idea. And as for this Charly person, whoever is he? Charly's a boy's name, and we don't know anyone by the name of Charly, or Lucy or Annie for that matter, do we, Frank?' She turned to Dad, but didn't give him time to answer. 'And didn't I ask you to incinerate all that junk, Frank? All those smelly old things the previous owner left?'

Dad stayed silent.

'Well you might want to do it now please,' she said.

'No don't burn the suitcase, Dad.' Charlotte gripped the handle tighter, desperate to keep it but suddenly not as convinced it *was* hers.

Mum's face crumpled into another frown. 'But why ever not, Charlotte? We have several of our own, much nicer suitcas —'

'I'm keeping the suitcase because I'm writing a story about an old object for an English class project,' Charlotte said, holding up the torn photo again. 'And the characters will be these people: Lucy, Annie and Char-something, who I'm going to call Charly.'

Dad choked and spluttered, as if his beer had gone down the wrong way. Spittles of it spurted onto Mum's clean carpet.

Charlotte's mind swirled like the beach rock pools in a storm. A whirlpool of confusion. Could she believe Mum, that the suitcase belonged to the previous owners? Because if it didn't, if it really was hers, nothing made sense.

But Charlotte promised herself she'd find out more about this suitcase, until everything *did* make sense.

43

Ben had kept his promise four years ago, that May afternoon of 1968 when he picked me up on the roadside and brought me to Wollongong.

For a week, his friend Eileen hadn't asked me to pay for my bed, food, the roof over my head. Hard as I'd tried though, I never did find a job. My skills weren't good enough; weren't *formal* apparently.

At first I had no clue what work Eileen's girls did, but seeing those "special guests" come and go through the day, through the night, I figured it out soon enough.

Special guests, my arse. Nothing special about the boozed up young blokes who never looked you in the eye, or the pathetic fawners who looked you in the eye too much, or the wrinkly old farts with saggy bellies that swallowed up their dicks, who couldn't even see you clearly.

But by then I'd become fond of Benito's little square tabs with Superman stamped on them. Made my shitty life a bright, amazing rainbow, stopped me thinking about Milton Fucken Yates. About how I'd lost everything – my home, my mother, my sister, my childhood. How I'd ended up, at age twenty, without a single thing.

So I'd thought, why not give it a go, Lucy? Screwing Nick Hurley had been the biggest non-event ever, so why would it be any different with Eileen's punters? Shagging doesn't *mean* anything, and if men are stupid enough to throw cash at you for barely any effort, why not?

And at first, it hadn't been bad at all, after a joint, half a bottle of bourbon, and a Superman trip. Besides, I was a master at shutting off my mind; pretending I wasn't somewhere I was supposed to be; that it wasn't my body they were thumping into. I was the perfect faker, being whatever they wanted me to be, forcing a smile, a coy 'gee, thanks so much!' when one of my regulars gave me an extra few tenners that Benito never knew about, or a sparkly piece of jewellery which might've been fake, who knew?

As long as the cash kept rolling in, my belly wasn't screaming out for grub and I didn't have the worry of a safe place to sleep, I could play their game. I let their boring conversation wash over me, slip around me, only snagging me for a second when they expected an answer to a question. Or a riff of laughter at some dickhead joke.

No worries, mate, I could look like everyone else, even as I felt broken, lost inside. I became a master at pulping my feelings, at hiding my scars; the inside and the outside ones.

But the loneliness grew in me like a stubborn weed till it became a pain in my chest that took the place of my heart. The weeks passed, the months. A year. Then four years. And not even the prettiest shell on the sand, the reddest sunset, the squawk of a brightly-coloured bird, eased that loneliness.

Then, today, everything changed.

* * *

'Sorry, Lucy, you gotta leave,' Eileen said. 'Can't have preggers girls here, or their sprogs. Ain't good for business.'

I'd known, yeah, had *suspected*, at least. Four years and no accidents, then one split Frenchie and my world was, once more, turned upside down. Only this time it wasn't just mine, but also the world of the alien thing growing inside me. Like a weed from the Seabreeze veggie patch that wasn't good enough to become a flower, a plant, a vegetable; a thing that should've been ripped out and got rid of. But they'd told me it was too late, the weed had taken deep root.

At your stage, Miss *Rivers, we can no longer recommend … not safe …*

I'd hoped to hide it from Eileen – from myself! – a bit longer, till I figured out what to do, find a place to slink off to. But that Wicked Witch of Wollongong had cottoned on, and kicked me out on the spot.

I'd packed my bag, said goodbye to the girls, almost friends after four years, but not really. Not like Vinnie. Just girls who'd been lumped together for the same, sad reasons. And I'd walked out of Eileen's dump. To nowhere.

But as I trudged down the street in my limbo, cock-eyed life, the cold wind nipping at my bones, I was glad I was gone from Eileen's. Even before I could only keep down weak tea and plain toast, my stomach heaving just at the thought of Ben's acid tabs – guess I had the alien to thank for stopping me from those bad trips! – a small voice had chipped away at me: 'I hate you, Lucy, hate what you've become.'

Everything I'd promised myself I'd never accept – men bossing me around, lying, treating me worse than a stray dog.

I stopped in front of a house, stared into the window at the reflection of Lucy Rivers. Despite the small belly mound, I looked skinnier than my Seabreeze days, hair limper, greasier. A pale ghost with no face. Nothing inside.

Look at you, stupid, worthless chick, you've ended up exactly like your mother and Bonnie Yates. And all those other women who let men push them around.

That small voice had been nagging me to rack off from Eileen's long before the alien took root. But like every time I'd wanted to run from somewhere, there'd been nowhere to go.

So, go back to Vinnie … back to Seabreeze.

But how could I go back? When all I had to take with me was shame and disgust.

Vinnie had begged me not to leave, warned me it was too risky, and I'd ignored her. Shouted at her. No way could I go back, my sweet friend would know straightaway that I'd failed. Failed myself, and her. I couldn't let her know that. Couldn't bear her pitying the filthy slut I'd become.

I trudged on, gooseflesh scrambling down my arms. I stopped to rub them, put my bag on the ground. I peered into another window, hoping to see a different Lucy. But this time I didn't even catch my own reflection; I was looking in at a family seated around a table, smiling, chatting, eating dinner together.

I scurried away before they saw me, looked in the next window. Another family, another dinner table. An entire street of families but none of them mine. Life going on all around me, but without me in it.

The icy July gales blew across those old North Wollongong weatherboard houses, flimsy-looking on the outside, so sturdy on the inside, and the whispering voice of that wind was close to me:

However hard you try, Lucy Rivers, you'll always be on the outside, looking into those windows.

I'd always found the strength before, to scramble out of whatever bog I'd fallen or been pushed into, to keep moving on. But now that bog had swallowed me up. Whichever way I turned things around, I really had no choice but to hitchhike back to Seabreeze. To swallow my pride and hang my head in shame.

I looked up ahead to a telephone booth, thought back to when I'd tried to phone the Ashwoods the day of the failed beach escape. Same phone booth that dirty slag, Lucy Rivers, hadn't had the guts, the energy, to use to try and find her sister in four whole years. Well, it was a bit late now.

I had no idea what the deal was, up at Seabreeze, I'd have to phone first and check. A shaky hand opened the door, and I squeezed inside.

Fumbly fingers flipping the directory pages, panicked thoughts stumbled about my brain.

Is Vinnie still at Seabreeze, after all this time? What if she's not? What if the job with that new owner didn't work out?

Where the hell will I go then, with no money, a bun in the oven and no husband?

44

Charlotte Dolores Ashwood
Wollongong, New South Wales
Winter 1973

'Ha ha, you're dead, Charlotte,' laughed Kirsty, Simone's cousin.

Kirsty's voice was almost lost to the icy wind that swept across the graveyard, and Charlotte wasn't sure she'd heard right. 'What did you say?'

Beneath the moon hanging in that black sky dotty with stars, she, Simone, Kirsty and two of Kirsty's friends huddled in a tight circle between two rows of tombstones.

Kirsty took another swig of vodka, their second bottle of the party night, and passed it to her spotty-faced friend, Rebecca. Charlotte hoped Kirsty wasn't going to throw up and mess up this birthday, like she'd wrecked Simone's fifteenth, a year and a half ago. Right before Charlotte had found the brown suitcase, and still didn't know for sure if it belonged to her, or to the previous owner of number 11 Frangipani Drive.

'I said you're dead.' Kirsty wore the snazzy rainbow-coloured crochet jumper Simone had given her for her sixteenth birthday. She pulled out her fag packet, cupped a hand around one of the joints she'd rolled before they'd left her house to come to the cemetery. The wind kept snatching the match light and she took five goes to light the joint.

'Yeah, Charlotte looks *so* dead.' Simone giggled as she took the joint from her cousin, almost toppling sideways. She took a few puffs, passed it to Charlotte.

'Bit of a dickhead thing to say,' Charlotte said, glaring at Kirsty. She held the smoke in her lungs, the Pacific Ocean rumbling below that graveyard, shrouds of vapour clinging to the cliff tops.

As the clouds parted and the moon shone through, Charlotte glimpsed white patches of wake on those huge crags of waves rearing up, lurching forwards, swallowing the cliff's underbelly.

Tonight was Kirsty Jardine's slumber party, and Charlotte had been so excited she could barely sit still when Dad drove her and Simone up to Kirsty's house in the northern suburbs of Wollongong that chilly afternoon.

Dad had finally convinced Mum to let her go to her first ever slumber party. Simone and Kirsty and all Charlotte's other friends had already been to loads of them.

'Why won't you let me go, Mum?' Charlotte had stamped her foot like a kid, wanted to slap her mother when she'd said that Kirsty's slumber party was "an unsound idea". 'When will you let me grow up? I'm *sixteen* for God's sake, only one more year of high school and I'll be out there in the big, adult world, Mum.' She didn't hide her sarcasm.

'I'm sure it'll be fine, Dolly,' Dad had said. 'We practically know Kirsty's family, all the times over the years we've seen them next door at the Jardines.'

'But we've only actually met them once, Frank,' Mum said, 'at that barbecue, which is hardly *knowing* someone.'

'They seemed like normal, decent people,' Dad said. 'Really, Dolly, it'll be okay, you can't wrap Charlotte in cotton wool her whole life.'

'No, you can't, Mum!' Charlotte had snapped.

'Oh you two, always in cahoots against me,' Mum said, tears springing to her eyes. 'I don't stand a chance, do I?'

Charlotte had reached out, wrapped her arms around her mother's thin waist. 'Don't cry, Mum, I promise I'll be fine.'

She hated seeing her mother cry, though why she wasn't used to it, Charlotte hadn't a clue, since her mum so often broke down in tears. But just as suddenly, the tears would dry up and she'd be cackling like a kookaburra.

'Well alright, if you insist,' Mum had said. 'But I doubt I'll get a wink of sleep all night.'

Kirsty swallowed the last mouthful from the second vodka bottle as another wave crashed far below, sending up a blast of spray as if someone were flinging it up at them, over the cliff edge. 'Yep, Charlotte's dead as a dead frigging … I dunno … *dinosaur*.'

Kirsty threw an arm across her cousin's shoulder, gave Simone a silly grin.

'Are you calling Charlotte a *dinosaur*?' Simone laughed, giving her cousin a friendly punch.

Charlotte's nostrils flaring with the wind that surged down from the escarpment across the road, she tried to quash her jealousy watching Kirsty and Simone mucking about together. Tried not to wish she too had a cousin.

Ever since Charlotte had known Simone, she'd wanted a big family, like the Jardines. Being an only child was especially lonely when there were no cousins, aunties or uncles, a grandma or grandpa.

Mum had told Charlotte that her four grandparents had died young, and that neither she nor Dad had any brothers or sisters.

'You talk such bullshit, Kirsty,' Charlotte said, her voice light, as if Kirsty's drunken, stoned remarks were just silly jokes.

In fact, Kirsty Jardine irritated the crap out of Charlotte, but if she wanted to hang with Simone, she often had to put up with Kirsty, more Simone's sister than her cousin.

Besides wanting a big family, Charlotte too, had always wanted a sister. Often, though, she sensed she *did* have one, especially after finding that suitcase and the photo last year. This Lucy who she dreamed about, who whispered in her ear – words she couldn't quite catch – and who gripped her hand too tightly.

But that was a mad, impossible thought that Charlotte still couldn't bend her mind around. The chill night air, thick with sea salt, sent shivers down her spine and she folded her arms around her bent-up knees.

'Why do you keep saying Charlotte's dead?' Simone asked, taking the joint again from Kirsty.

''Cos I saw her grave when my boyfriend brought me here last week.' Kirsty blew a chain of smoke rings that the wind immediately snatched away across the gravestones – rows and rows of sleeping people who the rhythmic crash of waves had rocked to sleep, forever. 'Why else do you reckon I brought you all here?' Her giggle was loud enough to pierce the gales, the foggy darkness.

'Yeah, I was wondering why you made us walk half an hour in this freezing wind,' Rebecca said. She puffed on the joint. 'Only to end up in some spooky graveyard.'

'Yeah, bit creepy here,' Simone said, 'and we could've smoked our fags and joints and drunk the vodka in the park right across from your house instead of trudging all the way to a spooky cemetery.'

They all glanced around at the gravestones, silent with secrets buried deep in the earth, as the ocean below pounded its fury against the cliff face and the wind wheezed through the pine trees, flinging them about like flimsy dresses.

'You're all giant sooks,' Kirsty said, with a mock-pout. 'August's *always* windy. And why should a little cold wind stop us having fun? Besides I wanted to show Charlotte her own grave.' She burst into giggles again.

'Don't be a goon, Kirsty,' said the other friend, Mandy, a tall girl wearing a heavy bead necklace. 'It's just someone with the same name.'

'*Obviously*,' Charlotte said, trying to hide her annoyance, not wanting to start an argument and spoil the party. She lit a fag, blew out her own smoke rings.

'So where's this grave then?' Rebecca asked.

Kirsty pointed towards the far edge of the cemetery, where the gravestones seemed to lean backwards, as if about to topple down into those rolling waves. Killing the dead people once more. 'Come on, I'll show you,' Kirsty said, wobbling on her cork-heeled shoes as she lurched upright, 'since none of you believe me.'

Charlotte had drunk a bit of vodka, had a few puffs of the joints, but she was far less blitzed than Kirsty, and Simone, who clutched her arm as they stumbled, in the black-purple light of the Milky Way, towards the sea-torn cliff edge.

Kirsty stopped at the last row of graves, before the grassy slope fell away into the hissing coils of sea. She gathered them all in a tight knot around her, in front of a neat grave with flowers so fresh they looked like they'd been placed there that very day.

'See, told you you're dead, Charlotte,' Kirsty said triumphantly, and read aloud the gold-lettered gravestone inscription:

'*Charlotte Dolores Ashwood*
7 January 1957 – 4 February 1961
Precious daughter of Dolores and Frank.'

Everyone, except Kirsty, gasped. Charlotte's heart stopped still, the blood chilling her to the core. She was aware of nothing besides the slight shiver of those bodies close to hers.

'Oh shit!' Simone clamped a hand across her mouth. 'Even born the same *day* as you, Charlotte.'

'Far out, how creepy is that?' said Rebecca.

'It still has to be a coincidence,' said Mandy, 'since Charlotte is *obviously* alive.'

Dry-mouthed and shaky, Charlotte's mind froze, and she barely heard their comments. The sea swell rose beneath her like someone taking in quick, sharp breaths and, as the wind pushed the moon behind a cloud, and darkness shrouded the gravestone inscription, a welter of spray blinded her.

In that instant, in the ghost-filled graveyard, Charlotte's life stood still. Time stopped. The earth no longer spun.

Only her head spun, as the truth came screaming at her from the belly of a wave.

* * *

The hairs on the back of Charlotte's neck bristled, the wind sweeping through her in a circle, in and out, bringing – and taking – with it those fragments of memory that now flooded her mind like the surging sea below: how she couldn't recall a single thing from before the Frangipani Drive house, couldn't remember the pony accident, the hospital.

Only in her dreams, night *and* day dreams, could she recall those long-ago things, but they were always hazy and faraway. Things she could never catch or hold in her mind.

Then a clear picture of her sister *did* snap into her mind. Lucy, who had the same black hair as hers, same blue eyes. Lucy, who called her Charly.

Charly, Charly, Charly …

Charlotte's whole body tingled, shook. And, on that swirling gale, her nostrils flared with the stink of pickled herrings. She inhaled sharply, recoiled from the man's purple-veined nose and stubbly beard framed in wild, dark hair. The ragged, filthy fingernails as he raised a hand to her.

Another image flashed – two dark-haired girls sitting on the top step of a cold and bare landing, a woman cuddling them.

… don't you girls say nothin' … nobody must ever know what really 'appened … But if anybody does ask … say it was an accident … if they take me away, tell them to take you to Aunty Edna.

Aunty Edna. Aunty Edna's moffs. Yes, that's who said "moff" instead of "moth"! But who was this Aunty Edna?

She thought of the brown suitcase full of a little girl's clothes. *Her* clothes, not the previous owner's. She saw again the torn and faded photograph she kept in her bedside table, of Lucy, Annie and "Ch —".

Charly.

Charly's a boy's name … no it's not, I'm a girl.

Where are you, Lucy? Where did you go, my sister? Why did you leave Charly on her own?

In the blue-black night, she tried to grab all those memories, to line them up into an ordered story, but they just scrambled about her brain in a dead-end maze.

Charlotte wanted to scream, trying to understand, but her mind couldn't settle, whirled so fast as if her head might spin right off her neck and explode with all those pressing, squeezing, senseless thoughts.

* * *

Simone and Charlotte remained silent in the car the next morning as Mr Jardine drove them back down the coast road, past all the beaches and rock pools shimmering beneath the morning sun.

'Everything hunky dory girls?' Mr Jardine said, glancing up at them in his rear-vision mirror. 'You're both very quiet, wasn't the party fun?'

'Super cool,' Simone said. She was hung over, face pale and sweaty, swallowing hard trying not to throw up in her dad's new Holden. 'We're just tired, didn't sleep much.'

Didn't sleep much! Charlotte hadn't slept at all, thinking about dead Charlotte Dolores Ashwood. About Charly, Lucy and Annie Rivers. Her family.

She gazed out the window, at the coastline pine trees flashing past, still now, as the wind had belted itself out overnight.

'She died at four years old!' she mumbled to Simone.

'Maybe it *is* a coincidence?' Simone whispered back. Mr Jardine glanced back at them, frowned.

'Hell of a coincidence, exactly the same name, birthday *and* parents, as me?'

'Remember, years ago, when I said you were adopted?' Simone said. 'And you never believed me?'

'I know.' Charlotte nodded. She didn't want to talk about this with Simone, until she'd confronted her parents. And this time she would demand the truth – whatever that could be. Because right now, that truth was still upside down, inside out. No right way to it. She fidgeted with the window handle, winding it up and down, itching to be home.

Mr Jardine finally drove up the Frangipani Drive slope, parked the Holden in the driveway of number 9.

'Thanks for the lift,' Charlotte mumbled, grabbing her Indian bag. She tumbled out of the car, rushed up the gravel driveway of number 11 and flung open the front door.

Mum and Dad were sitting at the kitchen table, eating breakfast. Breathing hard, Charlotte stared at her parents, from one to the other.

'Who is Charlotte Dolores Ashwood, beloved daughter of Dolores and Frank? And what did she die of in February 1961 at age four?'

Mum's face paled to snow-white, Dad's deepened to scarlet, as he laid the *Illawarra Mercury* newspaper on the table. A fly buzzed around his plate of Vegemite toast, settled, rubbed its legs together. He didn't shoo it away. Neither of them spoke.

'Well?' Charlotte said.

Mum's Special K spoon clanged into her bowl. Milk splattered across the table, droplets flying up onto her chin. The noise sounded loud in that silence stretching like a never-ending gasp. A gasp where none of them could take a breath and get their breathing back to normal.

Normal? Charlotte didn't know what was going on, but she felt, in that instant, there was no more normal. That normal was only a fantasy in those *Famous Five* and *Secret Seven* stories she'd devoured as a kid.

'Wh-what are y-you talking about, Ch-Charlotte?' Mum stammered.

Dad looked at Mum, placed a palm on her forearm.

'I saw a grave in a cemetery near Kirsty's place. It was the grave of a four-year —'

Mum cut her off. 'A *cemetery*? Weren't you at Kirsty Jardine's for a slumber party?'

'Who cares what I was doing in the cemetery,' Charlotte snapped. 'I know you're hiding something from me, I know that old brown suitcase is mine. Where was our house before this one? Was it in the same suburb as Kirsty Jardine's, near that cemetery? I've always felt you two were keeping some big secret from me … *why* won't you tell me what's going on?'

'Oh, Frank, I need to go and lie down with a Vincent's,' Mum said, clapping a palm over her heart. 'I cannot cope with this madness.' She went to get up, swayed, grabbed the table edge. She steadied herself, sank back down onto the kitchen chair.

'*Dad?*' Charlotte shrieked, ignoring her quivering mother. 'Tell me, *please*.'

Her father gave her a small nod and patted the chair beside him, the look on his face filled with sadness, pain and something that might've been guilt.

'Sit down, Charlotte, it's time you knew. I'll tell you everything.'

45

Annie Rivers
London East End
1973

Five years now, that Annie Rivers has been living – no, not living, *surviving* – in her dark, bleak Hell. Five years of trying, with no luck, to find Charly; of living with the terrible truth that Lucy is dead and gone. Annie's insides are empty. A dried-out seashell lying on the sand without even the sound of the waves inside it.

Annie gets up from the narrow, saggy bed in her bedsit, shuffles over to the cupboard above the sink. She doesn't look in the cracked mirror, doesn't want to see the broken mind behind the drawn, sad face. She's glad that soon she'll never have to see that face again; never have to drag one foot in front of the other to get to work, and the end of a day.

She opens the cupboard, takes the jar of pills the doctor prescribed for her. 'Help you sleep, make you less anxious. Make you happy again.' Well bugger that for a game of soldiers, them pills didn't help Annie one bit.

She fills a glass with water, shuffles back to the bed and puts the glass and the jar of pills on the wooden crate that is her bedside table. From the crate, she takes the pen, the scrap of paper.

Dear Edna,

When they tell you what I've done, don't think badly of me. Just know I tried, tried really hard to carry on without them. But I can't, there's no point without my girls. Both of them lost to me forever one way or another. 'Cos with no money I'll never find them, only money can get you information like that.

This isn't any life for a mother and I only want to be with Lucy now. And once I'm gone I'll know where Lucy is. I'll be with one of my girls, at least.

And I just want to remember my little Charly how she was at five years old.

Much love from your sister, Annie.

She wants it over with now. Annie takes the jar of pills, tips what's left of them into her palm. Swallows them down with a gulp of water. She takes off her shoes, lies down, stares at the grimy, paint-peeled ceiling.

Outside, a lone dog howls. A car whooshes down the rain-slicked road.

She ignores the light tap on her door, her sister's voice.

'Annie? It's me, Edna, let me in.'

Annie doesn't answer, hopes Edna will go away and leave her alone if she doesn't open the door.

She crosses her arms over her chest, to save someone the trouble later, closes her eyes and waits for peace.

46

Charly Rivers
Wollongong, New South Wales,
August 1973

You could say this was the moment when what the doctor later called Charlotte's mother's second nervous breakdown began: a slight, almost invisible quiver of her whole body.

'What do you mean, Frank, tell her *everything*?' Mum frowned at Dad from where she was lying on the couch. 'Time she knew *what*? You do speak such rubbish sometimes.'

Dad kept motioning at Charlotte to sit in an armchair, but she stood in the kitchen-living-room doorway, arms clamped across her chest, teeth gritted.

'*No*, I don't want to sit ... time I knew *what*, Dad?'

'I can't keep up this charade forever, Dolly,' Dad said. 'I've gone along with it for eleven years now, to try and make you happy ... to keep the peace. It's time now.'

'*Charade*? Have you gone altogether bonkers, Frank?'

'Shut up, Mum,' Charlotte snapped. 'What charade? Tell me, Dad!' She stamped a foot, banged a fist so hard against the sideboard, that inside, her mother's crystal glasses shook. One fell, banged against another, setting off a dominoes game of glasses falling, cracking, shattering.

'Our daughter, Charlotte,' Dad began, sitting beside Mum on the couch, stroking her brow, 'our biological daughter *did* fall off a pony and hit her head when she'd just turned four. She *was* unconscious in hospital for a long time.' His blue eyes misted up.

'So I *am* adopt —?'

Dad held up a palm. 'Please, let me finish, then I'll answer all your questions.'

Wary of getting too close to her parents – of what she was about to hear – Charlotte didn't move, didn't glance at the mess of glass in the sideboard. Didn't even swat at the fly droning around her face.

Dad inhaled a deep breath, rubbed a hand through his hair. 'But our little Charlotte's brain had died, the doctors said, didn't they, Dolly? Our beautiful precious Charlotte was gone. You knew that deep down didn't you, Dolly?'

'Oh, oh, oh,' Mum wailed. 'Charlotte's not gone, no, Frank, she's all better … '

Charlotte's legs wobbly as jelly, she slid into the armchair opposite them. Dad's face was so twisted in pain, anguish, sadness, that a stab of pity jabbed at her chest. But she was plunging so deep into this terrible nightmare that she couldn't comfort her father. Because this really could not be true.

He patted Mum's arm. 'I knew Charlotte was gone, but your mum could never let her go, could you, Dolly?'

'Charlotte's well now, Frank … no more bump on the head.' Eyes wide, staring. Voice soft, strangled faraway. A ghost's.

'It's tragic for a father to lose a child,' Dad went on, 'but I think it's even worse for a mother, who has felt that little one growing inside her right from the beginning.'

'Charlotte's better now.'

'When I heard someone at work talking about this scheme,' Dad said, 'where England was transporting orphans for new lives in Australia —'

'Transporting orphans! Am I one … an orphan? Did I come from England?' Charlotte's words gushed out in a tangled snarl.

Dad held up a hand again. 'Please let me finish.'

Charlotte breathed deep. It was torture trying to be patient, to make sense of this craziness. She clenched her hands into fists.

'I thought if we could adopt an orphaned little girl, it would give her a better life and also help your mother with her grief,' Dad said. 'Another little girl to love might help her recover from losing Charlotte.' He squeezed Mum's hand. 'Not everyone wants to adopt a baby – nappies, night feeds, sleeplessness, toddler trouble – some want an older child. So when Miss Sutherland from Easthaven Home for Girls in London was accepting donations in exchange —'

'*Easthaven*?' Charlotte cut in. 'I've heard that name … is that where I came from … London? Where was I before? Who's my real family? Are my parents really dead?'

Dad nodded. 'I'm sorry, Charlotte, they *did* assure me only orphans were transported. As I was saying, when the Easthaven people told me they had a little girl who resembled our Charlotte – even born on the exact same day! – it was so … so uncanny. It was a sign. At first I worried I'd made the wrong decision, that it might send your mother spiralling even deeper.' He smiled down at Mum. 'Then when I saw how she reacted to you … how she loved you just like our own daughter, how she even convinced herself you *were* her real Charlotte, I believed, until now that is, I'd made the right decision.'

Mum sobbed. Great, heaving gulps. Dad stroked her arm. 'Relax, Dolly, everything's going to be alright.'

He looked back at Charlotte. 'When we lost our daughter, I couldn't bear your mum's misery. When you came to us, Dolly was happy again, and I didn't want to upset the apple cart, didn't want to destroy our lives once more. So I went along with her, never had the heart to remind her that you weren't the Charlotte she'd given birth to. All I wanted was our happy little family back.'

'You used me.' Charlotte's breath strangled in her throat, words coming out hoarse, cracked. 'You lied to me about the adoption, the brown suitcase, the photo. Everything! Every single thing is a lie. My whole life is a lie!'

'Not deliberate lies,' Dad said. 'Weeks, months, would go by and I'd never even think you were anything but ours; I'd forget you weren't actually our biological daughter. I barely ever thought about this whole charade … this pantomime I'd let happen, *willingly*.'

'Wh-what are you s-saying, Frank?' Mum stammered. 'Why are y-you s-speaking such non-nonsense?'

'The Easthaven people told me you had a sister,' Dad went on, still patting Mum's arm, 'who I'd also wanted to adopt —'

'Lucy, isn't it? What happened to her? Where is she?'

Charlotte spat the questions at him, angry flames of a fire that only burned harder, faster, the more she kindled the terrible truth from him. 'I've always known, always felt in here,' she thumped a fist against her heart, 'that I had a sister. As far back as I can remember, I *knew* it. Then, when I saw that torn photo … ' She glared at her mother. 'It was no dream, no story. I really do have a real, live sister.'

Dad nodded. 'Yes, Lucy was ten years old and, as I said, I wanted to adopt her too but presenting your mum with two girls was too risky. While I hoped you alone could help her grief, I was sure an extra girl would've backfired the whole idea.'

'Was Lucy adopted too?' Charlotte said.

He shook his head. 'Only the very young orphans like you were adopted. I believe the woman on the docks mentioned a farm.' He frowned, licked his lips. 'Yes, that's right, Seabreeze Farm, up on the Southern Highlands.'

'I want you to drive me to this Seabreeze Farm place right now.'

Mum's quivers rose to violent shakes, as if she was in the throes of some kind of fit. She screamed, tears tracking her cheeks. Her howls like those of a wild wolf.

'Good God!' Dad lurched upright, held her shuddering shoulders. 'I was afraid she might react this way when she had to face up to it, finally.'

The screams dwindled as he covered her with a blanket, raised her feet on a cushion.

'It's alright, Dolly, relax now,' Dad said, emptying a Vincent's

Powder into her cup of tea. With a shaky hand, he lifted her head and coaxed her to drink the tea.

'Just let me make sure your mother's okay, then I'll take you to Seabreeze, Charlot —'

'I'm Charly!' she screeched, her five-year-old voice echoing in her ears, right across a decade.

I'm Charly, Charly, Charly.

Dad nodded. 'I'll help you find your sister, I promise.' Sadness stretched into the lines across his face, his sagging shoulders. Well that was too bad, Charly too was drowning in misery. Sad and angry and going mental with this freak-out truth.

'And you're not Dad, and she's not Mum.' The scarlet rage, the sorrow, the pain, all swirled in the pit of her belly, surged into her throat, a spurt of bitter liquid. She almost threw up, but swallowed it down. It all hurt, so badly. Charly un-fisted her hands, flung her arms in the air. 'You're just Frank and Dolly … fake parents!'

Mum shrieked, bolted from the couch, scurried to a corner of the living room. She collapsed like a used handkerchief, crunched in a tight ball, arms tight around hunched up knees, and clawed at her face.

'I'm your mother. I am, I am, I am ...'

Red stripes criss-crossed her mother's cheeks, spots of blood oozed, and Charly remembered Mummy Dolly.

The new mother wants me to call her "Mummy". But I already have a mother, so I'll call this one "Mummy Dolly", but only in my head. She doesn't like it.

'No, Dolly, stop!' Dad gripped her hands, trying to stop her gouging out her cheeks. 'Come and lie down again … you'll be alright.'

But anyone could see that she was not alright, that she'd turned into a madwoman.

And, in that instant, Charly was too angry, shocked and stupefied to care, to help Dad – Frank – with the crazy woman, so she just watched him pick up the phone and call for help.

All she could think of was that her parents, no they were *not* her parents, that these imposters had stolen her homeland, her sister. They'd taken – no *bought* her – like some piece of furniture, to replace the broken piece, the Real Charlotte.

' … yes that's right, 11 Frangipani Drive,' Dad was saying. 'Thanks, come quickly please.'

Her mother had fallen quiet; too quiet, Charly thought, compared with the chaos of a few moments ago. She might be silent but, eyes wide, gaze fixed on the ceiling, arms clasped across her chest like a corpse, the smell of madness clung to her like poison to the oleander bush.

The room was silent, except for the tick-tock of the wall clock. Second after second, minute after minute, like a heart still beating in an almost-dead person.

As soon as the ambulance arrived, Charly stomped upstairs to her bedroom, plucked a book from the shelf – any book, she didn't bother checking the title – and sank down on her bed.

Through that haze of disbelief, the pages white fog, Charly couldn't focus on a single word, and she certainly didn't go back downstairs and wave to the fake mother as the ambulance men carted her off to hospital.

* * *

Charly had vowed never to talk to her parents again. Dad was rattling around in the kitchen, emptying broken glass into the bin by the sounds of it, and when he fell silent she couldn't resist slipping back downstairs. She had to know more. To know *everything*.

He was sitting at the kitchen table, cradling his head in his hands, a half-drunk beer in front of him and outside, a vicious wind hurled leaves across the backyard.

'I should get up to the hospital,' he said as Charly opened the fridge, poured a glass of milk, and spooned in Milo. 'See how your mother's getting on. I don't suppose you want to come?'

He only cares about how she's feeling, not me.

'She's not my mother, and I don't give a damn how she's getting on.' Charly sat in the chair furthest from Frank, crunched the Milo bits floating on top of the milk. 'Those so-called dreams all this time were just Mum's – Dolly's – lies, the voices, shadows, ghosts that always hovered around me, it all makes sense now.'

Simone's words over the years, other conversations, sped through Charly's mind like someone turning the pages of a book too fast for her to properly read the words. Like the magnetic pull to England, in the stories of those books.

'Simone was right, I *am* adopted. Those baby photos *were* the Real Charlotte, not me. And did the Noumea cruise even happen, or was that something you invented to confuse my memories with the ship from England?'

A tear slid down Frank's cheek. 'No, that was real, and I *did* drop the camera into the water, truly. I'm so sorry, Charlotte … Charly. I never imagined this … this pantomime would go on so long. I kept thinking – hoping! – Dolly would come to her senses, accept the truth. Then we could tell you where you came from, I always knew I owed it to you to explain all that.'

He heaved a sigh. 'But your mother never did come to her senses, and the years kept slipping by, and everything was fine until … ' He bowed his head again, held it like a lead ball.

'But when you brought me here as a five-year-old, I must've known I'd come from somewhere else, that I wasn't your real daughter?'

'Certainly you knew you'd sailed here on a ship from England, with your sister,' Frank said. 'But gradually, over the years – with no reminders of that other life, no *photos* – your memories faded. You forgot your English life and grew up with us a happy, smart and lovely girl who I'm very proud of.'

'I always believed I was an Australian,' she said, 'but I'm not. So what am I?'

He attempted a weak smile, blew out long and hard. 'You're as much an Aussie as we are. And I know I should've told you about the adoption before, but Dolly wouldn't hear of the word "adopted". Because for her you're *not* adopted; you *are* Charlotte.'

Charly gulped down the Milo. 'She must know I'm not the Real Charlotte?'

'Deep down she certainly knows the truth,' Frank said. 'But that truth is too awful to accept. No, it was far easier for her tortured mind to convince herself she never lost Charlotte. Her doctor told me many grieving parents have the same thoughts as Dolly, but generally only for a short time. He said her delusions were at the extreme end of the range … the intensity and how long they were going on. He said that "in delusion, there is safety". He gave a heavy sigh. 'He also spoke with a psychiatrist mate of his, who doubted that any anti-psychotic treatment would've helped her.'

'Her doctor just let you both continue this *farce*?'

Frank shook his head. 'No, but he understood I wanted to keep your mum happy.' He took a gulp of beer, gave her a weak, teary smile. 'When Dolly first saw you, when I brought you to the car at the Pyrmont docks, I don't suppose you remember how her face lit up … the sparkle in her eyes? I was surprised, and *pleased*, when she immediately believed you *were* our little Charlotte, recovered from her terrible injury.' He waved an arm. 'Or whatever other fantasy Dolly had invented to avoid the raw, horrible truth. And, since that day, she's never believed otherwise.'

'So all I am is a replacement for a dead girl?'

'No, it wasn't … it's not like that. I've never regretted adopting you for a single second. After Charlotte died, you became our reason to go on living.'

He swallowed more beer, tapped his fingers on the table. 'But what a mess I've made, when all I wanted was the best for everyone.'

'You moved here, to Frangipani Drive, to hide the lie of my adoption?' Charly said.

Frank nodded. 'All our old neighbours in the northern

suburbs knew about Charlotte's accident, that she was in hospital. But nobody here, down south, knew us. The doctor assured me you'd lose your English accent and your memories easily, as children do at the age you were, especially with so much love and care, and that you'd adapt quickly to new surroundings.'

He flung an arm in the air. 'And you *did*. I was surprised myself, at how quickly and easily you adapted. It truly was as if you'd been born to us.'

Outside, the wind blowing through the jasmine, bottlebrush and wattle bushes whispered to Charly:

You've got a Pommie accent. Are you one of those ten-pound Poms?

'I did panic a bit when you insisted on going to Kirsty Jardine's party in our old neighbourhood,' he went on. 'But I thought, what were the chances you'd go to that cemetery ... that you'd stumble across Charlotte's grave? Besides, she was already buried when I decided to adopt you. We couldn't move away from Wollongong – not with my job at the Steelworks – and I certainly couldn't unbury Charlotte and bury her somewhere further away.'

'Was it you who put the flowers on her grave?' Charly said. 'You who keeps it neat?'

Frank nodded. 'After I dropped you at Kirsty's, I laid fresh flowers. I go every couple of months, but your mother never goes. Because, for her, Charlotte has no grave because Charlotte is *alive*.'

Things from her childhood, growing up as the Australian girl, Charlotte Dolores Ashwood at number 11 Frangipani Drive, hurtled through Charly's mind. A stream of things that had been skewed but now made perfect sense.

'That's why she'd only ever let me eat food the Real Charlotte ate, when I was a kid,' Charly said. 'Why she only wanted me to wear the Real Charlotte's clothes, play with her toys, her favourite doll, Heidi? My God, I get it all now.'

Frank didn't have to say anything, Charly knew she was right.

'I'm so sorry, Charlo – Charly,' Frank said. 'I know it was

wrong to lie, but we *have* given you what you'd lost – a home, a family. Haven't we?'

Buried beneath the anger, hate and injustice, and despite Dolly's overbearing and protective mothering, she had to admit that, yes, they had been good parents. Charly's heart was ripping apart with all the love she'd built up for them, but still she couldn't forgive this monstrous deception.

She clenched the hand holding the drink so tightly that the glass shattered, chocolatey milk and glass shards spattering across the table. 'My whole life, from age five years old, has been one huge lie.'

She jumped up, jabbed a forefinger at Frank. 'You stole me from … from who I was. You stole Charly Rivers. It's like you killed her. I'll never forgive you … I hate you and I hate *her!*'

She slammed a fist onto the table, spilling more glass onto the lino. 'And if you *really* care about me, you'll drive me to this Seabreeze Farm place. I need to find Lucy right now.'

PART 3
1973 – 1988

47

Charly Rivers
Wollongong, New South Wales
August 1973

'I'm *never* going to the hospital to see *her*,' Charly said that same windblown Sunday afternoon, as Frank drove up the steep Macquarie Pass, gales swaying the car as if it were a Matchbox toy. 'Never want to see her again.'

'Well, I can't make you, but I hope one day you change your mind,' Frank said quietly. 'Anyway, when I called Wollongong Hospital, they said she was sedated, might not be up for visitors for some time.'

Charly gave him an exaggerated shrug, so he'd know she didn't care about Dolly, or him.

The thoughts still lashing her mind like the windswept trees outside, she refused to look at Frank, kept her gaze on the endless thread of eucalypts.

After Dolly had gone off in the ambulance, Frank had tried to insist Charly have a lie-down before they drove up to Seabreeze. 'I'm betting you didn't sleep much at Kirsty's,' he'd said. 'And after this shock, you must be exhausted.'

'No way!' she'd snapped, flicking the telephone directory pages, tearing a few in her rush to find the Seabreeze Farm address. 'I won't be able to lie down till I find Lucy, till I find out about Charly Rivers; about *me.*'

Seabreeze Farm wasn't listed in the directory.

'It might've closed down by now,' Frank had said.

'No, they forgot to put it in the directory,' Charly had said, knowing even as she spoke, it sounded ridiculous. 'We should still go up there, ask around … locals would've heard of the place.'

Frank had sighed, mumbled something about a wild goose chase, but Charly had insisted.

And he hadn't argued about Charly's lie-down. He'd grilled cheese, bacon and tomato on toast, with a sprinkling of Worcestershire sauce – one of her favourite snacks – and plonked a fresh glass of Milo milk on the table. And while she was eating, he'd cleaned up the mess of the other milk and shattered glass.

And now, as they drove up to the highlands, a flurry of questions chased through the maze of her mind, rounding corners, racing up another path, around another bend, only to hit dead end after dead end.

Where do I come from? How did my real parents die? Do I have any other sisters, brothers? Cousins, aunts, uncles, grandparents? Where in England was I born, where did I live?

She thought of the torn photo, a wood shard splintering her heart. 'That's my mother in the photograph in that suitcase I found under the house, isn't it? Well, half of her … and the girl is my sister, Lucy?'

Frank nodded, his face so crumpled into sad, pained lines, that once more, she felt a stab of pity for him.

A tall man is holding me like you'd hold a baby. A girl with wavy black hair, can't see her face, is tearing a photo in half, shoving it into the man's hand. Please make sure my sister gets this.

'Lucy gave you that torn photo when you took me away from her, on the docks in Sydney, didn't she? Why didn't you give it to me?' Acidy liquid filled her throat. She swallowed, took deep breaths.

Frank sighed, nodded again. 'I'm sorry I couldn't give you the photo, I thought it best … no memories.'

She thumped a fist against the dashboard. 'You're both liars, and when we get home, I'm going to Simone's place and I doubt I'll ever come back to number 11.'

'I know you're angry and upset but please, Charly, try and calm down.' His voice was still hushed, gentle, but she wanted to punch him, to hurt him as much as he'd hurt her. 'I'll do everything I can to help you find your sister … look I know it's all so hard to understa —.'

'You can say that again,' Charly said, as Frank pulled off the road, into the petrol station.

'Ask him if he's heard of Seabreeze Farm,' Charly said, as the attendant filled up the petrol tank.

As it turned out, the petrol station attendant *had* heard of Seabreeze.

'Farm for orphans up past Mittagong way … closed down about five years ago,' he shouted, over the wind. 'Bit of trouble up there, I heard on the bush telegraph. Farmer's wife shot him, Bonnie Yates her name was. Heard she got around ten years … got off lightly, self-defence or something. Husband was a bit of a brute apparently. Kicked her around, and the kids.'

Oh no, I hope he didn't kick Lucy around!

'I heard they shipped off all the orphans when the new owners turned the place into a vineyard … well-known winery now, is Hennikson's. They make a decent drop, though I'm more of a beer man, meself.'

'Someone from the Seabreeze days might still be there,' Charly said, trying to quash her disappointment, her frustration. '*Someone* might know where they sent the orphans.'

'I'm really not sure there's any point,' Frank said. 'Your sister surely won't be there now.'

'But what if she is still there?' Charly grasped at those thin dangling threads. 'Anyway, we're so close, you *have* to take me.'

Frank nodded, let a couple of big trucks pass, and pulled out again. He kept his gaze on the road ahead, knuckles white as he gripped the steering wheel. Charly's mind churned with all the information she'd grown up with, and now questioned.

'What you always said, about us not having any relatives – no grandparents, cousins, aunts, uncles – was that more lies?'

'There are no grandparents, and I'm an only child,' Frank said. 'But your mother has a sister, and two daughters a few years older than you. When Charlotte died and Dolly went … when she became not herself, every time she saw her nieces there were scenes … sad, very upsetting for all of us. Her sister, Joanie, understood Dolly was grieving deeply, but she couldn't put herself or her daughters through it anymore, so they cut contact with us.'

'Which was handy for you,' Charly said spitefully. 'Since if they'd ever met me they'd have known I wasn't the Real Charlotte … the only people who might tell everyone about your big *charade*.'

They continued driving in silence, Charly's mind still reeling.

Does Lucy remember her little sister, Charly? She's older than me … why didn't she ever come and find me? Has she even missed me the last eleven years?

Charly so hoped she'd find the answers to those questions flooding her brain like a storm-washed sea.

'The petrol attendant said the turnoff's about ten minutes out of Mittagong,' Frank said, checking his watch, 'which should be in a couple of minutes.'

Charly could hardly contain her excitement, her fear, her jangling nerves. Couldn't believe she might soon see Lucy, or at least find out about her.

'There's the turnoff!' She shot a finger at a fancy sign with a picture of grapes, a wine bottle, intertwining the painted lettering, "Hennikson Vineyard". She tried not to bounce in the seat; to bolt from the car and sprint the rest of the way.

'Please don't be too disappointed,' Frank said, 'if nobody knows about your sister.'

But it was too late. As they pulled into the driveway of a large and cosy-looking homestead with bright red eaves and veranda railings, swathes of grapevines stretching into the distance, Charly was convinced Lucy would still be here.

'Wait for me in the car,' Charly said, tumbling out into the wind. Clumps of dark hair lashed at her face as she hurdled the three steps, almost tripping over a wallaby lying on the veranda that two little orange-haired boys were patting.

Charly rang the doorbell.

Maybe Lucy will answer!

* * *

Lucy didn't open the door. If Charly's suspicions were right, that she and her sister looked alike, this tall girl with green eyes, orange hair and a freckled face wasn't a bit like them. She did look about Lucy's age though, around twenty-one.

'Hi,' Charly said. 'I'm hoping you can help me, I'm looking for my sister. She was sent here from England, eleven years ago.'

'I'm sorry,' the girl said, with a friendly smile, as a very old-looking dog with greyish-blue fur tottered out onto the veranda. 'Seabreeze was sold five years ago. The Henniksons bought the farm and turned it into a winery, as you probably saw, on the sign?'

She patted the dog, smiled at the little boys playing with the wallaby, all of them protected from the wind beneath the veranda eaves. 'Child Welfare, I think it was, sent the orphans to other places, but I don't know where. There's only me and my husband, and a friend of ours, left from the Seabreeze days. We're the caretakers here at Hennikson's.'

Charly's heart plummeted to her feet.

'My husband Tommy's studying to become a winemaker,' she said, nodding and waving at a ginger-haired guy hammering something into the ground with another guy. 'I look after this place, and our little ones.' She smiled again at her boys, cuddling the wallaby. 'Thank God it's a different place now, nothing like before. We're really happy here, the Henniksons are good people.'

'Are there any records from the Seabreeze Farm days?' Charly asked, more out of desperation than hope, 'about where the orphans were sent?'

The girl fell silent. Her lips quivered. 'Would you keep records of child slave labour … of how you abused kids? 'Cos that's what Milton Yates was running here at Seabreeze … a slave camp for his own greedy benefit.'

Charly glanced back at the car, where Frank was waiting, fingers tapping the steering wheel. And when she turned back, the girl was squinting at her. 'Who's your sister?'

'Lucy … Lucy Rivers.'

The girl's eyes sparkled like two large emeralds, and she let out a hooting laugh. 'I knew it! Charly, it's you, isn't it?'

Charly nodded. 'But who are you? How do you know me?'

The girl opened her arms, grabbed Charly in a bear hug. 'It really *is* you! Oh wow, eleven years? Are you alright? You look alright … poor Lucy, for so long she wondered what became of you —'

'You know Lucy?' A flicker of hope shot through Charly.

'She was my best friend, even before we came to Australia. But don't you remember me? Vinnie – Lavinia – Anderson … well Oakley now, since Tommy and me got hitched.'

'I don't remember much from before I arrived in Australia, flashes of things,' Charly said. 'I've only just found out that Lucy's my sister, and I really want to find her. Have you any idea, even the faintest clue, where she went?'

'When Seabreeze was sold, Lucy wanted to make the break so she hitched down to Wollongong —'

'*Wollongong*? That's where I live!' Tears smarted Charly's eyes; she couldn't believe she'd been so close to Lucy but not found her.

'She worried so much about you,' Vinnie went on, 'but didn't have a hope of finding you, at least not while we were prisoners here – 'cos that's what we were.'

Vinnie took a breath, bent down to scratch the old dog's belly. 'Ah … Lucy didn't phone your house – the Ashwoods' – in the end …?'

Vinnie's voice trailed off, though Charly sensed she'd wanted to say more.

'But how would Lucy know my address or phone number?' Charly said.

'Oh, okay … I guess not,' Vinnie said, and Charly wondered why her pale face flushed crimson.

'Lucy promised we'd keep in touch,' Vinnie went on. 'But sadly we didn't. We had a bit of a tiff the day she left. But she did phone me once, the day after she got to Wollongong, to give me her phone number and address. Then nothing. I called her back a few times, but this woman kept saying Lucy was busy, couldn't come to the phone.'

'Can you give me that phone number?'

'Sure, but it was four years ago, Lucy mightn't be there anymore,' she said, walking back into the homestead.

'I've noted our number here too,' Vinnie said, back with a scrap of paper she pressed into Charly's hand. 'And if you do find Lucy, tell her I miss her, and would love to see her … it's been too long. I guessed she wanted to be left alone, to live her new life, so I didn't bother her. Then I got busy with kids, the job, Tommy, and everything.'

'Thanks, I will,' Charly said, shoving the scrap of paper into her jeans' pocket. 'Can I call you soon, Vinnie? I've got a million questions about my life before Australia, but right now I need to get back to Wollongong to try and find Lucy.'

'Oh, I'd love that!' Vinnie said with another smile. 'And come back for a proper visit, Charly. Bye for now.'

'Bye-bye,' called the older boy, holding up the wallaby's paw in a wave.

Charly gave the little boy her biggest smile, despite her frustration at not finding Lucy. But certain she'd find her at this Wollongong address, she skipped back to the car, across the neat gravel drive where every pebble was perfectly aligned, every bordering plant perfectly pruned.

* * *

'I need to hang at your pad for a while,' Charly said, when Simone answered the door of number 9. 'Maybe for longer than *a while*.'

The wind had died down by the time she and Frank got back from Hennikson Vineyard and, as he parked in the driveway, Charly had told him she was going straight to Simone's.

'Whatever you think's best, Charly. I'll be heading up to the hospital, but later we could go to Pizza Hut or Kentucky Fried Chicken?'

'I'll eat dinner at Simone's,' Charly had said, not looking back at Frank as she hurried off.

'For sure, you can stay here,' Simone said as they tramped upstairs to her bedroom. 'Oh shit, what's wrong? Is it about that grave we saw last night?'

Was it really only last night? So much has happened since.

Charly nodded, dumped her bag on the shag pile carpet, same as in number 11, and slumped onto Simone's bed. 'I'm not Charlotte, my name's Charly.'

Simone sat beside her. 'Charly? Where've I heard that name before?'

'Probably when I first came to Frangipani Drive from England, as an adopted orphan.'

Simone frowned, freckles clumping together. 'So you *are* adopted?'

Charly nodded, and when she'd finished telling Simone the whole muddy story, Mrs Jardine tip-toed into the bedroom.

'We never knew the truth, but something wasn't right from

the beginning, Charlotte ... er, Charly,' she said, placing a tray of snacks on Simone's desk. It was obvious she'd overheard their whole conversation. 'The English accent, the fact that you didn't look like a sick girl who'd spent months in hospital. You looked too healthy.'

'That's because I was,' Charly said. 'After six weeks on a fancy ship eating awesome food and playing all day.'

Mrs Jardine patted her leg. 'Such a terrible shock for you, dear ... anyway, I'll leave you girls while I pop out to get Edward from his piano lesson. Then we'll all have something nice for dinner.'

'Thanks, Mrs Jardine.'

'But however awful it all appears,' Simone's mum said, 'remember they *have* been good parents, haven't they? They *have* given you a marvellous childhood.'

Charly nodded. 'Yeah, I know that.' She'd barely eaten or drunk all day and gulped down a glass of orange in one go. Then gobbled two Shortbread Cream biscuits.

'My whole life has been a lie built on a little girl's tragic death,' she said, brushing biscuit crumbs from the bedspread. 'What would she've grown up like if she'd lived, the Real Charlotte? What would I've grown up like, as Charly Rivers?'

'Real different than growing up as an Aussie,' Simone said. 'Wow, that is one far out story, Charlo ... er, Charly. I'll have to get used to calling you "Charly" now.'

'And since I know my sister is right here in Wollongong, I really want to find her right now. She showed Simone Vinnie's paper scrap. 'But Dad – Frank – wouldn't take me, said it was too late today, and he'd take me tomorrow. But he just wanted to rush off to the hospital, to see *her* – Dolly. Anyway, I don't want him to come with me.'

Simone glanced at her watch. 'I'll help you find your sister, but it really is too late now, and there's no more buses at this time on a Sunday.'

'We'll go tomorrow then,' Charly said. 'We'll catch the North Wollongong bus straight from school.'

* * *

'How can I help youse?' said the scabby-looking woman who answered the door of the address Vinnie had given Charly – an old weatherboard place with peeling paint, a rusted fence and a weed-choked garden. A broken armchair lay sideways amidst long brown weeds.

The woman squinted at Charly and Simone, eyed them from head to toe. Foundation filled her wrinkles like mud in bicycle ruts. She wore thick black eyeliner, mascara and bright red lipstick. Her eyelashes looked fake and, from the short denim skirt showing off veiny legs, it was obvious she was trying to look much younger than her age.

'I'm Eileen, youse two looking for work? Well sorry I don't employ schoolkids.' She smiled, showing off crooked, brown-stained teeth. 'Then again, some punters go for a girl in uniform.'

'I'm looking for my sister, Lucy Rivers,' Charly said. 'A friend told me she was living here?'

'Nope,' Eileen said, hair rollers dancing like moths around a light as she shook her head and pulled a pack of cigarettes from her pocket. 'Lucy *was* here, stayed about four years, she did.' Eileen struck match after match, trying to light it, but the breeze kept snatching away the flame.

'But she's not here now?' Charly said, anxious to get the whole story out of Eileen, who was in no hurry, flicking each failed match onto the weeds. She wanted to snatch the fag and matches from Eileen, and light the cigarette herself.

Finally, after about five goes, the fag tip fired up. Eileen leaned against the crooked doorway, blew out a stream of smoke, leaving lipstick marks around the butt. 'I had to ask Lucy to leave. About a year ago it was, when I found out she was preggers. Can't have kids here, ain't good for clients. Can't keep working either, with a kid.'

A clump of ash dropped onto the stained porch wood. 'No john likes a sloppy fanny, does he, eh?' Eileen's smile showed off yellow-stained teeth, gaps where two were missing.

'A kid? Lucy had a *baby*?' Charly said. 'Well what about this John, is he Lucy's boyfriend? Where did they go?'

Eileen let out a husky laugh, took another drag on the cigarette. 'No boyfriend, and I dunno where she went, no concern of mine.' She shrugged. 'Accidents happen, but the silly girl should'a got rid of it before it was too late.'

48

Lucy Rivers
Wollongong, New South Wales
August 1973

'Your kid's whimpering again, Lucy.' Jenny's voice. That judgy bitch.

I looked up to the doorway where Jenny stood, holding the baby, patting his back. 'You'll have to get up, he's hungry.'

She bent down to my floor mattress, tried to push the baby at me. But I didn't have the energy to hold him, let alone figure out his bottle.

'Can't you feed him?' I said. 'Just this once?'

I rolled away from Jenny and the baby, upturning the ashtray of fag butts, smearing streaks of ash across the sheet. Empty bourbon bottles clinked, the stink from a nappy flared my nostrils, made me want to throw back my head and howl with sadness like that dog, Bluey.

But I no longer had the strength to cry, so I fixed my gaze on the wall stains: Joey Joe's paw, my invisible blackbird's beak, a cocky's crest, the wall marks I'd stared at since that bitch, Eileen had kicked me out a year ago. My only comfort since these house-share people had turned nasty.

I was sorry I'd come here; should've gone back to Vinnie at Seabreeze. I'd even picked up the receiver and dialled the number, when one of Eileen's girls had tapped on the phone-booth glass.

'I heard Eileen kicked you out,' she'd said. 'I know of a room going in a share-house down the road … bunch of cool people, you'll be right there.'

Snatches of the cool people's whispers I now overheard, through the bedroom door Jenny had left open.

' … *you* ask her for rent money, I've tried … '

' … spends all … booze and pot … hopeless … '

'*You* ask her to move out.'

I'd almost forgotten Jenny was standing in the doorway, until she made that annoying *tsk tsk* tongue click. 'Just this once, that's what you say every time, Lucy … really gotta get your shit together, snap out of this downer.'

Did *get my shit together, Jenny … morning sickness put a stop to Ben's little blue pills quick smart, and what's the big deal about a joint now and again, a swig of booze? Nothing, I say. Squeaky clean, I say, compared with before.*

But snap out of this downer? Well, that was something else; a hurdle my lead-jelly legs couldn't jump.

Jenny's bare feet slapped off down the hallway. She'd left my door open, and I heard her mumbling with the others in the living room.

'Not *my* kid … she never should've had … '

' … God's sake, Lucy's twenty-one … old enough to look after … '

'The baby's not my fault,' I wanted to tell them; that I hadn't wanted him, despised him, hated myself for that. But at the same time, deep in my gut, loving him intensely. I wanted them to understand how hard it was to wake up each morning with that burden of having to care for another person. The weight of responsibility.

Sometime later, I had no idea how long, but Jenny must've come back into my bedroom because the baby's whimpers buzzed in my ear like those annoying sleeping-shed mozzies from the Seabreeze days.

'I've changed his nappy and fed him,' Jenny said, laying the baby on the mattress beside me. 'And I reckon you'd be less miserable if you got up, Lucy, if you had a shower and got into some clean clothes.'

'Maybe,' I said, though I didn't have an ounce of strength to get up, let alone have a shower. Such mountainous chores.

Jenny padded off again and I wished I could cuddle that bundle close to me, warm and dry and sleepy after his bottle. But I had no energy for this little stranger. A stranger with no place in my pitiful life.

A pitiful life where no one loved you. Nobody cared the slightest about you. Where you just hung about waiting for something but not knowing what. All you knew was that your life was aimless, sick, pointless. That the loneliness was drying out your insides.

Jenny wouldn't take care of the baby forever, she kept telling me that.

And maybe I *could* snap out of this downer if those ghosts would stop stalking – my father, Mr Zachary, Mr Yates, Ben. The cops who took my mother, and Bonnie Yates, away from me. If their pressing hands weren't pushing me this way and that, but never where I wanted to go. If their voices weren't filling every silence.

Because really I didn't want much. A simple, safe place to live, food, clothes. Peace and order. For the nightmares to end. For someone to take away this baby and care for him.

I wanted to go to the beach and dig my toes into the sand; for a clear, green wave to lift me high, far away over that vast blue horizon.

After all, hadn't I come to Wollongong for the beach? Not to find Charly, no, not that.

But after that first afternoon I climbed out of Ben's fancy car at Eileen's pad, a handful of his little blue pills nestled in my pocket, I'd been too busy or too stoned to get to North Beach more than a handful of times.

Then the baby stole my drive, my force, my soul.

49

Charly Rivers
Wollongong, New South Wales
August 1973

Eileen dropped her cigarette butt, adding to the stack on the ground, and crushed it beneath a velvet slipper. 'So you can't help me find Lucy at all?' Charly said, the panic, the frustration spiralling inside her.

Eileen shook her head as a girl appeared from the dim hallway. 'I know where Lucy went,' she said. 'Why, who wants to know?'

She squeezed past Eileen, and stood on the porch in a silky red dress and very high heels. She also wore a ton of makeup, and flashy jewellery.

'She's my sister … we were separated a long time ago,' Charly said. 'I really need to find her.'

The girl pointed down the street. 'She moved into number 49 about a year ago, with a bunch of hippy bludgers.'

'Thanks so much!' Charly cried, wanting to hug the girl, but sensing she wasn't the huggy type. She grabbed Simone's arm and they scuttled back out onto the footpath.

'Was that a *brothel*?' Simone said, as Charly hurried her away.

'How would I know?' Charly dragged Simone along the footpath.

'Pretty sure it was,' Simone said. 'You know what that means, don't you?'

'What?' Charly wished Simone would shut up, and walk faster.

'It means your sister was working there as a prostitute.'

'No, surely not!' Charly said, but she couldn't think about that right now; couldn't think about the baby either. She'd worry about all that later. All she could focus on, in that instant, was finding Lucy.

* * *

'This is it, number 49.' Charly tried to calm her speeding pulse, to stop herself bouncing up and down on the footpath, as she and Simone stood before a weatherboard house as rundown as Eileen's.

Along one side, she caught a glimpse of a washing line full of greyish-coloured nappies flapping in the wind like elephant ears. Not white, as Edward's had been, when Simone's brother was still in nappies.

An image flashed into Charly's mind: she's running, with some other girls, beneath lengths of line stretched across the street, crowded with sheets and nappies. They're giggling as they slap at the washing blowing in the breeze.

She shook her head to clear the confusion, inhaled sharply, nervous, excited and terrified all at once. She gripped Simone's arm and, since there was no doorbell, she tapped on the grimy, frosted-glass front door.

No answer. She knocked again, harder. Still no answer.

Charly's hopes plummeted. 'Don't tell me there's no one home.'

Simone pressed an ear against the door. 'There is, I can hear music, a guitar.'

A sandy-haired girl appeared from around the back of the house. She wore an Indian bead necklace over a crochet top, and a long flowery skirt that the cool winter wind swirled about her ankles.

'Hi there,' she said with a smile. 'I'm Jenny.'

'I'm looking for my sister,' Charly said. 'I was told she lives here … Lucy Rivers.'

The girl's blue eyes widened. 'Lucy? She never mentioned a *sister*. She told us she had no family, that she was an orphan. We've kept letting her off the rent money 'cos we feel sorry for her.'

'I'm Charly, Lucy's sister,' she said, briefly explaining to Jenny how they were separated eleven years ago. 'I was told she was here … is she, *really*?'

'Yes, she's here, come in.' Jenny nodded to a similar dim hallway as Eileen's. Same stained and peeling wallpaper. Same stink of stale food and rubbish, toilet and mildew, all mixed together.

They passed the kitchen doorway where, behind a beaded fly curtain, Charly glimpsed a stack of grungy plates, saucepans and mugs piled in and beside the sink. Flies buzzed around an overflowing bin.

'Have a seat in the living room,' Jenny said, pointing to a door just down from the kitchen. 'Say hi to the others, I'll go and see if I can get Lucy out of bed.'

'Out of *bed*?' Charly said. 'But it's four o'clock in the afternoon?'

'Is Charly's sister sick?' Simone said.

Jenny shook her head. 'Not sick, sad more like it. We all reckon it's the baby that brought it on. I know 'cos my mum got down like that after my sister was born.'

'Poor Lucy,' Charly said.

'That, and the misery of her life up at the farm,' Jenny said. 'She never told me the lot of it but I knew right from when she moved into the spare room – preggers with nowhere to go – that some really uncool things had happened to her at that place.'

'Oh God,' Charly whispered, as they followed Jenny into a room with faded wallpaper that might once have been pink-flowered, and the stink of washing forgotten overnight in the machine.

Three people were slouched in a saggy, rust-coloured couch,

a guy with long, sun-bleached hair strumming a guitar. Two girls sat cross-legged on the floor in front of a lopsided coffee table on which sat packs of fags, stained tea cups, an empty Scotch Finger biscuits packet, half-drunk cordial in empty Vegemite jars, an overflowing ashtray, and a bowl filled with chopped-up dope.

They were all humming along to the guitar song, which sounded like Neil Young's 'Heart of Gold', and staring at a television screen. But there was no picture, only white noise.

A girl with long dark hair, wearing a kaftan and beads, sucked on the same dolphin-shaped bong as Kirsty Jardine's. She exhaled a thick stream of smoke, adding to the already heavy layer that veiled the room. With the raggedy curtains pulled shut, it was dim too, musty and dust-smothered, as if the window was never opened.

'G'day,' the guitar-strumming guy said, as Jenny disappeared further down the hallway, hopefully to get Lucy. 'Have a seat, have a bong.'

'Sit here,' said one of the cross-legged girls with a lazy smile, patting the brown carpet beside her.

Charly shuddered at the thought of sitting on that filthy carpet. 'Thanks, but I only came to see my sister ... Lucy.'

'Oh, Lucy,' the guitar guy said, rolling his eyes.

Charly kept glancing down the hallway. No sign of Jenny or Lucy. She wanted to race to her sister – so close now! – but this wasn't her house; she couldn't go poking into every room.

After five more minutes of nothing but white television noise, Charly whispered to Simone, 'maybe Jenny got distracted, or forgot we're waiting?' These people might be friendly, but their red eyes and crooked smiles told Charly they weren't the reliable type.

'Could I go to Lucy's room myself?' she asked the circle of people staring at the television.

One of the girls pointed down the hallway where Jenny had disappeared. 'Sure, Lucy's room's last on the right.'

But as Charly reached the room, Jenny came out, shut the door behind her. 'Sorry, Lucy doesn't want to see you.'

'But I haven't seen my sister for *eleven years*,' Charly said, a pinpoint of panic deep inside her skull. 'Why doesn't she want to see me?' She took a step, pushed past Jenny.

'Well, go in if you want,' Jenny said with a shrug. 'But your sister insists she doesn't want to see you.'

As Jenny ambled back to the living room, Indian beads click-clicking, a voice came from the bedroom.

'Rack off, Charly, and don't ever come back!'

50

'**B**est if I try and talk to her on my own,' Charly said to Simone as they stood in that dank hallway outside Lucy's bedroom. 'Wait for me in the living room?'

Simone nodded and Charly tapped on the door, heard the baby whimper. 'It's me, Charly.'

'Didn't I tell you to rack off?'

The venom, the hiss of a deadly snake, in Lucy's voice shook Charly.

'But *why*? I'm your sister.' The baby's mewls grew louder.

' … haven't got a sister … took her away … September 1962.'

On the edge of Lucy's Aussie twang, Charly recognised, from the ten-pound Poms at school, traces of an English accent. The accent Charly now realised she'd completely lost.

'I've just found out about that whole terrible thing,' Charly said, 'but I'm here now and I'm coming in anyway … to see my nephew, I think that's him crying?' Charly opened the door, a gust of the same stale, musty air that filled this whole dump of a pad spiking her nostrils.

Twilight had almost given way to darkness on that cold winter night and, in the grey dimness, Charly felt around for a light switch, flicked it on. But all the light did was reveal the bleakest, grubbiest bedroom she'd ever seen.

She gazed around at the pile of adult and baby clothes littering the stained, threadbare carpet. Tried not to show her shock, to gag on the stink of dirty nappies and baby puke; had to stop her hands flying to her mouth in disgust and dismay at finding her sister living like this.

From where she lay on the stained mattress, without even a sheet, Lucy's eyes sat deep in their sockets, cheekbones sticking out like bird bones. Her greasy hair was pulled back in a rubber band, strands hanging over her face. So thin, she looked, in that baggy, faded dress. So tired, shaky and sad, that both tenderness and revulsion rushed through Charly.

She wanted to ask Lucy how she'd ended up so desperate and obviously miserable, but she remembered what Jenny had said about Lucy's bad memories making her unhappy, worse after the baby came. She recalled Vinnie's words. *Would you keep records of child slave labour … of how you used and abused kids?* And she didn't dare, not straight off.

The baby, a boy she thought, was lying on a grubby blanket on the floor, sucking his thumb, little face red from crying. Charly picked him up. 'I think someone needs a cuddle.'

'And who the fuck do you think you are marching in here, judging me?' Lucy snapped, gnawing on a thumbnail, though she hadn't the slightest bit of nail on any finger. Unlike Charly's pink, polished nails. 'You, the posh little snob in your spick-and-span school uniform? You definitely walked the Yellow Brick Road, didn't you? *You* made it to the Emerald City.'

'Emerald City?' Charly frowned, held the bawling child over one shoulder, patting his back.

'Oh never mind, put that baby down and piss off,' Lucy said. 'I can take care of him myself.'

'And don't we all wish *that* was true,' Jenny cut in, slipping into the bedroom. 'Here, give him to me,' she said, taking the wailing baby from Charly. 'I froze some Vegemite toasts for him to gnaw on … good for teething, then I'll get him to sleep, like *always*. You try and get your sister to snap out of this downer, Charly.'

'I was so excited when I found you. It's been hard tracking

you down … I thought you'd be excited too. So why *don't* you want to see me?' To hide her nerves, Charly bent down, flipped the ashtray the right way up, gathered up the butts.

She shovelled the butts into the ashtray, brushed ash from her hands, sat back on her knees, and fixed her gaze on her sister. 'Is it because of what you were doing at that old bat Eileen's place? Because you had a baby and you're not married? Well I don't care about any of that, you're still my sister. A sister was all I ever wanted and now, finally, I find out I *do* have one, and she won't even look at me! I don't get it.'

'No, you don't get anything do you, Princess Charly?' Lucy heaved herself to a sitting position, leaned against the wall, took a slug from a bottle of bourbon. She grabbed a cigarette pack from the floor, fumbled for a fag.

'Fuck.' She crumpled the empty pack, flung it aside. 'Chuck me over a new one, will you?' She pointed to a battered dressing table. Charly opened the pack, lit a cigarette and passed it to her sister.

The room fell silent. Lucy smoked. 'Look at you, look at me,' she said, waving an arm at Charly. 'We got nothing in common apart from the same parents. So just get out of my life and stay out of it. I don't want you or need you.'

'Yes, we have the same parents … parents I don't remember,' Charly said, 'and you're the only one who can tell me about them. About me, about *us*. How did we become orphans?'

Lucy tapped ash from her fag, missed the ashtray. 'We're not orphans.'

'Our parents are *alive*? Where? How?' The tension, the not knowing – like about the Real Charlotte – was freaking her out. 'Please tell me, Lucy.'

'Our father's dead, but *you* should know all about that. Our mother was alive last I heard, but that was eleven years ago, might be dead by now.'

'Is our mother Annie Rivers?' Charly said. 'I have this photo, torn down the middle … I think you left it with me when we got separated in Sydney? I'm guessing you have the other half?'

Lucy gestured towards the dressing table again. 'Top drawer. And yeah, our mother's Annie Rivers and our father was Albert-the-bully-Rivers.' Her lip curled. 'But surely you remember *him*, at least the day he died?'

'I barely remember anything of my life before Wollongong, only fragments of things that don't make sense. But why are you talking in riddles, Lucy? Why can't you tell me everything?'

Their gazes locked, Charly determined she wasn't going to look away first.

'You want me to tell you how you murdered your own father?' Lucy finally said.

'*Murder* —?'

'How you pushed him down the stairs?' Lucy took a drag, blew out a stream of smoke. 'My life wrecked, and all of it your fault.'

Charly couldn't speak, couldn't believe what her sister was saying. She must've got it wrong because all she could hear was her pulse thundering in her eardrums. 'I k-killed our f-father?' she stammered. 'But how, why? That can't be true, I was only five years old! Did you see me do it?'

'No, I was hiding in our bedroom, or the bastard would've beaten me too. It was only much later I figured out you must've pushed him. Mum guessed straightaway though, and she took the blame … went to prison for manslaughter, to protect *you*.'

'Wh-when w-was this?' Without asking Lucy's permission, Charly took a cigarette, hands trembling as she lit it. She took deep drags, trying to calm her racing pulse.

'January 1962 right after both our birthdays. Dad was pissed, as usual. Mum was out at the shops, that's why *she* couldn't have done it. He tripped over your toy on the stairs, this wind-up blackbird, and was swaying about, yelling at you for leaving your toys lying around.' She tapped ash from the fag. 'Then little Charly just gave him a shove and down he toppled like a sack of potatoes. Dead when he hit the concrete at the bottom.'

Charly frowned, tried to force her mind back eleven years.

But the only thing she'd ever recalled about her father – only now, she realised – was his stinky pickled-herring breath. There was a hazy image too now, of barrels of those pickled herrings, on a pavement somewhere.

She puffed on the cigarette, unsure whether to believe Lucy's accusation. In this state, her sister wasn't exactly trustworthy. But why would she invent such a terrible lie?

'You said our mother took the blame … went to prison to protect me?'

Lucy nodded. 'That's why they shoved us in Easthaven Hell for Girls, with those bitchy care workers, that snooty house mother, Miss Sutherland, who never gave a shit about us. Then we got conned into coming to Australia. So that's how you wrecked my life and our mother's.' She sneered. 'But not yours. No, Charly Rivers ended up with a pretty neato life.'

Truth or not, her sister's claim that she'd murdered her own father came as a violent punch to Charly's stomach.

'What can I say?' Charly asked. 'Sorry? That sounds pathetic, but I don't know what else to say. I don't even remember any of this.'

Lucy stabbed out her fag in the ashtray, her voice quiet, faraway. 'Why don't you go away and leave me alone? Enjoy your nice life and don't come here bothering me again.'

'Okay, I'll leave … for now,' Charly said, sensing she wasn't going to get any further with Lucy right now. 'But I'll be back, I'm not giving up on my sister.'

Shocked, hurt, confused, she slung her crochet bag over her shoulder and shuffled back to Simone in the living room. Nobody had moved, everyone still staring at the white-noise television, the bleach-haired guy still strumming his guitar.

Simone was squeezed on the couch between a girl and the guitar guy, sucking on a bong. She looked up at Charly, blew out a hard stream of smoke. 'How'd it go? Oh my God, you're white as a ghost.'

'Yeah, you look like shit,' one of the girls said. 'Sit down, have a bong.'

Another girl held out the dolphin bong to her. 'Here you go, this'll make you feel better.'

Charly shook her head. 'No, but thanks.'

She tugged Simone off the saggy couch. 'Let's go home.'

* * *

I killed my father. Murderer. Killer. Murderer.

Thank God Simone was stoned, staring out the bus window at the night seascape, rather than hammering Charly with questions. As the bus rumbled down Crown Street, Wollongong's main road, they both gazed out at the closed shops.

Was she a killer, or had Lucy just invented such a lie to get back at Charly because she believed she had a neato life? Was this only another in the thread of lies Charly's life had become? And how could she find out the truth? As she and Simone got off the bus and trundled up Frangipani Drive, she couldn't think straight, couldn't focus on a single thing.

'Oh I wondered where you two had got to,' Mrs Jardine said, as Simone opened the front door. 'Anyway, you're here now, just in time for dinner.' She frowned at Simone's red eyes. 'What's wrong, have you been crying?'

'I'm cool, Mum.' Simone giggled, and Charly wished she had accepted that bong; got stoned too, so she wouldn't have to think about whether she'd actually killed another human being. Or not.

'Oh, your father, Frank, called over, Charly,' Mrs Jardine said. 'He'd been up at the hosp —'

'I don't want to know anything about *her*,' Charly said. 'And I already told him I'm not going back to number 11 … if that's okay with you?'

'Of course, dear,' Mrs Jardine said. 'You know this has always been your second home, but your father's so upset, it'd be nice for him if you thought about going home sometime … and right, well, just so you know, they're keeping her – Dolly – in, giving her some medication to sort out her troubled mind.'

Her *troubled mind?*

Charly couldn't face dinner, pushed the lamb chops, mash and green beans around her plate.

Simone's dad and her brother, Edward, kept eyeing her, but didn't say anything. Charly wondered how much they knew. Everything probably. She guessed the whole neighbourhood would know it all soon enough.

Mrs Jardine kept asking if she was alright. 'Can I get you something else, dear? Toast and Vegemite?'

Charly shook her head. 'I'm fine thanks, not that hungry.'

Edward gawped at Charly's plate. 'Can I have hers then, if she's not going to eat it?'

'Sure,' Charly said, and pushed her plate towards Edward.

'He's a growing boy,' Mrs Jardine said with a smile, as Edward chowed down Charly's meal.

After dinner, in her bedroom, Simone put on The Beatles 'Blackbird' song. 'Are you going to tell me what happened with Lucy?' she said, 'or just stew and frown about it the whole night?'

Charly dropped onto the mattress Mrs Jardine had made up beside Simone's bed, and told her friend everything – about Lucy's misery, her accusation that Charly had killed their father.

'And you believe her?' Simone said. 'She's not the most reliable person, you know, so angry, so miserable.'

'I know, but how will I ever find out?'

A light knock and Mrs Jardine popped her head around the door. 'Mum!' Simone said, 'you're eavesdropping *again*?'

'I'm simply worried about your friend,' she said, handing Charly a tablet and a glass of water. 'Take this, dear, half a Valium does wonders for my nerves.'

Charly swallowed the pill as Mrs Jardine went on: 'I'm so glad you've found your sister but from what I heard it sounds like she's got the baby blues. Just between us girls, Shirley Penfold from down at number 1 suffered from the baby blues after her last one, before the doctor got her on the right pills.' She smiled, turned to leave. 'Now don't you two stay up too long,'

'Close the door, Mum,' Simone said, with a wink at Charly. 'She's such a nosey parker.'

She and Simone lay there, listening to the 'Blackbird' song, and as soon as Charly closed her eyes, her heart juddered like a lizard trapped beneath a rock. And, clear as the nightbirds' calls outside, an old slow-motion, soundless film of her father's death rolled across her mind.

He stamps his boot on her blackbird. The ball that was the bird's head spins off, rolls across the landing.

Why you broke my birdie?

Teach yer not to leave stuff lyin' around for me to trip over.

He lunges, palm flat, taut. Herring-whisky stink rushes at her in the sweep of his raised arm.

… you'll get a beltin' …

… she moves far quicker than he does.

He stumbles, a foot slipping on that little ball that was once her blackbird's head … tumbles backwards, and down he goes.

51

When the knock came on my bedroom door the next morning I knew it was Charly.

Shit, not that pest again.

I'd tried not to think about my sister during the night, awake most of it with this screamer of a baby. Yesterday I'd acted as if I hated her, but I didn't. I just cursed what had happened to me because of what she'd done. Angry that Charly's life had worked out so well, and mine so shitty.

'What do you want, now? Aren't you supposed to be at school?' I said as she barged into the room, hands clamped on her hips. 'And don't talk loud 'cos if you wake that grouch, you'll have to get him back to sleep.' I nodded at the little bundle curled up beside me, his early-morning bottle beside him, half-drunk.

'I decided to skip school today, and I did *not* push our father … didn't kill him,' she said. 'I remembered, it all came back to me. I saw him trip over my wind-up bird, well the tiny ball that was once its head. It had come away from the body, he didn't see it and tripped over it … fell backwards down the stairs.' Charly's garbled words spilled out so fast I had to concentrate to make sense of them. 'I *know* that's what happened, I'm no murderer,' she went on. 'He was drunk and he fell, you have to believe me, Lucy.'

'But the police reckoned he was pushed,' I said, 'though that bitch of a neighbour, Iris Palmer, probably gave them that idea.'

'I don't remember what the police said, but I did not push him.'

'Well our mother thought you did.' I lit the first fag of the day, swallowed a slug of bourbon. I smoked in silence, staring at Charly, that innocent face, her fancy pin-stripe flares, turtleneck jumper, trendy shag haircut.

'Our father stumbled over that bird's head, I *know* that's what happened. You have to believe me, Lucy. Do you … believe me?'

I took another drag, exhaled a stream of smoke and, slowly, I nodded, because I really did believe her. 'Shit, so Mum *did* go to prison for an accident. What a total fuck up! All this, for *nothing*.'

I stared around at my grungy room, the filthy clothes, the rubbish. And, suddenly, I was ashamed.

'Park your bum,' I said, pointing to a clean-ish corner of the mattress. 'Excuse the mess … place isn't usually like this. It's just, I had a bad night with the baby. Teething, Jenny reckons.' I offered her the pack of cigarettes.

'Bit early for me, and don't you think it's a bit early for *that*?' Charly nodded at the bourbon, glanced at her fancy watch, glossy pink and perfect fingernails flashing. I made a fist with the hand that wasn't holding the fag, to hide my gnawed stumps.

'I'm twenty-one, can do what I like. Besides, I told you yesterday, who are you to judge me?'

'I'm your sister who cares about you, and him.' Charly pointed to the sleeping baby. 'How old is he?'

The baby rolled over, and started crying before he even opened his eyes.

'Told you not to talk loud, now you've gone and woken him up!' I snapped. 'If it's not enough, having him yell half the night.'

'Poor little one, he's soaking wet,' she said, picking him up.

I snapped again, couldn't stand her hoity-toity carping. 'Well if I'm such a bad mother, put him down and get lost. Even better, take him with you.'

Charly ignored me, unpinned his nappy, frowned at his red-raw bum. 'Got any cream?' I pointed to the nappy cream on the dressing table. She smeared it on and took a nappy from the teetering pile on the floor in a corner.

'They're clean stains,' I said, seeing for the first time how badly marked and grey the nappies were. 'Washing machine's a bit busted.'

'Never mind,' Charly said, trying to fold the nappy.

I leaned over, took the nappy from her. 'You gotta make a triangle, like this. And, since you asked, though it's none of your business, the baby's seven months old, born in January, same as us.'

'Okay,' Charly said, and fastened the nappy pin. She snagged a vest and a jumpsuit from the jumble of baby clothes, reminding me I really should put his clothes in the wardrobe. Mine too. I just never had a spare moment, or the energy, for extra jobs.

Charly picked up the half-empty bottle. 'Right, where can I heat this up, Lucy?'

'Jug in the kitchen,' I said, and when she came back, bottle warming in a jug of hot water, she swept the clothes off the chair, sat down with the baby on her lap and fed him.

The crying, the trembling lips, the little waving fists, stopped like someone had switched him off.

Not only pretty and smart, efficient too! What can't *Charly do?*

Look at her. Look at me. Nobody would guess we were sisters; we might as well be two different species.

'Let's go for a walk down the beach?' she said, when he'd finished the bottle. She held the baby over her shoulder, burping him, as if she'd been doing it for years.

'A *walk*, whatever for?'

No way, can't go out.

'Because it's a nice sunny morning,' Charly said, glancing out the window at the blue sky, the trees still now the wind had finally blown out over the Pacific Ocean. 'And because the fresh air will be good for the baby, and for you. Come on, up you get, put on some clothes, find me a clean sheet for this pram.'

From a nook beside the wardrobe, Charly wheeled out the

battered pram Jenny had got me from somewhere. Anyway, I hardly ever used it, except to take the baby to the Baby Health Clinic after he was born. Before he leached all the life out of me.

'No clean sheets right now,' I said. 'I told you, machine's not working properly.'

Charly grabbed a beach towel, held it up to the window. 'This'll do for a sheet.' She didn't flatten the towel out in the pram though, just kept holding it up, staring at it. 'This towel ... the dolphin pattern ... I've seen it before.'

I looked at Charly, and the realisation crashed through my skull like thunder before a raging storm. 'It *was* your beach towel? It *was* you, that day we escaped to the beach?'

As Charly put back on the snazzy jean jacket she'd taken off when she arrived, I told her about our escape from Seabreeze, and how a girl had given us her beach towel.

'Oh wow, I *do* remember that,' Charly said, blue eyes sparkling. 'There *was* something about those girls ... they gave me goosebumps. To think I was so close to you, Lucy!'

'I know,' I said, unable to stop the shadow of a smile escaping my lips.

'What's funny?' Charly said.

I frowned. 'Funny?'

'You smiled. You look nice when you smile.'

'I was thinking that it was always me looking after you,' I said, slipping into the half-decent tartan dress Charly held out. 'Now who's looking after who? But I s'pose it's only fair that it's your turn,' I said, tucking the bourbon into the pram, at the baby's feet.

'Well if I am looking after you,' Charly said, removing the bottle, flinging it onto my bed, 'you won't be needing this for a beach walk.'

I shrugged. 'Guess not. Our mum counted on me to look after you, and I always did, which made it even worse when that man – your new father – took you away.'

Charly wheeled the pram down the hallway, and out into the morning sun. Distant, winter sun, but it still hurt my eyes.

Sullen puffs of smoke from the Port Kembla Steelworks stack pumping into the sky in the distance, we walked along the beachfront road, where blokes in souped-up panel vans were burning rubber, surfies lugging boards to and from the water. I glanced at the groovy chicks in jeans and thongs, lounging against cool-looking panel vans, wished I was one of them. But I'd never be like them, free and happy.

'You know, Mum was counting on me to look after you ... the day he died,' I said as Charly pushed the pram along the footpath and I struggled along behind, trying to keep up. She walked so fast, so *healthily*, as if she had a real purpose. 'I should've been there for you when she was out at the shops ... when Dad smashed your toy and fell down the stairs.'

As we reached Cliff Road, streaming with cars, I stared out across the harbour, and beyond to the Pacific, my insides empty and rusted as a shipwreck forgotten on the seabed.

'Because if I'd stuck up for you, Charly, none of this would've happened.'

'You can't blame yourself, you were only ten, I was only five,' Charly said as they sat down on the grass at Belmore Basin. 'Both of us, only kids. None of it was our fault.'

My sweet little sister touched her fingertips to my arm, smiled. Straight, white teeth. The way she held herself, the gloss on her, the words she used, told me how far she'd come from the bed-wetting cry-baby of Easthaven Home for Girls.

Yeah, life had turned out good for Charly, and shitty for me. But none of it was my little sister's fault. It was all down to the toss of a dice.

I smiled back at her, squeezed the hand she held out to me. I hadn't been to the beach in so long, well before the baby came, and now I hankered after that sea.

I breathed in the fresh, salty air, gazed at the carking seagulls, the little harbour waves curling onto the shore. And I welcomed it all like a long lost friend.

* * *

'We could walk over to North Beach?' I said, pointing into the distance, at the crashing breakers, the empty stretch of winter sand. 'If you can handle pushing the pram all that way?'

Charly smiled. 'Sure!'

'I was glad, in fact, when our father was gone,' I said, as we took the dusty pathway, walked past the Continental pool lap-swimmers. 'He was a drunken prick. You were too young to remember how he'd bash Mum when he was boozed. How he hit us too.'

'Oh gosh, I had no idea.' Charly gave me a sharp look, hungry for more details.

'But when the cops arrested Mum, this childcare officer sent us to her sister's place. But we only stayed a few days 'cos, like us, Aunty Edna was poor as shit and couldn't take us in. I remember her whole flat stank of mothballs ... obsessed about those "moffs" putting holes in her old clothes!'

Charly laughed. 'I *did* remember an Aunty Edna and her *moffs*, but could never figure out who she might be.'

I told her about those cold Easthaven bitches, creepy Mr Zachary and our journey on the *Star of New South Wales*.

'I do remember parts of the boat trip,' Charly said, 'especially this nice lady teaching me to read.'

I nodded. 'Hazel. Books were your way of escaping.'

'Still are,' Charly said as we walked past the Gentlemen's Baths, waves rising up, curling back down and swallowing those crumbling stone walls.

'I hope to write my own books one day, in the future. I'm going to study journalism first though, at uni, after I finish high school next year.'

I never thought about *my* future. All I could cope with was getting from one day to the next. Couldn't see any kind of future for me, only a dark, endless tunnel, the baby's screams drilling holes through my skull.

'Is our mother still in prison?' Charly asked.

I shook my head. 'No idea.' As the foamy breakers crashed down into the rockpool, tossing about the one swimmer as if he were a rowboat in a sea storm, I told Charly how I'd tried, and failed, to get a letter to Mum.

'We should try again,' Charly said. 'I so hope she's still alive.'

'She was a bonzer mum,' I said, the pram wincing and grinding along the dusty track that led to North Beach. 'Did her best for us, worked nights looking after old people ... tried to hide her wages from Dad to stop him drinking them away.'

I realised that, since leaving Seabreeze, I'd not thought about trying to get in touch with Mum. Once at Eileen's, what with Ben's Superman tabs, not to mention the *job*, I just forgot about everything else. Which was how I'd wanted it. 'But I wouldn't have a clue where to write to her. And if she *is* out of prison, Mum wouldn't be back living in our flat ... council would've given it to some other poor family.'

I couldn't admit to Charly I'd never have the strength to do anything as complicated as writing a letter.

'I'll try and think of something,' Charly said, as we reached North Beach, and she nodded towards the kiosk. 'Fancy a Paddle Pop? Chocolate's my favourite, what's yours?'

'Chocolate too,' I said.

The baby slept on, and we sat on the grass licking our chocolate ice-creams, watching the high tide come in.

'So now I've told you stuff,' I said, savouring the creamy Paddle Pop, 'why don't you tell me about your adopted family?'

'Well you were right, it *does* look like I have a neato life,' I said, 'but it was all a big lie.'

I frowned. 'A big lie?'

'I'm just a replacement for a dead girl.'

'A *dead* girl?' The baby stirred, I must've spoken too loud.

'None of my memories are real. No memories that are truly my own, anyway,' Charly said and, rocking the pram, poured out the whole adoption story.

'Since I found out the truth, it's like I've come out of these half-forgotten, half-remembered, shards of time. Splinters of things I filled with made-up memories.' She shrugged. 'Maybe it was just my mind trying to make sense of all that unknown stuff? Which is why I'm glad you're telling me everything, Lucy.'

I checked the baby. He'd dozed off again, thank God.

'I can't really know where my made-up memories end and the real ones begin. Maybe first memories are like that for everyone, but mine are more blurred, more *jagged*. And it's worse because I have no family stories to go with the memories, nothing real. All I have is a single, torn photograph.' She looked at me, teary blue eyes gleaming in that faraway wintery sunshine. 'It's as if I wasn't born at all. That I just happened.'

'You know your name really *is* Charlotte?' I said. 'Like mine's Lucille. But we were only ever called Charly and Lucy.'

'Really, how ironic. See how much I *don't* know about myself?' she said and I felt almost as sorry for my sister as I did for myself.

The baby whimpered. Charly stood up, rubbed her arms. 'We'd better get him home, it's getting chilly.'

* * *

'I'm sorry about whatever happened to you at that Seabreeze place,' Charly said as we got back to the house, and she parked the pram in the hallway. 'Even though I don't know the details. When I saw your friend, Vinnie – Lavinia – she just hinted, was it really so bad?'

I shrugged. 'Nah, was okay.'

'You're a hopeless liar,' she said, with a small smile. 'But I understand if you don't want to talk about it.'

'Nothing much to tell, really. Anyway, the baby's looking hungry so I'd better prepare another bottle.' Charly followed me into the kitchen, rattling the beaded fly curtain. She filled the kettle, put it on to boil and washed out two teacups.

'My life, a never-ending round of bottles and nappies,' I said. 'Jenny reckons I should start him on solid food, but how am I supposed to know what to do? And, before you suggest it, I'm not going back to those judgy Baby Health Clinic bitches.'

'I'd love to take my nephew to the clinic,' Charly said. 'Ask them about solids.'

'Oh? Well why not,' I said, making up the formula as Charly sat at the table with the two cups of tea.

After we'd drunk the tea, as the baby sucked contentedly, Charly washed up the pile of dirty dishes. Outside the window, in the late morning sun, I caught the scarlet flash of a parrot's wing high in a tree. A flame amongst the leaves. First spark of a bushfire.

'I was going to deal with those nappies this morning, but then you turned up,' I said, as she took the bucket of soiled nappies I'd shoved beneath the sink. 'I normally rinse them off in the dunny before I soak them,' I said, 'but I haven't had time.'

'You really can't take proper care of a baby in a house like this,' Charly said, wrinkling her nose at the shit-caked nappies.

I gave her a cold stare. 'I'm doing my best, Miss Perfect Charly, and as I said before, if you don't like it go away and take the baby with you.'

'Could the baby's father maybe help?' Charly said. 'I can see you're not with him now but is he still around? Did you love him?'

'What's the baby's father or love got to do with anything?' I said.

'Doesn't it have *everything* to do with it?' she said. 'You had a baby together, surely you two were in love?'

'My God, you really have been wrapped in cotton wool, haven't you? I had to sleep with men to get money for what I needed – food, clothes, rent at Eileen's dump.' I was too ashamed to add "Superman acid tabs" to my list of needs.

'I don't have a clue who the father is, the baby was an accident, a mistake. Like my whole life.'

I plonked the baby down without even burping him, and lit a fag with shaky fingers. 'Sex is just another thing people buy and sell, Charly, like anything else.'

Charly took the red-faced baby, slung him over a shoulder, patted his back. 'I'm not judging you, I want to help you get over these baby blues.'

With her free hand, Charly took mine, squeezed it. It felt strange, but I didn't pull away.

'I love you, Lucy,' she said.

Love? What's that?

'Anyway, you never told me what you called my nephew,' she went on, cuddling him now he was burped.

'No point you knowing his name,' I said, as Charly put the baby back in his pram, 'because I won't have him much longer. As you said, I'm in no state to bring up a baby, especially not in *this* house. I'm adopting him out, just haven't got around to it yet. Some other parents will take better care of him, and they'll give him a different name.'

'Oh no! How could you?' Charly raised a hand as if to slap me. 'After what you told me about those mean women at Easthaven, after I told you about the lies of *my* adoption, how could you even think about giving him away?'

'Look at me, I'm no mother.'

'Please don't give him away,' she said. 'I'm sure you'll regret it. *I'll* regret it. After all that's happened to us, shouldn't family be the most important thing?'

We both fell silent. Charly reached out, touched my arm. I pulled away from the tears in my sister's eyes.

'Don't cry, for God's sake, it's bad enough having *him* crying all the time.' I nodded at the pram. 'Anyway, I reckon you should just go away and leave me alone, I'm crap at all this soppy stuff.'

'I want to help you and my nephew,' Charly said. 'Why don't you come and live at the Ashwoods' with me? Only till you get on your feet again, till we get your baby blues fixed up. They have pills to treat that. You *can* get better, you know?'

'*Baby blues*, what the hell's that? Live at the Ashwoods'? Oh yeah, just by looking at you, I can imagine what those people are like. I bet they'll be dead keen to take in an ex-druggy, ex-hooker sister and her bastard kid. I can see that going down well in a posh house in some swanky neighbourhood.'

'Yes, but what do you care if the house is posh, in a swanky neighbourhood?' Charly said. 'Anyway, my fake mother's in hospital and Dad – Frank – will never refuse. After what he's done, he'll do anything to make it up to me. And, however much it's hard to admit, to not hate how they lied to me, he *is* a good, kind man … the best father.'

I shook my head. 'No way, I bet this Frank's the same as every other man who's let me down.'

Charly took a scrap of paper and pen from her fancy crochet bag, scribbled a phone number on it, and slid it beneath my teacup. 'That's my friend, Simone's number. She lives next door. I'm staying with her for a while … till I can forgive my parents, and go back home; go home with you and my nephew, hopefully.'

She rinsed the teacups, walked to the front door. 'Will you at least think about it?'

'Maybe,' I said, 'but it's a shitty idea.'

52

'You're *sure* me and Adam being here won't be too much for your mum?' Lucy said, for the tenth time that day. 'That she'll cope with us living in her house, right after a nervous breakdown?'

It was a warm October morning and she and Lucy were sitting in the backyard beside Adam in his pram, where he'd finally dozed off after a nasty teething bout.

After two months in hospital, Charly's second mum – as Lucy had convinced her to call Dolly once more – was coming home. Dad had only just left to pick her up, but already Charly's pulse beat hard against her temple.

'You know Dad's been telling Mum about you right from the beginning,' Charly said, swiping sweaty palms down her front. 'And you heard him say, only last night, how excited she is about meeting you and Adam.'

Lucy nodded, kept jiggling the pram parked beneath the gum tree, bright with crimson blossoms. 'But I'm still a bit nervous … like you are, little sis, I can tell.' She patted Charly's shoulder, smiled. 'I told you a hundred times, your mum and dad's reasons for adopting you mightn't have been the coolest – the most *honest* – but they really did give you the best childhood, didn't they?'

'I know they did,' Charly said, breathing in the fragrance of the new jasmine, honeysuckle, jacaranda and wattle.

In the two months since Lucy had dragged her heavy baggage – from Seabreeze Farm *and* Eileen's place – to Frangipani Drive, she'd made Charly see how lucky she'd been to grow up in Dolly and Frank Ashwood's privileged home. Charly knew it could easily have been Lucy adopted into a loving family, and her suffering at Seabreeze, working at Eileen's dump, then depressed with a baby and no husband.

'I have forgiven Mum,' Charly said, 'forgiven *both* of them, but it's not easy to forget they did steal my childhood memories. And I couldn't bring myself to visit her in hospital … didn't know what to say to her. And now she'll be home soon, I'm still not sure.'

When Charly had left her sister at that filthy North Wollongong house, she'd been stoked when Lucy had phoned Simone's number the very next day, and told her the housemates wanted her to leave.

'They whinge the baby's screaming keeps them awake all night,' Lucy had said, the exhaustion, the desperation, stretching down that phone line. 'Not my fault he's teething. Anyway, I thought of your place … since you asked. And yeah, it'd only be for a couple of days till I can sort out another pad.'

Charly had told Frank, who hadn't hesitated for a second. They'd driven straight over to North Wollongong. He'd paid the rent Lucy owed, piled the baby and all their things – except the bourbon bottles – into the car. They'd driven back to Frangipani Drive and Charly had come home from Simone's that same night. Now Charly felt like Lucy and her sweet nephew, Adam, had always lived with them.

Despite Lucy's protests – "I'm okay, leave me alone" – Dad had insisted on taking her to the doctor, same one who'd looked after Mum for her nervous breakdowns. He'd diagnosed Lucy with postnatal depression and had got her to take some pills.

Her sister certainly hadn't got over those baby blues in the wave of a magic wand though. No, it had taken over a month before Charly saw a flicker of improvement.

She still hadn't learned every terrible detail about Seabreeze Farm; had eked out from Lucy what she guessed was only part of her sister's harrowing past. And she didn't believe Lucy would've told her a single thing if Charly hadn't walked in on her in the bathroom; hadn't glimpsed the ugly red scars criss-crossing her backside, before Lucy had quickly covered herself with a towel.

Around the front, a car crunched over the gravel driveway. They squeezed hands, Lucy picked up Adam, and they hurried into the house as Dad opened the front door.

* * *

Dad came inside first, Mum cowering behind him, lingering on the doorstep.

'So, how's the most handsome grandson in the world?' Dad smiled, taking Adam from Lucy's arms. 'Were you a good boy for Mummy and Aunty Charly?'

'Oh, Dad, you've only been gone an hour and Adam's slept the whole time,' Charly said with a shrill laugh. She darted a nervy glance at Mum, still standing in the doorway as if she didn't dare step inside her own house. Like it was no longer her house.

'Hi, M-mum,' Charly said. 'N-nice to have you home.' Her words came out stilted, nervy, not altogether sincere.

'Hello, Charly.' Mum's voice shook as she stepped inside. 'It's wonderful to be home too.'

Charly caught Lucy's glance, the same unspoken words – Charly, not "*Charlotte*" —rattling in her own mind.

'What if I take Adam out to the yard, show him the new flowers?' Frank said, 'while you three girls have a chat?'

'No, please don't take him away, Frank,' Mum said. She shuffled over to the baby, placed a hand on a little leg poking out from the light shawl Lucy had wrapped around him. She stared at his sleeping face. 'You were right, Frank, he truly is the most gorgeous boy.'

She looked at Lucy. 'Hello, you must be Lucy. I'm so happy to meet Charly's sister … really I am.'

She took Lucy's hands in hers, held them for a moment. 'And I'm so glad you've come to live with us; Frank's told me how happy Charly is, to finally have her sister back.'

Things were going better than Charly had imagined, Mum appeared more recovered than she'd dared hope, but still, these first moments were filled with bouts of awkward silence.

'Who's on for a nice cuppa?' Dad said, escaping to the kitchen to fetch tea and biscuits. 'Why don't you all go into the living room, instead of standing at the door?'

Mum and Charly sat on the sofa and Lucy, still cradling Adam, sat in an armchair opposite them.

'Would you like to give Adam a cuddle, Mrs Ashwood?' Lucy said.

'Oh please, call me Dolly.' Mum fiddled with a pearl button on her cashmere cardigan. It was her favourite, the mauve one, that Charly thought suited her dark blue eyes the best. 'Or Aunt Dolly … if you'd like to? And yes, I'd love nothing better than a cuddle.'

Lucy placed him in Mum's outstretched arms, and she smiled down at him, a fingertip stroking his dark hair.

She looked up at Lucy. 'May I call him my grandson? Would that be alright with you?'

Lucy clapped her hands, nodded, and Charly couldn't stop her big silly grin.

'There are no words to say how sorry I am, Charly,' Mum said, after a few moments, passing Adam back to Lucy.

'You know I'm not your Charlotte now, right?' she said. 'That I'm Charly, a different girl?'

Charly was well aware that Mum did know that now but she wanted to hear her say it out loud.

Mum nodded, spoke in a voice softer, slower than her usual one. 'I always did, deep down. But it was simply too … too terrible. But yes, now I've *accepted* that Charlotte is … '

Her eyes glimmered with tears and the hard crust of Charly's heart melted. In that instant, more than ever, she understood her mum's illness, and how she'd reacted to avoid grieving for the Real Charlotte.

She hovered a hand close to her mother's quivering ones. 'I understand, Mum.'

And she did. All those excuses Mum had made for Charly's flashes of memory – "only a dream, something you read in a book, imaginary sister," were things her mother had completely believed.

Mum grabbed her hands, squeezed them tight. 'We'll be alright, won't we, Charly?' she said.

Charly gathered her in a hug. 'Yes, I think we will.'

She threw Lucy a smile and a wink over Mum's shoulder. 'If you and Lucy promise to stop always squeezing my hand so tight.'

53

It was only mid-morning on that steamy Christmas Day of 1974 but the lemony sun had already baked the scrubby grass to hot spikes.

'You have to tell me the surprise, Charly,' Lucy said, as they sat with Simone on the rug Mum had spread out beneath the back-yard gum tree. 'Please?'

Charly shook her head. 'You'll have to be patient a bit longer,' she said, over the din of nectar-hungry lorikeets, their green, orange and blue feathers flashing through the gum tree. 'Though I've learned patience isn't one of my sister's strong points.'

She fired a warning wink at Dad, not to give away the secret, but her father was too busy sailing toy boats around the paddling pool with Adam. Cute in his Batman cossies, one of a dozen Mum had sewed for him, Adam squealed, jumped up and down and flicked water everywhere.

From the kitchen, where Mum was rattling pots and pans, the delicious smell of roasting turkey and crispy potatoes wafted across the yard.

'He's *so* cute,' Simone said, as Adam chucked the boats out of the pool, Dad madly picking them up and "setting sail" yet again. 'Almost makes me want my own kids.' She grimaced, crunched on a handful of chips. 'Not quite though. How old is he now, Lucy?'

'He'll be two next month ... January.' Lucy smiled at her

little boy, drained her glass of cordial, and stood up, sending a blue-tongued lizard scurrying beneath the hydrangea bush. 'I'm popping up to the kitchen to try and convince Aunt Dolly to let me give her a hand basting that turkey, Bonnie Yates didn't teach me all that stuff about cooking for nothing.'

'Good luck with that!' Charly said, brushing stray gum-tree blossoms from her hot-pants.

Her mother had refused everyone's help in preparing this Christmas lunch. Finally on solid ground again after the nervous breakdown, Mum needed to be back at the controls of her spaceship.

'You still okay to watch Adam, Uncle Frank?' Lucy said.

'Sure!' Dad cried, smiling at the giggling little boy, splashing water about the paddling pool. 'Adam and I have our work cut out sailing these yachts all the way around the world, haven't we, young man?' He pushed Adam's dark, wavy hair out of the little boy's eyes.

'Bon voyage then!' Lucy said with a laugh, the sweet frangipani scent trailing her up to the house, past the new swing, seesaw and sandpit Dad had bought for Adam, to replace Charly's childhood toys, rusted the same shade as the summer earth.

'Your sister's *so* much better,' Simone said.

'Yep, she's doing really well,' Charly said. 'The doctor weaned both her and Mum off their pills ages ago, but they still go to these psychotherapy sessions. Funny thing is, they go *together*, and they love their coffee and cake at the café afterwards!'

'Weird, isn't it,' Simone said, nodding at Dad and Adam, still fooling around in the pool, 'like that little boy really *is* their grandson?'

'Blood bonds aren't really that important,' Charly said, 'in the end.'

Simone nodded, swallowed the last of her cordial. 'Talking about blood bonds, any luck finding your real mother?

Charly shook her head. 'You'd be the first to know. We've tried everything. Lucy still remembers our old London address, but says our mum wouldn't be there. We sent a letter anyway, which eventually came back with "Unknown at This Address". We also wrote to Easthaven Home for Girls to see if she'd gone looking for us there, or phoned them, or something. But they never wrote back.'

Charly swallowed the last of her cordial. 'Dad even phoned Easthaven, all the way to England. But they said they couldn't give out any kind of information. Refused to tell him a single thing, it's all so frustrating.'

'Hey, look what the cat dragged in!' Simone called out to her cousin, Kirsty, sauntering down the yard towards them.

Charly hadn't seen Kirsty Jardine since the slumber party; the tombstone that had changed her life when the Real Charlotte's ghost had woken, and started walking in Charly's footsteps. But, in the end, she'd found Charlotte's presence comforting rather than creepy or alarming. This other girl, kind of like a twin sister, growing up in her shadow.

She felt she knew the Real Charlotte, had a special link to her. And she loved her like her Mum and Dad loved them both.

'Aunty Irma said I'd find you over here ... as usual,' Kirsty said, rolling her eyes as if Simone was an idiot to spend so much time at number 11. She plonked down beside her cousin, and grabbed a handful of chips. 'Hi, Charlotte.' She clamped a palm over her mouth. 'Oops, I heard you're "Charly" now.'

Charly glanced over at Dad, making sure he was out of earshot. 'You were right, Kirsty, Charlotte *is* dead,' she said, with a sly smile. 'But Charly's so alive.'

'Yep, okay, cool,' Kirsty said, blushing, unable to think of a smart-arse answer on the spot. 'Come on, Simone, we need to get back to yours for lunch.'

She and Simone stood up, brushing off olive-coloured gum leaves. 'See you at the beach later, Charly?' Simone said.

'Yeah, sure.'

'Yeah, sure!' shrieked little Adam, as Dad wrapped him in his Winnie-the-Pooh towel.

'Let's get you into some dry shorts for lunch, cheeky man,'

Dad said, carrying Adam up to the house, even though Charly's little nephew was quite capable of walking. And even better at running.

'Batman shorts!' Adam cried, and everyone laughed.

And later, as Lucy and Mum were about to serve out lunch on the table beneath the grapevine-shaded pergola, a car crunched onto the gravel driveway around the front.

'Who's that?' Lucy said, as car doors slammed, kids' voices bubbling and streaming on the hot air.

Charly and Dad exchanged a grin. 'I think your surprise has arrived, Lucy.'

54

'Strewth, if it isn't Vinnie Armstrong!' I cried. My friend bellowed one of her irresistible donkey-laughs as I hurtled across the driveway, and we flung our arms around each other.

'But it's Oakley now, isn't it?' I said. 'Charly told me she saw you at Seabreeze, that you and Tommy'd got hitched.' I grinned at Tommy. 'Not that I ever doubted you two would end up together.'

I looked back at Vinnie, both of us silent, searching each other's gazes. I'm sure she saw the same in mine as what I saw in her wide green eyes – happiness and relief riding on that ripple of sadness, the sinister rip in the surf that would always try and pull you far out to sea, even if you swam between the yellow and red flags. 'Sorry I didn't phone, Vinnie … I wanted to. I've just, well … you know, things haven't been easy.'

Vinnie waved an arm. 'No sweat, I could've called you, too, but I wasn't sure you'd want to speak to me. And then I got so busy running the winery, and chasing these kids around the whole day.'

Tommy was trying to hug Lucy too, in between calming down three excited kids – two boys, around five and three, and a little girl tottering about on chubby, unsteady legs, plucking out frangipani petals.

'They're all so cute,' I said. 'And with that orange hair, green eyes and freckled faces, there's no doubt who their parents are.'

In the buzz of seeing Vinnie, I hadn't noticed Nick Hurley at first. But I saw him now, as he got out of the car, and stood apart from the Oakley crowd.

'It was Dad's idea to invite Vinnie and her family … a Christmas surprise for you,' Charly said. 'And when I spoke to Vinnie on the phone a few weeks ago, she asked if she could bring Nick along.'

'Yeah, bonzer idea,' I said, unable to hide my smile, the distant glow sifting through that hard core of my heart.

Gone was the blushing, awkward teenager. Nick was taller, more muscled, and sun-bronzed than at age sixteen, and now stood tall, solid, sure of himself. But those same mesmerising honey-coloured eyes stared right into my mind.

'Good to see you, Nick,' I said. 'How's things?'

'Fine, great actually, Tommy's almost a rich and famous winemaker.' He gave his mate a friendly punch on the arm.

'Ha, as if,' Tommy said.

'I'm doing alright for myself, still working up at Hennikson's, I'm chief caretaker now,' Nick said. I sensed him checking me out and was glad I'd washed my hair, shiny and shag-cut like Charly's; glad I'd worn the cool hot-pants I'd sewed on Dolly's machine. Glad there wasn't a trace of the stoned, sad and starved waif Charly had found in bed sixteen months ago. 'Looks like you've come a long way too, Lucy … from our dark old days.'

My face flushed. 'Yeah, I have … finally.'

'Come on, lunch is ready, we'll talk while we eat,' Frank said, shooing everyone around to the backyard. 'Let's get you folks a drink, you must all be thirsty and starving after the trip.'

* * *

After lunch, Adam and Heather – Vinnie and Tommy's little girl – had a nap, and later, when the afternoon heat threatened to pummel us into comas, we all headed to North Beach.

'Looks like every family in Wollongong's got the same idea,' Nick said, as we hurried across the hot, crowded sand down to the cool shoreline. To the heads bobbing in that inviting, turquoise water. To the beachgoers jumping over waves, and others bodysurfing into shore. Outside the flags, surfers paddled into the high rollers that carried them, grinning and hooting, into the beach.

'Cooling off after Mum's big meal is always the best part of Christmas Day,' Charly said as we all stripped down to our cossies. I too felt bloated as a dead possum, from the huge lunch of turkey, roast potatoes and veg, and Dolly's creamy pavlova laced with passionfruit from the backyard vine.

Nick sat beside me, on my towel, the threadbare dolphin-patterned one I couldn't throw out, even though Aunt Dolly had bought me a pretty flower-patterned one.

Charly had found Simone and they were swimming out past the breakers, way further out than I'd dare. Vinnie and Tommy were splashing in the shallows with their three little ones, Dolly and Frank beside them, each holding one of Adam's hands.

'Whee!' they cried, swinging Adam up and over the breaking eddies.

'Whee!' shrieked Adam, giggling so much my little boy's face was scarlet.

'You okay keeping Adam for a bit?' I said to Frank and Dolly. 'Nick and I thought we'd go for a walk, over to the park?'

'We're fine!' Frank said, 'and after our swim, we're going to build the biggest sandcastle in history, isn't that right, Adam?'

'Off you go, sweetie,' Dolly said with a smile. 'Nick seems a nice chap.'

'Yeah, he is,' I said, 'real nice.'

'So, any plans for the new year?' Nick said, as we walked past the kiosk, towards Stuart Park, a gentle breeze cooling the last of that hot summer day.

'I'm going to study to be a social worker,' I said. 'Help people like … like me, like us. Dolly was the one who suggested it – just like a real mum! – and says she'll look after Adam. Well she actually jumped at the chance to have her grandson all to herself.'

'Little Adam sure is a cutie,' Nick said and we sat together, cross-legged, in a nice possy beneath a pine tree, like we were old people who'd sat beside each other for years.

Neither of us spoke at first, watching people playing cricket on the grass, jumping up and down and screeching when someone was caught or bowled out.

'Reminds me of England,' I said, nodding at the cricketers.

Nick nodded, plucked out bits of dried grass. 'Vinnie told me about your father,' he said. 'My dad belted my mum too. She finally got so scared he'd kill her that she ran away.' He shredded the grass, let it fall through his fingers. 'Then she couldn't afford to keep us kids, so she had to put us in homes. Told us it was only for a while, till she could get some money together.'

'Like poor old Jane Baxter,' I said.

Nick nodded, tugged out more grass, rubbed the fragile stalks between his palms. A bright-green dragonfly – a magical insect I always thought – hovered above us, a heron pecked at litter. 'But then we all got shipped to Australia before Mum could come back for us. I got separated from my sisters on the dock in Sydney, like you and Charly. I have no idea where they sent my sisters, and no clue how to get in touch with them, or our mother.'

He rubbed his hands together, harder, faster. I prised them apart, took one, squeezed it between my palms. 'I'm sorry, I get how awful it is. Charly and me haven't had any luck finding our mother either.' I edged closer to Nick, felt the electricity stretched between us like taut wire.

'I know you get it,' he said. 'You get it that we were nothing, nobody. That's why I can tell you all this. And you know what, I reckon they only shipped us here to get rid of us because the kids' homes in England were overcrowded, and because the Aussies needed slave labour.'

'Those medical tests were a farce too,' I said. 'When Charly told me Uncle Frank had got in touch with Easthaven to adopt a girl who resembled their Charlotte, I knew Charly had only been shipped out because she'd been handpicked and paid for! I even said it back then, she was no healthy physical specimen.'

'Thankfully we had each other, I had Tommy, you had Vinnie,' Nick said. 'Reckon that's the only way we made it through. And thank God we'll never, ever have to see that Yates prick ever again.'

'I wonder how poor Bonnie is?' I said. 'Now that I'm feeling better myself, I'd love to catch up with her, wherever she ended up.'

A bold lizard darted out from beneath a bush. As it sunned itself on a small rock, fat tongue lolling, the last rays of the sun hopped between the pine leaves, throwing patchworks of sun and shade across our side-by-side bodies.

'Lucy?'

'What?'

Nick held my chin up, forced me to meet his soft honey-coloured gaze. As soon as he kissed me, I recalled those lips, smooth and raspberry-red as six and a half years ago.

'I've got a few days off,' he said, as he drew away from me, ran his tongue over his lips. 'I don't have to get back to Hennikson's this evening with Tommy and Vinnie.' He swept a strand of hair from my cheek. 'When Charly phoned a few weeks ago and I found out where you were I thought, you know, maybe …?'

He smiled, blushed. 'I've booked a hotel for a few nights at the Beachcomber.' He waved an arm across the park in the direction of the hotel, but I knew where it was. 'I promise it won't be like that time in the orchard, when we were sixteen. I've learnt to control myself a bit since then.' He laughed and I laughed with him.

'I always thought you were a bit cool, Nick Hurley, I just couldn't admit it to myself, and definitely not to you. I couldn't trust men. Maybe I should've stayed at Seabreeze with you and Tommy and Vinnie back in '68 but I was shit-scared that new owner would back out of his promise to give us jobs. I was terrified we'd find ourselves in yet another prison.'

I didn't mention that back then I hadn't believed that I deserved to be happy with someone.

I looked away from Nick, across the park, to the lagoon coiling like some thick intestine from the sea into the greeny-purple bush, and I shivered. But I wasn't cold. 'Thankfully Dolly and Frank, and Charly, changed all that. But I'm not the same girl as before, Nick. I've done some things … things I'm not proud of. And now I have Adam to think about. It'd be complicated if you and I … '

Nick rubbed my goose-fleshed arms. 'I don't care what's happened in between,' he said, 'I'm pretty stoked in you, Lucy Rivers, always have been.'

I threw him a sly smile. 'You reckon I should give you another chance, Nick Hurley? Well, I'll think about it, but I want to be at Frangipani Drive tomorrow morning, when Dolly's sister, Joanie, arrives with her husband and their two daughters, Charly's – *our* – cousins. Family's pretty important to me, these days.'

'Oh I get that. So tomorrow night then?' Nick pulled me upright. 'And what if we get back for a swim now, before the sun sets and we end up as shark bait?'

'I said I'd *think* about it,' I said, as we strolled back across Stuart Park, arm in arm. 'What's your room number?'

55

Charly and Lucy
London
1988

The plane hits a patch of turbulence, shakes, shudders. 'Oh, Mum, the plane's going to crash!' Suzy-Jane grips my arm, honey-coloured eyes – Nick's eyes – widen in fright.

'Don't be a cry-baby, it's only turbulence,' her fifteen-year-old brother, Adam says, from where he's seated with Nick in the row behind Charly and me. 'Pilot's got it covered.'

But as I pat Suzy-Jane's arm, reassure my daughter, I think how much of what happens to us *is* down to luck. We might be able to help shape, and even change, much of our lives, but really our destiny is as random as the throw of a dice.

Like the plane journey Charly and I, our husbands and kids are on, might never have come about if Uncle Frank hadn't been sent, by chance, to work in Melbourne last year. If he hadn't bought a copy of the Melbourne daily, *The Sun*, and happened to see the advertisement about child migrants as young as three years old being shipped from Britain to Australia.

Uncle Frank had called Charly and me straightaway, told us there was a number to ring for information.

And later, through the Child Migrants Trust, Charly and I were finally, after all those years of hope, disappointment and grief, given an address in the East End of London for our mother, Annie Rivers. The Trust told us Mum was living there with her sister, Edna and that they'd been in touch with her, and she couldn't wait to hear from us.

We tried to stop ourselves getting too keyed up, afraid of being let down yet again, as we posted that letter.

But Mum *did* write back. And I can still hardly believe we'll see our long-lost mother in a few hours. I open my purse again, pull out her crinkled letter Charly and I have read a dozen times.

Suzy-Jane and Charly's kids are glued to the Disney film showing on the big screen, Adam is listening to music, Charly's husband and Nick are dozing and, together, my sister and I read our mother's letter yet again.

To my beautiful girls, Lucy and Charly,

I almost fainted with excitement when your letter came, when I found out the both of you were alive! All my Christmases come at once.

I was proper sorry when Edna told me they'd put you in Easthaven, right sorry Edna couldn't take care of you. Don't know what I was thinking that night, when I told you to tell the police to take you to my sister's, but I wasn't thinking clearly. It all happened so fast, so sudden, and – what with Nan gone – there wasn't anybody else what could take in you girls.

Anyway, soon as they let me out, back in '68 it was, I went straight to that Easthaven place, but they told me you died, Lucy, and Charly had got adopted by a family up north. They refused to give me any names, not a single bit of information. Said their records were confidential or some such.

So I couldn't even lay flowers on my little Lucy's grave. Had no idea where you were, Charly, what family you were with, if my baby girl was alright. It was torture. I thought my life was over.

Never in a million years did I imagine they'd shipped the both of you all the way to Australia! They never asked me, I never gave my permission for them to send you over there. Boiling mad as a vat of hot oil, I was about that, still am! But there wasn't a thing I could do about it.

Anyway I won't go on too much, I'm not much of a one for

letters, just to say the day can't come quick enough when I can cuddle my angels again.

Hugs and kisses till I see you both,

your loving mum,

Annie Rivers.

'And today's the day!' Charly squeezes my arm. 'How strange it'll be for her, meeting adults aged thirty-one and thirty-six, rather than a five- and a ten-year-old.'

'I was a bit worried finding Mum might upset Dolly,' I say. 'I know how … how possessive she is over you, even though you left Frangipani Drive over ten years ago. But she was the opposite, wasn't she?'

Charly nods, brushes a tear from her cheek. 'I'll never forget that she and Dad gave me the best childhood. And Dolly knows I think of it as having two mothers, and now I'm going to visit the first one.'

I blink against the tears smarting my own eyes. But they're happy tears these days, for which I feel incredibly lucky. Unlike so many of the child migrants Charly and I met up with through the Trust; all those desperate people still trying to track down English relatives.

Carol and Fiona Mulligan had been put in touch with some family members in England, as had my other sleeping-shed mates, the Liverpool girls, Bessy and Helen. But little Sarah and Georgie – I'll always think of those kids as little – still haven't found out a thing about their English relatives, or even if they have any.

We never found out where Patty Hampton was sent from Sydney Harbour, or what has become of her, but Vinnie and I are half-glad about that. How could we have ever broken the news about the tragic suicide of her beloved Suzy?

After a few weeks in London with Mum, we're all heading up to Halifax to reunite with Nick's mother, and his three sisters who arrived in Yorkshire a few days ago. My husband's been bouncing about for weeks, like an over-excited kid.

I think of my dear friend, Vinnie, still waiting, still hoping, to find the brothers she left behind. She tells me she'll never give up.

Nick and I and the kids, and Charly's family, often visit the Oakley Vineyard, well-known estate up on the Southern Highlands. And, in my suitcase, I have one of their best bottles Vinnie gave me to take to Mum.

Tommy found a brother, living in Perth, who apparently survived terrible abuse from the Christian brothers. And that was far from the only terrible story we heard about those religious bastards.

Christian, how ironic is that?

'We're now beginning our descent,' the pilot announces and my heart leaps in my chest. A clammy hand grabs my sister's and we smile at each other. Take a deep breath.

Once we found out where our mother was, and after a few excited phone calls with her, Uncle Frank insisted we all plan a trip back to England. He also insisted on paying everyone's fare.

There was barely time to organise our workers and volunteers to cover for Nick and me at the women's shelter we run, the refuge Uncle Frank had generously funded, buying and renovating the old weatherboard place we'd named "Sisters House".

But in true "Mum-style", Bonnie Yates – who worked with us at the shelter, even though she was of retiring age – took over and shooed us out the door.

'Off youse go and don't worry about a thing, sweet chooks,' she said. 'I got Sisters House in hand.'

I smile to myself, thinking yet again how lucky I am to have *three* mums – Annie, Bonnie and Dolly when, at one time, I hadn't had a single one.

'You think Mum will like Australia?' Charly says, pointing down to the rolling green countryside, so different from dry, barren Australia, that vast expanse of desert we flew across when we left Sydney.

'I bet she'll end up loving it, like we do,' I say. 'Anyway we've got a month to tell her all about it.'

'She did sound keen on coming back to Australia to live with us, when I asked her on the phone,' Charly says, 'in that strange cockney accent of hers, the accent you've *still* kept a bit.'

''Cos I was speaking mainly with other Poms,' I say, 'unlike you, a little Aussie kangaroo right from the start. Besides, you were only five when you got shipped, more chance you'd lose your accent than a ten-year-old.'

'Anyway, we've got *more* than a month to convince her,' Charly says. 'The boat trip back to Australia will take six weeks, remember? I can't wait to visit all those places you told me we saw on the way over. More pieces of the jigsaw for me to slot together.'

I laugh, remembering. 'Back at Easthaven, I was so shocked that any kind of journey could take six whole weeks. And I want to visit those places again too, if only to see, even after everything that's happened, that our new lives in Australia turned out pretty neat.' I place a hand over Charly's, on the book she's been reading most of the journey.

'Thinking of books,' I say, 'have you got a title yet, for your new one?'

'I'm calling it "The Lost Blackbird".'

I frown. 'Why a blackbird?'

'Didn't this whole story start with a wind-up blackbird toy?' Charly says. 'And did you know that blackbirds aren't native to Australia; that they were introduced?'

'Really, Miss Bookworm?' I laugh, as the cabin crew glide down the aisle, checking seatbelts are fastened.

'The English likely brought blackbirds to cattle and sheep stations in Australia around the mid-1800s,' Charly says, 'for their songs and to remind them of home. They're migratory too apparently. And I also came across something else – blackbirding.'

'What's blackbirding?'

'Describes people who've been forced, either deceived or kidnapped, to work as unpaid or poorly-paid labourers,' Charly says, 'in countries a long way from their homeland.'

'My God.' I press a palm against my heart.

Our plane touches down at Heathrow, and I stare out at the tarmac, sleek with rain and sleet. This is what I remember most about England – grey skies, a numbing nip in the air. But despite the grim weather, it's like I've come home. My other home.

As the plane winces to a halt, I think about the Lucy Rivers who left England twenty-six years ago, and the person she's become today: the girl with the coolest husband and kids, the most satisfying job helping people. Tough, yeah, but with so many rewards.

I barely think about those Seabreeze Farm days – the taste of sludgy porridge, the smell of his temper, the fear of his violent mood shifts, the sound of his whip slashing tender, young flesh. The place that turned my heart as calloused as the soles of my feet.

These days, weeks, *months* even, go by without a single thought of Seabreeze Farm. The ache and hollow of it, all pushed to cobwebby nooks of my mind. And Suzy-Jane will never know her name has immortalised my lost Seabreeze friends, at least for my daughter's lifetime.

* * *

In the Arrivals area, I recognise Jamie, our Child Migrants Trust contact, from the photo he'd sent. He smiles, holds up a hand in a wave.

Right from the beginning, Jamie said it was best he meets us at the airport, then drive Charly and me to Mum and Edna's place.

'Best not to overwhelm your mum with the whole family for a first reunion,' Jamie said.

Nick kisses my cheek, smiles at Charly. 'Good luck, girls, we'll catch up later, at the hotel.'

I nod, belly flipping, nerves crackling, a sweaty hand

clutching Charly's as Jamie opens his car door for us, then heads off in the direction of London's East End.

'Countryside and fields are so green, aren't they?' Charly says. 'So different from the dry Aussie bush and scrubland.'

I nod. 'Just what I was thinking. And I'd forgotten England's fog too, this misty rain … you remember how it hung, almost permanently in the air?'

Charly shakes her head. 'Sort of, maybe. I don't know what I remember, really. It's all mixed up with those Enid Blyton books, the dreams, the flashbacks. I'm still working out what's real.'

'This is it,' Jamie says, pulling up in front of an old back-to-back terrace house that I now remember clearly. Aunty Edna's place. I'm glad Mum's been living with her sister all this time, rather than on her own.

My heart leaps as the front window curtain twitches, a face darts out of sight.

'Here goes,' Charly says as we get out of the car.

'Right, I'll leave you alone with your mum,' Jamie says. 'But I'll be back later, to take you to the hotel in Islington.'

We thank Jamie, my legs shaky as Charly and I stand on the footpath, neither of us game to take those few steps to the front door. But then the door opens, and Mum's standing there, still as a statue, staring at us like she's afraid to believe it's really her daughters.

The mother we lost all those years ago looks just how I remember her – like Charly and me – small, with shining blue eyes and dark wavy hair. Though grey strands streak hers.

Then, as if invisible, friendly hands are reaching across those twenty-six years, snapping that long thread of time, we're all smiling, laughing, crying as Charly and I run the few steps to her.

Every second of that stolen time peels away as we throw our arms around our mother, all of us sobbing tears of utter joy.

MESSAGE FROM LIZA

I hope you enjoyed *The Lost Blackbird*. If you did, I would really appreciate it if you could spare a minute to leave a short review – even one line is enough – at the retailer where you purchased the book. Reviews make a huge difference to authors, in that they help books to get discovered by other readers. Thank you so much, your review is really important!

LIZA'S NEWSLETTER

If you would like updates on the book I am currently writing, as well as all book-related news and promotions, why not subscribe to my very occasional newsletter? Don't worry, I would NEVER share your email address with a third party.

I love hearing from readers and will answer all my newsletter replies.

As a thank you for subscribing, I'll send you a free download of Friends & Other Strangers, my award-winning Australian short story collection.

Sign-up form on my Website or blog.

AUTHOR'S NOTE

I hope you enjoyed reading *The Lost Blackbird*.

You may be wondering how much of it is true. All the characters, as well as the *Star of New South Wales* and *Seabreeze Farm*, are the product of my imagination. However the heart-breaking truth is that these fictional characters mirror many of the true-life experiences of thousands of child migrants.

These children were a burden, costing society too much, and overflowing orphanages and care homes. So a cheaper solution was found: ship off this potentially good British stock to populate Australia, Canada, New Zealand and the former Rhodesia – parts of the Empire whose wide-open spaces were in need of labour.

The perfect solution, so it seemed.

Sadly, the reality was far from perfect. Many of the children's documents were illegal or forged, and they became prisoners, half-starved in what were little more than slave camps. They were given barely any schooling, and suffered public degradation and beatings, mental and sexual abuse.

In these cruel, desolate and isolated institutions, there were no hugs or comfort if you felt homesick, no care if you grazed your knee. No love for a child even as young as three years old.

Without a soul to turn to for help, the wounds of many child migrants have never healed, and they have carried their burdens of guilt, shame and rage into adulthood. Many suffer from sleep disorders, inability to form relationships, anxiety, lack of self-confidence and suicidal tendencies. Some search solace in drugs and alcohol, or end up in jail.

The following six paragraphs are quoted with permission

from the Child Migrants Trust website, founded in 1987 by its Director, Margaret Humphreys, to address the devastating impact of British child migration schemes:

In 1986 Margaret Humphreys, a Nottinghamshire Social Worker, received a letter from a woman who claimed that at the age of four she was shipped to a children's home in Australia, and now wanted help to find her parents or relatives in Britain.

Gradually, the enormity of child migration was exposed. Incredibly, up to 150,000 children had been deported from children's homes in Britain and shipped off to a "new life" in distant parts of the Empire.

Many were told their parents were dead. Parents were told their children had been adopted. In fact, for many children it was to be a life of horrendous physical and sexual abuse far away from everything they knew.

Her investigations led to the establishment of the Child Migrants Trust in 1987, whose main aims are to enable former British child migrants to reclaim their personal identity, restore their dignity and to reunite them with family.

Margaret Humphreys and her team have reunited thousands of families, before it was too late, brought authorities to account and worldwide attention to an outrageous miscarriage of justice.

For readers wishing to learn more about the Child Migration Scheme and the Child Migrants Trust I highly recommend Margaret Humphreys' book, Empty Cradles (Oranges & Sunshine), which was very helpful in my research. The book was dramatised as the 2011 feature, Oranges and Sunshine, a British-Australian drama film telling the story of Margaret Humphreys' struggle to help the child migrants.

David Hill, a former ABC chair and managing director, was shipped from England to Fairbridge Farm at Molong in 1959. His book, The Forgotten Children, in which he describes the mistreatment of children at Fairbridge Farm, was another valuable research resource, which I would highly recommend for factual reading on this subject.

In actual fact, only a third of the child migrants were true orphans. The rest were either abandoned by their parents, or stolen from them. As was common practice at that time, parents facing financial difficulties would place their children into care as a temporary solution, which I have portrayed in the characters of Jane Baxter and Nick Hurley. But often, when the parent returned for them, they were told the children had died or been adopted.

Despite the fact that the last children were shipped in 1970, this tragic miscarriage of justice has only become public far more recently. And even though my main characters, Charly and Lucy Rivers, managed to find their birth mother, this is sadly not the case for many child migrants.

Former Australian prime minister, Kevin Rudd made a public apology in 2009 on behalf of the nation, for Australia's role in the program.

In 2010, the British prime minister, Gordon Brown publicly apologised for Britain's role in sending thousands of children overseas.

Not having endured this myself, I cannot claim to know the extent to which the child migrants suffered but I hope, as an author, my characters will help to make people aware of this scandal and its consequences, and to better understand what these children went through.

This book is dedicated to all the child migrants,
with my greatest respect.

ACKNOWLEDGEMENTS

Many thanks to this group of generous people who gave their time and effort in making *The Lost Blackbird* a better story. To JD Smith for the cover design; Julia Gibbs for her proofreading expertise; Catriona Troth for her fine editing skills; fellow authors and fabulous Beta readers: Vanessa Couchman, Chris Curran, Jane Darmanthé, Jane Davis, Tricia Gilbey, Gwenda Lansbury, John Lynch, Jill Marsh, Claire Morgan, Jan Patterson, Camille Perrat, Wendy Quiggin, Barbara Scott-Emmett, Margaret Southan, Cindy Taylor, Susan Van der Spuy, Claire Whatley; Debbie Young for checking Cockney speech patterns; Courtney Adams for checking young child speech patterns; Clare Flynn for the cover quote; Joan Lipscomb for information on blackbirds; Alison Morton for directing me towards "blackbirding"; Dr Norman James for help with psychiatry information and treatment from that era; JJ Marsh for her blurb expertise; fellow 70s "party-girls" Sharon Pusell, Bev Thomas and Bettina Mow for help with 1970s research; Facebook group, Lost Wollongong for information on the area in the 70s; my lovely author friends from The Sanctuary for their invaluable help with the cover, title and blurb, as well as their ongoing support and encouragement; Karen Rowe-Nurse for Wollongong research information; former child migrant, David Hill; Ian Thwaites from the Child Migrants Trust for helpful information on behalf of Margaret Humphreys.

Thanks, as always, to my wonderful husband for his infinite patience, support and encouragement.

And, most of all, thank you to my loyal readers who make writing such a joy!

OTHER NOVELS BY LIZA PERRAT

FRENCH HISTORICAL NOVELS

(all standalones)

Spirit of Lost Angels
Book 1 in *The Bone Angel* trilogy

A Paris lunatic asylum. A woman imprisoned. Plunge into
France on the brink of Revolution.

Wolfsangel
Book 2 in *The Bone Angel* trilogy

France under Nazi Occupation. Lives colliding unpredictably.
One woman's fatal choice.

Blood Rose Angel
Book 3 in *The Bone Angel* trilogy

1348. As Bubonic Plague makes its first inroads into Europe,
medicine, religion, family traditions and love intertwine in a
woman's search for identity and her battle to heal the sick in a
world ruled by superstition.

AUSTRALIAN DRAMA NOVELS

(all standalones)

The Silent Kookaburra

Embracing the social changes of 1970s
Australia, against a backdrop of native fauna and flora,
The Silent Kookaburra is a haunting exploration of the
blessings, curses and tyranny of memory.

The Swooping Magpie

A heartbreaking drama of lost innocence, deceit and a scandal
that shook Australia.

Friends & Other Strangers

An award-winning, eclectic collection of funny, shocking,
heart-breaking and distinctly Australian short stories, each
with its own message.

ABOUT THE AUTHOR

Liza grew up in Wollongong, Australia, where she worked as a general nurse and midwife. She has now lived in rural France for twenty-seven years, working as a medical translator and a novelist. For more information on Liza and her writing:

Website: https://www.lizaperrat.com/
Blog: http://lizaperrat.blogspot.com/
Facebook: https://www.facebook.com/
Liza-Perrat-232382930192297
Twitter: @LizaPerrat

For occasional book news and a free copy of Friends & Other Strangers, Liza's award-winning Australian short story collection sign-up on her website or blog.

Printed in Great Britain
by Amazon